Praise for Nancy G
By M

BOUND

"*Bound by Moonlight* has everything I want in a romance! Sizzling passion, a sexy hero, and paranormal love to last the ages."

—Gena Showalter, *New York Times* bestselling author

CAPTURED BY MOONLIGHT

"These lovers have much to overcome, including their own self-sabotaging character traits. Gideon adds new clues and layers to her world while placing her protagonists in terrible danger, both physically and emotionally. Terrific series!"

—*Romantic Times**

"Exhilarating adventure . . . and extremely erotic sex."

—Fresh Fiction

"*Captured by Moonlight* is profoundly moving as emotional challenges endlessly crop up amid the perilous danger."

—Single Titles

"As good as if not better than its predecessors . . . Gideon has written the perfect paranormal romances."

—Romance Junkies

"A deliciously complex novel full of love and devotion, personal angst and paranormal intrigue. I highly recommend it."

—Night Owl Reviews

CHASED BY MOONLIGHT

"Gideon does a terrific job with her world-building as her characters and readers discover dark and hidden secrets."

—*Romantic Times*

"Another dynamic thriller in this series filled with exciting drama and erotic romance... This book will keep your senses alert and the blood pounding."

—Fresh Fiction

"An outstanding romance overflowing with emotional issues and innovative supernatural elements."

—Single Titles

"The boiling-hot duo of Max Savoie and Charlotte Caissie returns, and the thrillride just keeps getting better.... This series is a must-read!"

—Bitten by Books

MASKED BY MOONLIGHT

"A paranormal romance series with intriguing characters and zippy action... Gideon masters the tension required to keep her complex and engaging story moving."

—*Publishers Weekly* (starred review)

"Definitely a series to keep an eye on!"

—*Romantic Times*

"Sizzling . . . dark and compelling!"

—Susan Sizemore, *New York Times* bestselling author

"Vivid, dark, and memorable . . . I couldn't put it down."

—Janet Chapman, *New York Times* bestselling author

"The reader won't find more excitement anywhere."

—*Fresh Fiction*

"Brilliantly spellbinding with fascinating supernatural aspects, heated passions, and unanticipated dangers."

—*Single Titles*

"An exceptional read. It will have the reader laughing one minute, crying the next. It's a compelling story and a tremendous first book in Gideon's new series."

—Reader to Reader, NewandUsedBooks.com

"Darkness and danger never seemed more appealing. Gideon's paranormal world comes alive with dynamic characters and seductive werewolf lore. A must-read!"

—ParaNormal Romance Reviews

These titles are also available as eBooks

NANCY
GIDEON

*Hunter of
Shadows*

Pocket Books

New York   London   Toronto   Sydney   New Delhi

Pocket Books
A Division of Simon & Schuster, Inc.
1230 Avenue of the Americas
New York, NY 10020

This book is a work of fiction. Names, characters, places, and incidents either are products of the author's imagination or are used fictitiously. Any resemblance to actual events or locales or persons, living or dead, is entirely coincidental.

First Pocket Books paperback edition December 2011

POCKET and colophon are registered trademarks of Simon & Schuster, Inc.

For information about special discounts for bulk purchases, please contact Simon & Schuster Special Sales at 1-866-506-1949 or business@simonandschuster.com.

The Simon & Schuster Speakers Bureau can bring authors to your live event. For more information or to book an event contact the Simon & Schuster Speakers Bureau at 1-866-248-3049 or visit our website at www.simonspeakers.com.

Cover illustration by Craig White

Manufactured in the United States of America

10 9 8 7 6 5 4 3 2 1

ISBN 978-1-4391-9950-3
ISBN 978-1-4391-9953-4 (ebook)

For my Pocket team: Micki, Parisa, Ayelet, Min,
Julia, and, of course, Louise

Hunter of
Shadows

Prologue

Silas MacCreedy identified certain sounds with New Orleans: the mournful wail of a saxophone on the corner of the Square, the whine of mopeds darting along the narrow streets like flies needing a good swat, a hard blues backbeat and drunken laughter drifting out from open doorways.

A sharp female cry wasn't one of them.

He'd lost sight of the men he'd been following, and he couldn't afford to let the trail grow cold. But no one else on the early evening street had reacted to the possible call for help. Either they couldn't be bothered, or the sound was too faint to reach their ears. He should continue on; he had vital things to do. Yet...

Aw, hell. MacCreedy shut out the city soundtrack, listening.

A scuffle on loose stone. The crack of a hand against vulnerable skin.

He sighed and turned down the shadowed side street, his tread light with caution. "Better ready than dead" was the motto that got him home safely at night.

The dark, narrow alley ahead was the perfect place for bad things to go unnoticed. He breathed deeply through his nose, drawing in a taste of what he was walking into. A female. Four males. Not human. He could separate their scent signatures, now that he was closer, and he smiled at his good fortune. These were the same men he'd been tracking.

His job was surveillance, to stay hidden and see where they'd lead him. But he couldn't just watch while they indulged their nasty habit of preying on women.

He eased into the mouth of the alley, knowing he had only a moment to assess the situation before they saw him. Not good. The woman was on the ground with one man crouching over her. The three others crowded in close, their breaths quick and raw with anticipation.

"Am I interrupting something?" Silas said politely.

All eyes flashed to where he stood in shadow, where they could see his large, looming figure but not his face. He expected the dangerous glares of challenge from the males. In the dim alley their eyes glowed with an unnatural brilliance. They were big men, roughly dressed, smelling salty from gulf water and exertion. Dockworkers. Shape-shifters, needing no weapons other than their rough strength and preternatural abilities.

His own kind.

MacCreedy took his hand away from his holster. He would enjoy dealing with them as soon as he got their victim to safety. But maybe they'd just run like the bullying pack animals they were, rather than face consequences. He could see hesitation in their feral gazes and fleetingly hoped they'd make a stand so he could teach them a lesson. That would almost be worth having his cover blown.

Fight or flee, you cowards.

He was ready for them, hands fisted, muscles loose and lethal. But a quick glance at the female caught him off guard.

Beneath a tangle of long black hair, her cheek was red from the slap he'd heard. She was slender, dressed in a sweat jacket and jeans, nothing provocative that would draw her attackers' attention. A battered backpack lay on the dirty stones beside her. Though her face was partially cloaked by her hair, he got the impression of sharp angles and a wide mouth.

And instead of the wild-eyed plea for help he expected, her stare was steady and ice cold.

Her voice was a sudden slash of lightning. "Unfortunately, you're intruding on a private party."

In an instant, Silas realized he'd confused predator with prey.

Her arm made a quick arc. She must have held a blade within the loose sleeve of her jacket, for the male straddling her fell back, gripping his throat as if he could stop the sudden geyser of blood. She agilely rolled free of him, was on her feet and, just as fast, was on the next man with an inhuman snarl. Gripping her arms to jerk her away, another of her would-be attackers sealed his own fate.

Eyes blazing hot and golden, she turned in his clumsy hold and took his face between her hands. With a sickening crack, she broke his neck.

MacCreedy's instincts finally overcame his astonishment. He needed the remaining two men breathing, so he ignored the terrified pair scrambling for their lives to deal with the female determined to kill them. The instant he grabbed her slender upper arms and felt whipcord muscles tighten beneath his grip, he realized his mistake. A possibly fatal mistake.

"What have you done?" she snarled, whirling to confront him.

She had beautiful eyes, deep blue, as sultry as the twilight sky. Something sparked within him as he got his first good look at her, a quick flame of recognition of someone he'd never seen before. It made him slow to respond.

"I thought I was saving your life."

The upward swing of her elbow caught his chin with a force that made him stumble. The sweep of her leg clipped behind his knees, dropping him to the ground, where his head cracked onto the cold cobbles, making the world spin. Then she straddled him, her strong features and lovely eyes harsh.

"You should have stuck to saving your own," she said grimly. "Too late now."

Knowing she would kill him, he hit her with everything he had, the force knocking her head back. She simply gave it a shake, then smiled at him.

"It's not nice to hit a lady," she chastised with short jabs to his midsection.

MacCreedy twisted, trying to throw her off,

growling, "If I thought you were a lady, I wouldn't have done it."

She was quick and impossibly strong. Even though he could have taken down the four males, he couldn't get the best of her despite all his training.

When his jacket fell open, the metallic flash of his badge didn't make her hesitate. But the sight of his inner wrist as she wrenched his hand away from his gun made her pause. Her gaze fixed on the scarred brand burned into it.

Then she eased back with a small laugh. "This is your lucky night. You get to live through it."

He *had* to know who she was.

When she started to lift off him, MacCreedy gripped her arm in a staying gesture. "Wait."

Clearly surprised, she cocked her head as she studied his face. A slight, amused smile curved her lips as she said, "As much as I've enjoyed the tussle, I'm in a hurry, hero. But I guess there's enough time for a quick thank-you."

Braced for another attack, Silas was stunned by the sweetness of her assault. She took his mouth with hers, engaging his tongue in a tangling flash of desire and cool mint before she pushed back to whisper, "Thanks for the rescue, even though it was bad timing."

Then she was gone, leaving MacCreedy lying between two bodies, with the taste of her on his breath and her heat burning in his blood.

One

A quick glance at the clock over the bar told Monica Fraser she was twenty minutes late. Not a good start for her first week on the job.

She slipped into the small servers' galley and stuffed her jacket into a cubby next to the cash register so no one would notice any bloodstains. A quick brush of her palms smoothed her hastily braided hair, then she snatched up her change pouch to secure it about her waist.

"Sorry I'm late," she began as another woman came in to ring up some drinks.

"Don't worry about it," Amber James reassured her. "We haven't been busy and I covered for you. Told Jacques you were in the back taking care of female things." She grinned. "That shut him up."

Not sure how to respond, Nica returned the smile. She wasn't used to kindnesses with no strings attached. "Thanks."

Amber shrugged it off. "That's what friends are for."

To the softhearted waitress, it was that simple. Amber had enthusiastically scooped her into that huge category titled "friends" without knowing a thing about her, without first weighing and negotiating terms for their association. She had no idea what a foreign concept that was to Nica.

Nica should have thought her foolish for having such uncomplicated views, yet part of her was reluctantly envious. While her coworker's vision was carefree and rose-colored, Nica's was as fiercely narrowed as a sniper scope. But then, Amber's life expectancy was measured in decades, not in seconds. There was no real comparison.

"I owe you one," Nica insisted, feeling the need to pay her way.

"If you insist, I'll let you take care of table four. They're loud and seem to have no control over their hands."

"Maybe I'll have to teach them some manners." She winked with an aggressive confidence that made Amber chuckle.

Cheveux du Chien was just starting to fill up with the evening's patrons; an exclusive clientele gathering under the unsuspecting nose of New Orleans. Though the city was proud of its diverse cultures, discovery of this hidden pocket of preternatural citizens would have been far from welcome news. In much the same way, Nica knew she'd be ostracized and feared if these clannish souls recognized her for what *she* was. The four she'd met in the alley had. Two of them wouldn't be describing what they'd seen; that left a pair of loose ends to deal with when her shift was over.

Blending in was how she'd managed to survive for so long in her dangerous profession. Though she chafed with urgency, Nica forced an outward calm. *Draw no attention. Break no patterns.* Even if it meant a nerve-tautening delay. The pair would go to ground like frightened rabbits, but she'd find them again. They'd been easy to lure into that alleyway, where her secret would have been successfully laid to rest if not for her misguided savior.

Suppressing a growl of irritation, she efficiently cleared the glasses and empties off the nearest table, then gave it a polish with the cloth tucked in the back pocket of her tight black jeans. *Hero?* Meddler was more like it. Bursting onto her scene with a cop's unerring instinct to be just where he wasn't wanted. A cop who also wore the brand of the powerful Terriot shape-shifter clan. Interesting, but none of her concern as long as he didn't interfere in her business.

Interesting and a damned good kisser, she thought as her tongue touched her lower lip.

It had been careless not to kill him, especially when the stakes were so high—not only professionally but personally as well. She was so close to obtaining her freedom, she could taste it.

The way she could still taste him.

"Leave no witnesses" was a cold but necessary practice that could mean life or death for her. But what an unfair reward for a good deed that would have been, for a stranger willing to risk all on her behalf. She stacked more glasses until her tray teetered as precariously as her reasoning . . . a tall, rugged reason clad in a dark suit coat, blue chambray shirt, and tie, over snug jeans.

There was something about a man in a tie and jeans. She sighed. Something best left alone. A male bearing a clan mark wasn't someone to be taken lightly.

Nica slid her tray across the bar so owner Jacques LaRoche could unload it.

"Is, umm, everything okay?" he asked with the squeamish distaste males had for female matters.

She liked Jacques LaRoche, and lying to him wasn't a necessity. "I was late for work," she confessed. "No excuses. It won't happen again. I didn't ask Amber to cover for me."

LaRoche's brow lifted at her bold honesty. "She was being a friend."

Nica nodded. "I'm taking table four for her."

Jacques watched her walk away with a smile. Monica Fraser had saved a friend of his with her quick thinking, and he wouldn't forget that. He'd given her a job as a way to thank her, and he'd been thanking his lucky stars ever since.

It took a special kind of female to work his crowd. She had to be easy on the eye without being easy in other areas. She had to have a sense of humor to handle bawdy talk without offense, and enough sense of self to know when to say enough was enough. Nica managed both things. She wasn't beautiful or swimsuit-issue curvy like the rest of his girls, but she had her own kind of appeal with her long, lean, tomboyish shape hugged by a white knit tank top and skinny jeans. The fact that she didn't bother with a padded bra in the air-conditioned room also appealed to the customers' base instincts. The quick flash of her wide smile said she could give as good as she got, and that mass of glossy black hair made every male dream of sinking his fingers into it. She'd come out of nowhere, made his life easier, and he had no complaints.

He watched her handling the difficult customers at table four. They worked for him on the docks and would behave themselves if he stepped in. He let her take care of it in her own way, though he was ready to intercede if necessary. No one disrespected his crew, on the docks or in his bar.

She exchanged tart comments with a friendly smile, just the right balance of sass and flirtation. Two of the fellas grinned and enjoyed the teasing, but the third placed his big hand on her ass for an uninvited squeeze. Without spilling a drop from pitcher to glasses, she caught his hand with her free one, gripping his thumb for an almost casual twist that brought him to his knees on the floor in an instant. After she let go without a glance or a word of reproof, he slipped back into his seat to the demoralizing chuckles of his friends.

Jacques grinned and went back to clearing the bar.

Just then, a slight prickle of sensation disturbed him; a signal from his checker at the door that possible trouble had entered the club. His gaze lifted casually to the stranger at the edge of the room. A tall male with conservatively short brown hair and a five-o'clock stubble, wearing a suit coat and tie, and an attitude that said he could handle himself. He locked stares with Jacques, then started across the room with a purposeful stride. Maybe not trouble, but definitely something. LaRoche made a subtle gesture to stay his men, letting the visitor approach.

"Are you LaRoche?" His voice was deep and smooth, betraying no hint of his intentions.

"I am. And you?"

"Let's say I'm an interested party."

"And what are you interested in, friend?"

"I didn't say I was a friend." Very smooth.

Jacques smiled thinly. "Guess you didn't. Best state your business, then."

The visitor stood straight and sure, with no posturing or aggression, maintaining eye contact. His manner said, *I could kick your ass, but I choose not to.* Maybe he could, maybe he couldn't. Jacques relaxed, knowing he wasn't going to have to prove anything one way or the other. At least not yet.

"I was told you take care of things around here," the man continued.

"By whom?"

He didn't answer that. "I happened upon an awkward situation a few minutes ago that needs cleaning up before questions get asked. I don't have the resources."

Now he had Jacques's attention. "Explain."

"Two of our kind got themselves dead, not by my hand." He gave the location. "Maybe you know them, maybe you don't care. Just thought I'd give you a neighborly heads-up before the police get wind of it and start poking around."

Jacques signaled a couple of his crew over and gave them the necessary details, along with brusque instructions to tidy the scene. Then he put a glass on the bar. "Thanks for the tip. Drink on the house?"

Silas MacCreedy shook his head. "Gotta be going. Have a nice evening."

As he stepped away from the bar, Silas hoped it wasn't a mistake to make himself known to the local clan. He'd been aware of this spot since his arrival in New Orleans, and had made it a point to stay away so they wouldn't sense him. The success of his plans demanded he conceal what he was and what he was after.

He thought of that drink with a brief wistfulness. How long had it been since he'd shared a companionable glass with one of his kind? Too long to even remember. Too dangerous to even consider.

His mission was completed. He'd alerted them so they could protect the secrecy by which they all lived. Police involvement meant unnecessary attention. Let the clan of outcasts take care of their own, and he'd take care of himself. No need to get involved.

And then Silas caught her scent.

Just that hint, teasing like a whisper across his senses, sent a jolt through his system. His skin sizzled, his blood grew thick and hot, and his breath raspy. The instinctual response came from some unknown place deep inside.

His gaze swept the room, not pausing when it caught

her tucked back in the shadows. Hiding from his notice? Perhaps.

The fact that his mysterious and fierce lone wolf chose to conceal herself amongst trusting sheep wasn't his concern, so he continued out into the sultry night. There he rubbed his arms restlessly until the staticlike sensations eased.

This female was nothing to him. Nothing but trouble.

He remembered his younger sister Brigit teasing him that someday he'd be brought to his knees by fated sexual chemistry, by an irresistible pheromone drawing him to his mate. Then he remembered how he'd laughed at her, calling her a foolish romantic.

He wasn't laughing now. But he *was* unbearably—and probably unwisely—curious.

Two

She must have left her backpack in the alley. Was there any chance it would still be there?

Nica watched the clock, anxious for her shift to end. Panic and nearly unmanageable waves of loss pushed her to make an excuse, any excuse, to race back and recover her property. Discipline held her in check. Pragmatism dashed her hopes.

It was gone. Gone, with all links to her identity.

No use crying about it now, she told herself as she blinked the hot anguish from her eyes.

The past was the past. She needed to concentrate on her soon-to-be-reclaimed future.

It was all that Shifter cop's fault.

Had he followed her to the club? Had he been asking LaRoche about her? Maybe not, since Jacques had hardly glanced her way as business picked up and kept them scrambling. She had no doubt the quick deployment of his men had been to clean up after her. Usually she saw to that herself, but her would-be rescuer had upset her normal routine—and cost her the only thing she valued.

Nica waited impatiently behind two other waitresses

so she could close out her drawer. They were taking a long time, chatting about their personal lives and musing over the mysterious stranger who'd come in. Her stranger.

Outsiders always caused a stir. These castoffs survived by keeping their existence secret not only from humans, but from others of their own kind as well. A current of uneasiness surrounded them, a fear that had been an obstacle on her first few days of the job, until Amber decided to take her under her wing and make her into a confidante.

The outgoing Amber had proved a fount of information. Nica only had to ask why one of the back tables was held in reserve to hear all about their almost mythical leader, Max Savoie, and his human mate. They were currently out of the city, and without Savoie's stabilizing presence, a nervous anxiety jittered through his clan.

Nica had no interest in local politics, nor did she want to involve herself with their worries. What she did need to do was remain invisible while she waited for instructions. But somewhere out in the night, two males knew she was not what she seemed, and had seen what she was desperate to hide.

So tonight she would go hunting to make sure her secret stayed secret. She'd seek her lost treasures afterward, even though it was killing her to wait.

Preoccupied by her dark intentions, Nica moved swiftly through the Quarter. Well after midnight, the streets still held pockets of activity: college kids scoring illegal drugs, businessmen bartering for sex in dark doorways, tourists happily barhopping, and local workers heading home. Neon and loud music beckoned along Chartres, but she passed those open doors without glancing in.

She needed to make a quick stop at home to restock supplies before getting down to business. With a quick swipe of her passkey, Nica waited for the green light and welcoming click, leaving the night's humidity for a blast of air-conditioning inside the historic building remade into condos. She headed down the hall, across the inviting courtyard and into the other part of the building, where she pushed the button for the elevator. When the door opened, she stepped in and pressed four, just as another figure ducked inside. As the doors closed, she gave a restless sigh, her attention distracted.

"Tough night?"

There was no way to mistake that low, rumbling baritone with just a slight drag of the South beneath its cool, educated clip.

Nica made a quick sidestep but he was quick, too, snaking his arm about her waist to tug her close against him. He pressed the emergency stop button so the car shuddered to a halt between the third and fourth floors.

"Don't get excited," he cautioned. "I just wanted to make sure you were all right."

She laughed. "You should worry about your own safety, Mr. Hero. As you can see, I'm fine." She twisted and gave him a push. His arm opened so she could move away. Her back against the reflective wall of the elevator, Nica assessed him warily.

In the small space, he appeared intimidatingly large. He towered over her even though she was tall for a female, and she found herself rather breathless at that slight sense of disadvantage. Not many males could gain one over her. He was big without being bulky, handsome without prettiness. That forbidden interest niggled its way back to the forefront.

"Those two who got away might come looking for payback," he told her.

She sniffed. "Those two *you* let get away are looking for the deepest hole they can find. But that won't save them."

"Pretty ballsy of you to say so, considering I'm an officer of the law."

"Here to arrest me?"

"No. That wouldn't be in either of our best interests."

"So which part of you is stalking me? The cop or the Shifter?"

"Actually, I wanted to return something to you."

Her vision blurred as he lifted her backpack. She hesitated just an instant before taking it from him, then clutched the scarred leather protectively to her chest, her emotions swelling dangerously out of control.

"You didn't have it with you when you came into the club," she said faintly.

"I checked it at the door."

She carefully felt for the lock that held the zipper

closed—still intact. Relief shook through her as she whispered, "Thank you."

She breathed his scent in—clean, steely, and cool. Powerful but not overwhelming, subtle without softness. She liked it. She gestured toward the stop button. "Do you mind?"

He nodded and let her put the car in motion.

"So," she began as her confidence returned, "are you a Good Samaritan, or just stupid for wading into the middle of things that didn't concern you?"

He chuckled. "That's the thanks I get?"

"I already thanked you once," she reminded him, her gaze going to his mouth before returning to his eyes. Gray eyes without the slightest warming of blue, beneath thick, short, dark lashes. Intense eyes that could cut like lasers. That made her cautious, but she liked playing with even a cool flame.

As the doors opened on four he followed her the few steps to her apartment, then waited while she inserted her key card and got the green light to go in.

"Maybe I should check things out for you," he offered. Again, the chivalrous male.

She laughed and placed a hand upon the chest pocket of his shirt. Beneath it was firm, hard muscle. "If anyone's waiting in there for me, they'll regret their foolishness."

A lift of one eyebrow. "Intriguing females have been known to make even clever men foolish."

This chuckle had a husky warmth. "I doubt that happens often in your case."

"Only when I'm distracted."

"Are you distracted by me?" Her fingertips traced over impressive pectoral terrain before giving his tie a playful flip.

"By your purpose here in New Orleans."

Nica's eyes narrowed slightly. She didn't want to consider him a threat. That wouldn't be nearly as enjoyable.

"I'm working as a waitress at *Cheveux du Chien*."

He wasn't buying it. "And you can afford a posh place like this on tips?"

"I'm very frugal with my money."

"And with your facts."

"Is this going to be an interrogation, or would you like to come inside so it can develop into something more pleasant?" She leaned toward him with a hint of invitation, her lips parting, her gaze warming suggestively.

His posture straightened to put a cautious distance between them, and it took Nica a moment to realize he was refusing her offer. She laughed to cover her surprise ... and disappointment. Honorable males were so difficult. Especially when they were smart.

"Why did you coax those men into the alley to kill them?"

She blinked in pretended surprise. "Why would you think that? Those men attacked me. You saw that for yourself. Who knows what might have happened if you hadn't come along when you did?"

"I suspect LaRoche's men would have had four bodies

to contend with. I'm not sure what you are, but innocent isn't part of it."

"What I am," she told him, "is an independent, and none of your concern." Her words were brusque and razor sharp. "I'll make sure we don't get in each other's way so you won't be inconvenienced further, on the job or off."

He smiled then, displaying even white teeth and too much charm. "I wouldn't call meeting you an inconvenience." He nodded good night. "Make sure you lock your door. The Quarter can be a dangerous place. All sorts of predators here."

Nica watched him return to the elevator, unsure whether she was relieved or regretful. When the door opened, she called, "What's your name?"

He grinned. "Hero." He stepped into the elevator and the doors closed.

Potential pain in the ass is more like it.

But she smiled as she shut the door and engaged both locks. He'd returned everything that meant the most to her in the world. She quickly spun the combination lock to get inside the pack, then pushed past the tools of her trade to get to the interior pouch. Nothing was disturbed. She sighed in relief as her hands stroked the battered bag.

He'd done her a great service, so she couldn't reward him with death. But just because he hadn't broken the lock didn't mean her undeniably appealing hero wouldn't pry into her other secrets. The prospect of their paths crossing again stirred a shiver of anticipation.

What was his game? A cop who didn't arrest a killer. A Shifter who shied away from his own kind. There were several ways to find out what she needed to. Why had she tried seduction, her least favorite tool? He was annoyingly immune to temptation—and she was in danger of becoming intrigued, when indifference would serve her better.

Nica moved through the condo. Posh, he'd called it. She never paid attention to her living situation. Her first dozen years of life had been stripped to the basics, and those that followed were ones of discipline and deprivation. These rooms had been rented for convenience; comfort didn't enter into it. Used to passing through as quickly as possible, she needed only a place to sleep and plan. But because he had mentioned it, she glanced around now, noticing how nice her accommodations were.

The walls were old brick, the local art bold with a jazz theme. Overstuffed furniture offered an oasis of comfort, as did the freestanding bar and small, gleamingly efficient kitchen area. A dining table for four stood unused. She ate her takeout meals from the cartons in front of the TV she'd yet to turn on. The high, pitched ceiling boasted a huge fan and a skylight offering a view of one of the massive City Central hotels. But it was the window-seat nook she focused on, where a pair of stained glass windows opened outward.

Kneeling on the cushioned seat, she cranked one window open all the way and slipped through it, pulling her backpack behind her. With the lights from the hotel to guide her, she moved in a low crouch along the tarred roof of the third floor until she reached the front of the building. Perched on the edge like a gargoyle, she smelled his scent on the warm evening air, its crisp note teasing beneath the odors of grease from the fryers next door and the trash set curbside for pickup.

Hunching down to be less visible, Nica scanned the parking garage across the street. In one of the darkened drives she saw a shadow that could have been a man. He was watching her—waiting for her to make a move.

Her handsome protector had just become a major inconvenience.

Three

Pretending to be who and what he was not was an inbred means of survival. It made Silas a natural for undercover work. His quickness to adapt under pressure and absolute fearlessness in the face of danger put him right where he needed to be, under the nose of mobster Carmen Blutafino, and exactly where he wanted to be, partnered temporarily with Detective Alain Babineau of the NOPD. The need was professional, the want strictly personal, and his current job as dealer at Manny Blu's private card table served both purposes well.

MacCreedy had suggested the pairing when he and Babineau were soloed by partners on leave. Babineau, who was already undercover in Blu's operation working a complex extortion case with Vice, got him in once they discovered a niche for his talents.

Silas was good with cards. In a life so bereft of freedoms, a deck offering risk and chance, as well as financial rewards, had been infinitely appealing when he was younger. Not that he gambled. He had a cautious respect for the odds. But manipulating them was altogether different. He didn't have to cheat, although he could do so without detection. He just had a flair for the table, shuffling and flicking out the various suits almost too quickly for the eye to follow, using dexterity and an uncanny knack for numbers to ensure that the house ruled.

MacCreedy read Blutafino easily at their first meeting: a cheap hood longing for the polish of a respectable criminal. So Silas gave him what he wanted—the impression of class. He had his hands manicured and wore a tuxedo on his first night. He kept his face smooth, his short hair slick, and his expression one of elitist snobbery behind a pair of dark-rimmed glasses. The other employees thought him too pretentious for a strip club, but Manny loved it. After the first night Silas was moved to the private game behind closed doors, where the upper echelons of New Orleans came to indulge their vices. Right where he needed to be. Jackpot.

Developer and mayoral candidate Simon Cummings sat at his table tonight, along with a midlevel arms dealer and a member of the archdiocese. Silas dealt, making no conversation and very little eye contact.

After a few hands, Manny dropped by to chat with the players. The gun runner Artie Culper, who was knocking back scotch fairly liberally, pointed his glass at MacCreedy.

"New dress code, Manny? Trying to give the joint a little sophistication?"

Blutafino smiled easily. "He came with the monkey suit. Afraid a little style will rub off on you, Artie?"

Artie took a long swallow, studying Silas over the rim

of his glass with hard, suspicious eyes. "What happened to your other dealer?"

"Dennis got himself picked up for a third DUI. He'll be out of circulation for a while. Creed came highly recommended. He runs an honest table, don't you, Mac?"

"Yessir, Mr. Blutafino."

"There's nothing honest about this place," Artie scoffed. "And I don't like strangers."

"We're all friends here, Arthur." Blutafino's gaze chilled. "If you don't think so, you can go elsewhere."

Artie gestured for a refill, sputtering, "I was just funning with you, Manny. You always show a fella a good time. I just don't like putting my coin and trust in the hands of fellas I don't know." Another gauging look at MacCreedy.

"Mac, show him your hands." When Silas did so, Manny gripped one and crushed the fingers together, grinding until Silas winced. "These hands are his livelihood. Creed knows if there's even the hint of something not on the level, he won't be able to feed himself, let alone flip another card. Isn't that right, Mac?"

"Yessir, Mr. Blutafino," he managed with just enough strain in his voice for Manny to release him to massage his hand.

"Our employees are smart enough to be loyal, but in case a fool slips through, everyone on this level gets searched before leaving. What they do and see here stays here."

"Can we get back to the game, Culper, or does the man need to sit there in his Fruit of the Looms to prove he's not taping something to sell for an exposé?" Cummings complained.

The arms dealer laughed and shrugged. "No hard feelings."

"Of course not, sir." Silas smiled thinly and called for a new deck.

Once Blutafino moved away, Culper drew a pack of cigarettes out of his pocket. "Anyone mind if I smoke?"

MacCreedy produced an expensive gold lighter. "Allow me, sir."

Culper eyed him for a moment, then leaned forward to the suck flame into tobacco. "Thanks." When Silas left the lighter out on the table, Artie felt generous enough, after insulting the man's dignity, to ask, "You want one, or don't they let you smoke?"

"Not when I'm dealing, sir. 'Sides, my lady would have my head if she tasted smoke on me after I told her I'd quit."

The men chuckled and got back to cards, forgetting about the lighter that MacCreedy toyed with occasionally, using the tiny camera inside to document the faces of those present.

Players came and went as the night wore on, and Silas began to wonder how he was going to get the lighter out of the room. It would pass casual scrutiny, but if viewed close up, the modifications were apparent. He excused himself from the table, letting another dealer take his place. He was heading for the men's room when a new arrival caught his attention.

Warren Brady. The police commissioner?

Silas eased out of sight, just inside the hall leading to the bathrooms. Had the commissioner been advised of their undercover operation, or had he been purposefully kept out of the loop? What exactly was he here to discover? That corruption went all the way to the top?

He doubted Brady would recognize him, given that he was newly transferred and rarely reported in person, but Babineau would be familiar to him. Hopefully their paths wouldn't cross, since attendees of these games came and went through a private entrance.

Was Brady careless enough to think his presence would go unnoticed? Was he stupid enough to be unaware of the dangerous compromise to his office? Or was he simply at home among his own kind? The investigation had just gotten a helluva lot more interesting.

MacCreedy bummed a cigarette from one of the passing waitresses, then took his time lighting it, clicking off several shots of the commissioner and Blutafino shaking hands and laughing with Simon Cummings. And then a few snaps of something he hadn't expected to see: Simon Cummings and undercover detective Alain Babineau with their heads together near the stairs, just outside the bustle of activity. It might have been nothing. It might have been a very big something. He needed to get the potentially damning photos out of the building, but handing the lighter off to Babineau suddenly didn't look like a good idea.

Mingling with a trio of high rollers calling it a night,

Silas quickly took the stairs down to the main floor. In the glare of bright lights from the showroom where exotic dancers displayed their agility, MacCreedy cast about for a place to conceal his smuggled evidence.

"Hey, Creed," came a loud call. "What are you doing down here? You ain't supposed to leave the game rooms until your shift is over."

He turned to see one of the massive bouncers striding his way. Damn. Now he'd not only have to explain, but also would most likely be searched on the spot. He had the lighter in his hand, readying to give it a toss when another voice intruded.

"There you are, lover. I've been looking all over for you."

He got a quick glimpse of glossy black hair and deep sapphire eyes. Then slender arms encircled his neck, pulling him down for a long, lusty kiss that had him gripping her narrow waist to keep his knees steady. Finally, she slid from his mouth to whisper against his cheek, "You looked like you might need some assistance."

He rubbed his hands up under the skimpy lace top she was wearing. There was no time to question her presence or motives as he tucked the lighter into the waistband of her scandalously short skirt, murmuring, "Take this for me. I'll owe you one."

With his arm about her hips, Silas turned to the glowering bouncer, Todd, with an awkward smile. "Sorry—had to let my lady know I was working late, and they don't allow phone calls from upstairs. I didn't know I wasn't supposed to come down on my break."

She immediately produced a welling of tears. "You're not going to get fired, are you? Because of me?" Her voice trembled.

"No, miss," Todd assured her quickly. "I'll make sure he don't. I'll tell them he came down with me. Just this once."

She gave him a wide, wobbly smile that would have melted a heart of stone. "Thank you. It won't happen again. I promise."

He flushed as she stroked his arm, then stammered gruffly to MacCreedy, "We'd better get you back before Mr. Blu sees you're gone."

"Right away." Then he turned his attention to the enigmatic woman at his side. "I'll be by later to pick up where we left off."

She touched a soft kiss to his lips and said serenely, "I'm sure you will."

She answered his knock wearing loose black lounging pajamas with wide-legged pants and a cropped top. The fluid knit skimmed her long, sleek lines. Spaghetti straps bared pale shoulders and arms delineated by firm muscle. Her hair was loose, cascading to the middle of her back in soft, thick waves. Her feet were bare. Silas found the look dangerously alluring for its femininity and display of unapologetic strength. And his chest was suddenly so tight, he could barely take a breath.

Simple sexual chemistry. An irresistible pheromone drawing him to his mate.

Nonsense.

He inhaled, holding his breath until his mind cleared and the clutch about his ribs relaxed.

She handed him a glass of wine and let her gaze caress him. He'd come straight from the club, still wearing the tux. The tie hung loose about his neck and the first few buttons of his dress shirt were open. Her stare went to the chest hair revealed in that careless V, her deep blue eyes going a shade darker.

"I feel seriously underdressed," she murmured in that smoky voice.

He didn't react as her fingertips traced down the lapel of his jacket. "I don't know your name."

She smiled. "Nica."

His heartbeat quickened as her touch traced over him, and he kept his tone brusque. "I believe you have something of mine, Nica."

Her smile faded at his abruptness. "Come in, Detective MacCreedy." She turned away to start down a long hall.

Silas had no choice but to follow. He'd been naïve to hope she'd just hand him his property at the threshold. "How did you find me?" he asked, trying to keep his gaze from the hypnotic sway of her hips.

"I called your station, said one of their detectives had done me a great service and I wanted to write a note of appreciation. When I described you, they told me your name. Then I staked out your district office and followed you to the strip club."

Simple, logical, efficient. He admired practicality. And he more than admired *her*, even if her intentions were highly suspect. Following him wouldn't have been an easy task; he was extra careful in his undercover role not to invite a tail. He had a very good idea of what she was and what she did, but that didn't lessen the attraction. It should have.

Why was his brain having such trouble keeping up with his libido?

The wine, the sexy outfit, made him wary and aroused. If there'd been candles and music he would have backed away, recognizing a sensual trap. But the living area was well lit, and she headed for a laptop open on the coffee table. She sat on the couch, not the love seat, and patted the ample space next to her. As he sat, he looked to the computer to see one of his photos of the commissioner, Cummings, and Blutafino filling the screen—she'd already downloaded his images. Alarm stirred.

He'd respected her privacy with the backpack, but she hadn't returned the favor.

Nica leaned back into the cushions and sipped her wine, watching his expression tighten. "What are you up to, MacCreedy? Indictment or extortion?"

"That's my business, not yours." His tone was gruff with displeasure.

"I believe you invited me to make it mine when you

passed me these interesting snapshots to smuggle out. Try the wine. It's an excellent pinot gris."

He ignored the glass on the table and gave her a challenging glare. "I want my property and any copies you might have made from it. And I want these erased."

"You want a lot and give little." Her jaw squared with equal belligerence. "You make it sound as though I'm your enemy."

"I don't know what you are." He couldn't seem to pull himself from her hypnotic gaze, and he fought the attraction threatening to drown him.

"I told you, I have no stake in this game you're playing. I'm merely a spectator intrigued by the entertainment value."

"I'm glad you've been amused. Give me my property."

Her tone could have frosted the glass in her hand. "Ask nicely."

His fierce expression didn't soften as he drawled, "Pleeeease give me my property so I can go home."

She held his gaze for a long moment, then turned to the laptop, closing down the program and deleting the file from her hard drive. Surging up from the sofa, she stalked to the bar, reaching over it to find the lighter on the shelf behind it. Then she returned to the couch, tossing the lighter to him.

"Apparently the Terriots still don't train their beasts to have manners. Get out."

The smart thing would have been to go. Yet Silas hesitated, angered by her tone and words, shamed by his behavior toward a female who'd had no reason to help him, yet had. And agitated by the way her scent tormented his senses into a painful awareness, even as she glared at him with disdain. An apology started to form, but couldn't best his abused pride.

"I'm not on a leash to the Terriots," he growled.

"No?" she sneered. "If you wear their mark seared into your flesh, you obey their command. Expecting me to believe otherwise insults me even more than you have with your rudeness."

"I don't care what you believe. You say you're an independent? Don't pretend you have any more freedom than the rest of us."

She grew even colder. "You don't know anything about me."

"I know you're a slave to whoever holds your reins. We're all bound by someone's chains—so don't act as if you have no master."

Visibly trembling, she said with a contemptuous chill, "You no longer amuse me. I was wrong to think I saw something in you. You're a waste of my time."

"And you'll take up no more of mine."

Silas surged to his feet, towering over her. She held her ground, clearly unimpressed by his size or his temper, fearless in her fury and purposely barring his exit.

"You're in my way," he snarled. When she remained planted, he took her by the upper arms, intending to move her aside.

But the feel of her bare skin shocked through him, awaking strange, overwhelming emotions. His focus faltered, then fixed upon her incredibly warm, smooth skin. So soft and deliciously scented. Desire rumbled and his hands lingered, lightly stroking, drifting upward to the firm curve of her shoulders. An earthquake of urgency shook him, and even as frantic logic argued against it, Silas knew he'd never wanted anything as desperately as he wanted this female.

Nica's pupils widened. She took a shuddering breath, then clasped the back of his head in her hands to drag him down to her parted lips.

Explosive pleasure shut out all else.

They kissed as if starved for the taste of each other, as if no other meal had ever satisfied. Deep, plunging, lapping kisses that quickly overpowered reason and resistance.

Nica's will weakened beneath the drugging sensation. This mindless, careless passion was a shock. Things she'd always avoided seemed a necessity with this overbearing male. She lost herself in the tight wrap of his arms, surrendering to a wild, hot madness.

She let her legs give way, using the sudden slackening weight of her body to unbalance him. Then it was easy to toss him down to her carpet, where she was instantly astride him. As the volcanic kisses continued, his hands clasped her waist to move her over the massive ridge of his erection until she was panting raggedly. She lifted off his lips just far enough to meet his gaze, those cool gray depths now an iridescent blue that confirmed he was as desperate for her as she for him.

With a last tattered effort, Silas asked, "Do you still want me to go?"

"No." Her hand reached for the zipper of his tux pants. "I want you to come."

Her impatient growl lit a firestorm of need, inflaming desires Silas couldn't comprehend or contain. His fingers hooked in the elastic band of her pants to shuck them down her sleek legs as he rolled her abruptly beneath him. An answering urgency kindled in her eyes as he palmed her hot sex, then plunged fingers into her molten core with rough repetitions until her eyes glazed and fluttered shut.

She shuddered beneath him. Her hoarse cry broke into hurried gasps as she tugged his pants open and wrestled them down his hard flanks, then urged him to sink between the legs that quickly locked about his waist. His deep, claiming thrust and fierce, greedy demands rushed them toward a devastating pleasure that shattered them.

Dazed, Silas wondered, *What the hell just happened?*

"Am I mistaken, or did a Category Five just rip through here?"

Nica's slightly breathless and admiring question made Silas laugh as he toppled onto his back beside her. His senses surged and ebbed in a luxuriously intimate tide as he lay there with closed eyes. Her hand remained entwined with his as they slowly recovered.

A soft, sensual sound purred from Nica, and Silas brought her hand to his lips for a gentle kiss. Bemused by his overwhelming sense of contentment, he opened his eyes and gazed through the skylight at the lit windows of the hotel looming over them.

He chuckled. "I wonder if any of your neighbors were turned on by the show."

She gazed up, then smiled. She looked wonderfully relaxed. She looked wonderful.

Her hand stirred within his and her thumb began a sensuous rub at the base of his, moving down to feel the slowing pulse at his wrist, pausing over the raised scars branded there.

And his mood started to cool as reality began to poke holes in their blissful bubble.

"I'm sorry, but I've got go," he said.

Closing her eyes, she brushed off his awkward words. "That's all right. I never let my lovers stay over."

He tried to shrug. "Oww." Surprised he looked down at the mark on his shoulder where she'd pulled his shirt aside. Her impassioned bite had left puncture wounds.

"No offense meant. I'm funny about my privacy," she offered in explanation, not as an apology, still not looking at him.

She hadn't been laughing as he invaded every aspect of it only minutes ago.

Still lying beside her, he pulled up his pants, oddly reluctant to go. The way she gazed up through the skylight hinted that she'd prefer he leave, and ordinarily that would be fine with him.

But not tonight. Not with her.

He rolled above her, supporting himself with palms

placed in the spill of her hair to hold her captive. He slowly touched his lips to hers, and lingered as hers sweetly parted.

"No offense taken," he whispered.

As he started to sit back he felt her hand in his jacket pocket, and watched in puzzlement as she drew out his phone. She programmed her number into his cell, then replaced it.

"In case you need me," she told him simply. "For anything."

His smile was a quick, white flash as he got to his feet. He put down his hand, but she shook her head.

"I'm just going to relax here for a minute." Nica returned his smile as she looked up at him. What craziness had possessed her, making love to a potential enemy? Enjoying it so much she was tempted to have him stay, not just for sex, but for his company? For someone to relax with? Insanity.

He cautioned, "Don't forget to lock your door."

"I won't. Good night, MacCreedy." Nica closed her eyes, curious when he remained a moment longer, wondering what he was doing until she heard his sigh of appreciation and the clink on his wineglass being put back on the coffee table.

"That *is* good. Crisp and sharp-edged, with just a hint of sweetness. Like you. Good night, and thank you. For everything."

She listened to his footsteps going down the hall, followed by the click of her front door. *Lock your door.*

Smiling at his unneeded concern, she inhaled deeply, enjoying his scent upon her. Her hand ruffled over the carpet nap as if it still retained his heat. Sex usually left her anxious to shower and put the encounter behind her as inconsequential. Now she languished in the moment, unwilling to leave it, letting the sights and sounds and sensations return so she could revel in him all over again.

Silas MacCreedy had neatly slipped through her guard. He'd turned her fight into sexual excitement at the first hot taste of his mouth. And she'd loved every angry, sweaty, sensational minute of it. He'd had her so mindlessly panting for him that she'd actually bitten him in the throes of pleasure. Leaving two distinct punctures.

Nica sat up, the lethargy of fantastic sex falling away in the face of her dismay. MacCreedy was a cop with a Shifter's intuitive senses, used to latching onto even the most insignificant clue. And she'd left one impossible for him to miss.

The mark of her fangs.

A sudden sharp pain pierced through her head, replacing worry with blinding agony. She fell to the floor, clasping her temples, writhing helplessly as a stern voice stabbed her with each empathic syllable.

"What do you think you're doing, rolling around like a careless bitch in heat, jeopardizing everything just to scratch an itch?"

Moaning, she rolled to her knees, balling up as if she could protect herself against the splintering pain that punished her. She struggled to fight it, even though she knew it was impossible. There was only surrender.

"Please," she cried out. "He'll be useful. Stop!"

And just like that, the pain was gone.

She huddled, shivering weakly, thoughts of Silas replaced by razoring memories of the consequences of past infractions. Consequences she didn't dare incur lest she not survive.

After a time, her strength returned enough for her to crawl to her hands and knees, and finally get to her feet. Sick and dizzy, she made her way to the bathroom where a hot shower rinsed away all traces of her lover. The cold, lashing spray that followed reminded her of where her focus needed to be.

On the lives she needed to save. Her own included.

Four

Silas and his temporary partner sat in their small, economical import with the wrappings of their fast food meal on the seat between them, the windows down to let the damp early evening breeze drift through. Alain Babineau was studying the photos from the gambling floor that Silas could afford to show him now that the originals were safely tucked away while he watched the front of the club through a telephoto camera lens.

"Holy crap," Babineau gasped. "That's Titus King. He heads up the Committee for Urban Advancement. I wonder if his wife knows he goes for transvestites?"

MacCreedy glanced at the photo. His eyebrow arched high. "Are you sure?"

Babineau chuckled. "I busted Gino before he became Gina. He was working the streets to pay for his hormone therapy. Nice kid. Very polite."

"Nice legs. I can understand the confusion."

"Since Gina hasn't had the operation yet, I don't think Mr. King is confused." He nodded toward the image of the prominent community leader's hand beneath a very, very short skirt.

"Huh. I wonder if Manny's put the squeeze on him

yet. I'm sure he's got a file full of shots just like this one to pad his retirement."

"Probably. Manny's like a slug. He's in no hurry, and he leaves a slimy trail." Babineau looked at the last photo. "Is this it?"

MacCreedy thought he heard relief in that question. He didn't want to believe Babineau was a dirty cop; he wanted to think there was a good explanation for his partner's tête-à-tête with Cummings. But maybe he was padding *his* retirement by supplying Cummings with insider information.

Either way, Silas wouldn't be here long enough for it to matter. His job with the NOPD was almost concluded.

"That's all I got before I had to smuggle the camera out. I didn't want to risk getting caught with it."

Babineau nodded and tucked the pictures back into the envelope. "Got some good stuff here." He shook his head. "How could Brady get tied in with someone like Blutafino? He's got to know that if a whiff of that got out, it would be a career killer."

Two furtive males crossed the street a block down and approached the club. One of them clutched his shoulder, and Silas was instantly alert. Babineau glanced over as he opened the car door.

"Spotted somebody I need to have a word with," Silas said before slipping out into the foggy drizzle. He hunched his shoulders and jogged across the street, slipping inside the neon glare of the Sweat Shop.

The two men were approaching the bar. Silas recognized their scent the minute he entered the building, and now he could see their faces. He didn't think they'd recognize him from the alley since he was backlit in the shadows, but the next few seconds would tell.

Silas went up to them quickly. "Help you fellas?"

They turned to him with a mixture of annoyance and wariness. He'd been keeping unofficial tabs on them for the past couple of weeks, ever since their names surfaced in loose talk from his former partner, Stan Schoenbaum, concerning missing girls and an alleged confrontation with a policewoman. The guy with the bad shoulder—whom Detective Charlotte Caissie had shot when they attacked her—looked pasty and ill. The other looked just plain scared.

"We need to see Mr. Blutafino. Tell him Nash and Willis are here to talk some business."

"Sorry, but Mr. Blu is out of town. My name's Creed. Maybe I can help you. I handle things for Mr. Blu when he's away."

The two exchanged anxious looks, but when Silas's friendly nod to the mammoth bouncer, Todd, was returned, they started to relax.

"Why don't I get us a couple of drinks and you can tell me what I can do for you." MacCreedy steered them to one of the corner booths where they wouldn't be overheard, and ordered double shots for his nervous companions. He slid in next to the injured one, Willis, and casually pressed his hand down on his shoulder. Willis went gray and broke a cold sweat. "What's the trouble, boys?" At their hesitation, he smiled reassuringly. "Don't worry, you can tell me anything. I know all Manny's secrets." Or soon would.

"We need money to get outta town. Tonight," Nash urged, his gaze flicking about the room fearfully.

"What's the hurry?"

"Some she-devil is out to kill us," Willis cried, "just like she done our two pals."

"Shut your face, Willis," Nash commanded. "Don't forget who you're talking to."

A human, was the inference, Silas guessed. He took the drinks from the waitress and set them in front of the men, who sucked them down as he paid her. When he looked back at them, he let his eyes flash red and gold, then murmured, "I'm not an Upright, so those secrets will be safe, too."

Nash heaved a shaky breath. "I never seen one of our females change, but she was on us with fangs out and dripping."

"*What?* Are you telling me this female shape-changed?" He leaned in close. What they were saying was impossible.

"Not all the way, but enough to near rip off poor Mickey's head," Nash said.

Silas leaned back in the cushioned booth, thinking of the two puncture marks on his shoulder. The wounds had healed but the memory of them remained.

Nica could shape-shift.

He needed time to consider what this might mean. "Is there someplace outside the city where you'd be safe while I get some funds together?"

Relief made them grab his hands gratefully, gushing their thanks. He shushed them.

"Tell me where I can find you. Someplace no one will think to look."

Nash gave Willis a glance. "Cousin Troy's?" Willis nodded.

Silas took out his phone and cued the GPS app. "Show me."

"Out Bayou Barataria in Crown Point. He gots a shanty tucked back in the swamp. We used to go there when we was younger to fish." *Poach, more likely,* thought Silas. "Ain't no roads. You ax one of them tour captains to take you out to Troy DuPree's. They bring you in if you show them this." Nash reached under his shirt to pull off a leather cord that held a huge alligator tooth. "Tell them that were left in Troy's hip when the gator helped hisself to a steak."

MacCreedy pocketed the necklace and pushed four twenty-dollar bills at them. "Leave the city right now. Don't talk to anyone. Don't stop for anything. I'll be there in the next day or two, so sit tight. I'll take care of everything."

Starting with the answers to his questions.

Nica's feet and shoulders ached from the busy night at *Cheveux du Chien,* and she was looking forward to a long, steamy shower. Then she saw Silas MacCreedy waiting at her door and her priorities changed.

He sat on the cold-air register against the wall of windows that overlooked the central courtyard. He was wearing jeans, tennis shoes, and an olive green T-shirt that temptingly accentuated his powerful chest and arms. The need to run her palms over that masculine terrain made her greeting a bit breathless.

"MacCreedy. This is a surprise."

He rose smoothly to his feet as her hungry gaze followed. She was wondering how long it would take to get him undressed and horizontal, until she focused on his expression. He was unsmiling, his mouth and eyes narrowed. No trace of her fiery lover from the night before warmed his posture or his tone when he said, "Let's talk inside."

She ran her key card across the lock, a wary caution building. She was very aware of him, big and powerful and potentially trouble at her back. He clearly wasn't here for let's-get-better-acquainted sex. Too bad for them both.

"I had to close out for Amber. Her little girl was sick," she chatted as she moved down the hall in front of him, all of her muscles tight and her senses alert. "I hope you haven't been waiting long."

"No. Not long."

Something in his voice had her nerves taut and tingling.

Don't start something I'll have to finish, MacCreedy. I really like you.

She placed her backpack on the coffee table and pulled off the white shirt she wore over a snug black tank top. "Can I get you something? I have—"

"No. This isn't a social visit."

Damn.

"So why are you here?" She gestured toward the couch, hoping to maneuver him from his squared and readied stance.

"I think I'll stand."

So that's how it's going to be. What a waste. She sighed. "What's on your mind, MacCreedy?"

"I found those two men."

Her attention targeted like a gun sight. "Where?"

"I have them on ice. They're part of my ongoing investigation."

Investigation? It all came together with an unpleasant click, like a well-hidden trap.

MacCreedy hadn't been in that alley by chance. He hadn't stepped in just to save her life. His plan all along was to save the two who could destroy her.

"I don't care about your investigation," she told him. His cop business wasn't a blip on her radar—unlike their personal business. Few moments had passed throughout the day where intimate thoughts of him hadn't hovered.

And he'd been using her. How . . . disappointing.

"I don't expect you do," he replied. "But I have to keep those two alive long enough to give statements."

How much did he know about her? How much had he guessed? Why was he here, alone, to confront her?

Nica stepped closer, her movements deceivingly relaxed, until they were toe-to-toe. She placed her palm on his chest. His heartbeat was strong and steady. If he knew anything, he had nerves of iron to stand there so cool and composed.

"What have they told you?" Her gaze held his while her hand eased upward to distractedly stroke his neck and the side of his face. Not a muscle moved beneath her light touch.

"All sorts of interesting things." His tongue grazed her fingertips as they glided over his mouth, but his stare remained unblinking.

She stretched up to nuzzle his warm throat, to breathe in his scent and taste the heat of his skin with her lips. As she rubbed her cheek against his, she whispered, "What sort of things?" She glanced up to find his steel gaze upon her.

"Impossible things," he replied. "Things I never would have believed if you hadn't left your fang prints behind."

"You know Shifter females can't change shape," she reasoned quietly. Her pulse pounded wildly. *He knew.* She couldn't let him leave this room with that knowledge, couldn't let him tell anyone what he'd discovered. Everything she'd worked for, every sacrifice she'd made would be for nothing.

Primal self-preservation kicked in, and she backed away.

"So," Silas asked, watching her closely, "if you're not one of our females, what does that make you?"

"More dangerous than you could ever imagine. Tell me where they are, MacCreedy. I'd rather take you back into the bedroom for a nice long tumble than scoop your remains into a plastic bag."

Silas laughed. "Having sex with you is about the last thing on my mind." Not exactly true. "Don't get out the plastic yet. You need me alive to find them."

Nica laughed, too, a low, throaty sound completely without amusement. "You're wrong, hero. I can scent out those cowards without your help. So I guess that makes you . . . unnecessary."

She sprang.

Even ready for her, Silas hadn't anticipated her speed. She was on him before he could blink, and he was barely able to keep her snapping teeth from his neck.

She was everything he feared . . . and more.

Nica's strength was unimaginable as she began to shape-shift. He struggled to contain her while dodging the vicious swipes of her claws. Pain streaked across his face, his chest, his neck, but it was her bite he needed to avoid, those massive fangs that sought to rip out his throat.

Her eyes were bloodred and merciless as the beast within her took control. If she could get him on the floor, she'd tear him to pieces in seconds. He didn't want to kill her, but he wasn't sure he could stop her from killing HIM without doing her serious harm.

As Silas fended off her aggressive moves with lessening success, the cold reality of his possible death shocked through him. If he died, what would happen to those he loved?

His legs bumped the arm of the couch and Silas tumbled back onto the cushions under the juggernaut of her determined fury. He allowed his arms to buckle, letting her fall upon him with a victorious roar. As her jaws opened wide and began to descend, he used his last breath to cry, "Nica, wait!"

She hesitated; for an instant, she didn't move.

That was all the time Silas needed. As a surge of strength rushed through him, he tucked his knees, planted his feet squarely against her, then kicked out with all his might. She gave a furious screech as he sent her flying into the brick wall. In the second it took for her to shake off her daze, he'd reached the door.

He burst out of her apartment, threw his arms up in front of his face, and hurled himself through the window on the other side of the hall.

Hearing the crash, Nica stumbled out into the corridor. She stared incomprehensibly at the shattered glass, then moved to gaze down at the figure sprawled four floors below. He'd landed on his back in the courtyard's decorative pool. The impact had broken the brick ledge and cracked its tiled interior. As the water turned red, startled tenants began to gather. Nica ducked back to avoid their uplifted gazes. When she dared risk another look, the pool below was empty.

Silas MacCreedy had managed to escape her—

carrying with him a secret she would do anything to protect.

"What the hell happened to you?"

Under the glow of Alain Babineau's porch light, MacCreedy looked like he'd gone twelve rounds with a cement mixer and lost.

"Girl trouble. Got someplace I can crash?"

Babineau opened his door wide. "C'mon in." He glanced around the cul-de-sac. "How'd you get here?"

"Cab."

When Babineau got a better look at him inside the tiny living room, he gave a low whistle. "What'd she do? Run over you with a rototiller?"

"She let her big, very nasty dog off its chain." He glanced at the wall clock. "Sorry. Didn't mean to wake you up."

"Wasn't sleeping." Babineau smiled wryly. "Girl trouble."

"Ah. Where can I wash up?"

Following Babineau's gesture, Silas went to the cheery bathroom and slumped over the sink. As it filled with water, he assessed the damage.

He didn't look too bad for someone who should be dead.

The claw marks had already healed to thin scratches. He hurt too much to dare wonder what kind of internal injuries he'd sustained in the fall. Even though the water had absorbed most of the impact, he could hardly draw a breath, and was sure everything across the back of his shoulders had been broken when he'd hit the lip of the pool. His head rang like church bells on Easter Sunday with the slightest movement. Not something a human could have walked away from. He'd managed to crawl.

Silas turned off the tap and submerged his face in the icy water, letting the chill clear his mind.

He hated bringing potential trouble to Babineau's door, but he'd had nowhere else to go and desperately needed a place to recover.

Nica would be coming after him. She couldn't afford not to. And he couldn't count on her momentary weakness to ever happen again. She'd be prepared next time and she'd be unstoppable.

How had he allowed that first taste of desire to maneuver him into this catastrophic position? Why hadn't he just put Nica behind him without a thought?

He'd always been hit-and-run in his sexual encounters, though up front about it. He didn't have the time or the resources to sustain a relationship. The brand on his wrist said it all: he wasn't his own man. He had nothing to offer beyond a night's pleasures. As the hot blood of youth eased and revenge had chilled to a dish best served cold, his constant focus became those he loved and needed to protect. His sister and their best friend; all that remained of his past. For them, he'd yielded to the Terriots.

For Nica, he'd yielded his resolve.

Why did she hesitate?

He couldn't afford to speculate. She was dangerous not only because of her unnatural abilities, but because of her strangely powerful hold over him. He had to be careful, and he had to be smart.

When he returned to the living room, Alain Babineau had a tumbler in each hand and extended one. Silas took a sip and let the cheap tequila slide down, grimacing at its medicinal bite. As he glanced around, his gaze settled on several framed photos. Babineau with a petite, dark-haired woman and a small boy.

"Is this your family?"

Babineau gave a quick nod, then opened the glass slider to step outside to the deck.

Silas continued to study the pictures until the cramp of longing in his heart got too painful to endure. He took another long drink and joined his partner in the heavy evening air.

"Where are they?"

"Who?" Babineau glanced up from where he sat on the top step of the deck.

"Your wife and son."

"He's not my son." Melancholy weighed down his voice.

When he offered nothing further, MacCreedy eased himself down. "How long have you been married?"

"Little over a year."

"She's very pretty."

A slight smile. "Yes, she is."

"What are their names?"

"Tina and Oscar."

"Tina and Oscar." Silas spoke the names softly, almost reverently. "Are you separated?"

Babineau gave him a sharp look. "You're getting pretty damn personal."

"Sorry. It's just that I haven't gotten to know anyone here and . . . It's none of my business."

They sipped their drinks in silence for several minutes, staring out at nothing.

"I guess we are separated," Babineau admitted at last. "We had some trouble a few months back. Bad business involving the boy. Scared my wife plenty and she got to thinking that I couldn't protect them." He shrugged. "Could be she was right. Anyway, they're living with Oscar's older brother." He said that as if it tasted sour on his tongue.

"Here in New Orleans?"

"Out in one of those big-ass plantations along the river. With all his mob money, he can hire an army to protect them."

"What's this fella's name?"

"Savoie. Max Savoie."

Silas looked down into the glass clutched between his hands and struggled to keep his voice level. "Savoie. As in your partner's . . ."

"Lover?" he supplied bitterly. "Yeah. Small world, huh? Just swooped in bold as you please, and snatched them right out from under my nose."

"I thought he was out of town with your partner. Why not just go out there and get them back?"

"It's not that simple."

"It is if you still love her."

"You don't understand."

"I understand family just fine." His tone hardened. "You love each other. You stay together. You protect each other."

"Yeah, that's what I thought, too." Alain tossed back the rest of his drink. "It's complicated, Mac. See, Tina's not who or what I thought she was when we got married. She's not that woman at all."

And then Silas understood everything.

Alain Babineau knew his wife and adopted son were shape-shifters.

Five

Silas arrived at the club midafternoon to pick up his check and get his schedule for next week. He was also anxious to hear if his interaction with the two men the night before had been noted.

He'd managed to sleep most of the day on Babineau's couch and could move with only slight discomfort now. As a precaution, he'd bought new clothes rather than return to his apartment, in case trouble was waiting for him there.

"Hey, Mac," Todd called to him. "She's been waiting on you about an hour."

Silas turned to follow his pointing finger and froze.

Trouble was closer than he'd anticipated, and she had the nerve to smile at him.

Because there was nothing else he could do, Silas waited as Nica rose from the table where she'd been watching for his arrival. Her hair was bound back in a heavy braid, leaving her pale features dramatically exposed. A tiny white T-shirt and low-slung black jeans showed a wide patch of toned midsection, making him think of how soft her skin was. Her approach was fluid and predatory.

"You look no worse for wear," came her casual purr.

His response was a low growl. "No thanks to you."

"Don't be that way, lover," she crooned, swaying toward him as her arms reached up to go around his neck. He took a quick step back to avoid the embrace. She let her fingertips trail lightly down his arms. "I just came to say I'm sorry. I got a little bit carried away by your surprise."

"Get away from me," he warned, gripping her wrists and pushing her back. "I don't want things to get unpleasant."

"You aren't going to let a little fight get in the way of what's between us, are you?"

He stared down into those seductive eyes and said flatly, "Yeah, I think I am. Todd, escort the lady to the door, please. Don't let her back inside unless I clear it first."

She pouted, her eyes glittering dangerously. Then she stretched up to kiss Silas's cheek and whispered, "I'll see you again soon. Our business isn't finished."

As she walked away, Silas felt unsettled. Her bold appearance tore away his illusion of safety. Would she be brazen enough to attack in front of so many witnesses, at the risk of revealing what they were? If they went toe-to-toe out in the open, it would be an evening news event.

Even worse than the overt threat was the subliminal one: the way the scent of her shuddered through him even now, leaving him raw and pulsing with the need to grab her, to taste her, to take her down to the floor, right here, right now in a roaring madness so out of his control it terrified him. Some kind of hoodoo spell? Some scientific trap to seduce him with pheromones? Whatever she was using to entrance him, it was making self-preservation damned difficult.

It's destined. She's your mate.

He shook off the words his sister had planted in his brain. There was nothing fated about this unnatural attraction. There was another explanation. And he would find it and use it to sever the dangerous fascination—before it killed him.

Nica stepped out of the club, her expression fierce enough to make the bouncer take a quick step back.

What was *wrong* with her? What was it about this insignificant Shifter male that tied her intentions up in knots? As she'd waited for him to arrive, she'd swiftly considered ways to eliminate him. She could lure him out to the alley and silently kill him in an instant. With her knife, with her bare hands. Let him drop, then just walk away. An undercover cop killed behind the den of a notorious criminal? No one would look too far to find a motive for his murder.

But the instant she'd seen his face, she wanted to go for his lips, not his throat.

Why? He wasn't *that* astonishingly good-looking. Only his intensity pushed him a notch above merely handsome. He was subtle as a cool breeze, prickling over her arms, tightening her nipples just at the thought of him. Maybe it was his voice, that silky baritone that both soothed and projected powerfully. She couldn't pinpoint the attraction.

Now she'd alerted him to the danger, and he was going to run for cover—or for assistance, either from the law or from the clans. The last thing she needed was a war with the Terriots.

She'd have to finish off the two little weasels, and then MacCreedy, before she could safely await her orders. She couldn't afford to have her presence compromised. Too much was in the balance this time.

She was passing the alley next to the Sweat Shop when a side door opened and a figure slipped outside. Nica eased back into the shadows, wondering if she'd just gotten lucky.

But it was a woman. A voluptuous strawberry blonde whom she would have mistaken for a dancer if not for her pale peach Chanel suit. The sound of quiet weeping reached her and Nica started to move on. None of her business. Then the woman caught her high heel on the step and fell hard onto her hands and knees.

Oh, hell.

Nica went down the alley, crouching beside the now sobbing female. "Hey, it's okay. Let me help you up."

A slender hand with long nails painted to match the suit, and a diamond the size of a grape, took hold of Nica's offered arm. The woman tottered to her feet. Her stockings were shredded, her palms and knees oozing blood. But that wasn't what caught Nica's attention.

The huge sunglasses had slipped down her bloodied nose, exposing an eyelid already beginning to swell shut. And because nothing upset her more than helplessness, Nica's protective instincts growled into play.

She steered the battered woman over to the stairs to the loading dock, easing her down on the metal steps. "You just sit here for a second. I'll go get some ice."

Surprisingly steely fingers gripped her wrist. "No! No, it's all right. I'm fine. Thank you."

"Someone smacked the shit out of you and it's all right? I don't think so."

A sigh lifted the generously augmented breasts beneath a white silk blouse now speckled with dots of crimson. "It's my fault. I'm stupid. I should never have come here."

Nica sat down on the step beside her. "He hits you and it's *your* fault? Don't you see something wrong with that logic? No one has the right to treat you like a punching bag."

Plump lips painted a smeary tangerine curved up in a smile. "You don't even know who I am."

"I don't need to know who you are." A pause. "Who are you?"

"Lena Blutafino. My husband owns this place."

"And apparently thinks he owns you, too."

Lena blew her nose loudly on a lacy scrap she pulled out of her tiny purse, then sniffled, "He does. He took me from a stripper pole to a mansion. He married me, Manny did, gave me a big house in the Garden District, and all these flashy trinkets."

"And a black eye and a bloody nose. I think that kind of cancels out the trinkets."

A sad smile. "And a son. I have a son. And Manny would never, ever let me leave with him. So," she gave a shrug, "I guess I just need to get smarter."

Why did humans take their freedoms for granted? "Leave him. Divorce him. Take him for everything he's got. You've got grounds right here, and you look like you can afford a good attorney."

"He might let me go, but he'd kill me before he'd let me take Paulie—and I couldn't leave him behind." She looked stronger, squaring up now that the shock and pain began to subside, accepting her lot with maddening stoicism.

"Maybe something bad will happen to good old Manny. Ever think of that? Of what you'd do?"

A rather wry smile. "Only every night. I'd open my own interior design studio. I took classes when me and Manny first got married. I wanted to decorate our house, but Manny said I had the taste of a whore." Her shoulders slumped. "I think it would have looked real nice."

Nica's arm went around her, squeezing awkwardly in support. "I bet it would. You just hang on to that dream, Lena. You never know."

"You've been so nice, and I don't even know your name."

"It's Nica. I'm staying at the Quarter House. My... friend Mac Creed is one of your husband's dealers. If you have any more trouble, you can talk to him. He'll help you out or get a message to me." Now why had she involved MacCreedy? It wasn't like he'd be willing to go out of his way to do her a favor, after she'd nearly killed him.

"Maybe for now you can just help me to my car," Lena said wearily.

Nica hoisted Lena up on her ice pick heels and steadied her across the uneven stones. At the curb, Lena straightened, pushed up her dark glasses, and smiled gratefully.

"Thank you, Nica. I won't forget your kindness." And she slid into her dove-gray Mercedes and drove away.

Kindness. Since when was she *kind*?

Her honorable hero was becoming a really bad influence on her.

Carmen Blutafino's office was a porn star's fantasy: all mirrors and shine and sleaze. MacCreedy had been inside only once, when he was hired, and he'd had to suppress the urge to use an antiseptic wipe on the chair before sitting down. When he knocked this time and was told to enter, he saw there was another visitor. He didn't need an introduction, he knew the man's name and history from the news and police reports he'd scoured.

Max Savoie lounged in an expensive suit paired with red high-tops, one of which bobbed indolently at the end of his crossed leg. He'd inherited an empire from the mobster he'd protected since making a name for himself as a teen. That name was whispered in awe and fear, allegedly soaked in the blood of those who challenged Jimmy Legere.

Since assuming Legere's mantle, Savoie had embraced public life by appearing at high-profile social events, by being a partner in a huge urban reclamation project called Trinity Towers, by becoming very involved with a detective in the NOPD. Some said he was moving his business toward legality, but the fact that he was with Blutafino cast doubt on that.

Silas wasn't interested in what people speculated about Savoie, though: because he knew the truth. The man's surface sophistication couldn't hide what he really was.

Max Savoie was damned by the unavenged souls of Silas's family. And their wailing for justice nearly drowned out all reason as Silas stood rigidly in the doorway.

"Creed, come in," Manny called. "Freshen my drink and pour one for yourself while I finish my business here. I'll just be a minute."

An amiable smile spread across gritted teeth. "Can I get you anything, Mr. Savoie?"

The sleek killer gave him a cool glance. "No. Thank you."

Crossing behind Savoie's chair on his way to the well-stocked bar, MacCreedy drew in the man's scent. Savoie twitched at the subtle intrusion, picking up the fact that he was being psychically touched, but he didn't acknowledge it. Now they both knew each other for what they were, and were not. What they were not, was human.

Silas fought to steady hands that still felt his mother's blood upon them as he mixed Blutafino's drink. He blinked hard to dispel the image of his father's dismembered body gruesomely strewn at his feet. His stomach pitched and tightened as the scorching stench returned to his nose at the agony of the Terriots' mark being burned into his skin. He fiercely buried the shock, the horror, the pain, and quieted the shrieks for retribution with a promise. *The time is coming. Justice will be done.*

Behind him, he heard Manny say, "Now that you're back, it's time to make good on your promises, Max."

"Remind me, Carmen," came Savoie's smooth reply.

Silas could feel his employer's displeasure without seeing it color his florid face.

"We had a deal, Savoie. You were going to move some special cargo for me. I have a shipment that needs to go out, and you have a freighter all ready to head to a mutually profitable destination. Why are you hedging on our agreement?"

"I'm not hedging. I just got back into town. This is the first business stop I've made in response to your excessive number of messages, some of which had a rather unfriendly tone. I'm wondering why you thought you needed to bring threats to the table for an arrangement between friends and gentlemen?" That cool drawl of reproach was about as subtle as a slap, and Blutafino responded with poorly concealed rage.

"Stop acting like you're either of those things. You're a lying crook, just like that bastard Legere. I'm not going to let you screw me over and say thank you. I'm not your cop bitch girlfriend."

Silence, then a low rumble. " 'Cuse me? What did you just say to me? Something like, 'Please kill me now for being stupid enough to let these words come out of my mouth'? I think I'd like an apology. Now."

"I'm not scared of you, Savoie. This is my place and I can say what I please. If you don't like it, get the hell out and consider our arrangement ended. And you can expect your cop whore to receive a tape of your 'getting to know you' meeting with that sweet little stripper you've got on the side."

Silas heard a deep, amused chuckle. "Send it, Carmen. We'll watch it together. I think we'd enjoy that." His chair skidded back and Silas turned to see Savoie rising out of it with a powerful thrust that brought him halfway across Blutafino's desk with his palms planted flat and their noses inches apart. "Don't you ever think to blackmail me, or I'll make gravy from your cowardly marrow and eat you for lunch with a side of red beans and rice. And I *don't* make threats."

Blutafino sat frozen, a trembling mouse beneath the gaping jaws of a lion.

Then Savoie straightened to assume that civil mask once more. "I think we should adjourn this meeting until cooler heads prevail. We'll speak again, Carmen. And I'll want that apology."

As Savoie crossed to the door with an arrogant strut, Silas set Blutafino's martini on the desk, noting the deep grooves Savoie had torn into the leather desk pad with his nails.

Savoie softly closed the door, and Carmen Blutafino's glass shattered against it as he screamed, "You son of a bitch! No one talks to me like that. No one! You're going to regret it with your last breath!"

Jacques LaRoche glanced up from the beer tap into the mirror to see a familiar face behind him. Grinning, he turned. "Charlotte, when did you find time to sit still long enough to get that tan?"

Despite the deeper color of her café au lait skin, Detective Charlotte Caissie looked far from rested. Her eyes were shadowed by sorrow, her brow creased with worry. But her smile for the big bartender was genuine.

"Sun, sand, and sex. Just what the doctor ordered."

"You're killing me," he groaned. "I haven't had a vacation in . . . ever. Did you bring Savoie back with you, or did you use him up and leave him behind?"

"He's meeting me here in a while. I was in the mood for something familiar."

"Like my face?" His grin widened. He liked and admired Savoie's Upright girlfriend, who joined Jacques in fearlessly protecting their clan leader's back. She was one of the few humans allowed in his club and, after several rocky, distrustful months, was accepted there. "Get you your usual?"

A husky voice said, "Hello, Lottie. You don't remember me, do you?"

Cee Cee swiveled on the bar stool toward the new waitress at *Cheveux du Chien*. Jacques had given her the job after her intercession had stopped a group of Shifters from attacking Charlotte out front.

Charlotte smiled her gratitude. "Of course I do. And thank you again. How's Jacques treating you?"

"He works me like a dockhand, but I have no complaints." Then a mysterious smile. "We've met before. A long time ago, when we were children."

Cee Cee studied her closely, then gave a small cry. "Oh my God! Mony? I don't believe it!" She told Jacques, "We grew up at St. Bart's together. We haven't seen each other for, what, fifteen years?"

"So long ago. It's Nica, now. Mony makes me sound like a tweenager."

Cee Cee remembered the toughly independent kid with the hard, suspicious eyes. She hadn't been young or innocent when she'd been brought as an orphan under Father Furness's sheltering wing. Most of the children were afraid of her glowering stares and moody silences, which only Mary Kate Malone could draw her out of. She'd followed the effervescent Mary Kate around like a stray puppy—and then she'd disappeared, a runaway at twelve.

"You took off without a word to anyone. Why?"

Nica rolled her eyes and gestured to the room of patrons behind her. "Let's just say I had an identity crisis."

Cee Cee understood: she'd discovered her Shifter heritage.

"Have you seen Father Furness yet?"

Nica smiled evasively. "I plan to. I have a lot to thank him for. How's Mary Kate? Married and raising a basketball team of her own?"

"No. I just got back from seeing her. She's in a rehabilitation facility in California."

Nica's eyebrows shot up. "Rehab?"

"Not that kind." The truth was much more painful. "She was involved in a shooting and a fire. For a while they didn't think she'd live, or ever wake up."

Nica's hand rested gently on her forearm. "Is she better now?"

"Hey," came a loud shout from a table. "What happened to my drink?"

"I'm giving you time to absorb the gallon you've already put away," Nica called, blowing the customer a kiss to make him grin. Then she looked at Cee Cee. "I've got to get back to work. It was nice seeing you."

"Let's get together and catch up. Soon, okay?"

Nica nodded and gave her drink orders to Jacques. *Yes, soon.*

"Mr. Savoie."

Max paused with a hand atop his big town car, one step from getting inside. He knew who was approaching him before he even turned.

"I don't think I know you," he said as he sized up the

man from Manny's office. He was tall, meeting him eye to eye with a direct, steely gaze. He carried himself well, clearly confident and capable of getting things done.

But there was something else, too. When Max first looked around, there was a glint of emotion in the man's face, like intense light flashing off the barrel of an assassin's gun before a killing shot. Then it was gone, masked behind a narrow smile.

"I wanted to make myself known to you out of respect for your position in the local clan." He reached for Max's hand, bowing over it slightly with stiff formality. "I'm Silas MacCreedy. I'm working undercover with Alain Babineau."

A detective and a shape-shifter, Max mused. "How long have you been in New Orleans?"

"I transferred in from Baton Rouge to work the Tides that Bind case with Detectives Caissie and Schoenbaum. I wanted to speak to you about a rather delicate situation before you heard the details from Jacques LaRoche."

Max's attention sharpened. "Heard what, exactly?"

"About the four Shifters who attacked Detective Caissie."

Charlotte had said nothing about the confrontation, and finding out about it secondhand did *not* please him. "Go on."

"Two of them are dead. LaRoche took care of their bodies so no questions would be asked."

"And the other two?" he asked, figuring that was where this conversation was going.

"They're in hiding at my suggestion. They're working for Blutafino."

His people aligned with Manny? That couldn't be good. "Where are they now?"

"They're in the bayou near Marrero, expecting me to bring them get-out-of-town money. I thought you might like to come along and ask some questions of your own."

Max knew from harsh experience that being an officer of the law didn't necessarily mean abiding by it. The vibes he was getting from MacCreedy were all over the place, too subtle to pin down. A fierce rip and ebb was going on under his smooth surface, but Max couldn't tell which way that current flowed until he waded in.

"Let me make a quick call."

Max walked to the end of the block and keyed a number into his cell. "What do you know about a Silas MacCreedy?"

"MacCreedy?" Charlotte's curiosity was audible over the loud background revelry of *Cheveux du Chien*. "He got temporarily assigned to work that last case with us. He was partnered with Stan until he was put on disciplinary leave. Good cop: tough, smart, coolheaded."

"Beyond the badge, is he someone you trust, *sha*?"

"I haven't spent much time with him, but yes, I got that impression. What's this about?"

"He and I are going to do a little sightseeing. I might be late. Wait for me at the house. I have things to discuss with you."

"What kind of things?" she asked warily.

"That's what I plan to find out."

"Max, be careful. I don't know him well."

"Noted." He closed the phone and returned to smile easily at MacCreedy. "We'll take my car."

The interior of the plush vehicle was silent as they crossed over the Mississippi River Bridge and headed for LA 45.

Silas stared intently ahead, so aware of Savoie beside him his nerves were jumping. A prime opportunity was slipping by with every mile, but he couldn't manage interrogative small talk. Usually he had no trouble remaining stoic even under the most trying circumstances, a survival skill he'd cultivated in the dangerous political clime where he'd grown into manhood. To show one's emotions was to reveal weakness or betray an advantage. That gift of impassiveness that served him well at Blutafino's gaming table had also kept him and his loved ones alive after the brutal purge.

He caught himself rubbing the scars on his wrist, and stopped before Savoie took notice.

The Terriots had scoffed at rumors of Savoie's unusual powers of perception, but Silas believed them. He'd found the most bizarre impossibilities, like the superstitions so steeped in their culture, were usually based in fact.

As they left the sprawl of clustered communities behind for long stretches of wilderness, Silas used all his concentration to control his breathing, his heartbeat, even his perspiration, lest Savoie scent something was wrong. If the ruthless clan leader sensed the darkness swirling through his soul at being within reach of the cause of his ruin, Max would act without mercy. As his father had before him.

So Silas quieted his fevered thirst for revenge and played the role of cop and submissive rather than that of avenger, even as it beat savagely in his heart.

Wait. Patience will be rewarded.

By making this offering to Savoie, he hoped to gain a level of trust that would give him access to other key opportunities. And if Nica became too great a danger, having Savoie as an ally wouldn't be a bad thing. She wasn't afraid to go boldly after him, but Savoie's presence might give her pause. He didn't want to be the one to take her life, and he didn't want to order it done, either. If an alliance with Savoie could get her to stand down and give him room to finish his business, Silas would make it. He'd see to his family's future, then satisfy his need for restitution. And maybe both he and Nica would walk out alive.

"Where do your loyalties lie, MacCreedy?"

Savoie's question startled him. Had the mobster sensed the direction of this thoughts? "What do you mean?"

"Are you a cop or are you of the clans? Which comes first if you have to choose?"

"I enjoy being a detective, but it doesn't define what I am inside." He looked over to meet Savoie's intent stare. "Just like you're a criminal, but that's not who you are down deep where it counts."

A smile quirked Savoie's lips. "Then we are much the same. On the surface. You've taken off your glasses."

Silas withdrew them from his pocket. "They're just for appearances." He put them on. "Clark Kent." Took them off. "Superman." At Max's puzzled frown, he laughed. "Never mind."

"What's that mark you bear?"

Silas extended his wrist as if it was no big thing. "It's a clan tattoo of allegiance from when I was too young to be on my own."

Max's thumb traced over the brand, following the scars that resembled the symbol for pi, measuring the pulse beneath it as he asked, "What clan?"

"Terriot. I'm a distant relation. Do you know of them?"

"I've heard the name," he said, giving no indication of what it might mean to him or what he knew about their history with his own family. He released Silas's wrist and asked bluntly, "Did they send you here to kill me?"

For a moment, Silas didn't breathe. Nor did he blink at the other's hard scrutiny. "No," he answered. "Whatever beef they might have with you isn't my concern. I look out for my own family. The Terriots have done me no great favors; I don't owe them anything. My job brought me here."

"Your job as a cop?"

"To see justice done."

"And are you good at your job?"

"Yes. Very."

Savoie gave that closed-lipped smile again, then told his driver, "Pete, take a right on three-oh-one."

The swamp tour office was a small Quonset in a yard draped with souvenirs. Silas wondered if his own teeth and claws would be hanging up with those luckless predators' when this trip was finished.

He asked about a private charter, and the teenage girl selling tickets to a busload of tourists pointed over to a group of boat captains wearing logo T-shirts.

Savoie was standing at the car, stripping out of his suit jacket and tie in the steamy late-afternoon heat, then tossing them and his dress shirt into the backseat before joining MacCreedy. In the snug white A-shirt, he looked lean and powerful, making Silas weigh whether he'd be able to hold his own if things got ugly. If rumors were true, that Savoie had ripped seven Trackers sent down from the North into pieces too small to find, it wasn't a slam dunk.

Soberly, he approached the captains to ask about a ride to Troy DuPree's while dangling the alligator tooth he'd been given to earn their cooperation. Captain Ray Bob Pascal, a barrel-chested man with a Cajun accent so thick he could spread it on biscuits, said he'd take them and named an outrageous fee. Savoie stared at the man through impenetrable sunglasses, then silently opened his wallet.

Captain Ray Bob took the high seat in front of the huge caged blades on the flat-bottomed airboat, and Silas and Max settled into two of the six seats in the bow, buckling up and securing noise-canceling headphones. What began as a low putter as they glided away from the dock soon racheted up to a jet engine roar that whined and throbbed through their ear protection. The airboat pounded over Bayou Barataria with a surprising speed until the captain turned off into one of the narrow ribbons threading into the wetlands and swamps. With no breeze or cooling spray, the broiling sun glittered blindingly off the water.

As an asphalt and steel city boy, Silas was used to targeting dangers in dark alleys and empty buildings, not in this muggy backwater jungle. He kept a cautious eye on the shadowed shoreline as they steered in close, searching the exposed roots, low-hanging branches, and the wispy gray beards of moss for signs of anything living.

Savoie eased off his headphones to turn to their captain, who cut the engine down low to hear him.

"Are we almost there?"

"Jus' round dat bend a piece. Troy gots a little shack back dare on da right."

"Let me off here."

Silas glanced at the ominous network of vines and stumps choking the bank and looked at Savoie like he was crazy.

"They're not expecting you to have company," Max explained. "Better that you go in alone so we don't spook them."

"Knock yourself out." As long as he didn't have to get

out on anything less solid than a dock, it was okay with MacCreedy.

Max unbuckled his seat belt and moved to the narrow platformed edge on the side of the boat. With a quick leap, he was out and perched upon one of the twisted tree branches. Silas motioned for the captain to continue. He didn't look back to watch Savoie's progress because if he went into the water, there was no way in hell Silas was going in after him.

As soon as they rounded the bend, he could see Du-Pree's rickety cabin balancing on precariously thin stilts like a water bird. Captain Ray Bob nudged the airboat up against a long wooden dock that led to the front porch, making it sway. Something large moved out from under its shadow to slip underwater, and Silas's stomach tightened.

He eased out of the boat onto the warped boards, instructing the captain to return in a half hour. As the boat started away, the dock rocked with its wake. Silas rode out the motion, then worked his way cautiously to the porch. He crossed to the door and was about to knock, when it opened.

And he found himself staring down double barrels.

Six

Get that out of my face," MacCreedy growled.

The shotgun lowered. "Was beginning to think you weren't gonna show," Nash said.

He moved aside so Silas could enter. The rustic shanty contained one all-purpose room. A cracked sink basin, a hot plate, and a refrigerator probably as old as he was, along with a card table and four folding chairs, were on one side. Two army surplus cots, a portable television tuned to a loud game show, and a stack of tattered porn magazines made up the living area. Empty bottles were scattered on every surface. A curtain in the back portioned off the bathroom. The room reeked of sweat, stale beer, pot, and fear.

Willis was lying on a tangled sleeping bag atop one of the army surplus cots, his face fever-flushed, his eyes glazed.

"What's with him?"

Nash pushed shaky fingers through unkempt hair. "Took one in the shoulder a few weeks back. By the time I dug it out, infection was already spreading. He's getting better." There wasn't much hope in that claim, clearly made for Willis's benefit. His features tightened. "Upright bitch had silver bullets."

"I don't appreciate you calling my girlfriend a bitch," a deep voice rumbled. "And I *really* don't like that you tried to kill her."

The sight of Max Savoie in the doorway like a dark, avenging spirit made Nash go deathly gray. Uttering a hoarse cry, he fell to his knees.

"We didn't mean her no harm, Mr. Savoie. Honest. We was just trying to scare her off so she'd stay out of our business."

"What business is that?"

Nearly blubbering in terror, Nash forgot all other loyalties. "We was making extra cash working for Mr. Blutafino. Please don't kill us!"

Max stared dispassionately at the groveling figure clutching at his pantleg. "What kind of work?"

"He'd give us a list of names and we'd bring 'em to him. We didn't hurt 'em, I swear we didn't."

"Shifter females?"

The bowed head bobbed rapidly.

Max exchanged a look with Silas, who was equally puzzled. "What did he do with them? Turn them out as prostitutes?" he asked Nash.

"No. I don't know."

"Which is it?" Max demanded.

"He was selling them," Nash cried out. "I think he was selling them to some medical clinic up north." He cowered on the bare board floor, watching Savoie's inscrutable features for a clue to his fate.

Selling their own kind, *females*, for God knew what

kind of abuse. If Savoie wanted to kill them, MacCreedy wouldn't stop him. These two scum were witnesses whose testimony could never be permitted to come out into the open for fear of what they might give away. So, what to do with them?

Savoie glanced from the huddled creature on the floor to Silas. "You said there were four of them. Who killed the other two?"

MacCreedy's jaw tightened.

"It was that she-wolf what got them," Nash spoke up. "The one I was telling Mr. Creed about."

Max gave Silas a stare that silently asked, *Why is this the first I'm hearing about this?* Then he turned back to Nash. "Tell me."

Eager to earn his favor, Nash spilled everything. How Amber, a waitress at the bar, had tipped them that the Upright cop was asking questions about the females who'd gone missing, and how LaRoche had made Amber give up their names to the detective. How they'd waited for Caissie to come out of the bar alone—to *scare* her, Nash emphasized, not to harm her.

"She doesn't scare," Max advised flatly.

Nash swallowed hard. "Nossir, she don't. She put one in Willis and things kinda got outta hand."

"And did you put those hands on my mate?" Savoie asked, as low and deadly as a suddenly unsheathed blade.

No male who wanted to go on breathing touched another's mate. It was quick and violent suicide. Realizing that, Nash amended, "That was Mickey. He roughed her

up some and then . . . and then the other one, she was just
there. Red eyes and fangs and ready to tear us to shreds,
until LaRoche came outside and she changed back so he
wouldn't see what she was."

"A female shape-shifter," Max said, apparently having
no trouble believing it

Nash nodded. "Scared us spitless. We musta run miles
just to make sure she wasn't behind us."

"Who is she?"

"Never seen her before. Never want to again. Ask
your buddy there. He got up close and personal with her
after she tricked us into coming after her in that alley the
other night. Wasn't sure until just now, but he was the
one who grabbed onto her while we was getting away,
after she kilt Mickey and Len."

Again, Max's reassessing gaze touched on Mac-
Creedy before he replied, "You saw what she is, and now
she wants you dead. Is that about it?"

"And Creed said he'd help us get outta town 'fore the
law or Mr. Blutafino was the wiser."

"Sounds like a smart plan. Let me talk a minute with
Mr. Creed while you get your belongings together."

Silas followed Max out onto the porch.

"Tell me about this female who changes shape."

Silas had no obligation to protect Nica after she'd
tried to rip out his throat. And he knew it was in his
best interest to hand the matter over to Savoie and walk
away, safe from her retaliation. But he'd tasted her lips.
He'd known a harshly beautiful pleasure within her body.

To betray her as if she meant nothing went against his conscience, stirring up a rebellion between his heart and mind. He *knew* she was a danger to him and his plans, yet he couldn't suppress the fierce, possessive need to keep her from harm at his enemy's hands.

"I can introduce you," Silas began carefully. "If you promise to keep things civil."

Complex emotions flickered across Savoie's face: annoyance, amusement, curiosity. Then he smiled, showing his teeth. "No need for it to become anything else. I'll call our transportation back while you see to our friends."

Silas watched Savoie move to the end of the dock, his steps sure and relaxed. Could he be trusted? Absolutely not. Was there any other choice? None came to mind. MacCreedy reminded himself that this was where he needed to be in order to see his goals accomplished. That's where he needed to focus.

The sounds that came from within the shanty could have been Nash gathering their meager possessions, but instinct told MacCreedy to be wary as he approached. His senses were suddenly alive and tingling.

But caution couldn't prepare him for the bloodbath inside the small room. Arterial spray striped the walls, and what was left of Nash and Willis would tell no tales.

"Son of a—"

A hand clutched his throat, squeezing off further sound as he was pushed against the wall with a force that made it tremble. Another hand clamped over his mouth.

MacCreedy hadn't felt her presence but now her

scent overwhelmed him, rushing to his head like brain freeze to ache and paralyze. When he tried to struggle she began a slow compression, blocking his airway until dots of blackness swirled across his vision, obscuring her cold, deadly features. She leaned close. He couldn't turn his head away.

"I'm sorry, lover," Nica whispered against his ear, her breath soft and warm. "Try not to feel used. I couldn't afford to let them live, not after what they'd seen."

He'd led her right to them! Humiliated fury returned strength to his resistance, but she quashed it easily with the press of her body, with the tightening of her hand. His senses swam and began to fade as she advised, "Don't fight. I don't want to hurt you."

He reached up, clasping the hand over his mouth. She let him pull it away without loosening her stranglehold.

"I've seen what you are, too," he goaded hoarsely, too angry for fear as he felt the sting of her claws at his jugular. "Aren't you going to kill me, too?"

She chuckled and leaned in closer, until her lips caressed over his with a taunting tenderness. "Shhh. Not yet, hero."

She stared into his eyes, hers all glittery promise. Silas was lost in them as in a mesmerist's crystal, seduced by their dark brilliance, held prisoner there by his own confusion. He could feel her hot, smoky desire for him and crazy things drifted through his fogged thoughts. *Stay with me. Don't go. I can protect you.*

Maybe that desire was a two-edged sword.

The press of her lips softened, conforming to the shape of his. Her fingers relaxed at his throat, a second of weakness. He gripped her forearms, spinning her around so her back was to the wall and his formidable size imprisoned her there. She didn't resist, for the moment content to submit. They exchanged hurried breaths and fierce heartbeats.

Then they heard the sound of Savoie's approach.

Nica's glance darted to the door, her need to escape breaking the thick, sensual haze between them, and she struggled to free herself.

Once he saw the carnage strewn about the cabin, Savoie's first instinct would be to kill her. Silas's grasp loosened. Her lunge to the side unbalanced them, and they went down hard on the floor. As she scrambled over him, the door opened.

Max's first glance interpreted the situation as life threatening. The force of his backhanded blow sent Nica across the room. He swiftly knelt beside Silas to check his condition, then he rose up purposefully, nails lengthening into claws as his attention turned to the dazed assassin.

Silas's reaction was as instinctive as it was bewildering. He gripped Max's ankles, tangling his stride and bringing him crashing to the floor as Nica leapt to her feet and disappeared through the rear curtain.

As he held on to Savoie's writhing legs, Silas realized his foolishness, but contained him until he was certain of Nica's escape. The second he eased his grip Savoie was on him, his hand fitting the mark Nica's had left on his throat. Silas put up his hands.

"You better explain yourself before I bury you along with them," Savoie demanded, his grasp opening so Silas could breathe.

"They were already dead," he rasped out, rubbing his abused neck. "If she'd wanted to, she'd have killed me before I crossed the threshold."

"Why did you stop me from going after her?"

"Because she did what we couldn't make ourselves do. She got rid of a problem that was going to bite us in the ass." Seeing he had Savoie's attention, he continued, "They were taking money for the sale of innocent females. *Our* females. Do you seriously think any amount of cash or distance was going to keep them quiet about what they were doing, about what they saw? I don't have that kind of faith in their integrity. Do I approve of what she did? No. Do I regret it was done? I don't think I do." If Savoie wanted to kill him for that honesty, so be it.

Silence stretched out as Max considered his words. "I can still track her."

"No need. I know where she's going." He smiled wryly. "She's not afraid of us, and she's not going to hide."

"Let's clean up this mess." Max put down his hand, grasping MacCreedy by the forearm to haul him to his feet. "Then it's time for that introduction."

It took a lot of hot water and lather to scrub the stench of the swamp off her skin. Wrapped in an oversize towel,

Nica padded into the bedroom to pull a tube of scented body lotion from her backpack. Warming it first in her palms, she began to smooth it over her legs as her mind spun.

Leaving MacCreedy and Savoie alive was a problem, but one she could handle. She had no doubt about her abilities. What she'd begun to doubt were her intentions.

Her MO was quick in-and-out, no time for attachments. She never got close enough to care, so if she had to exterminate an unexpected risk, she could take care of it without hesitation.

MacCreedy made her hesitate. And damned if she knew why.

She rubbed on the moisturizer with quick, aggravated motions. He stirred feelings up inside her. Agitation, uncertainty, and worst of all, anticipation. She looked forward to their confrontations. MacCreedy made her feel restless and unsettled, unsatisfied.

It was more than sex. She could indulge lust without conscience or complication. She'd enjoyed other attractive males before, slaking her needs and her interest in them on her own terms and timetable. MacCreedy was upsetting both.

He'd kept Savoie from pursuing her. Why? It wasn't a logical choice. She'd pegged Silas as methodically intelligent and admired that about him. He should have let Savoie go after her rather than creating tension between himself and the dangerous Shifter king. As a stranger to New Orleans he needed strong connections, yet he'd risked them for her. Finding no answer why chafed her uneasiness.

The soothing vanilla notes of the lotion warmed with the heat of her skin, but for once the familiar scent and its subliminal associations failed to calm her. She rested her cheek upon her updrawn knee, her brow furrowing.

What was MacCreedy's angle? He had to be up to something, want something. Her anxiety twisted tighter. She shouldn't be analyzing her feelings for MacCreedy. She shouldn't be thinking about him at all, except as a potential liability.

And now there was Savoie to worry about, as well.

How could she gain the upper hand? Though it went against her independent nature, she needed someone to have her back.

Going into the kitchen, Nica poured a glass of the pinot gris and as she sipped, she began to smile. She needed an ace, an unexpected card that would flip things in her favor, and her past would provide it.

Nica reached for her phone and dialed. "Hello, Lottie. I know it's late, but could you meet me for a drink?"

Nica had lived at St. Bart's from the time she was seven until she ran away at twelve. Unlike most of the orphans there, she hadn't thought of it as a home or salvation. To her, it was a prison.

Having survived on the streets, roaming the shadows with a feral band of discarded children, she'd learned the skills necessary to escape notice and capture: how to hide, how to lie, how to steal, how to kill, and how not to trust. The walls and rules of St. Bart's smothered her. Overtures of care or affection were greeted with hostility and suspicion. Only three breached her instinctive guard. Father Furness, who'd refused to give up on her, she respected; Mary Kate Malone, who was like a fairy princess in the storybooks she devoured, dazzled her; and Charlotte Caissie, who treated her like an annoyance, was her idol.

Father Furness took her in without question. He told her she'd have a safe place to sleep, eat, and learn, if she'd abide by the ten very difficult commandments that governed his spiritual life. At seven she'd already broken a considerable number of them, but he told her with infinite patience what was past was past.

He didn't understand. She didn't need or want his rules or forgiveness.

At first she'd considered him a foolish mark, with his unrealistic ideals and tender heart. Then he'd come upon some street toughs who'd surprised her on her way back from school. He'd waded into them like a holy fury, then carried her the remaining blocks home within the strong wrap of his arms. In those moments, she'd felt a security she'd never known before. He was the only one who'd ever come to her defense without an agenda—until Silas MacCreedy. Or so she'd wanted to believe.

Truth had a way of crushing trust. Father Furness had sheltered her because of the special talents he'd kept a secret from her. MacCreedy had been working on a case.

But still, in those first moments, when he'd thought she was the victim, he'd risked breaking cover to come to her aid. And he'd kept Savoie from coming after her today. Neither intervention had been necessary, and both left a trembly confusion in the pit of her belly whenever she thought of him.

So she wouldn't think of him. She'd look into her past.

Mary Kate Malone had been everything Nica dreamed of becoming, but knew she never would. Beautiful, care-free, generous, filled with laughter and love. She'd adopted Nica like a little stray, showering her with attention and small gifts and affection, which were received with wary caution. It simply astounded Nica to think such things could be so freely given, with no strings attached. So she watched for them, waiting for the trap to spring. It never did. Mary Kate Malone might have been the first and only human she'd loved with a child's desperate greed.

Lottie Caissie was as different from her best friend Mary Kate as night and sunny day. Like Nica, Charlotte was dark souled and distant, an outsider who preferred to observe rather than participate. Her father was a cop, which made her immediately suspect. But when the older girl had caught Nica lifting her cigarettes and change, instead of reporting the theft, Charlotte had told her to apologize and mean it. Nica had and did, because Lottie had told her if she tried to steal from her again, she'd be in a body cast. Nica believed her, and admired that honorable fierceness. Honor was a mystery to her, a luxury she couldn't afford, balanced against survival.

It was Charlotte who taught her how to throw a punch and how to roll with them. From her stoic tutor, Nica had learned to adapt without submission, and how to get what she wanted without guile or lies, though her own way was far easier. While she coveted Mary Kate's glamour and femininity, it was Charlotte's impressive swagger she mimicked.

It still impressed her. She smiled as she watched the detective stride through the room of unnatural beings as if she were walking up a church aisle, without any fear or awareness of her precarious situation. Her façade still bristled with self-assurance and "Get the fuck outta my way" aggression. But there was something else, too. Something that surprised her.

Charlotte Caissie gave off a glimmer.

Though it was faint and probably undetectable to the baser shape-shifters inside the club, Nica picked up on that psychic vibration that existed in all her kind. But Charlotte was *human*. So how could she exude that signature of power? Unless . . .

Unless she'd bonded with Max Savoie.

A human and a Shifter. Impossible. Unheard of.

Fascinating.

And in light of Nica's purpose in New Orleans, dangerous.

Seven

They were on their second round, Nica drinking dark beer and Charlotte tonic water.

"Tell me about this Max Savoie I've been hearing so much about," Nica prompted after they'd gotten through the "Bring me up to date" talk. "Is he as badass as the rumors say?"

Charlotte leaned back in her chair, her smile smug, her eyes gleaming. "They don't even come close. Max is ... complicated."

"And you're in love with him."

Charlotte grinned.

"So how did a nice little red-white-and-badge like you get hooked up with America's Most Wanted?"

Even before Charlotte spoke, Nica saw the shadow of terrible things in her eyes.

"About a year after you left, Mary Kate and I got nabbed by some mobster knee breakers to keep my father from giving damaging testimony. They took their job above and beyond what they'd been ordered to do."

"Bad?"

"As bad as it gets," she said flatly. "Until Max rescued us."

Nica leaned forward, elbows on the table, chin on her

laced fingers, intrigued. "But wasn't he working *for* the mob?"

"For Jimmy Legere, the one I always suspected was behind the kidnapping and my father's murder."

"So why did he do it? Why did he risk everything for the two of you?"

"Because he couldn't look away. And I've been in love with him since the first moment I saw him, because I couldn't, either."

Nica was amazed. "Even though he's a shape-shifter?"

Charlotte shrugged. "By the time I found out, it didn't matter. That probably sounds crazy to you, doesn't it?"

No. It sounded wonderful, like one of Mary Kate's fairy tales come true. What was crazy was the way the memory of MacCreedy's touch immediately flamed through her.

Charlotte's features suddenly softened and her gaze took on a sultry glow. Without looking behind her, Nica knew Savoie had just entered the room. Was he here for her? She tensed, readying for fight or flight, until large hands settled on her shoulders, pressing her into her seat.

MacCreedy's lips brushed lightly against her cheek. "Don't run," he whispered.

His remark made her stiffen. As if fear would send her rabbiting underground! She turned, her gaze filled with indignation.

"I've been waiting for you," she purred. Her hand

went to the back of his neck, but he didn't wince as her claws dug in. "What took you so long?"

"We took the scenic route." He pulled her hand away, then held it in his. "Did you order me something?" he asked, sitting in the chair beside her.

"I wasn't sure what you wanted."

A slight smile. "Oh, I think you know what I like."

Their gazes held, challenging, searching, smoldering.

Charlotte looked between MacCreedy and Max with the same curious intent with which Max was staring at her and Nica.

"Your friend and I haven't been formally introduced," Max drawled. He pinned Nica with an icy glare. "I'm Max Savoie."

Nica extended her hand with a flirtatious "Ah, the legend. Nice to officially meet you. Lottie and I have been friends since we were children. I didn't think she could surprise me, but she certainly did when it came to you."

He let her hand hang there for a moment while processing that news. "She's surprised me, too," Max murmured, accepting the firm handshake before taking the seat next to his mate. "In several things lately."

Cee Cee avoided the comment by directing hers at MacCreedy. "And what sort of surprises have you been hiding, Mac?"

"Me? Nothing. No one asked me my political, religious, sexual, or species orientation when I came on board at the NOPD. I assumed the status quo was Don't ask, don't tell."

Conversation stopped when their waitress approached. She smiled at Nica, then asked them, "Get you anything from the bar?"

"We'll have a couple of these." Silas gestured to Nica's beer.

Max shook his head. "No, thank you, Amber."

MacCreedy grabbed her wrist, startling a gasp from her. His stare was rapier sharp. "*You* tipped off the four who attacked Detective Caissie?" She paled and tried to tug away, her frightened eyes flashing over to Max.

"MacCreedy," Nica said quietly as her hand settled over his, "let her go. It's all right, Amber. Bring us those drinks. Silas, please." More softly still, "This isn't the time."

The waitress darted away the instant she was freed, leaving them in a contemplative silence Max finally broke. "I think we should make time."

Cee Cee and Silas's pagers went off together, and they pulled out their phones to see the same number: Babineau's.

"Give you a ride, Detective?" Cee Cee offered, grateful to escape Max's interrogation.

"Sure." MacCreedy also rose up.

"I'll walk you out," Nica offered.

Max looked at the three of them with obvious displeasure. "This matter isn't finished. We need a more private venue. You'll come out to the house tomorrow night for dinner."

"I have to work," Nica said quickly.

"I have paperwork to go over with Detective Babineau," Silas spoke up.

"Amber will cover for you," Max told Nica, "and you can bring Babineau with you. He has matters to settle, too." His pointed stare slid to Cee Cee. "Any objections you'd like to make, *cher*?"

"How does seven sound to everyone?" At the reluctant couple's nods, she looked at the glowering Max. "I don't know how late I'll be tonight. Depends on what's going on here. I'll let you know if I'm going to be staying in town."

Max's smile quirked at her obvious attempt at avoidance. "You do that. I'll have Helen make arrangements for tomorrow."

While Cee Cee went to get her car, Nica pulled Silas inside the dark doorway. She stood close, tucking her hands into the back pockets of his jeans, rubbing her nose into his soft cotton T-shirt and inhaling his scent. He stood very still, barely breathing.

"Did you bring him here to find me?" she asked.

"He would have done so eventually. I thought it might be better if I came along."

"To protect my back or his?"

"My own."

She laughed, not believing him. Her hands began to knead through the denim. "You could come over after you're finished with your call."

His palms settled easily on the subtle curve of her hips. "I could, but I'm not going to."

"You're still angry with me." Her gaze lifted, teasing, tempting. "Or are you playing hard to get?"

"That would be silly, considering we both know how easily you get to me."

She smiled, her chin lifting in invitation. He lowered his head until their lips touched, once very softly, again very silkily, then with enough heat to set off the fire alarms.

"Come over," she sighed into his kisses. "You've tried the floor. The bed is more comfortable."

He nipped at her lips, tasting and parting them so his tongue could slip inside for a quick, sensual dance.

"I don't think so. I don't trust you enough to close my eyes around you."

She gave a husky chuckle as she tugged his hips against her. "I promise you won't be sleeping."

His hold tightened, pulling her against the rock-hard proof of his interest, until her eyes closed and her head fell back. When his mouth pressed to her neck, she moaned. When he set her away from him, she staggered.

"What do you want, Nica? Is this the way you keep your enemies closer?"

She drew a stabilizing breath before meeting his steady stare. Honorable men—God help her. She shrugged and said reasonably, "We're not enemies. I like you. I like having sex with you. Why should it be more complicated than that?"

"It's not going to happen."

As he slipped past her, she laughed. "Think again, MacCreedy."

"You're a Shifter." Cee Cee got right to the point as she drove her powerful car down the tight network of streets.

"I'm a lot of things."

"What are you doing in New Orleans?"

"I already went through all this with your boyfriend."

"Then you won't have to think very hard about the answer."

"My job."

Her dark eyes flashed over to assess him. "As what?"

"A detective. Those four who jumped you were kidnapping girls for Blutafino. And the girls weren't picked randomly."

"Why do you say that?"

"They were clan females, selected because they had something of interest to some clinic up north."

"The Chosen."

Silas angled toward her on the seat to demand, "What do you know about them?"

"Not damned near enough. But I know they're dangerous, and I know they've sent their Trackers down here to snoop around." She gave him a gauging look. "About the same time you showed up."

MacCreedy gave a snort. "I don't work for them. I avoid them." He paused. "How well do you know Nica?"

"Funny, Max asked me the same question about you.

Guess we'll all have time to get to know one another tomorrow night."

"I'm looking forward to it." He *was* looking forward to it. To getting inside those well-guarded walls, where he'd be closer to his goal than he could have ever hoped.

"Does Babs know what you are?"

"He knows I'm a cop and he trusts me to have his back."

"And do you?" Delivered like a knife jab.

"Yes. Your partner's safe with me. I *picked* this job, Detective. It wasn't assigned to me. I'm trained and skilled, just like you are. I take it seriously and I do it aboveboard. I'm not one of your boyfriend's undocumented outcasts, hiding out of the mainstream. I want to do things that matter."

Cee Cee chuckled at his defensiveness. "Have a pretty high opinion of yourself, don't you?"

"I earned it, working damned hard."

"Good. You don't need to get all pissy about it. Geez, I have to tiptoe around enough of that shit at home."

Silas enjoyed a laugh at his own expense and relaxed. "Sorry. Habit."

She smiled. "I hear you. Try being a woman."

They drove in silence for a moment. She slowed down as they entered the dockside area Babineau had called from. Then she asked, "How did you get mainstreamed in with us humans?"

"Clan connections. They arranged an identity for me, hoping I'd be useful."

"And are you?"

"When I have to be." He pointed ahead. "There he is."

Cee Cee eased her car next to Babineau's and cut the engine. Her partner came over to lean on her open window.

"Nice tan," he observed, then nodded to Silas. "Got lucky. Spotted Manny slipping out of the club with some interesting company, so I followed. They've been on the ship for about a half hour."

Cee Cee studied the vessel and frowned. "That's one of LEI's. Who took him on board, Babs?"

"You're going to love this. Francis Petitjohn. Question is, does Savoie know about it?"

"I doubt it," MacCreedy said, then gave them a brief summary of the confrontation between Manny and Max he'd overheard in Manny's office.

"So," Babineau mused, "if Max isn't in on this little get-together, could be T-John is planning to make a move on him. Wouldn't have thought he had the balls for it."

"Weasels have sharp teeth, but only strike when they have a sure advantage. Why would T-John be thinking that he does?" Charlotte mused. "Something's going on, and we'd better figure out what pretty damned quick."

"To protect your boyfriend's interests?" Babineau drawled.

Cee Cee wouldn't let it get personal. "Who'd you rather have at the head of Legere Enterprises? Savoie, who's not giving us any grief, or Petitjohn, who'll have the streets running red in no time?"

"Got a point."

Babineau began to straighten when suddenly he was yanked out of sight without a sound.

"Alain?"

Hand going for her gun, Cee Cee was getting out of the car when a large figure loomed up between the parked vehicles. The door came smashing shut, catching her in the temple. As she slumped forward, huge clawed hands gripped her under the arms to drag her out.

Silas saw three of them, already transformed into hulking bestial shapes. As he unbuckled, the car began to rock violently. He was tumbled around as the vehicle went over onto its roof in a slow roll, but as soon as the car settled he came shooting out through an open side window.

Babineau was struggling with one of the man-beasts and Cee Cee sprawled unmoving on the cement. He had two challengers to overcome before he could be of any help to them, and there was only one way to accomplish that quickly.

He shifted.

The astonishment in their eyes was satisfying as the two hired watchdogs saw MacCreedy's T-shirt stretch and tear as his mass increased with explosive power. Taking advantage of their surprise, Silas used that second of hesitation to rip through the throat of the one closest to him. Then the other was on him, knocking him back against the overturned car. Locked together in combat, they grappled for momentum until MacCreedy managed to throw the other down and was instantly on top to quickly finish him.

Covered with blood and deep gouges, Silas leapt over the car to confront the third attacker. He was bigger than the first two, with a massive chest and curling claws. Seeing MacCreedy's rush, he flung Babineau to the ground and charged with the force of an oncoming train. They both went down, snarling and snapping. Silas managed to flip him, got his forearm around the other's neck and an arm wedged up behind his back, and planted the creature's altered face into the pavement.

"Who are you working for?" Silas growled, his voice as harsh and deep as death. "Who hired you to turn against your own kind? Blutafino? Petitjohn?"

With a buck and a twist, the other got MacCreedy's arm between his teeth and would have severed it, if Silas hadn't seized the back of his attacker's neck in mighty jaws to crush his spine. Silas rolled off the lifeless body to clasp his mangled arm, letting go of his animal form to rock and curse in pain.

Babineau crouched over him, muttering, "Son of a bitch. Just when you think you know a guy, he turns into a fucking werewolf."

"You're welcome," Silas groaned as Babineau yanked off his cotton jacket to use as a compress, applying steady pressure to get the bleeding under control. By then, a groggy Cee Cee had come to kneel on the other side of him, and was swiping at the blood on Silas's face with her palm.

"Mac, you okay?"

"Get me up. We gotta get outta here before more of them come sniffing around."

The two humans hauled him to his feet, then were faced with the problem of the upended car.

"Help me," Silas told them simply as he gripped the door frame with both hands and began to lift. Crimson-glazed muscles bulged as he strained and groaned. As soon as the vehicle began to rock up onto its side, the awestruck detectives put their shoulders to it as well and momentum carried the vehicle over to bounce, then settle on its wheels.

Men started to appear on the deck of the ship, and lights began to shine across the dock.

"Tomorrow night, seven, out at the house." Cee Cee didn't give her partner a chance to argue as she shoved MacCreedy into her car, then quickly climbed in herself as Babineau got into his. Then the two cars spun away in different directions to blend into the darkness.

Silas leaned against the car door, eyes closed, cradling his arm to his chest.

"You need a hospital?" Cee Cee asked.

"No. I'll heal. It just takes a little time. Take me home."

Home was a subletted apartment on St. Peters. Cee Cee pulled up in front of the three-story building of salmon-colored stucco with blue shutters. He was on the second floor, and he thought grimly of that flight of stairs.

"What are you going to tell Savoie?"

Cee Cee frowned. "I've got some poking around to do before I drop that bomb on him. I'll stop by for a visit with Antoine D'Marco, LEI's attorney, first, and find out what the pecking order is for controlling interest. See if our buddy Petitjohn has been as busy behind the scenes as I'm beginning to think he's been. If he's planning to make a move on Max, it's going to be his last one."

In too much pain to care about Savoie's politics, Silas heaved himself upright with a groan and pushed open the car door. "I'll see you tomorrow night."

Cee Cee nodded, wincing as she touched her own bruised temple. "Yeah. Seven o'clock."

Moving gingerly up the three front steps, Silas heard her pull away from the curb with a squeal of tires. He took his time with the arduous climb inside, thinking of nothing but a long, hot shower, restorative red meat, and bed. Until he reached his apartment and saw a strip of light beneath the door. He used his key and entered cautiously.

His shotgun apartment was narrow and cramped, furnished for utility rather than comfort. The only thing classy about it was the fiery redhead who swept out of the galley kitchen.

"Don't you have a bottle of decent wine? Where have you been? I've been stuck here for hours waiting for you. And you don't even have cable."

She stood with her fists on curvy hips in a dress that probably cost more than his month's rent, the picture of impatient displeasure while he dripped blood on the carpet. Not a word about his ragged appearance, only her own inconvenience. Sometimes it was damned hard to love her, but he did.

"Nice to see you, too. A call would have probably made for a more gracious welcome."

She sniffed at that. "You would have told me not to come."

"Knowing that, why are you here?"

"Because you won't answer my calls. I don't think you fully appreciate how important this is to our future, or you'd be taking care of things instead of brawling like some animal." Her critical gaze took in his battered state with distaste.

His answer was testy. "I've got an invitation to Savoie's estate tomorrow night. So you see, I *have* been toiling diligently to see to your future happiness and self-indulgence."

She smiled then, and her tone softened like warm honey. "How clever of you. And it's for your happiness, too. It's to get both of us what we want, what we deserve. Or have you forgotten that while playing with your silly human associates?"

Silas growled, "I haven't forgotten anything. I know what the stakes are. Why else would that bastard still be breathing?"

She took a quick step toward him, gripping his arm just above the terrible wound. "You promised you wouldn't act against him, Silas. This isn't the time for vengeance. Stick to the plan, or we'll lose everything."

"What haven't we lost already?" He jerked away, ignoring the pain of that harsh movement as his temper heated. "I know what's in the balance. You have no idea how hard it is to be so close and do nothing."

"You'll have your blood for blood, but not until we regain our power. Remember your obligations."

"When have you ever let me forget them?"

Her gaze grew bittersweet. "You don't need me to punish your conscience, Silas. You take too much joy in that task already." She gently rubbed his tense shoulder, then drew him down to press a light kiss to his furrowed brow. "Are you all right? I've been worried." Finally, that soft note of concern.

A knock at his door was followed by its immediate opening. The two females regarded each other with territorial bristling.

"So," Nica drawled, "this one you can close your eyes around? What's your name, bitch, so I know what to tell the ambulance driver when they pick you up on the curb?"

"Brigit MacCreedy. His sister."

"Nica Fraser. His lover."

Eight

Your *lover?*" Brigit arched an indignant brow at her brother. "I see you *have* forgotten some things."

He fought not to flinch. "Good *night,* Brigit."

"We're not finished here, Silas."

"We are for now. Where are you staying?"

"I have a suite at the Sheraton."

"I'll call you."

"No, you won't, but you'll be hearing from me." Eyeing Nica with a dissecting precision, she sniffed her contempt and strode out into the hall. The door slammed behind her.

"Your sister? That explains a lot."

"What are you doing here?" MacCreedy asked, too tired and sore to pretend civility.

"Keeping you from falling down. Which way to the bathroom?"

She took his elbow carefully and guided him down the narrow hall to the closet-sized bathroom. Closing the lid on the toilet, she had him sit while she ran cold water in the sink and rummaged for supplies. In the cramped quarters, he leaned back against the sweaty tank to avoid the curve of her rump when she turned to soak a hand towel and then wring it out.

"Okay, let's see what we got here." Holding Silas's wrist to steady his arm, she unwrapped the saturated jacket, tossed it in the shower, and began to blot away the fresh blood. Her movements were brisk, her touch gentle. Silas drew a hissing breath as the ugly wounds were cleaned, and Nica whistled softly. "That's gonna leave a mark. Hurt much?"

"Only when I have to answer obvious questions."

She didn't look up. "Be nice or my bedside manner could get a lot worse." She arranged a line of gauze pads over the savage bites.

He watched her cautiously, unable to see her expression through the curtain of her hair.

She tied off the dressing with a purposeful tug. "That should hold you together. Let's get the rest of you cleaned up."

"I can manage," he grumbled.

"I'm sure you can. You managed to get yourself *into* this condition, after all." She took hold of the bottom of his ripped T-shirt as she spoke and carefully pulled it over his head. Checking for further injuries, she eased her hands over his hair-covered chest and hard abs. Definitely droolworthy; tough, firm, and detailed with muscle. Her fingertips circled a spectacular bruise forming on his side. "Ouch! What hit you here?"

"Car door handle. Went for an unexpected ride." His voice had gotten huskier, his stare never leaving her face.

Aware of his intent focus, she angled away to drain the discolored water from the sink and to wet a clean washcloth before turning back to him. His eyes were dark, stormy seas. Nica cupped his chin in her hand, holding him still while tending to his face. A very nice face, with strong, solid features and expressive brows that slashed boldly above that turbulent stare to hook like wings. Brows that lowered slightly as she caressed his square jaw.

The washcloth fell to the floor as she bent to snatch his lips for a quick, lusty plunder.

His hands clasped her waist. When he stood, he lifted her without surrendering her urgent mouth. Her arms and legs encircled him as he carried her down the hall, breaking from her kiss only long enough to rumble, "Time to check on that bedside manner."

The bedroom was in the front of the apartment. A king-size mattress in a wrought iron frame filled most of it. She saw nothing else but the lazy sweep of the ceiling fan as he laid her back on the thin comforter.

This time, he was as methodical as he'd previously been hurried. He skinned off her stretchy capri leggings, kneeling to remove her sandals. Then his mouth began an exquisitely torturous trail up her calf, along her inner thigh, sucking, nipping at her until she quivered in anticipation.

Then he parted her damp folds and began to feast. With his mouth. With his tongue. With his teeth. Until Nica reached down to grip his short hair, pulling him tighter as her hips undulated against him.

For Nica, sex had always been a fierce, hard ride to climax. She'd never wasted time with foreplay, anxious to find a quick relief with a partner with whom she'd share nothing more. But with Silas it was all about the explosive pleasures of the journey, each plateau a new sensual delight, from his hot, hungry kisses and steamy body to the devastating technique that had her writhing over a series of unexpected, control-shattering peaks.

Panting, moaning with a frustrated yearning, she clawed at the bedspread. "Silas . . . Si, please!"

He settled over her, pushing her knit top up her laboring rib cage, over her small, taut breasts. His mouth targeted one tight nipple, then the other, suckling until the delicious sensation pulled at her womb.

Nica thrashed helplessly, shaking, desperate as she pleaded, "Si, finish with me. *Please!*"

He silenced her with a slow, deep kiss. He palmed her cheeks, eyes burning down into hers as he whispered gruffly, "Don't beg, Nica. You only have to ask."

He filled her with a conquering thrust, his tongue plunging deep within her mouth, then withdrawing in tandem with his cock to wring another urgent cry from her. He finally settled into a fast, forceful rhythm that pounded the breath and strength from her until a glorious shock of tension tightened, squeezing, then releasing in a shuddering rush of pleasure.

Nica lay limp, gasping and dazed. She lost herself in his slow, thorough kiss, content to let him use her mouth in urgent exploration. Her palms rubbed over the hard cords of his shoulders, eager to luxuriate in the heavy, sated weight of him above her.

And then she realized in shock that he wasn't finished with her.

Nica's thoughts were as heavy as the darkness in the small room. A quiet snore made her smile. *Not going to close your eyes? Yeah, right.*

MacCreedy was stretched out on his belly beside her, dead to the world after the triathlon he'd pushed them through. She envied his slumber as she stared at the circling shadow of the fan and listened to him breathe.

After the last amazing bout he'd kissed her and rolled away without a word, apparently as guarded about his own space as she was. She wasn't a snuggler. She never allowed any cuddling not because she didn't like it, but because it might imply closeness. Commitment, caring. Things she couldn't invite into her life for fear they'd weaken her. If she didn't care, she couldn't be hurt, and she couldn't be betrayed. This was the first time she'd ever remained beside a partner once the final glow of satisfaction had winked out, and she had no desire to move.

She'd never felt so completely and thoroughly pleasured. Her bones were like liquid, her blood slow and warm. Her muscles had the consistency of overcooked pasta. The very last thing she wanted to do was get dressed and leave this bed where she'd experienced such bliss, or this male who'd shown her the way.

Exhausted, she wished she could curl up against his solid strength for the rest of the night. But she didn't dare sleep. She was afraid of what might come to her in dreams.

Silas woke with a start. He knew even before his hand touched the empty sheet that she was gone. Before disappointment had a chance to settle, he felt the languid stir of evening air across his bare skin and glanced over to find the window open.

Pulling on a pair of boxers, he stepped out onto the iron grillwork balcony, where steps zigzagged from floor to floor. She sat on the first step down, hugging her knees to her chest. Engulfed by his T-shirt, with her hair loose about her shoulders, she looked poignantly childlike.

Whether it was her unexpected vulnerability or the way something inside his chest took a slow, shuddering roll, Silas hesitated. Suddenly, everything had changed. His sister's arrival had called him back to his responsibilities. He'd been absent from those he loved for five long, lonely years, and he'd never had any reason for apology—until now. Because of the pull he felt toward Nica.

She didn't move as he settled on the gridded landing a step above her, bracketing her slender form with his knees. Silas scooped up the heavy spill of her hair, winding it around his hand until her neck was bared. Then he pressed his lips at the graceful base, eliciting a shiver.

"I thought you'd gone," he murmured.

"I couldn't. You sucked me dry." A soft laugh. "Both of us enjoyed that immensely."

"Several times."

She leaned back against his chest with a sigh. "Do you always have so much energy?"

"I found myself inspired."

"And I find myself unable to walk. You're incredible, did you know that?"

"So I've been told." It wasn't a boast. His previous sexploits had been pleasant diversions, quickly forgotten. The way he and Nica had intended this to be. When had that changed?

"So many times you get tired of hearing it?" she persisted.

"Not from you." His arms looped around her, possessive without being smothering. He'd never tire of hearing it from her. And that was what had his conscience churning.

Unaware of his brooding, Nica covered his hands with her own. "I look forward to saying it a lot."

"Then you'll be staying here in New Orleans for a while?" He should tell her his own plans were temporary. When had that begun to matter, sharing future plans?

She smiled, her head tipped back, her eyes contemplative. "I'm not sure yet. Would you mind if I did?"

"No. I like your company—when you're not trying to kill me."

"The value of your stock has just gone through the roof, lover. I don't think you have anything to worry about."

His cheek rubbed the top of her shoulder. "Let's go back inside."

"How could you possibly—?"

He chuckled. "To talk. I don't think I could manage anything else." It would be hard enough to manage what he needed to say to her.

"Let's talk out here. I like the night air. I like the sounds of the city getting ready for bed."

"I like the sounds *you* make when you're in mine."

Nica closed her eyes, absorbing the noises of the night world. "Your sister doesn't approve of me."

MacCreedy gave a snort. "I love Brigit, but I don't let her vet my relationships."

"Is that what we're in? A relationship?"

"You don't know?"

"Haven't a clue. You tell me."

She felt his smile against her hair. "Well, I like you. I like having sex with you. I like that you've stopped trying to kill me, at least for the moment. Haven't you ever been in a relationship before?"

"No. Never in one place long enough. What about you?"

He was silent for just a beat too long.

"Are you in one now?" Nica demanded quietly, holding her breath as she waited for his reply.

"I have obligations," was his evasive answer.

Which meant yes.

It felt like a knife to the heart.

"Are you mated?"

"No, nothing like that. We haven't even been intimate."

"Why not?"

"It's complicated," he told her, his tone getting tighter, more distant.

She wanted to smack him, hard. *Bastard!*

"Most things are," she agreed. "What's she like, this paragon you haven't had sex with? Obviously she doesn't know what she's missing."

"I really don't want to discuss this with you." Testy now, as well as guarded.

"Why not? I want to understand how relationships work. Enlighten me."

"She's someone I've known all my life. We always believed that someday . . . There was a change in my family's circumstances. It made any hope of a future together impossible. I'm no longer worthy of her consideration."

"So you're here to change those circumstances, to win her as your mate?"

"Yes." Then his voice gentled. "I'm sorry."

Her lips gave a bittersweet twist. "Why be sorry?"

Nica stood, taking a moment to steady her legs and her expression before she turned toward him. He looked so earnest, so apologetic. She wasn't sure which she wanted to do more: slap him or kiss him. "You didn't have to tell me any of this." How she wished he hadn't. "I never would have known the difference."

"I would have known. And you don't deserve to be lied to."

"You don't owe me anything, MacCreedy. Not explanations, not apologies. This was just kind of an 'Ooh, shiny' moment. It'll pass and we'll both move on—you to your noble plans and me to my selfish ones."

He didn't appear relieved. Before he could say anything sincere that would break her heart into even smaller pieces, she cupped his cheek and bent to kiss him. She meant it to be a quick good-bye, but his lips parted and for a moment she surrendered to the sweet taste of remorse. Then her fingertips slipped between their mouths, pressing against his as she lifted away.

"Good night."

"You don't have to go."

He didn't reach out to stop her; his expression held her. Such a complexity of passion, such longing. Such a trap she'd barely escaped.

"I always leave, MacCreedy. Always."

Silas sat out on the steps for long, miserable minutes. By the time he climbed back in through the window, all signs of Nica were gone except the scent on his skin and his sheets.

He'd known better. He should have backed away the second he'd felt interest change into something more complicated. With so much at stake, he couldn't afford to have his edge dulled by desire. Part of him still wanted to call her back, while the other saw blood on the floor and Kendra's trusting dark eyes lifted to him in adoration.

Guilt lashed him. There'd been no vows spoken, no commitments made, but he'd carried her memory as his talisman, his perfect glimpse of all the things he could aspire to. In those grim, desolate times when he didn't think he could pick himself up again, when there didn't seem to be a reason to go on, her pure, golden image would shine like a guiding star to lift him from despair. He had only to recall the moment when her lips had touched his so sweetly, offering a haven of peace where all the ugliness and pain that scarred him was healed.

I'll hold you safe in my soul until you return to me.

Her tender words carried him through the worst days and tided him over on lonely nights.

But those sentiments were just a faint whisper now. So much time had gone by. Hope had faded to near transparency. But now, with the reality of that dream at hand, he was reluctant to claim it. Because of Nica.

He couldn't have both things—the desire and the dream. So he closed off the discord in his mind by choosing as he always did, with his heart, where love of family ruled over any individual wants. Always.

Unable to return to bed, Silas carried a cold beer out onto the balcony, where he sat on the window ledge until the sky began to brighten with the promise of dawn. A new day that held nothing for him but duty and regret.

A knock at his door had him tugging up his jeans as he hurried to answer. Had Nica come back? He could explain, make her understand.

"I brought you breakfast." His sister stood in his hallway with a takeout bag from Café Beignet and a cup of coffee. "And I wanted to see how you were doing," she added.

Right. She wanted to see if he was alone.

"I appreciate your concern. I'm fine, but I'm going to be late for work if I don't get in the shower now."

As she stepped inside, Brigit's delicate nostrils flared, taking in the details of everything he'd done as clearly as if she'd read it in a tabloid.

"Is she still here?" Venom dripped from her tone.

"No. Not that that's any of your business."

Setting down her peace offering, she said with icy directness, "It is when it interferes with our business."

"*Our* business?" he bit out just as coldly. The anger was so sudden and strong, he didn't have time to catch it. "Since when has this involved *you*? Have you ever once gotten your hands dirty? Have you ever sacrificed or risked anything, except by association? *I've* made all the sacrifices. I've taken all the risks so you wouldn't have to. I have given my heart, soul, and blood since I was fourteen years old. So if I want to take an hour out of my whole fucking life to do something other than tend to *our* business, cut me some damned slack."

She stared up at him, eyes round with surprise. When she finally spoke, her words were faint and fragile.

"You're right. Of course you're right. You've taken care of everything without getting anything in return. We've depended on you for so long, we'd be lost without you." She looked down as if ashamed; then her words strengthened in determination. "But I *am* involved, Silas. Not a night goes by that I don't wake up hearing those screams. I haven't spent one single day free of fear. I'm tired of living with constant terror. We're so close, Silas—so close to having everything back the way it was."

"Not everything," he said, making her glance up at him again. "We can't get them back."

At the shimmer of tears in her eyes, his arms went about her, pulling her in to cradle her like he had when they were children. For a moment, she clung the way she had all those years ago, but soon her prideful starch returned and she levered away from his embrace. Though not too far away. She looked up at him somberly. "They'd be so proud of you."

Her sincerity struck like an unexpected blow and he reeled slightly, his vision swimming until he had to close his eyes to maintain control.

Brigit lightly brushed his cheek with her fingertips. "We're counting on you to do whatever's necessary until we have what they wanted for us. Eat your breakfast, take your shower, and remember that we love you."

She left him standing there, struggling with emotions only she and their mother had been able to manipulate with such ease, winding them up into a tight, aching knot with the keys to his heart: pride, guilt, and devotion.

When he finally reached for the coffee with shaky

hands, it was cold. By the time he stood under the shower spray, so were his intentions.

MacCreedy was waiting on the front steps, sipping from a hot cup of instant brew when Babineau pulled up. He climbed into the car, offering the bag of pastries before buckling up.

Babineau picked from the remaining selection. "I expected you to look like shit this morning."

Freshly shaven, in clean white shirt with jeans, suit jacket, and loosely knotted tie, Silas showed no sign of having been sliced and diced the night before.

"If it's any consolation, I feel like hell on the inside."

Babineau still stared, making Silas edgy.

"What?"

"I don't know." Babineau shook it off with a slight laugh. "I expected to see you differently this morning, is all."

"Like a werewolf in a suit instead of as a partner?"

Alain grinned. "Something like that."

"You should see me before I shave."

With a chuckle, Babineau put the car in gear. While he negotiated the narrow street, waiting for a group of picture-taking tourists in front of Reverend Zombie's Voodoo Shop to step back on the curb so he could pass, Silas pulled out his cell phone to make a call.

"Morning," he said.

"What do you want, MacCreedy?" Nica sounded as raw as he felt.

"I was wondering if you needed a ride tonight. Babineau and I can pick you up."

"I don't think—"

"It's no problem. You're on the way. See you at six thirty." He snapped the phone shut before she could respond.

Nine

A tropical storm barreled across the gulf, sending sheets of rain across the streets like a power washer.

Nica waited inside the front door as MacCreedy stepped out of Babineau's car, popping a big umbrella as an ineffective shield. Her stomach tensed at the sight of him, so tall and lean and lethally handsome with his raincoat flaring open in the wind to reveal jeans that seemed shrink-wrapped to his muscular thighs. When she opened the door, the roar of pounding rain greeted her along with his smile.

He angled the umbrella over her. "Hold this for a second." When she took the handle, he whipped off his long coat to whisk it about her shoulders, overwhelming her with his heat and scent. He opened the back door for her. When she didn't scoot over for him to join her, he rejoined his partner in front.

"Nica Fraser, Alain Babineau."

"Nice to meet you," Babineau murmured. "Not a fit night for man nor beast."

"I think we've got that covered," she muttered. Nica settled into her seat, shaking the rain off Silas's coat and trying to keep her stare from his broad shoulders. Traffic and the pounding rain on the roof prevented conversation, giving her thoughts too much leeway during the drive.

One of the reasons she was so successful was her ability to remain disconnected from those around her, never letting them touch her or make an impact upon her. As in a chess game, they were pieces to be moved to gain an advantage. Their lives before or after she passed through weren't her concern. Her goal was to make no impression, leave no memories.

Not this time.

She'd stayed too long in this place that still had distant ties to her soul. She'd been forced to integrate into the community, to deal with its members one-on-one, to interact as employee, friend...lover. She'd become caught up in the problems and passions of those around her. Even worse, she was beginning to like them.

LaRoche, Amber, Lottie, MacCreedy. They were far more than potential collateral damage. No longer pawns to play in order to win her deadly game, they'd pulled her in, involving her, making personal bonds that weren't going to be easy to sever. Making her recall things she hadn't experienced since she was a child: loyalty, belonging, trust, happiness, affection. Love. All things she'd thrust away as symptoms of weakness, as stepping stones to betrayal. If you didn't care, you couldn't be abandoned. A lesson learned so young, it marked her like that brand on MacCreedy's wrist.

She turned to look out the window, disgusted with

her treacherous desires and with herself. Because she was looking forward to this evening—not to gathering strategic information, but to enjoying the company, as if she had any business mingling socially amongst them. Professional suicide, that's what it was. Foolish, reckless, and so dangerous.

Yet she longed for the chance to laugh and reminisce. To respond naturally to what stirred within her heart as if she were their equal and not their prospective slayer. Didn't she deserve one such evening, one opportunity to know what it might have been like if she'd been born to other circumstances? Where she could be worthy of friendship, where she could explore the fascinating twists and turns of a relationship with a man like Silas MacCreedy?

But if she did, when the time came, would she be able to walk away with the blood of one of their lives on her hands?

It wasn't wise to tempt fate. Even when it was packaged as temptingly as the man sitting in front of her.

Max Savoie's home was surrounded by high walls and security cameras, as impressive as it was intimidating. When Babineau pulled up to the sturdy gates they immediately swung open, welcoming them inside the compound just as the rain gave way to steamy late-day sunshine.

The long, oak-shaded drive led to a sprawling antebellum plantation home, haloed by shafts of light that glittered with tiara-like brilliance upon the faded head of a grand dame. A wide veranda with a wraparound upper balcony, floor-to-ceiling shuttered French doors, and vine-covered pillars added to the aging elegance of Southern charm... if you didn't notice the subtly positioned well-armed guards.

Savoie came out to greet them, accompanied by a huge wall of a man. He waited on the porch, a dark, elegant shadow of hospitality.

MacCreedy opened the rear door and extended a helping hand, his gaze dipping briefly as Nica unfolded long bare legs ending in wicked stilettos. After one look between those precarious shoes and the water-saturated drive, he whisked her up from the backseat into his arms. Since struggling would have increased her embarrassment, she allowed him to carry her from the vehicle to the front steps.

He eased her down until she found a steady perch, then Nica took MacCreedy's hand, establishing a bond between them in Savoie's assessing gaze. She could feel Silas's startlement, but he quickly engulfed her hand in a firm claim.

"Good evening, Detectives, Ms. Fraser. Sorry for the soggy welcome. Charlotte's spiking the coffee with brandy, so you should warm up rather quickly. Giles will take your coats and your sidearms. No need to bring them to a civilized table."

"Guess that depends on your definition of *civilized*, doesn't it?" Babineau drawled, surrendering up his police issue.

Silas held his suit coat open for Giles's inspection, then told Max, "It won't be necessary to pat us down. We come bearing no weapons—unless you count Nica's rather sharp tongue."

She smiled at the suspicious Giles and then at an equally distrustful Max, who said, "I find lovely women are rarely unarmed in that regard. Please come in."

Silas helped Nica out of his coat and passed it to Giles, easing his hands along her sides and hips in a casual search before settling his arm about her waist.

"It's not like this dress was made to conceal anything," she grumbled. She was gratified by his quick survey of the silky red fabric held up by thin straps and ending in flirty swirl just above her knees. "If I had a weapon, it would be taped to my inner thigh. Would you like to warn Savoie's hulking bodyguard, so he can search there?"

"I think I'll keep your inner thighs to myself. They can be fairly lethal without a weapon, too."

The area in question grew as damp and steamy as their surroundings.

Cee Cee met them in the parlor with an unexpected flutter of nervousness that got Nica studying the group dynamics with an outsider's gift for clarity. Her childhood friend was hiding something from Max that was about to come to light. Savoie and Babineau circled one another like wary animals readying for combat. Silas was the only one who seemed relaxed, until two newcomers entered the room, a mother and child.

She heard his raspy inhalation and felt it shudder from him.

Nica's gaze flashed up, but his expression revealed nothing. No way had she imagined his reaction. She knew he had some secret agenda. She'd thought it had something to do with Max, but now she knew different.

She watched his tension gather until he practically vibrated with it, and a strained smile stretched his lips as Cee Cee brought them over.

"I'd like you to meet Nica Fraser, who's just returned to New Orleans. She and I knew each other as children when we were at St. Bart's. And Silas MacCreedy. He joined the team during our last case and is partnered with Alain until I'm back in the field. This is Tina Babineau and her son, Oscar."

Babineau?

Nica scrutinized the delicate female with her soft brown hair and doe eyes and her coltish son, knowing instantly that they were shape-shifters. She and Babineau were married, yet she was living here under Savoie's roof?

Silas put out his hand, taking Tina's as if it were made of glass. "I've enjoyed working with your husband. He talks about you all the time. I feel like we're almost family."

Tina looked flustered as she drew her hand away.

When MacCreedy turned to Oscar, Nica saw something bright and glittery in his eyes, turning cool slate to gleaming quicksilver.

"Hello, Oscar. I'm Silas and I'm very happy to finally meet you," he said in a deep, measured tone as he pressed the small hand between both of his.

It was the boy he was after.

Dinner was a mix of superficial conversation and fabulous food served up in a massive dining room that could have easily seated two dozen. While her mother, Helen, was busy in the kitchen, a pretty dark-haired girl Max called Jasmine delivered the courses. The girl was uncomfortable enough with the serving process for Nica to guess that entertaining wasn't regularly done under the trio of chandeliers.

Cups of corn-and-sweet-potato bisque were a hearty accompaniment to a light salad of melon and crabmeat over mixed greens. A savory main course followed; tender beef brisket served with a Creole remoulade, spicy shrimp, flavorful vegetables, and plenty of warm bread to absorb the heat. The wine was excellent, and Alain Babineau imbibed freely, refusing to relinquish his glass in favor of a coffee when dishes of bread pudding were brought out.

"So, Oscar, how do you like living here?" he began with a slightly aggressive slur. "Is Savoie teaching you the tricks of the trade?"

Oscar looked nervously to Max, who was silent at Cee Cee's side. Then he smiled tentatively at his stepfather. "I'm learning how to box."

"My father taught me when I was your age," Silas

said, earning the boy's grateful glance. "I used to have a pretty good jab to go along with a lot of bruises."

"Max lets me go to the gym at his office with him sometimes. He says it's never too early to start building stamina and strength. He's going to start teaching me martial arts in the fall."

"You're never too young to become an effective killer, right, Savoie? Is that what you're teaching my boy?"

Max returned Babineau's belligerent glare with one of ice. "There's nothing wrong with being able to take care of yourself if danger presents itself."

Then he looked at MacCreedy, his expression contemplative. "Do you like to run, as well as box?"

Silas laughed. "No. All that sweating to go nowhere? I prefer public transportation and a destination."

"I like to run," Nica said. "There's a path along the St. Charles streetcar line where you can really stretch your legs. But I'm competitive. It's no fun if there isn't a challenge."

She held Max's gaze with a smile, letting him know that she, not MacCreedy, had led him on an invigorating chase some weeks ago.

Babineau spoke up again. "How about hunting? With all this property, it seems like you'd take advantage of that, Savoie. You teaching the boy how to hunt, how to stalk game, how to bring down a kill?" A pause, then right for the throat. "Or do you take him down to the docks to learn that, the way you did under Legere?"

Silas pushed back his chair, reaching for his partner's

arm and jerking it up behind his back to bring him to his feet. "Excuse us for a minute. I think we need to get some air."

He marched the truculent Babineau out of the room and out the front door, giving him a shove so that he stumbled against the porch rail, where he clung for balance.

"You are just *full* of amusing table conversation tonight."

Babineau turned on him with a fierce cry. "You don't know what he is, what he's done."

"I know he's taken that boy in when you decided not to be a father to him anymore. If you don't give a damn about them, why should it bother you who puts a roof over their heads? You don't seem to want them under yours."

"It's because they're—" He choked off the rest.

Silas's eyes narrowed. "What? Animals? Monsters? Like me?"

"Because they're not human."

"Humanity isn't all that great, from what I've seen." MacCreedy crossed to the rail to lean next to Babineau. "I hadn't figured you for narrow-minded. Is it all our kind you object to, or just Savoie?"

That set Alain back and got him thinking. "I don't have any problem with you."

"Good to know. I'm a damned nice guy and a helluva partner. So it's Savoie who's got your shorts in a twist."

"The smug bastard. He's a criminal. A killer. *And* he's the boy's family."

"Does Oscar have other family? Would you rather he live with them while you get your shit together?"

"Tina's adopted parents are dead. She doesn't have anyone else to go to."

"And you can't make yourself take them back?"

"Not yet." He scrubbed shaking hands over his face. "I'm screwing everything up. If Savoie wasn't in the picture, maybe I could see things more clearly."

"Maybe you could," Silas agreed. "Go do a couple of laps around the porch, then head for the coffee instead of the liquor. You're acting like a real asshole, and you're embarrassing me in front of my date." He slapped Alain on the back with enough force to get him started on that walk, then he returned inside, where he was surprised by the sight of Oscar Babineau. Hopefully he hadn't heard the entire conversation.

Oscar nodded toward the door. "Is he okay?"

"Your dad?"

"He's . . . he's not my dad."

Silas placed a supportive hand on the boy's shoulder and squeezed. "He's pissed off and confused and not sure who he's mad at. Probably himself."

"It's because we're different, isn't it?"

Smart kid. Intuitive. Not many adult Shifters could read him as easily when he was trying to blend. "Yeah. It's kinda tough on 'em at first, accepting what we are, but he'll get over it."

"He likes you."

"What's not to like?"

That coaxed a reluctant grin.

"Oscar, if you could choose, would you leave here to go back with him?"

"If we could be a family again, sure. This is a great place and Max and Detective Caissie and everyone here are awesome, but it's not home. You know what I mean?"

The thin shoulders slumped, and Silas's emotions gave a worrisome plummet. He removed his hand to take a physical and mental step away.

He wasn't here to put this broken family back together.

He was here to kidnap a prince.

Ten

The others were still at the table when MacCreedy returned. The big guy, Giles, was speaking to Savoie, who looked somber.

"Giles tells me a tour bus went into a culvert up the road, causing a chain reaction involving half a dozen cars," Savoie announced. "The rescue workers won't have the area cleared for at least a couple of hours, about the time we get the whip end of that storm that just went through. Looks to be a long, ugly night, so I suggest you ride it out here. We've got plenty of room and a backup generator in case the power goes. Roads will be a lot safer in the morning."

"Sounds like the smart thing to do. I'm sure Alain will agree," Silas said.

Cee Cee gave a snort. "He's not all that reasonable when it comes to our hospitality, but I'll make sure he sees it's the best of two evils."

Tina pushed back from the table, looking fluttery and anxious. "I'll let Helen know we'll need extra rooms made up."

Giles saw Oscar lingering uncomfortably in the doorway and called, "C'mon, sport. You can help me batten down the hatches."

The boy was instantly at his heels.

After Nica excused herself to visit the restroom, Max leaned back in his chair to regard the detectives. "Now we'll have plenty of time to get certain things out in the open. How 'bout you start, *sha*?"

Cee Cee's gaze flashed to his. "With what?"

"With that question you've been dying to ask me since yesterday. Ask away."

She looked nervously toward their guest. "Max, I don't think this is the time."

"It's the perfect time. Ask."

She cursed softly under her breath, then squared her shoulders. Before she could form the question, Babineau asked it for her from the doorway.

"Are you running human cargo for Blutafino?"

Max regarded him unblinkingly. "Why would you think I am?"

"Is that the deal you made with him to get us undercover in his place?" Cee Cee asked in her hard-edged cop voice.

Babineau growled, "Manny met with your boy T-John on one of LEI's ships last night. I don't think he was there to discuss taking a cruise."

"He had Shifters on guard," Silas added. "They gave us a rather unpleasant time. It didn't seem like the type of greeting you would have ordered, considering it involved your housemate."

Max's gaze settled on Cee Cee. "And you were going to tell me this when? About the same time you planned to mention those four who jumped you outside *Cheveux du Chien?*"

"It was part of an investigation, Max. I didn't want to bring you into it."

"Because you thought I was already a part of it?"

"No, because I didn't want you to complicate it. What was your deal with Manny?"

"He wanted to use my ships to move his cargo up the Mississippi."

"And you agreed to that?"

"I said I would."

Cee Cee looked quickly at the two other detectives, realizing what he'd just admitted and to whom.

"Don't look so distressed, *cher*. I wasn't going to go through with it. We made a gentlemen's agreement and as you well know, Carmen is no gentleman. He just couldn't help trying to skew the deal in his favor. Then, of course, I became righteously indignant and walked away. MacCreedy can verify that for you. Jimmy was a shrewd businessman; he'd never work with Carmen. Why would you think I'd be that foolish?"

"I didn't think that at all," she replied indignantly. "What I'm wondering is why Francis Petitjohn thinks it's safe to make a move on you in a bid for LEI?"

"I don't know. Guess I'll have to find out." He pulled out his cell phone and made a call. "Francis, we need to set up a time to talk tomorrow. What do you have available? This and that. Four works for me. My office. Oh, and, Francis, I heard there was some commotion down on the docks last night. Do you know what that was about? I see. It's taken care of? Good. Four o'clock then." He put the phone away. "Rumor is, some of the dock-workers were making money on the side with the black market and the deal went sour. They were killed by a trio pretending to be undercover cops. Sound familiar?"

"Sounds like a cover-up," Silas murmured. "We need to find out what's in that hold."

"I'll put LaRoche on it. If Francis is scheming, using the Clan is better than depending on business connections."

"Max, be careful." Cee Cee covered his hand with hers. "T-John is treacherous, but he's a coward. He wouldn't go to Manny unless he felt safe to do so. So watch your back."

He brought her knuckles to his lips. "That's what I have you for."

MacCreedy strolled along the veranda under the pretext of having a cigarette. He rarely smoked but it provided a good excuse to use his tiny camera. The sudden loop of Nica's arm through his almost made him jump out of his shoes.

"Hi," she purred, nudging in close. "What did I miss?"

"When?"

"When talk turned to business the second I left the room."

"Just cop business. Nothing that would interest you."

"Anything that interests you, interests me. Like that motion detector over there. Did you catch that one?"

Silas followed her nod with a polite gaze and said, "I don't know what you're talking about."

"Planning to come calling without an invitation?"

"That would be just plain rude, wouldn't it?"

"And suicidal. There's no way you could take Savoie. You know that, don't you?"

"I've got nothing against Savoie."

She chuckled. "Liar. You hide it well, but I know you rather intimately. I could help you, you know."

"Help me what?"

"Keep from getting killed."

"Why would you do that? Because you *like* me? Because you like having *sex* with me? I think your allegiance goes for a little higher than that."

"Don't sell yourself short, lover. I'm bored. I need something to do. What can I do to help you?"

"Quit trying to create intrigue where there is none."

"Why do you want the boy?"

His hand was around her throat, shoving her hard against the shutters. Recovering from her surprise, she laughed at his ferociousness.

"Oooh, now I'm excited. I love it when you get all riled."

"Stay out of my affairs, Nica," came his warning growl.

"I thought I *was* one of your affairs."

He released her and strode off at a furious pace. Chuckling, she caught up to him, hugging his arm again.

"Stop being so grumpy," she chided. "We could be so good together."

"We're not together. Do you think I trust you, any more than I do him?"

"You're going to have to pick a side, MacCreedy."

"I pick my own side."

"Then you'll lose." She stepped in front of him, placing her palms on his chest. Her features were grim, her tone flat. "He'll kill you. He will rip out your heart, and then he'll eat it."

"Then I hope he chokes on it."

"What is so damn important that you're willing to throw your life away?"

He simply set her aside and continued his walk.

Let him go, she told herself. *Let him rush headlong to his own doom.* Any attempt on Savoie would be a perfect distraction, drawing attention from her and her job. But as she studied his arrogant, determined posture, something in her snapped.

She hurried to catch up to him again.

"You don't have the cards for this game, MacCreedy. Fold while you can."

"I can't. It's too late."

"Silas, don't be a *fool.*"

He stopped and turned to her, his expression fierce, stare intent. "Why do you care what happens to me?"

"Because I hate waste. And your dying for a lost cause would be a terrible one. Don't be a hero."

"Can't help it. It's the only hand I have to play, Nica. I have to see it through."

She touched his face, letting her fingertips glide over his cheek and her thumb graze his lips. "I'm not happy about this."

"I'm sorry. I don't have a choice."

They stood for a moment, eyes locked. Then she dropped her hand and stepped back with a bittersweet smile, letting him walk away.

The storm rolled in with window-rattling intensity just after nine o'clock. Lightning strobed and sizzled, with booms of thunder on its heels as the air grew thick and tense.

By ten, the power was out.

The backup generator came on, but since they had no idea how long they'd be without electricity, only the necessities were kept running: the refrigerator, emergency lighting, the water, and the security system.

Without ceiling fans, the house grew oppressively hot and sticky. Tina announced she was going to run a cool bath for her son, then take one herself. Her husband had no comment from where he stood at one of the windows, staring out into the darkness.

Max had gone outside with Giles to check the perimeter of the house for storm damage. A huge limb had come down, crushing one of the porch roofs at the back of the house, breaking out the windows in one of the pantries. MacCreedy coaxed Babineau into helping to move the dry goods to a safer location.

As they left the parlor, Cee Cee glanced at Nica, who was seated on the sofa beside her. "So?"

"What?"

"MacCreedy."

"What about him?"

Cee Cee made a fanning motion with her hand as if overheated.

Nica poked her index finger through a circle formed by her other hand, using the crude visual to trivialize what she had with the Shifter detective. "Isn't this the question you're asking?"

"So?" Cee Cee repeated.

"Yes, he's hot and yes, I've slept with him."

"Past tense?"

"I hope not." Uncomfortable, she changed the subject. "You and Savoie serious?"

"As a heart attack. There's nothing we wouldn't do for each other. How about you two?"

Nica gave a brittle smile. "Just having fun. He's got other plans."

"I'm sorry."

She shrugged. "You know me. Enjoy the ride. Roll with the punches."

"No, I really don't know you anymore."

"I'm no different. No strings, no ties. But you—swaggering law-and-order tough girl keeping house with a mobster shape-shifter? Who would have seen that coming?"

"Not me. A lot *has* changed, in ways I never could have imagined." She pulled the neckline of her knit dress to the side.

Nica's jaw dropped as she stared at the marks. "Holy shit! You *are* bonded to him." She leaned forward to whisper, "What's it like?"

"You've never mated with one of your males?"

Nica shook her head. "I was never that into any of them."

Liar. From the first time he'd taken her on the floor of her apartment, Nica had fantasized about Silas Mac-Creedy crouching over her in his beast form. Of him claiming her in that animal state until she lost all control. Imagining it now brought a flush to her face and a restless heat to other areas.

"Are you religious?" Charlotte asked suddenly.

Nica shrugged, grateful for a change in topic. "Father Furness tried, but it didn't really take. You?"

"It sneaks up on me at inconvenient moments."

When she brooded for a moment in silence, Nica prompted, "What's going on, Lottie?"

"I told you about the men who kidnapped me and Mary Kate, how we were abused before Max rescued us. It changed us, Nica. I followed in my father's footsteps with a vengeance, determined to single-handedly become a scourge against crime, and Mary Kate turned to God. She became a nun, Sister Catherine."

"Mary Kate?" Nica couldn't imagine the energetic,

free-spirited girl she'd known as a Bride of Christ. Then she understood. "Ah. What better way to avoid dating and marriage, if you're terrified of men."

"She wasn't exactly hiding. She found a way to strike back at those who victimized the women and children who came to St. Bart's for shelter. She used Max to avenge them."

"And you knew about this?"

"No. I hadn't a clue until after he and I got involved. When Jimmy found out, he threatened Mary Kate but she wouldn't back down. And when the son of a bitch sent someone to teach her a lesson, she shot herself rather than go through that horror again.

"Max had her sent to a rehabilitation facility in California. That's where we've been for the past couple of weeks. Mary Kate wanted to see me. She made them stop her pain meds long enough for her to tell me to let her go, to let her die. There's no chance for recovery, Nica. The doctors all told me she can't be conscious without incredible pain."

She gripped the hand Nica pressed over hers. "I can't let her go. Not like this. Even if you and I have flexible beliefs, she doesn't. If she dies, she'll be a suicide and she'll spend eternity in hell. That's what she believes. That's what she's asking me to condemn her to. I can't do it, Nica. I won't."

"I wish there was some way I could help."

Charlotte's gaze drilled into hers. "I think there might be."

Nica listened in shock and disbelief as her friend laid out her plan.

With the bond Charlotte and Max shared came other abilities that were unheard of amongst Shifter kind. They could communicate telepathically along a link so powerful, Max had actually been able to call her back from death. Cee Cee was able to heal herself, not as quickly but as completely as he himself could, repairing wounds both new and old. What if those strange and wonderful properties could be used to help heal Mary Kate's burned and shattered body?

Nica shook her head in confusion, not sure why that involved her.

"It has something to do with a secret you and Max's mother share. She could shape-change and, according to Max, so can you," Cee Cee said.

Nica recoiled.

"What makes the two of you so different from the other females of your kind?" Cee Cee asked. "Do you see things? Can you read minds? What do you know about your family, Nica? What do you remember?"

"Nothing," she whispered hoarsely. Then she sprang off the sofa, crying, "I don't remember anything," before she sprinted from the room, running from shadows and flames.

Nica paced as if caged.

The bedroom was stifling. She'd stripped down to a gauzy camisole and fluttery boy-cut panties, but sweat continued to bead on her skin, plastering strands of hair to her forehead and neck. She couldn't seem to draw a breath that didn't need to be wrung out first.

She hadn't thought about her past for years, nor did she dwell on the future. She preferred to exist in the now, rather than be influenced by things she couldn't change or control. She'd tunneled her focus into the immediate, keeping it narrow and crystal clear. When it expanded to the big picture, that's when things got confusing. That's when she began to question and doubt, and there was no place in her existence for those things. They'd kill her quicker than a dagger.

Things like what it would be like to have a life like Charlotte Caissie's, to be mated to Silas MacCreedy, to remain in New Orleans and make it her home, where she could have friends, get involved in their lives and have them involved hers . . .

It was the heat and this damned waiting. She needed to move, to act, to do something. *Anything.*

She saw a shadow pass by her French doors, and all her senses began to quiver.

Walking out onto the balcony was like stepping into a damp towel.

Hearing her step, MacCreedy turned, taking in her flushed features and scanty attire. "Hi."

"Hi, yourself." She gestured to his glass. "What do you have there?"

"Ice water. I was trying to decide whether I should pour it over my head or down the front of my shorts."

His gaze followed a trickle of perspiration as it trailed from collarbone to the valley between her breasts. "Definitely shorts."

"Would you share, first?"

"Sure."

He came toward her, his movements leisurely and sexy. He was wearing jeans and a white A-style undershirt that was glazed to his chest. His feet were bare and his eyes were smoky. Nica had been hot before; now she was on fire.

She took the glass from him, pressing it to her cheeks, then holding it against her chest with a sigh of pleasure. "That feels good."

Silas watched as she fished out an ice cube and popped it into her mouth, crunching it while closing her eyes and leaning elbows back on the rail. Her soft, throaty moan of contentment tightened everything from his molars to his balls.

"Better?"

"Almost as good as air-conditioning." Her eyes opened, as dark and depthless as the clearing night sky. She speared another cube between her fingers and glided it around her neck from ear to ear, from shoulder to shoulder, then down to the edge of her camisole.

"Heaven," she murmured. "Want some?" She touched the dripping cube to the skin just below his ear. The effect was jolting.

Then she pushed the cube into his mouth, and rubbed her cool fingers across his lips as he crunched on the ice.

"I was thinking," she began, dipping out another cube. "Since you're going to be dead soon and future plans will be a moot point, it would be a shame to waste what might be our last chance to have sex."

"That *would* be a shame, wouldn't it?"

"So, what would you say to a proper send-off to Shifter Valhalla?"

His smile spread slowly. "It wouldn't take much to send me off right here, right now."

She glanced down at the hard ridge behind his zipper, then hooked her index finger into the waistband of his jeans and underwear to drop the ice cube down inside. "Chill out, lover. The night's still young."

He did some frantic adjusting, then shook his right leg until the remaining chip of ice fell onto the balcony floor. He grinned. "What do you have in mind?"

Tugging him toward her open doors, she said, "Let me cool you down before things get heated up again."

Eleven

With MacCreedy stretched out on her bed, the heat became an inspiration.

Nica crouched beside him and ran her damp fingertips down the side of his face. "Close your eyes."

She lightly massaged his temples until the tension ebbed from his shoulders. Then she took a chip of ice and ran it over his closed lids, down his neck, lingering at his pulse points before putting it in her mouth.

She leaned over him, breathing a chilled exhalation against his lips, tracing their shape with her cold tongue. When he tried to kiss her she pulled away until he settled back with an understanding smile, placing himself completely in her hands.

And oh, what she wanted to do to him.

She licked the inviting curve of his mouth as she pushed up his undershirt, so she could run a cube around his nipples until they were temptingly tight. Then she shifted her mouth there, tugging with her lips, grazing with her teeth until his breaths were shaky and uneven.

"Is this your idea of foreplay or torture?" he whispered gruffly.

"You inspire me, lover. Before you, my idea of fore-play was turning out the light."

As he chuckled she ran the ice down to his navel, cir-cling there until he shivered.

"I want to get into your pants, MacCreedy."

"That's an excellent idea."

After his clothes hit the floor she ran the ice up the arch of his foot, making him jump. Then her mouth eased down his chest as the ice moved up the inside of his leg, both heading for the same destination.

Hot and cold. Fire and ice. Silas shuddered from the contrast.

Her mouth burned along his rigid shaft as the frigid shock below had his balls looking for a place to hide. The conflict of desperate desire and anxious denial scattered his self-control, and when she reversed directions the opposite polarity shorted out his circuits.

He grabbed her roughly by the shoulders to stop the exquisite torment, but she twisted away with a growl, gripping his wrists and pressing them hard into the mat-tress as she sat astride him. And then she began to move.

The narrow crotch of her panties was invitingly wet, taunting him, beckoning him as she slid up and down the length of him. His eyes rolled shut and his body trem-bled as need surged in a seething tide.

He tried to take control of the situation or at least participate, but he couldn't break free. Her hands were like shackles about his wrists, binding him, restricting his movements, his freedom.

And what had been playfully erotic darkened into something very different, triggering deeply suppressed emotions of claustrophobic panic and helplessness.

"Let me *go*." His words were filled with intimidating menace, but Nica exerted even greater pressure to control him. When he moved his legs for some leverage, she twined hers about them, imprisoning him.

Don't move. Don't react. Don't show fear or hate or pain.

He could smell his flesh burning, could hear screams ringing in his ears, could taste the bile in the back of his throat as horror upon horror surged up to choke him.

He couldn't catch his breath. Impotent fury raged, feeding extra adrenaline to muscles that bulged with effort. Thrashing beneath her, he roared, "Get off me! Damn it, Nica, let me *go*!"

He flung her off him and rolled above her, assuming a dominant position.

Nica stared up at his suddenly unfamiliar features, tight and dark. Fierce passion beat from him with every savage breath, blazed from eyes of laser blue. She'd woken something primal and shockingly dangerous.

This was what he hid behind his cool confidence. This panting rage, this wild emotion that ripped his composure away and left him raw to the bone.

Silas MacCreedy was a pressure cooker with no outlet for the steam, except through her.

And it made her want him madly.

Her body arched up to his in an undulating wave. Her eyes glowed, their sapphire brilliance lit by sparks of gold. "Take me, MacCreedy. Take me like I was yours."

Mine.

Silas's harsh breathing stilled, then exploded as his thrusting hips tore through the filmy barrier of her panties. He buried himself deep and hard inside her, immediately withdrawing and plunging again.

Mine!

That claim echoed with each frenzied thrust. He drove into her, over and over lost in the savage repetition, his actions fiercely possessive. The scent of her arousal, of her desire, was a drug. Her quick gasps in rhythm with their coupling urged him on. Faster. Harder. *Mine.* As he felt the tension gather in her body he redoubled his efforts, obsessed with the need to drive her into the same hot madness calling to him.

Her guttural moans encouraged him. "Yes, Silas, *yes.* I want you, want you, *want* you. Now. Now! *Please!*"

Her orgasm gripped him like a pumping fist, sucking his own climax from him along with a mighty roar.

Afterward, only the rasp of their breathing broke the silence. Then MacCreedy withdrew, rolling away from her.

It took Nica a while to become aware of the distance between them. He laid on his back, eyes closed, sweat glistening on his skin and dampening his hair. He looked like a pagan god.

When she chuckled, he slid her a look out of the corner of his eye.

"Think we made enough noise?" she asked.

His lips twitched. "We're not very considerate guests, are we?"

She'd never wanted post-sex touching, never dared to explore that level of intimacy. Until now. She lightly placed her hand on his forearm. When he allowed it, she moved her palm slowly up to his shoulder then back, enjoying the texture of his skin, the muscles beneath it.

Mine, he'd growled. *Mine*.

"I'm sorry if things got a little strange there," he said.

As she watched him absently rub the mark on his wrist, she pieced it together. Time to let a little more of that blistering steam vent.

"Don't apologize, Si. I understand."

That earned a scowl. "How could you?"

"Humility was never easy for me, either. I take it you didn't go willingly to the House of Terriot for protection, any more than they took you in graciously?"

He stared at her for a long moment before his gaze flickered away. "No."

Nica rose up on one elbow to study his profile. He was locked down tight. He wasn't about to let her in if she took a direct approach, but there were stealthier ways to get where she wanted to go. "Tell me about her. What's her name?"

Again, the quick dart of his gaze to her face. "Who?"

"Your ideal. Your love."

"Why would you want to know about her?"

"Maybe I want to know what makes her worth the sacrifice of your life."

"Kendra. Kendra Terriot."

"Of the same Terriots who branded your skin?"

"She's not like them. She's quiet, refined, intellectual, delicate."

Everything Nica was not.

"Her father and mine were distant cousins. Her mother died when she was very young and she came to live with us while her father traveled, taking care of clan business. Her father didn't want her to grow up surrounded by the intrigues and danger of the Terriot court. He was afraid she was too fragile, too like her mother."

He was relaxing in spite of himself, so she cracked open his reserve a little further. "And where did you grow up?"

"My father's clan came up from the Irish Channel, rough, earthy stock. His mother worked for a fine household in the Garden District and took him with her sometimes. He'd amuse himself by reading the books in their library while she cleaned their grand staircases and fancy silver. He became friends with a spirited little lass, as he called her, named Therese. Thinking she was the daughter of one of the other servants, he let her tag along with him. Later he read sonnets to her in the garden arbor, and about the time he discovered he was in love with her, he also learned her name was Guedry—daughter of the house."

"Ah, so this is a romantic story." Nica sighed. "The princess and the pauper."

Silas caught her hand between his. "It should have

been. They bonded as mates and married to live free, shunning clan politics. My father taught at a college in Baton Rouge and my mother was a photographer. Brigit and I, and then Kendra were all homeschooled, living in the middle of the human world while separate from it. We were all each other had."

"And you fell in love with her the same way your father did your mother."

The gentling of his features was her answer. He was silent for a time, then gave a heavy sigh. "I had simple dreams, Nica. To be an honorable man like my father, to look for the good in others as my mother taught me, to be of service to my kind in the manner of our families, and to find the contentment I saw between my mother and father every day of their lives, until the Terriots tore that all away. My father had thought living apart from them would keep us safe, but what it did isolated us from those who would have given their protection."

MacCreedy sat up, his legs over the side of the bed and his back to her. His damp undershirt revealed the tenseness of his muscles as he scrubbed his hands over his face and hair. Nica knelt behind him, leaning against his rigid back, her arms going around his middle, pressing her cheek to his shoulder.

"The Terriots came to our house," he said. "I could hear them downstairs, my father, who never raised his voice, shouting for them to get out. The girls were scared and begged me not to go down, but I wouldn't listen.

"I watched my parents die from where I stood on the

stairs. I did *nothing* to save them." His voice thickened with self-loathing. "I ran, Nica. I left them in their own blood."

"How old were you?"

"What difference—"

"How old?"

"Fourteen. Old enough. I could have done something, *anything*."

Her answer was a flat slap of logic. "You would have died with them. They would have killed you."

She could see Silas so clearly, on the cusp of manhood, confronted with horror and grief of a crippling magnitude. Yet he'd suppressed the shock and emotion to act, not on his own behalf, but for the sake of others.

"Any fool could have thrown himself to his death in self-serving vengeance." She felt his jerk of objection and hugged him tight. "A boy would have, without any thought of the consequences. And what good would that have done? But a man would control his fury, and think beyond it to the two still alive upstairs.

"You didn't run away, Silas. You ran *to* them, to see to their safety. You left a war you couldn't possibly win, to fight a battle where there was something left to gain."

"By groveling to our enemies like a dog, begging for mercy while my parents' blood was still on their hands," he said bitterly.

"Because if they'd considered you a threat, they would have killed you on the spot. So you had to make them believe you were harmless. You *had* to let them humiliate you, demoralize you, crush you. They wouldn't have let you live otherwise."

"I was very convincing," he spat out with contempt.

"Did your sister and Kendra realize how difficult that was for you? Did they understand the strength it took to hide all that rage and hate and fierceness, to submit to the Terriots' control?"

"It doesn't matter."

"It *does* matter. You saved them, Silas. None of you would have survived the night if you hadn't surrendered." She understood that kind of compromise with crystal clarity. The burn of it, the shame and self-contempt of it. The dire necessity of it. "What did you have to promise them?"

"I vowed that if they took Brigit and Kendra into the House of Terriot and cared for them, I would serve them."

"For how long?"

"Forever."

A monumental promise from a boy of fourteen. In effect, he *had* given his life to save them.

She gripped his chin, turning him to face her. His expression was granite hard, his gaze cold steel—and she shuddered inside with admiration.

"You did the right thing," she told him.

"*You* would have leapt right into the middle of—"

Nica pressed her fingertips to his mouth. "No. I would have done exactly as you did. I would have controlled my emotions, studied my options, and chosen survival. I would have realized that my death would serve no purpose, but if I lived, I could find a better time to take my vengeance."

A wry smile twisted his lips. "You would have considered all that in an instant?"

"Yes, just as you did. Because we're survivors who know how to play the odds. That doesn't make us weak. It makes us smart." Her tone roughened. "And I like that about you."

She touched her lips to his, then gently guided his head down to rest on her shoulder for a while.

After he finally sighed deeply, his muscles now relaxed, they settled into the big bed. Tucked into the curl of his arms, Nica drifted her palm across his chest, resting it over his steady heartbeat. She smiled as his big hand stroked her hair, and her eyes closed before she realized she was breaking a cardinal rule.

She was trusting him.

The fit of her lithe body against his stirred Silas's desire, but the quiet closeness felt too good to disturb. He'd had so few peaceful moments lately, so few times when he was completely at rest. And right now it felt more satisfying than sex.

Surrounded by her scent, her heat, by the sound of her even breaths, he sighed and relaxed. Her empathy sank deep like a healing balm, soothing his troubled mind, cradling his aching heart with a sense of comfort he hadn't known since childhood.

She understood him.

He hadn't realized how rare that was until now. Brigit would have expressed impatience with his failings. Kendra would have shown compassion with no comprehension. She would have been shocked by his confession, by the brutal force of such a wild, unrestrained mating. She would shrink away from the darkness, the violence, the passion, and knowing that, he never would have let himself go. Ever.

There were no such limits with Nica. Nothing he could say or do would make her recoil. He hadn't known how deeply gratifying that was. And when she'd said, *You did the right thing,* absolution had seeped into his anguished soul.

Because they were two of a kind.

And he didn't know if that pleased him or scared the ever-loving hell out of him.

Brigit MacCreedy lay in the darkness, waiting for the hotel air-conditioning to cool her flushed skin. Daniel Guedry was an inventive lover, but tonight he was becoming angry and tiresome. He'd been sweetly convincing and she'd been hot to have him, but now she'd listened to enough of his tirade.

"Daniel, I've told you. It's being taken care of."

"By your brother? He's done nothing."

She watched him pace. He was glorious in high temper. He was glorious anytime, with his thick black hair, flashing eyes, and sleek body made for pleasure. But his endless complaints were getting on her nerves.

"Silas is as coldly clever as you are impetuously ruthless. Both styles have their advantages."

"Saint Silas, the careful schemer," Guedry snarled. "He's not going to rise up against the Terriots. He's been on his belly to them for too long. I say we just kill Savoie and the kid. Then I can take the throne from the Terriots, and you can sit on it beside me. My family would welcome the match and you into our compound as their queen."

"Memphis is no better than here. It stinks of the river, and I hate being soggy all the time."

Daniel scowled at her, clearly incensed that she'd tossed aside his offer so casually. "Then I'll take the Terriot refuge in Tahoe over the bodies of their clan, and set you up on their mountaintop. Would you like that better?"

She stretched leisurely, kindling a flare of lust in his eyes as she'd intended. "I *would* like that. I always enjoyed living there, though the company was lacking."

"Let me take it for you," he growled, stalking toward her. "Let me give you the things you deserve."

She opened to him, welcoming him atop her, then within her.

"Now. No more waiting," he said insistently.

She shoved him away, barring his return with the brace of her hand.

"It takes patience as well as willingness for a coup of this magnitude, Daniel. Give Silas time to take care of things. He wants this as badly as I do, for his own reasons. Let him clear the way so that you can be king without spilling any blood. I've already seen too much of it. Promise me you'll wait, Daniel, that you'll do nothing foolish. I'll have your word—on your love for me."

He pouted deliciously for a moment, then his gaze roved over her nude body with ravenous intention, quickening her own appetite. "All right. I'll wait. But not forever. Not for my crown. And not another second for you."

And he lunged.

Even as he toiled to ignite a fire in her, Brigit found her thoughts drifting. Her brother had never failed her. So why did she feel this sudden uneasiness? Was it because of the human contamination? Or that brash female who claimed his bed?

It was time to call Silas on his loyalties, and she knew just which screw of guilt to tighten—after she rode out her approaching climax to its spectacular end.

Having a vigorous, if somewhat dim, lover rule beside her would have its advantages.

Twelve

Nica's "dreams" always began the same way, with a wild free fall through time and space.

First came the cold of a sudden void, an emptiness like the grave as she felt the pull on her psychic self. She struggled, even knowing she couldn't fight it. She could see MacCreedy asleep beside her, could feel the heat of his body fading as the chill seeped into her soul. She flung out her hands to reach him, screaming his name, but he and the room were gone in an instant.

Then there was only chaos, cold, dizzying, disorienting. The mad scramble of sight and sound always ended in the same place: a blindingly white chamber surrounded by a collage of her thoughts, her dreams, her past. All the flickering, distorted images were of MacCreedy, which alarmed her, as if an intensely private corner of her heart had just been turned inside out.

He'd been watching, spying. He'd seen . . . everything.

The montage flashed across her consciousness. MacCreedy sprawled in the pool with the water darkening around him. Striding through *Cheveux du Chien*, where the brief touch of his gaze sizzled across her skin. His sudden grin as he stood at the elevator when she asked his name.

"Hero."

Conversations they'd shared began to whisper atop one another at varying speeds, the sound buzzing like an angry rattlesnake.

Her voice echoing, raw with desperate yearning as he loomed over her, eyes like hot blue flames.

Take me, MacCreedy. Take me like I was yours.

Pain lanced through her head, dropping her to her knees in the searingly bright space.

The swirl of images now became one looping over and over again, soaring above her as if played in panoramic IMAX. One image. One scene. Over and over until she was screaming.

"Si!"

Nica's eyes flew open. She was back in her bed. MacCreedy was staring at her in startled concern. She was gripping his arm, her claws breaking the skin.

"Nica, what is it?"

She released him and scooted away to the far edge of the bed. Her heart pounded. Her body dissolved into fitful shivering.

"Nica?"

He sat up, reaching for her. She could barely see him through the juxtaposition of another image. Of him turned toward her, and eyebrow raised in question.

Nica slapped away his hand, hissing, "Don't touch me."

"What's wrong?"

"You have to go. Now. Just go."

MacCreedy frowned, alert now.

"You can't be here. Go! This was a mistake. I don't want you here. Get out!"

He responded slowly to her frenzied demand, his eyes darkening with worry. He got up and gathered his clothes, his gaze never leaving her as he pulled on his jeans.

She was up on her knees, panting like a wild thing, her hair in tangled snarls about her shoulders, her face pale. "Just go. Please!"

He finally took a few backward steps, then turned and left the room.

When the door closed Nica slumped to the mattress, burying her face in the sheets saturated with his heat and scent. Tears scorched down her cheeks as she replayed the vision.

Silas, his strong, squared shoulders in a dark suit coat, walking ahead of her.

Her voice calling to him. "MacCreedy?"

Turning toward her, the movement agonizingly slow, one eyebrow arching as he faced her. A blur of silver as her knife slashed cleanly across his neck. His eyes widening, filled with shock before going glassy. The front of his white shirt now red. The whisper of her name as life left his gaze, and he slowly dropped where he stood.

Her terrifying look into a future she couldn't change.

———

What the hell was that about?

MacCreedy stood in the hall outside the door to Nica's room, puzzling out her mercurial change of mood. A chill of gooseflesh crept over his skin at the recall of her fierce, feral glare, the urgent plea threading through her snarl. He rubbed his arms, pausing at the deep grooves she'd carved: four perfect crescents. A prickle of instinct told him that he'd just escaped a dangerous threat, only because she'd pushed him out of harm's way. Part of him wanted to go back and demand an explanation. The other urged that he'd be wise to run for his life from the suddenly demon-possessed woman he—

He what?

Liked, he concluded, using her own word. The woman he liked to the point of unreasonable fondness. Which could get him killed if he wasn't more careful.

Silas stopped into his room to retrieve his shirt, then went downstairs in search of caffeine and a cooler temperature. A glance at his watch told him it was nudging up to five in the morning. He went into the dining room, grateful to find a large urn of coffee warming. After pouring himself a cup, he glanced out through the French doors to gauge the weather and saw a figure seated on the veranda—Tina Babineau.

She looked up at his approach, her expression stark and eyes swollen, then quickly ducked her head to conceal her sorrow. Silas paused, his hand on the back of the chair next to hers.

"Mind if I join you? We seem to be the only two awake."

"I don't mind." Her soft voice was slightly rough from weeping.

He sat at the table, leaning on his elbows, hands cradling the warm cup. Despite its humidity, the air was cool. Unfortunately there was no breeze to carry away the moisture. Just as there was no hope to alleviate Tina Babineau's sadness.

Unless he gave her some. But would that be a kindness or cruelty?

"Alain still asleep?"

"I don't know," came her muffled reply. "He spent the night on the parlor sofa."

"My partner's an idiot."

She said nothing.

"He worries about you living here."

Tina glanced up at his cautious invitation to unburden herself. "It's safer here. He knows that."

"Safe from what?"

She looked away. "From things you wouldn't understand."

"I think I would." He placed his hand lightly over hers, sending a gentle glimmer to spark along her nervous system.

Her huge brown eyes fixed upon him. "Does Alain know you're—?" At his nod, she asked more warily, "And Max?" Another nod. "Cee Cee? Of course she would know. And your girlfriend, she's a—"

"Shifter," Silas supplied. "Yes. Like you and your son. Oscar and I have done a little talking about your situation."

Her features tightened and her tone grew harsh. "I'm always the last to discover these things. No wonder I can't protect him."

"From what, Tina?"

"From whoever killed my parents. From whoever or whatever almost killed Max and Cee Cee when Oscar was taken from us. I don't know what they want, only that they want Oscar. Even if Alain did still love us, he isn't strong enough to keep us safe if they come for him again." Wobbly tears filled her eyes. "I'm not sure even Max can stop them."

Silas carefully took up one small, cold hand between his. "What if there was someplace you could go where you wouldn't have to worry anymore? Someplace you'd both be safe?"

Her gaze searched his, desperate. "Does such a place exist?"

This was supposed to be quick and impersonal. A snatch-and-grab, not this quiet, impassioned coaxing. Not a baring of his own purposes, his own soul. But Silas couldn't back away from the pull of her misery.

"I've come to New Orleans to find you, Tina. To let you know that you and Oscar aren't alone. You have family."

Her hand began to tremble within his grip. "Max is family."

"I used to rock you in my arms when you were a baby. I used to sing you to sleep." A smile flickered across his lips. "It wasn't exactly a lullaby, but you seemed to like it."

Tina stared at him. Then she whispered, "Your mama don't dance, and your daddy don't rock and roll." Her voice broke and her eyes flooded up. "Who *are* you?"

"You were a baby when our mother took you to St. Bart's. I called you Chrissy. I'm your half brother. And I've been looking for you for twenty-two years."

There was a long silence, then Tina surged out of her chair into his arms.

Silas hadn't realized how difficult and how wonderful this would be. She'd been two and a half years old when she was taken from his life. Yet the instant her arms went around his neck, a flood of fragile memories drowned him. She was family, and he loved her with the same fierce devotion he held for Brigit and Kendra.

Tina sat back at last, wiping teary eyes filled with amazement and confusion. "I don't understand. Have you told Oscar that you're his uncle?"

"No. We need to keep this between the two of us for now, Tina. I'm not sure who we can trust."

"Max—"

"Not Max. Not Alain. Not Oscar. No one. You and Oscar are in danger here. I've come to take you someplace safe."

Her excitement cooled to cautious sensibility. "Why would I leave here with you? I don't know you. I remember a silly tune you may or may not have sung to me before—before I was given away. My family gave me away?"

The anguish in her voice twisted about his heart.

"Politics were involved; dangerous politics that I'll explain later. Right now, I just want you to listen. I don't want you to decide. Just listen."

She slid back into her chair, looking wary yet receptive. "Go on."

"You and Oscar are part of the Terriot clan. They're powerful and well-connected. They have a compound in Nevada where you and Oscar will be protected, cared for, and honored."

"Honored? What a strange word."

"Think of our families like a feudal society. The strongest are showered with prosperity and respect. The weaker clans pay homage to them in return for protection and favor. Leadership over the family clans comes down through the bloodlines, generation to generation. And the Terriot bloodline leads to Oscar. That's why he's so important. That's why he's in danger. Once he's within the Terriots' circle, he'll be out of the reach of those who'd kill or ransom him. He won't be safe until then. Neither will you."

He hated the quick spark of fear in her eyes, but would use it ruthlessly.

She swallowed hard and looked out over the fog-draped yard. "How do I know I can trust you not to be one of those I should fear?"

"You don't." That brutal answer got her full attention. "*Don't* trust me. Don't trust anyone. You can't afford to. There's too much at stake." And then he lied to her so shamefully, it was all he could do to keep his gaze steadily fixed upon hers. "I have no agenda here. I'm a MacCreedy, not a Terriot, even though I share some of their lineage through my father. I have nothing to gain . . . except family. I've spent too much time searching for you to lose you both now." His voice caught, and that unplanned snag was what convinced her.

She said, "Would you go with us to this place?"

"I would take you, yes."

"Would you stay there with us?"

"I would. It would be my privilege to act on your behalf until you're comfortable and confident enough to handle your own affairs. There are things you'd have to learn quickly for Oscar to take and hold his rightful place."

"And you could teach me those things?"

"Yes. I'd make sure you had all you were entitled to, all that you deserved." And in doing so, he, Brigit, and Kendra would go from outcasts to royalty. Their lives would be filled with comfort instead of fear. And he would finally be worthy of his dreams.

So why did he want to throw up?

"What about Max? Would he be welcomed there?"

Silas gave a snorting laugh. "No, never. There's too much bad blood between their families for him to ever be invited onto Terriot ground." Seeing her distress, he softened that claim. "But maybe once you're established there, you could bend their pride a bit. He is your blood, after all. It's an old grudge. Perhaps the venom has gone out of it." He smiled over clenched teeth. *Hardly.*

Tina leaned back in her chair, playing restlessly with the sash of her cotton floral dress. "What about my husband?" she asked hesitantly. "Would he be allowed to come with us?"

Silas blinked. He'd never actually considered that. "I don't know. A few human mates live among the clans. It wouldn't be easy for him, but I don't think it's impossible. Would he go?"

"No." No hesitation. "No, he wouldn't."

He covered her small hand with his. "I'm sorry these decisions are so hard. But you have to make up your mind soon. Maybe it would be easier if you just considered what would be best for Oscar."

What a shit he was, Silas thought as he held her gaze so earnestly. Where had he learned to deceive and connive with such aplomb? When had he decided to condone such despicable behavior? But he knew. It was when he'd stood with his mother's blood wet on his hands. When he'd labored, dry-eyed, to gather up the pieces of his father so he could see him properly buried. When he'd been forced to become the head of his family, responsible for all their futures, when little more than a child himself.

But that didn't make the bitter taste go down any easier.

He stood up and drank the remains of his coffee.

Tina got to her feet, as well, looking uncertain for a moment, then she slipped her arms about his middle and hugged tight. Holding her head to his chest, he reminded himself that it was all about family. He couldn't afford to look beyond that.

Not even when the electricity came on, illuminating the rooms behind them, and Max Savoie standing on the other side of the French doors, watching their embrace inscrutably. Silas dropped his gaze before Max could read the sentiments it contained, a truth that pounded hard and ferociously with every beat of his heart.

Try and stop me, you son of a bitch. I'm washing down that cold dish of vengeance with your blood.

The ride back into the city was long and silent. Nica's steady stare had the hair on Silas's nape prickling. She hadn't met his eyes since she'd come downstairs clad in the seductive red dress, her hair braided back from features so brutally angular, they looked like fractures in stone. When his gaze lifted to the turbulence of her own, their eyes locked briefly in a scramble of emotions. Then hers lowered first.

She avoided him when they all gathered for a quick buffet breakfast, drawing Cee Cee's curiosity when she glanced between them. Babineau spoke briefly to Oscar, who manfully contained his own upset, then nodded to his estranged wife before muttering that he was going to get the car. Silas found Cee Cee at his elbow, scowling after Alain.

"Asshole," she grumbled. "See if you can make any headway."

"I will." In his own direction, not hers. He told Savoie, "Thanks for the invite."

Savoie regarded him unblinkingly, then drawled, "Thanks for being such a considerate guest."

The not so subtle reference to his and Nica's rambunctious lovemaking brought a flush to MacCreedy's face until Savoie grinned and turned to Nica.

She accepted their host's hand and when he suggested they go jogging together someday soon, she returned his toothy smile with a "Yes, soon."

Was she in New Orleans to kill Savoie? Silas wondered during their tomb-quiet drive. If so, should he stop her?

Could he stop her?

When Babineau pulled up in front of the Quarter House, MacCreedy stepped out to open the door for Nica, extending his hand to help her from the small backseat.

On the sidewalk he lifted her hand to his cheek and touched a light kiss to the base of her thumb. Holding his stare, she withdrew her hand, letting her fingertips trail down the front of his shirt, briefly bunching the fabric up in her fist. Then she let him go.

"Good-bye, Silas."

She quickly turned away and went through the shadowed doorway.

MacCreedy looked after her, wondering if he was

watching something better than any dream he'd ever held escape him.

As Nica headed past the front desk, responding to cheerful greetings from the always pleasant staff, a soft call of her name brought her up short. Perched on the edge of an antique chair was Lena Blutafino. She wore the big, concealing glasses and an elegantly tailored shorts suit of ivory linen, its plunging neckline filled with ropes of pearls.

"Hello, Lena. This is a surprise."

Glancing nervously about, the buxom blonde asked, "Is there someplace we can talk?"

"Sure."

Lena didn't speak a word until the door to Nica's apartment locked behind them. Then she headed for the sofa and collapsed on it, her hands twisting together. "I've been thinking a lot about our conversation."

"Good." Nica went into the small kitchen to pour them tall glasses of sweet tea. "Sorry I wasn't here. The weather kept me from getting home last night."

"I want to leave Manny," Lena announced with a burst of courage.

Nica sat next to her on the love seat. "Good."

"But I don't want any of his money. I don't want Paulie growing up around all that . . . that stuff like I did. He's a good boy and I want good things for him."

"Any mother would want that for her child."

"I'm just not sure how to go about it. I thought you might have some ideas." Huge blue eyes, one with a hint of a bruise around it, gazed at her hopefully. "Though we don't really know each other, you're the only one I trust."

She didn't have time to get tangled up in this! She was on the cusp of the most important work she'd ever done, work that would launch her reputation as an independent. Work that would guarantee freedom for more than just herself. She had to stay detached, focused. It was bad enough with MacCreedy terrorizing her hormones until she couldn't come up with a single simple plan to get rid of him. Now this.

Tears welled up, threatening Lena's elaborate eye makeup.

Oh, hell. "I might have a few ideas."

Lena smiled and reached for her tea.

Just shoot me now. "You'll need your own money tucked away someplace safe," Nica said.

"Getaway money." Lena nodded, liking the sound of that.

"You said you had a lot of expensive jewelry. You could start by selling it off very discreetly."

"Manny has people watching me. He keeps track of my things. He'd know if something was missing."

"Okay, then we'll have to throw up some kind of smoke screen to distract him."

While Lena sipped her tea, her knees bouncing anxiously, Nica suddenly smiled.

"I've got an idea. I have a friend who could use a decorator." She picked up her cell and tapped in a number.

"Detective Caissie," came the growl on the other end.

"Chili? This is Nica. I think I found the answer to your problem."

After an icy shower and quick shave, MacCreedy pulled on fresh jeans, a black T-shirt, and sturdy boots, then picked up a gray suit jacket and his sunglasses. The blinking message light on his landline caught his attention and he paused to push play.

"Where the hell have you been? I've left four messages. You can't dodge me that easily, Silas."

He pressed stop. "Love you, too, sis." Then he was out the door, jogging down the stairs.

As he paused on the front steps to put on his dark glasses, a gleaming black town car slid up next to the curb. The darkly tinted back window came down soundlessly and Max Savoie gave him a narrow smile.

"Let's go for a ride."

Thirteen

A mobster wanting to take you for a ride wasn't generally a good thing.

Silas opened the door and sank down on the black leather seat. "I'm on my way to work."

"You're going to be late." Max nodded to his driver. The window went up, the door latches engaged, and the big car purred away from the curb.

Oh, shit. He was going to die.

They ended up down by the wharves in front of the huge, partially occupied Trinity Towers project, in which Savoie was a partner with Simon Cummings. Savoie left the car, striding to a corner of the main spire, where he keyed open a private smoked glass elevator that ran up the side of the building. He and Silas rode up in silence, both staring out over the city, postures deceptively relaxed, expressions impassive.

On twelve, the top floor, the doors opened to a huge unoccupied apartment, its main room facing a wall of glass that ran the width of the building. Max walked up to those floor-to-ceiling windows with Silas following cautiously.

"I built this tower as a haven for my clan here in New

Orleans. Its walls will shelter them and their families. It'll be the first time some of them have ever lived together under the same roof, the first time some of them have ever dared to stand upright like free men to protect their own children and give them a better life. This will be our fortress against those who think to take those freedoms away from us."

Good luck with that.

MacCreedy glanced away, measuring the dimensions of the room, checking exits, searching for weapons. He had his police issue, but its bullets would never take down Savoie. Just as he could never take Savoie one-on-one, not if the rumors were true. And he suspected they were, or these frightened, outcast Shifters wouldn't have accepted him so readily as their leader. Had he been brought here to discuss clan business and the nebulous hope of freedom?

When he turned back, Max was nose to nose with him. His eyes were hot gold disks swimming in red. His hand caught Silas about the throat.

"Did you think I was going to let you take my brother? Think again."

Keeping his arms at his sides was the most difficult thing MacCreedy had ever done. *Don't react. Don't give him an excuse to kill you.*

Savoie's hand squeezed tight and Silas's world went dark. Instead of struggling against that suffocating hand, he gathered every last ounce of strength and spat in Savoie's face. "Fuck you."

Savoie's expression blanked as he wiped his face with his free hand. Then, with one mighty gesture, he flung MacCreedy the length of the room, through the glass sliding doors, and out onto the rooftop patio.

Silas heard Max crunch his way purposefully across the broken glass as he struggled onto his knees. Savoie gripped the back of his head, smashing his face into the pebbled floor.

"Who are you? What is your clan?"

"I have no clan," Silas snarled. He hooked his arm back to snag Savoie about the neck and pulled him off his feet, giving Silas time to stagger to his own. He reeled back to put some distance between them, then assumed a boldly offensive position.

Savoie rose up with a lethally powerful grace. "Who are your people?" Max demanded again.

"I have no people. They're all dead because of your father." He spat again, this time blood from a split lip, right between Savoie's feet.

Max's rage chilled to a somber intensity. "Who sent you?"

There was no reason to lie completely, not when he could wield a partial truth like a double-edged sword. "The Terriots, my uncle's clan, to restore their heir. My half sister's son, your father's second son."

Max absorbed that information without a flicker of emotion. Then, surprisingly, he turned and went back into the apartment.

Breathing hard, seething with decades of rage, Mac-

Creedy followed. Part of him longed to push for conflict to settle his need for closure. He hungered to tear into the object of his frustration and pain. He'd thought of little else even as he promised Brigit to see to their business first. Why shouldn't he have both his revenge and his redemption?

Max stood behind the bar, pulling mineral water out of a small refrigerator to fill two glasses. He pushed one of them across the glossy top to MacCreedy, tense and ready on the other side. He took the glass, forcing the liquid past his bruised throat but refusing to grimace.

"Tell me," Max said.

"I'm not telling you a damned thing," Silas vowed fiercely.

"Tell me why you stand there with a thirst for my blood in your eyes. What have I ever done to you or your family? If the cause is just, we'll finish this between us right here and now."

Yes, they would. "When Rollo Moytes stole your mother before her contract with the Terriots was completed, he started a war between the clans. The Terriots were more powerful and unforgiving. They decimated the Moyteses, every male, female, and child, but that didn't end things. Failing to bring your mother's bloodline in with their own created an imbalance within the houses. The Terriots were challenged by the Guedrys and by several other smaller clans who wouldn't have dared before. The only way the Terriots could hold their position was to make a strong political match."

MacCreedy broke off, swallowing the rest of the water. It went down like shards of glass, the way retelling this story did. But he wanted Max Savoie to know how his father's selfish act had created ripples of destruction that shattered so many lives.

"My mother was a Guedry, far above my father in standing, but she loved him enough to mate with and marry him. She loved our quiet life outside the ugly conflicts of the clans, and she loved me and my sister. Too much to resist when the Terriots forced a bargain: her family's lives in exchange for a Terriot heir."

So without telling her husband, Therese MacCreedy mated with Bram Terriot, who was to have fathered a child with Marie Savory, but instead created a baby girl with her. And for almost three years, the MacCreedys raised that child, Christina, believing her to be part of their family. Until Bram Terriot sent word that he would be coming for his progeny.

"What did your father do when he learned the truth?"

Silas glanced up at Max, having forgotten him. "He loved Christina and still thought of her as his own, and he loved my mother above his pride. He didn't blame her for what she'd done, only that she hadn't trusted him with it sooner."

"So they decided that, rather than surrender this child they loved, they would hide her away," Max surmised. "They gave her to Father Furness at St. Bart's."

"Yes."

"And when Terriot came for his child?"

"My parents refused to tell him where she was. He gave them twenty-four hours to produce her."

"And when they didn't?"

Instead of giving a direct answer, MacCreedy approached it gradually, keeping tight control on his emotions. "My parents sat us down—me, my sister, and Kendra, the child of my father's cousin, who lived with us—and told us what they'd done and how that could affect us all. We all agreed to protect Christina with our silence because she was family, part of us." His eyes became an eerie bright blue. "We had no idea what they were capable of.

"At the end of that twenty-four hours, they brought us the heads of all our relatives and threw them down on the floor of our living room. My mother's sisters, her nieces and nephews, Kendra's father, who refused to co-operate with his own family by betraying mine, my uncles, my cousins." He paused, remembering the shocking sight of all those familiar faces with expressions caught in silent screams. "When my parents still refused to tell him where they'd hidden Christina, they took my father apart piece by piece in front of my mother. When she still wouldn't speak, they threatened to do the same to her children. She knew she wouldn't be able to keep her silence, so she attacked one of them and died to protect us."

Max reached beneath the bar and produced a bottle of bourbon, pouring a liberal amount into each of their glasses.

"To family," he said quietly, "and the sacrifices they make for one another."

MacCreedy tossed back the contents, letting the liquid burn all the way down.

"How did you manage to stay alive?" Max asked.

"I convinced them that my sister, Kendra, and I would be valuable assets to the House of Terriot. As hostages at first, in case any of the other houses objected to their barbarity, then as loyal and grateful subjects."

"And they believed you?"

"My parents were well-known pacifists. After my intentions were tested for a few days, I managed to impress them with my humility and a promise we wouldn't rise up against them."

Max didn't need it spelled out. They'd tortured him. "You didn't tell them where Tina was."

"I didn't know." His voice roughened. "I wouldn't have told them if I did. I'd dishonor myself to save the girls, but I would have died before dishonoring my father."

Max refilled their glasses. "And I would die before becoming like mine." He studied the rich golden liquor for a moment. "I recently made the error of thinking a father's sins could be purged through the punishment of his daughter. I wouldn't want you to make that same mistake. Rollo Moytes was a coward, a liar, and a thief who sold me to a mobster to become his obedient killer. He was a man without honor, who cared for himself above all else, and he died the same way. My father was everything you believed him to be and worse." He took a quick, fierce swallow.

"You were wronged by my father's actions. Though I took no part in them, I honor your right for revenge. I don't want your blood on my hands, but if you're determined to go after mine, it's only fair that you take the first swing."

If he was fast and fearless, that first strike would decapitate Savoie. MacCreedy's nails began to lengthen into wicked claws. He was strong enough to mete out that killing blow—but suddenly he lacked the desire to.

Slightly dazed by the revelation, Silas murmured, "You weren't responsible for my family's slaughter. And killing you won't bring them back or lessen their loss."

Max shrugged. "I'm not my father's son, but you are obviously yours."

Surprised by that sudden assessment, Silas felt his throat tighten. Then as quickly as it was given, the compliment was torn away.

"So you plan to steal my brother, and let the monsters who murdered your family raise him? Where's the honor in that?"

MacCreedy fought the sickness inside him to speak his practiced argument. "They'll protect him from other, more dangerous threats."

"I can protect him."

Silas shook his head. "I don't think you can. You're alone, with only that ragged band of leftovers at your back. They have an army trained only to fight and die."

"My clan will fight—"

"And they *will* die. Didn't you wonder why I didn't fight back against the Terriots? Why I didn't fight back against you a few minutes ago?"

Max lifted a curious brow and waited.

"Because I couldn't beat the odds, so I have to be smart and patient and play the cards I've been given. It's a shitty hand, but it's all I have. And as long as the Terriots don't see me as a threat, I can keep my promise to my parents and see my family's security and name restored."

"By giving them their heir."

"Yes."

"That's not going to happen."

"He'll be well cared for. He'll have the best of everything. And he'll be safe. He'll be with family."

"A family of greedy, savage killers? Where he can learn to be just like them?"

"And what is he learning from you, Max?"

It was a blow Max couldn't defend as easily as he wished, so he changed tactics. "You lived amongst them. Is that how you'd see your nephew raised?"

"I lived with them, not amongst them," MacCreedy clarified. His eyes again took on that eerie blue flame. "I was the son of a traitor and they never let me forget that shame."

"Yet you'd go back there?"

"If I returned with their prodigal, acting on his behalf, things would be very different."

"They'd welcome you with open arms and embrace

you," Max drawled. "So you can have your share of the power and wealth?"

"No. I'll have their respect. And then no one will dare challenge my family; my sister and Kendra will be safe. They'll be able to make good matches, strong alliances, have good futures instead of living in disgrace and fear. All the things they deserve."

"You think surrendering freedom will guarantee your safety?" Max chuckled. "Is that the life your mother and father wanted for you? Living under the thumb of those who don't give a damn about you? What they wanted for you, you won't find there with your enemies. They *won't* respect you. They'll fear you because they couldn't break you, and because of that, they'll never trust you. They'll send someone like your deadly little girlfriend to take care of the problem you've become."

"I don't care what happens to me."

"If you let them use you as their tool, you'll never become more than the blunt instrument of their greed. I know something about that. Your sacrifices will be for nothing, and your family will lose their protection."

Silas held his stare, not blinking, not backing down.

Max sighed and shook his head. "Tina and Oscar are your family, too. Don't forget what others were willing to sacrifice for them. Unless it's Tina's choice to go with you, I'll do everything in my power to stop you."

"I understand."

"But you won't change your mind?"

"I can't."

"It won't please me to kill you."

"I can't say I'll be too happy about it, either."

Max placed a hand on his shoulder. "I'll drop you off at the precinct."

"No. Take me back to my apartment." Suddenly it seemed imperative for him to hear his sister's message.

Max scowled as he watched MacCreedy disappear inside his building. A shame to waste a man of such talent and integrity. Now the problem lay with Tina and what she'd decide was best for her son. And he wasn't as confident as he wanted to be in that regard. She had come to him with her concerns about MacCreedy's offer, but it might appeal to her in the end. There was no guessing what a mother was willing to do for her child.

"To the office, Pete. I've got a meeting to prepare for."

With Francis Petitjohn. Another problem he'd let go unchallenged for far too long.

As Pete guided the big vehicle through the crowded midmorning streets, Max pondered his many dilemmas. MacCreedy and his lethal lover. Petitjohn and Blutafino scheming together. Charlotte straying to just the other side of complete truthfulness. The awful possibility of having to let Oscar go. He closed his eyes, blanking his thoughts as Pete picked up speed and they left the Quarter.

Then the brakes locked up with a shriek and the stench of burning rubber. A loud thump sounded near the driver's front fender.

"I didn't see him, Mr. Savoie," Pete said, upset but still with the presence of mind to flip on the hazard flashers. "He just was there. I couldn't avoid him."

Pete had opened the car door to check on the pedestrian, but there was no one lying in the street.

The quick blat of a silenced gunshot dropped Pete across the front seat, crimson blooming on his white polo shirt. A man leaned in through the door, firing three more shots into Max.

The impact took Max in the chest, flinging him backward. Fiery shafts of agony followed as the silver slugs burned deep. As he slumped down, stunned, with consciousness ebbing dangerously, Max saw an unfamiliar Shifter stretch over the seat to finish him. Max caught his assailant by the neck and hauled him inside, where they grappled for possession of the gun. Several more shots and subsequent jolts of pain.

Meanwhile the car slowly moved forward, picking up speed as Pete struggled to sit up behind the wheel to control the hurtling vehicle's trajectory. Right into the gas station across the intersection, where a startled teenager fueling up his Jeep saw them coming, his cigarette falling from his mouth as he leapt to safety while dropping the hose.

And Max's world burst into flames with a huge explosion.

Fourteen

Cee Cee entered the apartment, followed by Nica and Lena Blutafino. She was in her guise of Chili Pepper, former exotic dancer and now mistress of the wealthy heir to Jimmy Legere's mob fortune. She paused, puzzled by the sight of workmen reinstalling the patio slider.

"Oh, my," Lena murmured as she walked the length of the huge open space. "This is wonderful. You should do something organic, something that brings the river and the city together. A waterfall here on this wall against old stone and brick. Imagine the sound."

While Cee Cee took Lena on a tour, Nica was inexplicably drawn to the long ebony bar. She traced her fingers down the cool length, wondering what she was looking for until she touched a dried stain. Blood? She chipped at it with her nail, sniffed, then tasted. Her knees went weak.

Silas.

Her senses swam. Had Savoie killed him?

Why hadn't he taken her warning seriously?

She glanced at the replacement patio door with a terrible chill of knowledge, and alarm shook through her until her teeth chattered. A dizzying swirl of anguish made her clench her jaws against the need to wail out loud. Loss ripped open a void in her soul so cold and stark it sucked at her like an emotional black hole.

He couldn't be gone. She couldn't comprehend not seeing him again, hearing his low voice, feeling the eager anticipation his touch stirred inside her, mentally sparring with him, making love with him.

He can't be dead.

Beneath that surge of sorrow came a soft saving whisper.

At least he didn't die by my hand.

What kind of animal was she that she could find relief in the fact that she hadn't been the one to end his life? Would she have? Could she have? Fearing the answer made her sickness swell.

"Silk," Lena was saying as they came back from the bedrooms and bath. "Chocolate and cream. Rich, smooth, and sinful, with cream-colored lace edges, like whipped topping on a sundae. Gold lighting and bath fixtures. How's that for a start?"

"I can't wait to have a good long soak. I wish I'd had a setup like that when I was performing. Between the shower massage and the Jacuzzi, I might have been able to squeeze a little more enjoyment out of the evening."

Cee Cee and Lena shared a laugh before the undercover detective caught sight of Nica's pinched features.

"Nica, thanks for bringing Lena to my attention," she began. "I didn't have the slightest idea what to do with this place and she's full of great suggestions."

"They'll be expensive," Lena warned with an anxious smile.

Cee Cee waved a negligent hand. "Oh, Max doesn't care about the cost. He just wants me to be happy."

Lena's expression grew bittersweet. "Manny was like that when we first met."

Before Cee Cee could jump on that opening, Nica asked, "Have you talked to Max lately? Do you know where he is?"

Cee Cee gave her a stabbing glance to remind her of the roles they were playing. "He said something about meetings this afternoon. Then he said he'd try to slip over to see me." She looked around at the mostly bare space. "Once this is all nice and cozy, he won't be in such a hurry to rush off. When do you think you could get started?"

Lena's eyes grew glassy. "Really? You want to hire me?"

"I'd be crazy not to. You said you had some samples?"

They spread the books of fabric swatches on the bar. Nica stood silently beside them, her hand pressed over that dark stain as her insides continued to tremble. The excited chatter as Cee Cee worked a potential witness/informant dimmed into a low buzz, and her surroundings seemed to lose all color and depth. Nica's world compressed into one of flat, gray misery, until a knock at the apartment door quickened a sudden rush of expectation.

Cee Cee opened the door, and the sound of Mac-

Creedy's voice reached Nica at the same instant she breathed in his scent. Her senses spun, forcing her to grip the edge of the bar.

He entered the room behind Cee Cee and a behemoth of a man she remembered as Savoie's bodyguard. When Silas's cool gray eyes found her, Nica's bones went liquid. She looked for visible signs of injury, finding none. He seemed fit and all business in his dark suit coat over jeans and a crisp white shirt and tie. No bloodstains. He looked indescribably delicious.

He was here. He was all right.

Her mind swirled with relief.

Silas stepped forward to put his hand out to Lena Blutafino. "Mrs. Blutafino, I'm Mac Creed. I work at the club for your husband."

Panic at being discovered flashed across her features. "Did he send you to find me?"

An easy smile. "No, ma'am. In fact, he said something about meeting you after your spinning class to take you to lunch."

She returned Silas's smile nervously. "I guess I'd better go. I wouldn't want to miss him." She turned to Cee Cee. "I'll be in touch."

"Soon," Cee Cee insisted. She waited until the woman had left the room to turn to the burly bodyguard. "Giles, what's going on?"

Features stoic, Giles scooped her hand up in his, holding it so tightly she winced. "Charlotte—" His voice broke.

Alarmed, Cee Cee looked at Silas. "Mac? What's wrong?"

"There was an accident this morning. A driver apparently lost control of his vehicle and plowed into a gas pump. There was an explosion. There were two men in the car, one at the wheel, one in back, both burned beyond recognition. Closer examination at the scene showed that shots had been fired close range prior to the collision. Silver slugs were recovered. It's not looking like an accident anymore. Babineau's doing a follow-up at the scene because he figured you'd want to know . . ." He trailed off.

Cee Cee's hand crushed Giles's as she looked up at him to confirm what MacCreedy was getting to.

"Charlotte," he told her gruffly, "they think it's Max."

Everything about her stilled, then strengthened. "I don't believe it. If something had happened to him, I would know."

"It was the car he picked me up in this morning," MacCreedy said. "He was with his driver. It must have happened just after he dropped me off at my apartment."

"What did Max want with you?" Cee Cee asked, suspicion darkening her stare.

"We had some things to talk over."

His smooth evasion sharpened Nica's instincts. Her fingertips traced the bloodstain on the bar, drawing his attention there. "Things related to your case?"

"No," he said simply. "Clan related." He turned back to the detective. "The bodies are with Dovion. He said he'd make them a priority." A close friend of Max and Cee Cee, Devlin Dovion, the medical examiner, hadn't made that promise lightly. "Charlotte, Babineau said they found cuff links in the backseat. Large onyx stones set in gold."

"I helped Max put them on this morning." Her chin quivered, then squared. "Until I get word one way or another from Dev, I need to work this case with an open mind. I need to get to the scene." When she started for the door, MacCreedy put up his arm to block her. When she tried to go around it, he curled it about her waist, holding her still.

"Charlotte," Silas said gently, "this isn't your case. They're not going to let you on the scene. Word from the top, according to Babineau. He's checking things out for you, and wanted me to tell you to keep your distance if you don't want things complicated by the media circus. They're trying to keep a lid on it, but if you show up they'll start doing the math. By the book, Detective—unless you want the investigation tainted right off the bat."

"Screw that!" She flung off his arm and stormed to the wall of windows, pressing her palms against the glass, leaning her forehead there until she got her panting breaths under control. Until she tried to reach Max along the psychic connection they shared. And failed. Finally she straightened. "I know you're right, Mac. I know that's the right way to handle things, but dammit, I can't just do *nothing*. I can't just wait."

"Max had a meeting with T-John," Giles said quietly. "I wonder if that son of a bitch will be surprised by the news?"

Charlotte turned to him, her stare cold as the bore of a double barrel. "Maybe we should go ask him."

"I'm going to touch base with LaRoche at the club," Silas said. "If anything's going on down on the docks, he'll know about it. If you could drop me off—"

"I'm heading in to work," Nica interjected. "You can ride with me."

Silas glanced at her briefly. "Okay."

"If you hear anything," Cee Cee began.

"My first call." MacCreedy headed for the door, Nica on his heels.

Only then did Charlotte crumple in Giles's arms.

They rode down the elevator in silence. Nica knew he was waiting for her to set the tone after she'd booted him out of her bed at their last private meeting, but she didn't dare make a move. Her mood was fragile, barely in control. Just the scent of him reduced her to near emotional collapse.

Just knowing he was alive was enough for now.

Her car was a tiny rental. Nica slid behind the wheel while Silas contorted his 6'3" frame into the passenger seat. Once they were headed back into the Quarter, he broke the silence.

"Something's on your mind. What is it? Are you wondering if I killed Savoie?"

"You did get into an uncivilized conversation with him this morning in that apartment, didn't you?"

"We had a discussion about family matters that got briefly unpleasant, but we reached a tentative understanding. And where were *you* this morning?"

She gave him a scornful look. "If I'd killed him, I wouldn't have made such a mess."

"Oh? Like our first meeting?"

She sniffed. "I'm very tidy unless distracted."

"And I distract you?"

"You aggravate me."

"Enough to get in your way?"

She turned her attention back to the road. "Don't be silly. I'm a professional."

"A professional what?" When she didn't respond, he supplied the answer. "Assassin?"

"If I was, you'd be pretty foolish asking me about it. And I'd be even crazier to tell you."

"Is Savoie your target?"

"If I was an assassin and he was my target, that would certainly help you, wouldn't it? Unless someone else has already done you that favor."

"I don't want him dead."

"That's news. Since when?"

"It was a misunderstanding. We sorted it out."

"So he's not going to kill you if you try taking the boy?"

"We hadn't come to any terms on that yet."

"If you're planning to grab the kid, putting all Savoie's

people on high alert wouldn't be the smartest thing to do. So since you're a smart guy, I'm guessing it isn't a move you'd make. So who did?"

"I don't know, but it sure kicked open a hornet's nest."

"Try not to get stung."

She wheeled the little car into a parking space and cut the engine. When she got to the sidewalk, he put an instinctive hand to the small of her back. She jumped away and strode to the entrance of *Cheveux du Chien*. She was halfway down the long hall before his arm scooped about her waist.

"Nica."

The quiet, rumbling way he spoke her name was her undoing. She sagged back against his chest, her eyes closing.

"I thought he'd killed you," she whispered, shivering.

He simply held her, saying nothing, letting her gain her composure. When her breaths evened out, he turned her toward him.

Her eyes opened, shimmering as she blinked the tears away. "I'm late."

She pulled free and hurried toward the light and noise of the nightclub.

And Silas watched her go, grinning.

Even when they pulled the charred bodies from the remains of the vehicle, Alain Babineau didn't believe it. Even when they found the ruined onyx cuff links that had once belonged to Jimmy Legere, he wasn't convinced.

Max Savoie couldn't be out of his life for good. Some-one like that wouldn't be taken out in a hail of bullets and a funeral pyre. Not Savoie. The evidence didn't mean a damned thing. He wouldn't be content until he saw the son of a bitch grinning up at him from hell.

As the investigating officers combed the remains of the vehicle and the coroner's wagon pulled away, Babi-neau began his own search for proof that he was either right or wrong. Not daring to hope he'd seen the last of the smug bastard, Alain refused to think about it until he had a signed affidavit from Satan himself.

The smoldering car told him nothing. Two bodies, both crisped beyond identification, though witnesses stated Savoie and his driver had been inside. Holes rid-dled the interior, from bullets made of silver. While the team concentrated on the wreckage, Babineau widened his circumference, not sure what he was looking for until he was staring down at it.

The first droplets of a blood trail.

He purposefully scrubbed the sole of his shoe across the pebbled surface until the spots were obliterated. And then he began to follow splatters that became dragging smears on the pavement.

Another officer wouldn't have understood the sig-nificance. They would have been looking for a man, but Babineau didn't turn back at the first sign of an animal's paw print in the blood. And he found final proof in the large black dog lying behind an alley Dumpster. He was familiar with this animal.

On two legs or four, Max Savoie was the same unnatural being.

Babineau glanced about. They were alone. Cautiously, he knelt down to examine the motionless beast. Frothy blood pooled about the animal's muzzle. Its black coat was singed and punctured by countless bullets. When he leaned close, he could hear a death gurgle in the softly panted breaths.

All he had to do was nothing. Straighten up and walk away. Or just wait.

But Charlotte would take one look at him, and see her lover's death in his eyes.

Shit.

Cursing under his breath, he went to get his car, rationalizing that Savoie wasn't going to make it anyway. His efforts would appear heroic, a futile attempt to save a preternatural life and protect a dangerous secret.

He could live with that.

He parked in the alley and popped his trunk. After spreading out a tarp, he knelt beside the gravely injured creature. Surprisingly, its eyes opened, eyes that were green and eerily familiar.

"It's all right, Max. I'm going to get you out of here."

He put his arms around the beast's hindquarters and powerful chest, hesitating at the sound of a bubbly growl.

"Try to bite me, and I'll put one in your head. It wouldn't hurt my feelings to do it, either."

The animal coughed, almost sounding like a laugh. When Babineau struggled to stand, the heavy shape hung limp in his arms, not moving as he deposited the shaggy form in the trunk. He shut the lid and slid behind the wheel. What the hell was he going to do now? Take him to the vet? And have him shape-shift while on the table? What headlines that would make.

"Fuck me. Looks like you're going to be my guest."

For the first time, Babineau was glad his house was empty. He threw blankets down over the old leather couch in his office. Max never so much as twitched when he was carried inside and laid on the cushions.

Alain's first move should have been to call Cee Cee. But she'd come running to his side—and draw the attention of anyone still looking for Savoie.

"Now what?" Babineau said aloud. Did he call LEI to have someone come claim him? How did he know that Savoie's men weren't behind the attempt on his life? Not that he cared a damn, but he didn't want his family pulled into it. Why should he have to do anything more? He'd rescued the monster from discovery and immediate threat. He hadn't even owed him that much. Except for the fact that he'd saved Oscar's life. And that of Schoenbaum's daughter.

God, he hated being grateful to the son of a bitch.

Babineau sat at his desk, contemplating his options. Was there anything he hated more than the smirky criminal? The long-lost brother adored by his son, who used his illegal wealth to shower his family with luxuries a cop's salary could never come close to matching. Who was housing them in his mobster fortress as if they belonged to him. Who could protect them even as he brought threat into their lives. Who effortlessly and unworthily awoke love in those hearts he'd always wished would beat for him alone.

Who was now helpless and at his mercy.

Fever-bright eyes opened and a low rumble worked up from the damaged chest.

"Is that the thanks I get for taking you in off the street? Pretty big talk for having three paws in the grave."

The big animal grew quiet, studying him with a shrewd gaze. His legs began thrashing ineffectively as he tried to get up, and Babineau leaned in to place staying hands on his neck and hindquarters.

"Stop. You'll just hurt yourself. Relax. You go all Cujo on me, I'll chain your furry ass out in the yard."

The movements stilled, and a soft whimper escaped as the glittery eyes closed again. The instant Babineau realized his hand was stroking over the dark head soothingly, he pulled back.

"I don't like dogs, and I sure as hell have no fondness for you," he muttered. "Can you understand me?"

The dry, hot nose nudged into his palm, followed by the quick slap of the dog's tongue.

"Oh, for fuck's sake, don't kiss me. We don't have that kind of relationship."

The animal took several snorting breaths as if amused. And Babineau took a moment to examine the wounds.

"Can you talk? What am I saying? It's not like you're Mr. Ed. I don't know what to do for you, Max."

With a huge groan, the dog lifted his shaggy head and turned toward the bullet wound in his shoulder. At first Babineau thought he was licking it, but then he saw fresh blood and realized he was biting determinedly, whining not in mindless pain but with purpose. Babineau pressed his head back down, calmingly stroking his ears and neck to quiet him again.

"It's the silver, isn't it?"

Max heaved a thankful sigh.

"If I take them out, you'll be able to heal yourself. If I don't ... Kinda sucks to be you right now, doesn't it? Must be sweating it, thinking you should have been a little nicer to me, huh, Mr. Big Shot?"

Max's jowls curled back, not in a snarl, but more like an appreciative grin.

Ah, hell.

Babineau pulled his belt free. "No offense, but I don't want you nipping at me while I'm poking around. Okay?"

Max lay still, letting him use the belt to make a muzzle about his snout.

"And I want you to thank me for this later."

Fifteen

It was a long, miserable night at work. Nica's temper was short and her attention strained. The minute Mac-Creedy disappeared into the back office with LaRoche, she could think of nothing else but their conversation. What would happen to the New Orleans clan if Max Savoie was dead?

More important, what would it mean to her?

She wasn't just an assassin, she was considered the best. Though she didn't know the particulars, the fee for her services was enormous. She was in high demand because she was quick, deadly, left no traces, and she had no idea who hired her.

While Savoie was protecting his family and clan from the crude, mindless Trackers, he should have been fearing a more sophisticated enemy.

Her assignment in New Orleans had come so fast after her last one, she'd had little time to unwind. She'd been given little information. *Get in place, become invisible, and be ready on a moment's notice.* She hadn't been told who the assignment was, only that her success would guarantee her notoriety. As the only female in a highly competitive field, she'd won her accolades through diligence and an absolutely merciless success rate. Her targets were usually political, though she had no interest in views or causes, only in habits that would provide her with a single vulnerable moment.

She had no interest in fame, only in the promised reward.

She'd been in New Orleans for several weeks, longer than she'd been in one place since she'd started. She'd settled all too easily into the routine of her cover life, gotten comfortable here, dulling the razor sharpness of her edge. And she liked the sense of normalcy, of friendships. Of flirting with the idea of love.

But what she'd allowed to happen was beyond dangerous to her own situation. It jeopardized others.

She'd been lying to herself that having some hot fun with MacCreedy would do no harm. He was becoming a huge weakness in her armor of indifference. But she didn't need to worry; he was purely temporary. He'd made his future plans very clear, and the lucky woman in them wasn't her. There was no place for an itinerate assassin in his warm and fuzzy family ideals. There'd never been a place for her anywhere.

And with Savoie gone, they could both get on to their futures that much faster.

What she hadn't counted on was Savoie's impact. He was a remarkable philanthropist, a protector of the local clan, a moderate influence upon the fragile criminal balance, and the man of her childhood idol's dreams. If Savoie was dead, she was going to have to deal with it.

She was so deep in thought, the light touch of fingertips almost made her drop her tray. She turned abruptly, wedging it between her and MacCreedy.

He looked tired. He had taken off his tie and the first few buttons of his shirt were open, exposing crisp chest hair. She longed to bury her nose there.

"Any news?" Her voice sounded thin and strange.

He shook his head. "Nothing yet. What a mess."

Compassion snuck in before she could guard against it. "I'm off in about fifteen minutes. Have a drink and I'll take you home." She was careful not to put any suggestiveness into that offer and apparently he didn't look for any, as he nodded and headed toward the bar. Those strong shoulders, tall frame, and attitude really rocked his suit coat and jeans. And an unbidden chill rode through her as the image from her dream superimposed over it.

She turned away and quickly began to collect glasses.

Fifteen minutes later she leaned across MacCreedy's arm to pick up his beer bottle, draining the last inch. "Time to go."

"Ready when you are," he said.

She'd been ready since he'd shown up at Cee Cee's apartment alive and in one piece. Ready to be alone with him in the dark, to put her hands on his body, her tongue in his mouth, to rip off his clothes and mate with him furiously.

Mate with him?

She took a quick step back. MacCreedy intended

to bond with another. And casual matings weren't accepted because of the reproductive consequences.

MacCreedy's child.

The image was so tempting. A beautiful little boy riding atop those broad shoulders, tiny, trusting fingers clutched in his hair, MacCreedy's big hands curled protectively about little ankles.

Common sense gave her a firm slap. A child with MacCreedy? Nonsense. Who would trust her with a child? A man like him for a husband, the blessing of a baby, were not meant for her.

MacCreedy was headed for the door and Nica started after him, rattled by her thoughts. What was wrong with her? Maybe she just needed a good, quick kill and a change of scenery.

But she was liking the scenery here just fine. As her gaze lingered over Silas's body, lust began to rumble. Lust was good and honest, not like other sneaky emotions.

Outside, the night was surprisingly cool. As they walked up the narrow alley toward the street where she'd parked, Nica's awareness of MacCreedy's silhouette against the streetlights intensified. The rhythm of his movements grew mesmerizing. Her heartbeat quickened, her senses sharpened, tightening like a bowstring until they quivered. Her grasp of time and place fell away. There was nothing beyond him, and her focus narrowed like a sighting scope.

Now. Do it now.

The words whispered through her, so cold they

burned. She tried to shrink away from them, from the scorching pain, but the only way to escape was to obey.

Kill him. Quickly. Do it now!

Each syllable lashed along her nervous system, stinging, searing until she writhed inside. She dipped down, her hand snaking toward the top of the half boots she wore, slipping out the short blade sheathed in a pocket in the seam. In that feral crouch she moved up quickly, her steps soundless on the loose stones, yet he turned as if she'd called his name.

His features were haloed by the lights, his brows arched in a question he wouldn't have a chance to ask.

Nica moved swiftly, her arm arcing with a blurring speed, wrapping about his neck with near strangling urgency as her mouth took his. Between frantic kisses, she panted, "Take me home with you, MacCreedy. Make love to me until I can't think, until I can't breathe, until I can't remember my own name."

"Okay."

With her long legs cinched around his hips, her face burrowed against his throat, and her grip on his shoulders so tight it would have taken a tire iron to pry her loose, MacCreedy turned toward the street and caught a reflective glint off something lying at his feet.

A discarded knife.

He adjusted his arms about her, cradling her easily, and murmured, "I'll drive."

———

Max opened his eyes slowly. Everything hurt, from the roots of his hair to his toenails, as if he'd been tumbled dry with a yard of bricks. He didn't know where he was. He wasn't sure what form he was in, until he tried to sit up and heard a very human groan of protest.

He lay still, blinking slowly to soothe the scorch of his eyeballs, letting his surroundings ease into focus. Vaguely familiar objects emerged and he recognized the tools of the trade. A cop. A photo—his detective and her partner. Somehow, he'd ended up in Alain Babineau's spare room. Naked.

He'd have happily closed his eyes and let darkness reclaim him, except for the thirst. It baked his skin, tore down his throat, swelled his tongue as if he'd been staked out in a desert. To relieve it, he was willing to wake the agonies slumbering just below the surface.

Taking a bracing gulp of air, he rolled from the couch into an uncoordinated fall to the carpet on his hands and knees. *Sweet God!* Pain pierced through him and his right arm and leg buckled, spasming with injury and weakness. He swayed there for long minutes, afraid movement would lead to collapse or a return to comforting blackness. Finally, coaxed by the tantalizing scent of water, he began a torturous crawl from the bedroom into the dark hall.

What the hell had happened to him?

Shaking from the tremendous waves of sickness, he inched along on forearms and knees, pushing forward with bare toes until he encountered the cool tile of the bathroom floor. He let his cheek press against it for a long moment so the chill would steady his spinning senses. When he tried reaching up to the sink his world nearly upended, so he stayed low. The commode lid was up, the sign of a man alone in the house. Chuckling to himself in anticipation of the look on Babineau's face at finding him drinking out of the toilet bowl, Max raised up with a groan, then stared in dismay at the blue sanitized water.

Give a guy a break . . .

Turning to the tub, he hauled himself half over the side and stretched a shaky hand toward the faucets. An agonizing twist brought a cold jet thundering down and he scooped it up urgently, slurping out of his palm, splashing it on his face, drinking until the fever inside began to abate. Then he curled up on the bath mat and let awareness drift away.

Silas let Nica go up the stairs ahead of him. No sense being an idiot about it. Now wasn't the best time to have her at his back.

She'd spent the short ride through the Quarter practically in his lap, her arms tightly about his middle, her head tucked under his chin. He angled around her to shift gears and listened to the panicked rasp of her breathing. He didn't know what to do for her. He didn't know what do to *about* her.

But he certainly wasn't going to let her finish what she'd planned in the alley.

Instead of heading straight for the bedroom, Nica sat

on the couch, tucking her feet up and hugging her knees to her chest. Not exactly an "I want you now" pose.

"Coffee or beer?" he asked, draping his coat over the back of a dinette chair.

"Beer. I don't think I need to be wound any tighter."

Good thinking. He headed for the kitchen. Straightening from the refrigerator he turned right into her, her feverish eyes gleaming like black diamonds. It was all he could do not to drop the bottles.

"Do you have anything to eat? I haven't had a bite all day and I'm kind of shaky."

That was an understatement. She was in the middle of some kind of meltdown.

"Why don't you take these back to the couch and I'll put something together real quick?"

She took the beers and left the room, and Silas realized he was sweating. He let out a shaky breath and started rummaging in the fridge while keeping a cautious eye on the doorway. She'd want rare red meat, but could he afford to have her any stronger? He found some frozen cubed potatoes and tossed them into a skillet. While they sizzled, he began chopping up produce. After he'd scraped the peppers, onions, tomatoes, and mushrooms into the pan, his gaze lingered thoughtfully on the blade he held, then went to the knife block. He grabbed the set and hid it in the oven. As the vegetables sautéed he did a quick search of the drawers, cupboards, and dishwasher, adding anything that could perforate him before silently closing the oven door.

Whisking eggs, shredded cheese, and herbs together, he poured the mixture into the skillet and watched it until it set. No sound from the living room. He unclipped his service revolver and put it in the microwave, then divided the omelet, slid half onto each of two plates, frowned at the forks but decided spoons would arouse suspicion, added hot sauce, and headed out with their meal.

She'd taken her hair from its braid. Loose waves spun about her face and shoulders, making her look young and vulnerable.

He smiled grimly. "Eggs and beer, supper of champions."

"Sounds good. Thanks."

He set the plates on the coffee table, then settled beside her. His gaze lit on the letter opener on the lamp table. He'd been using it to open his mail.

"Let me get the light." He stretched across her, turning the switch, then quickly palmed the opener as he sat back, tucking it down into the cushions behind him. "Dig in."

She ate ravenously while he picked at his own plate, thinking furiously. Bathroom: razor blades, mirror. Bedroom: free weights, the pillows, wooden lamp base, belts, his damn shoelaces. Hell, she could take him out with almost anything he owned, including the gummed flap of the return envelope for his electric bill.

"Silas."

His attention leapt back to her and he held very still as her fingertips traced his jaw.

"Don't look so worried. I couldn't hurt you."

"I'm not afraid of you." He smiled wryly. "I just believe in preventive maintenance."

She swayed toward him until their lips just touched. "But you couldn't prevent this, could you?"

"No. And believe me, I tried."

He sank into her kiss, forgetting about weapons in lieu of pleasures.

Gone were the fierceness and fire as her lips parted beneath his, as if she'd surrendered herself to whatever this intense attraction was. She'd been afraid, this powerful, dangerous beauty—afraid for him, for his safety. That knowledge quickened a savage satisfaction more arousing than any of her direct overtures.

She remained sweetly responsive, her mouth soft and receptive, her tongue touching his lightly, then withdrawing to invite his to follow. With one hand at the back of his head, her other explored him with slow, tentative strokes, across his face, around his ear, down his neck, to knead his shoulder. His body thrummed to life. His blood surged in a warm tide.

"Let me stay with you," she breathed into his kisses.

"Yes. Stay."

"Si?" Her palms pressed to his cheeks so their gazes could meet. "Do you care for me just a little?" Her eyes sparkled like a starry heaven.

"I care for you a lot," he whispered.

Her smile trembled. "Then kiss me some more."

His deep, dreamy kisses soon had Nica's senses spinning delightfully. She relaxed, enjoying the textures, the heat, the taste of him. Drowning in those sensations until his hand moved to her breast. She slipped hers over his.

"Silas?"

"Hmmm?"

"I don't want to have sex with you."

His eyes flickered open. "What?"

Screwing up her courage, she said, "Make love to me."

He held her stare while she waited, breath suspended, for him to say something awful, like, *What? There's a difference?*

Then his mouth lifted in a sultry curve. "Just waiting for you to ask."

He carried her down the hall to his bedroom as she buried her face against the warmth of his throat, and laid her down on the bed in the dim room.

Then he slowly took off his clothes opening his shirt a button at a time, letting it slip gradually off his shoulders to slide down strong arms. Toeing out of his shoes, then bending to remove his socks so the light played over the muscles of his back. Straightening to open his jeans, easing them over hipbones until his impressive erection was freed, pushing them down his long legs instead of just letting them drop. Stepping out of them and straightening slowly so she could appreciate every bold line and powerful curve of his body.

Nica swallowed convulsively. He was the most glorious thing she's ever seen, solid, strong, breathtakingly male.

And then he leisurely undressed her. First with his eyes, then with his hands.

When he stretched out over her, balancing on toes and palms so only the heat of their skin was exchanged, he looked into her eyes. "Where would you like me to start?"

A wild fluttering began in her middle and spread until she tingled all over.

"Kiss me. Everywhere."

He started with her forehead, just a light brush of his mouth. Then her eyelids, her nose, her cheeks, her chin. Gentle touches sweeping down her neck, along her shoulder, down her sensitive inner arm to suck on her fingers. Restless and wanting, she pulled him up to satisfy her hungry lips.

"You're distracting me, Nica," he murmured with a nip at her chin. "You've given me a job to do. Let me finish."

He started up the fingertips of her other hand, up to her wrist and elbow, continuing that sensual journey until anticipation had her trembling. As her nipples ached for attention, he rolled her onto her stomach and lifted the heavy curtain of her hair so he could start at the nape of her neck and travel down the sleek slope of her back. By the time he reached the dip at her waist, she was pushing up onto her knees so his tongue could slip along the crevice of her backside to plunge deeply into her wet and ready core. But only for a maddening instant. Then he was nuzzling down the backs of her thighs, licking behind her knees, nipping down her calves to suckle on her toes.

Never had she been so agonizingly aware of her body, of each curve, each hollow he lavished with attentiveness. Even the arch of her foot, the taut pull of her Achilles tendon felt sexy and aroused. By the time he turned her onto her back her skin was alive with sensation, and when he pressed his lips to the smooth mound of her sex, she moaned and tried to trap him there with her legs. His hands on her knees, he continued up her quivering belly to pay homage to each breast, while her heart pounded madly and her senses spun.

"Now I know every inch of you by taste and scent," he whispered, and she was lost.

She wanted him so much, she thought she might die of need. Not for the carnal urgency pounding to be satisfied, but for this gentle sharing and trusting. She'd never trusted another soul enough to allow herself a moment of unguarded pleasure, and she didn't want it to end. She wanted to lie here with him forever.

His head rested on her shoulder, his breath warm against her throat. His hips adopted that same languorous rhythm as his weight settled over her, rocking in that easy, seductive motion. Primal. Irresistible.

Her eyes met his, so beautiful, like molten quicksilver. She could lose herself in them for a lifetime.

"What else can I do to please you?" he asked.

"Don't let me go." He had no idea how huge that request was.

"I won't."

Her body began to move beneath his. "Make me forget everything but you," she challenged.

"I will," he promised, sinking deep to claim her.

Sixteen

A flurry of knocking dragged Silas up from slumber. He squinted at his alarm clock. Not even four A.M.? Muttering obscenities, he started to sit up and discovered what he thought was a tangle of covers were actually arms and legs. Sleek, strong, sexy arms and legs.

Nica was entwined about him, sleeping soundly. But she wouldn't be for long if he didn't get to the door.

He began to extract himself and her hand rose to grip the back of his neck. He brushed a kiss over her cheek, whispering, "It's all right. Go back to sleep."

"Silas, don't go," she murmured, her eyes flickering open.

He kissed her eyes closed. "I'm not leaving. I'll be right back. Go to sleep."

He hurriedly pulled on his jeans, closed the door to his bedroom, went to look through the peephole—and gave a heartfelt curse as he undid the locks.

"Brigit, it's not even daylight."

Her hug nearly strangled him. "Silas, you have to help me. I might be in terrible trouble. Please say you'll help me."

He pulled her inside and secured the door, then

peeled her off him to find out what had her in such a panic.

"Calm down, Brigit. Calm down. I can't help unless you tell me what's wrong."

She stepped back, gulping for breath, her features stark and pale. The tears on her face appeared to be real. And Silas began to frown.

"Bree, what happened?"

"I told him to wait. I told him not to do anything stupid."

"Told who?"

"Daniel."

"I don't know who that is."

"We've been together for months now," she snapped in irritation. "Don't you ever pay attention to anything that involves me?"

"Bree, the only thing that changes faster than your affections is the weather. How do you expect me to keep up with every warm front that moves in?"

When she began to cry, Silas brought her into the protective curl of his arms. "I'm sorry. I'm sorry, Bree. What did Daniel do? How can I help?"

"I think he killed Max Savoie," she sniffed.

Silas went completely still. "What?"

"He got impatient because you were taking so long to act. He wanted us to be together. He figured if Savoie was dead, he could use the boy to bring down the Terriots. He wanted to make me his queen, to take care of me.

"I haven't seen him since yesterday. When he didn't come back, I got worried and turned on the news. It's everywhere, all over the television. My God, Silas, they're going to be coming for us!"

Silas set her away from him. "Daniel who?"

"G-Guedry."

"Guedry? Daniel *Guedry*!" he roared. Their mother's lineage, the proud family that had turned their backs on Therese MacCreedy's disgraced children. "What the hell have you done? You're damned right they'll be coming— from all sides, and they'll tear us apart! How could you make such a foolish alliance?"

At his harsh words, her teary eyes blazed. "For us. For you! I was afraid if you—"

"What? You were afraid if I took power, you wouldn't be able to control me as easily as you could someone you were leading around by the dick?"

They were both furious, breathing hard, when a reasonable voice interrupted.

"I'll just put on some coffee."

Brigit stared after Nica as she went into the kitchen, wearing only Silas's shirt. Then she blew up like a summer squall. "You dare speak to me like that when you're defiling your promises by boning that—"

His fingers pressed to her mouth as he growled, "Careful what you say to me, when you're begging a favor because of your lover's idiocy."

Brigit slapped his hand away and stalked over to the small window overlooking the rear courtyard. Silas stared after her, forcing his anger out with a hard blow of breath. There was little time for damage control.

"Do the Guedrys know you and Daniel are together?"

She glared at him over her shoulder. "Do you think he was too ashamed to tell them?"

"Brigit."

"No. I don't think so," she admitted sourly.

"Good. If we're careful, the local clan won't make the connection, either."

Nica came out of the kitchen carrying two cups. "All you had was instant. Did you know you left your gun in the microwave?"

Grateful for the distraction, he smiled at her as he took the cup. When she went up on her toes, he bent to kiss her slowly and thoroughly. She stroked his morning-rough cheek, then carried the other cup across the room to where Brigit eyed her malevolently.

"Take it or wear it," Nica said mildly.

Brigit took the cup.

"I'll just pick up a few things while you two make nice." She went to gather up the plates and bottles left on the coffee table from the night before, leaving the prideful siblings to work things out when she returned to the kitchen.

"When did you last see Guedry?" Silas asked, his tone all business.

"Yesterday morning. We had breakfast together."

"And he hasn't called you or spoken to you? Didn't mention any plans?"

"No." Brigit wrapped her arms around herself and sipped the coffee, nose wrinkling as she set it on the table. "How bad could this be for us?"

"Fatally bad, if we're not quick and clever."

She smiled faintly. "Good thing you're both."

He scowled at the flattery and reached for his phone. Babineau's cell went to voice mail. "Give me your room key."

She tossed it to him. "What are you going to do?"

"Get your things. Is the room in his name or yours?"

"His."

"You'll stay here. Nica?" When she emerged from the kitchen, he told her simply, "See she stays here and out of trouble. You can knock her unconscious if you need to."

Nica smiled. "Only if necessary."

He went into the bedroom for the rest of his clothes and when he came out, Nica was waiting with his gun.

"Will you be all right here?" he asked quietly while clipping it on his belt.

"I'm not the one you should worry about." Her brows knit for a moment. "Silas, why are there so many odd things in your oven?"

He laughed and kissed her hard. "I'm not much of a housekeeper. Be good. Go put your clothes on so you don't irritate my sister any more than necessary." He slapped a hand on her bottom to hurry her toward the bedroom. Then he looked at Brigit's stony stance.

"I won't be long."

She glared. "Afraid I'll hurt your little plaything?"

A snort. "Hardly, but you'd better be careful not to annoy her. We need to talk when I get back."

"Yes. We do. About several things."

"Try not to worry."

"I'm not worried about you."

A thin smile. "I know. I'll be back."

"No hurry. Your bitch and I can get acquainted."

"Don't call her that if you want to stay conscious."

And he closed the door behind him, doing all the worrying himself.

A jangle of shower curtain rings and the sound of the water cranking off awoke Max. With an instinctive snarl of warning, he scuttled back, wobbling up onto his hands and knees to blink blindly at the vanity lights. He squinted up at the blurry silhouette that could only be Alain Babineau.

"So that's the thanks I get? A higher water bill and you snapping at my ankles? You're welcome."

Max angled awkwardly onto his uninjured hip, slumping against the cheery flowered wallpaper, hugging his updrawn knees to fight off the sudden chills and the feel of being stripped bare. His voice rasped, low and dry. "How did I get here?"

"I found you in an alley, full of holes in your fleabag form. I brought you here in my trunk. I'll bill you if any cleaning is necessary."

"You saved my life."

Babineau looked none too happy. "Yeah, well, it was against my better judgment. I owed you. For Oscar."

Max accepted that with a nod.

"It doesn't make us pals or anything." Babineau left the bathroom briefly and returned to toss a pair of sweatpants at Max. "I don't enjoy the sight of you in your birthday suit before I've even had coffee."

After he left the bathroom, Max struggled to pull on the sweats. He twisted slightly to check out the pain in his hip and blinked at the evidence of mending bullet wounds, one in the fleshy part of his thigh and the other just above his pelvis. He remembered Babineau digging out the chunks of silver. Another made an in-and-out through his upper arm, just missing bone. Two more perforations were added to those already patterning his chest. Then the rest came flooding back. The unknown Shifter's attack. The whoosh of flames as he changed into his animal form to escape through the bullet-shattered window. He should have died. *Would* have died, if the surly detective hadn't removed the slugs when he did.

He was still shaky and ill and so weak it took him ten minutes to climb to his feet. Leaning into the wall for balance, he made his way toward the sound of the television in the living room. Babineau was there sipping his coffee. He didn't spare a glance toward his staggering guest.

"You're on the news."

Max glanced at the screen and stared at the sight of his car, mangled and smoldering, at the two body shapes on the ground shrouded by plastic. He heard the commentary through a sudden roar in his ears.

"—local millionaire entrepreneur and his driver, Peter Dugan, have yet to be positively identified by the coroner's office. An undisclosed witness called the scene reminiscent of a gangland-style slaying. Rumors of mob affiliations have been circulating since Savoie took over the vast holdings left him by his former employer, Jimmy Legere, himself the victim of violence."

"Any idea on who he was, and who wants you dead?"

Suddenly Max's heart began a frantic pounding. "Have you talked to Charlotte? Has she seen this?" More important, would she believe it?

"I haven't seen her, haven't talked to her. Kinda had my hands full."

Max reached for his nonexistent cell. "Call Giles St. Clair. Leave a message for him to be here in twenty. Don't tell him why."

"Who's after you, Savoie?"

"I need red meat, raw, and a shower. I don't have time for your questions."

Babineau gripped him by the upper arm, just below the fresh wound. "Make time."

It would have brought most men to their knees, wailing. But Max was all fierce control, speaking coldly through bared teeth. "Get your hand off me right now, unless you think you can take me out. It would be a mistake you wouldn't recover from. Step back, Detective."

Babineau shoved away from him. For a moment tension sizzled between them, then Max said, "I have to get to Charlotte. She might be in danger. We can get into the macho bullshit later."

He closed his eyes, then emptied his awareness to cast out a searching call. *Charlotte?*

No response. Either he was too weak, or she was already ... He was too weak. He wouldn't consider any other explanation.

Giles St. Clair was still reeling in shock as he pounded on Babineau's door. What the hell could Charlotte's pansy-assed partner say that was worth hearing when his world was crumbling?

The door opened.

"This better be good, Detective Babineau," he growled.

He'd barely finished when a figure walked toward him. His eyes widened incredulously.

"Blink, Giles. I'm really here."

Max *oofed* as the big man snatched him up for a bear hug, laughing.

"Crissake, don't *ever* do that to me again! I was a half second away from getting my suit cleaned and my résumé ready." He held Max away for a critical once-over. "You look like shit."

"So I've been told, but it's better than the alternative."

"Damn straight." Giles's face sobered. "So, who do I have the pleasure of breaking into little tiny pieces? Or maybe I should thank them for not sending someone more efficient."

"Pete's dead, Giles." Max drew a shaky breath, then squared his stance. "I want to see his family. I need to assure them that I'll take care of everything." His stare chilled. "Everything."

Babineau said, "No, Max. I'll be taking care of that."

Max regarded him unblinkingly. Dressed in borrowed clothes, living on stolen time, he still managed to convey a world of unbelievable hurt about to come down on some luckless fool's head. "Of course, Detective," he agreed smoothly. "That *is* your job."

"Max, if you take the law into your own hands, I'll come after you," he warned.

"I would expect you to try, Detective."

"What about Charlotte?" Giles interjected. "Does she know you're back from the dead?"

"No that's my next stop." Max looked coolly at Babineau. "I appreciate your hospitality. I'll be expecting your bill."

"Blow me, Savoie." He knew when he was being shut out and it pissed the hell out of him.

Max let Giles precede him past the glowering detective. When they were shoulder to shoulder, Max leaned over to press a noisy kiss on his cheek.

"Thanks, Dad."

Babineau stumbled back, scrubbing at his face. At Max's taunting grin, he snarled, "Next time I'll leave you on the street."

Seventeen

They stared at each other from across the room, like two female cats, each willing the other to make a move so a fight could ensue.

"Where did he find you?" Brigit finally asked, her tone cool with disapproval.

"In an alley where four men were trying to attack me. He stepped in to save me."

"Always quick to defend the lost cause," Brigit sneered.

Nica's eyes narrowed. "He's not the coward or fool you think he is."

Apparently that was the right hot button to push.

"Don't tell me what I think. Don't talk to me about what my brother is or is not. You don't know me and you don't know my brother."

"Oh, I know him. Intimately."

Brigit laughed at her. "You're the fool if you believe that. My brother cares for one thing only: restoring our family's pride to keep his promise to our father. He'll do anything to achieve that end—including sleeping with creatures like you. You must have something he wants"—she gave Nica a cold once-over—"besides the not so obvious."

"At least he doesn't hide and allow others to take all the risks."

A slow, baiting smile. "No, he doesn't. Because when he loves, it's with everything he has. That's the way he loves me. The way he loves Kendra. You think he has feelings for you? He'll wash your memory off like sweat, because there's only one future he's ever dreamed of: having Kendra for his mate.

"That's why he's sacrificed so much. So I can find the protection of a good match, and he can be worthy of the female he loves. My brother is clever, but he isn't complex. Love and honor—there's nothing else for him, except an occasional easily forgotten distraction."

Because she couldn't remain in the room for another minute without giving in to the need to dig through MacCreedy's oven stash of weapons, Nica went into the bedroom. But that was almost worse than listening to Brigit's barbed words. Here, she could feel the truth of them. MacCreedy's scent surrounded her. She could feel his touch on her skin, his breath soft upon her lips, his demanding strength possessing her body. But that was all she would ever have of him.

She should have been grateful; she could go her way and he his without regrets. He wouldn't try to stop her. Even if she might wish he would.

Nica pushed up the window and leaned out to inhale the dawn air. She could hear the whirl of the street cleaner's brushes, clearing the remains of the previous day. The same way Silas would rid himself of her memory.

A sudden sharpening of her senses overcame her brooding, then a cab stopped across the street. Silas got out and her heartbeat quickened in traitorous response. He pulled out his wallet as the driver unloaded several designer suitcases from the trunk, then paid the man with a nod of thanks. And as the vehicle drove away, his gaze lifted to where she stood in shadow.

He couldn't have seen her. The room was dark, hiding her well. Yet he still knew she was there. The corners of his mouth curved slightly as he bent to assemble the luggage and wrangle it across the street. With the bags at the foot of the steps, he was searching for his key when a dark, nondescript car stopped behind him. The rear door opened.

"No," Nica whispered. "Don't."

MacCreedy crossed the sidewalk and got in, then the car pulled away.

"Dammit!" Nica grabbed for her bag and shouted behind her, "Your stuff is down on the steps. Bring it up and lock the door behind you. Stay put!" Then she was out the window.

Instead of taking the fire escape down to the street, Nica went up. She raced along the rooftop, leaping from building to building, heart pounding frantically until she caught sight of the car. Then she took a settling breath, and became what she was inside. A predator on the hunt.

Even in the car's dark interior, MacCreedy could see the grim intention in the eyes of Savoie's bodyguard, glaring at him in the rearview mirror. The woman beside him wasn't as easy to read.

"My first guess was Francis Petitjohn," Cee Cee told him, "but he seemed genuinely surprised and annoyed when Max didn't keep their appointment. Then my friend Dovion confirmed what I suspected. The other body in that car wasn't human. And it wasn't Max, either."

"So Savoie is—"

"Really pissed off at you right now. You had to know we were tailing you, Mac. We were on you the second you left your apartment."

Charlotte Caissie was all professional courtesy, but Silas could feel the seismic tremors of a quake about to explode.

"If you'd been paying attention, you would have known a flash of my badge would give me the name Guedry. Who's the woman?"

"My sister. She has no part in this."

"So what exactly is your part?"

"Damage control. I just found out about it an hour ago. My sister came to me, afraid her lover had done something stupid to impress her. If that body is Daniel Guedry, I'd say he did."

"Maybe. Or maybe this story goes a different way. Your sister shows up a couple of days ago so you can coordinate your plans. Guedry is supposed to take out Max while you slip in and grab Oscar. Then either you take the Terriot crown, or you get it for Guedry in a nice little coup. Everybody wins. Except Max and Oscar."

"Could have happened that way, but it didn't. One, I'd never trust an impulsive idiot like Guedry to get anything right, and two, I would never put my sister in danger. Ever."

"I'd believe that if you really are the solid guy I thought you were. Now I'm not so sure. Power and politics can screw a decent person up big-time."

People like Babineau, Silas thought, who might be playing patty-cake with Blutafino and Cummings in some dirty dealings?

"I'm not interested in those things. I just want to take care of my family."

"Heading up the Terriot clan would do that, wouldn't it, Mac?"

He didn't answer the question. "Where are we going?"

"Neutral ground."

He didn't understand until Giles pulled into the tiny parking lot behind St. Bartholomew's.

MacCreedy had never met Father Furness, the founder of the small church with its women and children's shelter. He knew the priest had taken Cee Cee and Nica in, and that he was aware of the Shifter presence in New Orleans. He knew Savoie had sunk a fortune into the place because of both things.

"Bring him," Cee Cee told Giles as she started for the rear door.

MacCreedy exited the vehicle and gave the mammoth Giles a warning look. "No need for unpleasantness."

"Not yet." Giles waved him to follow the detective.

St. Bart's interior was simple, warm wood and cool, open space.

When a figure emerged from the shadows Cee Cee's steps faltered briefly, then she ran right into the arms of Max Savoie. They held on to each other for a long moment until Charlotte pushed away, slapping her palm against his chest.

"Stop scaring me."

"I'm sorry, *sha.*"

"Are you all right?"

His hand cupped her cheek. "Now, I am." Then his cool stare lifted to MacCreedy. "What's his story?"

Cee Cee briefed him on what was said in the car. Max listened without expression, then asked, "Do you believe him, *cher*?"

MacCreedy couldn't hear her reply, and got no hint from Savoie's stoic features. His future hung upon those whispered words.

"Touch him and I'll separate heads from shoulders."

And their futures now hung upon the words spoken loudly from the back of the cavernous room.

Nica moved up the aisle, her pace swift and light, her expression intense. She jerked the support rods from the frame of her backback, letting it drop as she held foot-long batons in either hand. Immediately, Max guided Cee Cee behind him, his actions lethally fluid.

"Nica, no. There's no need for this," Silas called, seeing everything about to go to hell in a hurry.

"Come here to me, MacCreedy." Her stare was riveted to Savoie's.

Giles wedged a pistol under Silas's chin, taking that decision from him as Max moved smoothly toward the aisle.

The batons Nica held sprouted deadly blades from both ends. She leapt onto the seat of one of the pews, then raced forward, jumping from back to back of the benches.

"Nica, stop!" MacCreedy caught Giles's wrist, angling the weapon away and quickly wrenching it from his hand. He ejected the clip and threw both pieces behind him.

He'd taken three steps when the tenacious Giles snagged him by the elbow and whipped him around, bowling him into the tiers of lighted prayer candles, scattering them like campfire embers. Before Silas could get his balance, he saw Nica launch her attack like a dark, graceful bird of prey.

In midleap she circled her leg about Savoie's neck, using her momentum to pull him off his feet. By the time they both went down, she'd used the crook of her knee to spin around him, coming up astride his chest, blades raised high for a killing downward stroke.

"Miss Fraser," came a booming voice. "The rules of this house still apply to you!"

Bringing the blade tips down to rest against Max's throat, she challenged, "What are you going to do? Make me say twenty Hail Marys?"

"It didn't help when you were twelve. I don't suppose it would do any good now."

The blades retracted. With a grim smile Nica bounded to her feet, using Max's sternum as a stepping-off point. "You still have no sense of fun, old man."

"You still have an irreverent mouth, little girl."

Max was instantly on his feet, his eyes glittering dangerously. He and Nica exchanged the same combative looks as Giles and Silas, but they all backed down as Father Furness moved into their midst.

Furness was like no priest MacCreedy had ever seen, a vigorous man with a stocky build and a brawler's stance. Silas got the impression that if words hadn't stopped the fight, Furness would have waded in to knock heads together.

Eyes that had sparked with ire were now warmed by emotion. The priest held his arms open wide in welcome, but Nica shied away to cross to MacCreedy.

She eyed his torn and singed T-shirt. "Looks like I got here just in time to keep you from becoming a burnt offering."

MacCreedy took her arrogant chin between thumb and forefinger and said sternly, "I wasn't in any danger until you arrived, determined to stir it up. You should have listened to me. I told you to stay with my sister."

She tossed her head to escape his grasp, her haughty tone disguising how his chastisement bruised her. "I'm not very good with the listening thing. I prefer action."

"They weren't the right actions to take. I don't need anyone to fight my battles for me."

She glared at him. "It would have been a very short one, MacCreedy. Sorry I interfered."

When she spun away, Silas caught her wrist and tugged her back around so that they bumped against each other. He saw confusion rather than anger on her face, and his temper softened. He bent so that his mouth brushed her ear. "Thank you."

The heat of both breath and sentiment caused her to shiver. Her gaze was unguarded as she told him gruffly, "You scared me when you got into that car." Her hand turned so that their fingers laced briefly together, then the attitude was back as she faced the others in the room.

Silas didn't know what to make of her. He was angry that she'd flouted his instructions, yet humbled to think she'd risk so much for him. He was always the one sheltering others, not the other way around—until now. He felt mystified. Gratified. Aroused.

"Monica, introduce me to your friend," the father said.

"Detective Silas MacCreedy, Father Furness."

"Detective MacCreedy?" His surprise became acknowledgment. "I knew your mother's family. I was very saddened by your loss. They'd be pleased to see what you've become."

Silas's gaze dropped; he was suddenly too ashamed to accept the compliment.

Would they view all he'd done with pride? He was

everything they'd given their lives to keep Oscar from becoming. A slave to the Terriots' will, instead of master of his own. Why hadn't he seen that until now?

The truth staggered him, but Nica's supportive arm about his middle helped him recover. She was staring up at him through those deep twilight eyes, uncertain of what was wrong.

Then Max came to place a hand on his shoulder.

"We need to talk."

Nica immediately bristled up, but Silas smoothed his hand over her hair and murmured, "I'll be right back."

"Don't leave with him," she whispered fiercely.

A faint smile. "I won't."

They walked a few yards, then Max said, "You didn't know of Guedry's plan."

"No. My sister would have told me if she'd been aware of it."

"Will your girlfriend try her hand in his place?"

"I hope not."

"Would you be able to do what's necessary to stop her?"

Silas's gaze lingered on Nica a moment too long before he admitted, "No." He didn't differentiate between a physical or an emotional barrier.

"She's dangerous."

"She's . . . misguided."

"And you're in love with her."

That conclusion stunned Silas speechless.

Max grinned wryly. "I remember the double-barrel

impact when it hit me. There's great comfort in knowing she would do anything for you, but also a great price."

MacCreedy looked wary. "What price?" Obligation, commitment . . .

"Trust."

Silas snorted. "It couldn't be something simple? Like a kidney?" Did he trust her? No. Could he? He wasn't sure. Love her? He didn't even want to consider that complication, yet once the seed was planted, it grew.

Thankfully, Max changed the subject. "Will the clans come after you because of Guedry?"

"If they make the connection, yes."

"I can protect you."

A laugh. "You couldn't protect yourself."

"There's strength in numbers. I would make as powerful a friend as I do an enemy."

"I'm not your enemy." It felt so strange to say that, to believe it.

"Then you can trust me with the truth about why you're here. The Terriots didn't send you after Oscar, did they?"

"No. They wouldn't have been so delicate about it. They sent me to learn what I could about the politics and law enforcement in the city."

Max's eyes narrowed. "Why?"

"So they can expand their territories by eliminating or assimilating the competition."

"And what have you discovered?"

"That corruption goes deep, and power could be

easily purchased. The police commissioner and Simon Cummings are in thick with Manny Blu. They create a vulnerable doorway to the city that the Terriots would exploit."

"And you've told them this?"

"No."

"Why not? Wouldn't it get you what you want more quickly? Just as my death would?"

"You think that I *want* to deal with them? With those sons of bitches who killed my family?" Silas walked in a tight circle to get on top of his rage, his hands working at his sides as if his parents' blood was still damp upon them. Then he stopped and turned to Savoie. "I think New Orleans already has the leader it needs. What it doesn't have is political leverage with the clans."

Max studied him for a moment. "Perhaps you could fill that position."

Silas reared back at the suggestion, laughing harshly. "No. Not me."

"Why? You know the clans—how they think, how they work. You come from a respectable lineage. You're smart, you're dedicated, you could teach me, and we could work together."

"Respectable? They consider me the son of a traitor. I'd be dead. And so would those who count on me to protect them. I can't risk any more. I won't."

Max smiled mildly and placed a hand on his arm. "Think about it. You've been without a home for too long." Then he turned away.

It should have been easy to dismiss Savoie's request. Silas should have brushed it off as sheer insanity. He should have chuckled at the ridiculousness of him in such a position. Except there was something so intrinsically right about it. Silas drew a tight breath, appalled, panicked, tempted.

"Max." When the other turned back, MacCreedy said quietly, "There's something you should know about Charlotte's partner, Babineau. He's taking money from Cummings. Money I think comes from Blutafino."

Clearly shocked, Max shook his head. "I don't believe that. He's the last person who would ever take a bribe."

"You have his family. You're stepping on his self-respect. Good men have gone bad over lesser things."

"I won't believe he's a dirty cop."

"Perhaps, he's a misguided one," Silas suggested. "Think about it."

Max nodded thoughtfully and returned to Cee Cee, put his arms around her, and rested his head on her shoulder.

Was that love? Silas wondered. Was that trust? A restless need squeezed like a fist inside him—the longing for someone to lean on, to share his burdens, his cares, his doubts. After carrying them alone for so long, that would be heaven. A distant concept that, like forgiveness, was out of his reach.

His gaze went to Nica, assessing her slender but strong build, the firm set of shoulders that might support his troubles. She met his tentative look unflinchingly.

Was he resting his future on all the wrong things? Could he trust this savage, unpredictable female, any more than he could Savoie's suicidal optimism?

"You've been in the city for weeks now," Furness told Nica, "yet this is the first I've seen of you."

"Why would I come here? To rehash the not-so-good old days?"

"To talk."

"You had years to talk to me, to tell me the things that I needed to know. You kept silent and let me learn those truths elsewhere. We have nothing to say to each other now."

Father Furness sighed. "You have every right to say those things. I didn't take care of you as I should have. I was afraid, and I waited too long to tell you the truth. And I fear worse things will happen if I don't let these secrets go now. That's why I wanted you all here. Come back to my office. I have a story to tell you."

Eighteen

Legend called them the Ancients. Mystical, magical beings able to change shape from humanlike form to that of a wolven beast, to manipulate the psyche, and to astral project. Power made them arrogant. Greed made them crave dominance of their own kind through perfection, until generations of careful selective breeding split their race into two groups: the Chosen, sleek, delicate intellectuals with amazing mental abilities; and the Shifters, fierce shape-changers used as weapons by the elite. Two parts of what was once a whole.

Max, Silas, and Charlotte sat in Father Furness's modest office as the priest paced and told his tale, revealing his purpose in New Orleans. Nica stood apart from them, her mood withdrawn and wary.

"I'm here to do more than save the immortal soul. I'm involved in a struggle to protect a race from extinction."

"These Ancients still exist?" MacCreedy frowned. "My mother told me that was a fairy tale."

"That's the story we wanted told."

"We?" Charlotte asked quickly,

"Very few of the original species survived with their genetic markers intact," Furness continued. "Unlike that of Shifters, where the male carries the dominant gene, the genetic code of the Ancients is passed on by the female. From your mother, Max. From Monica's mother. From Tina Babineau's."

Silas was slapped back in his chair by that news. Tina's mother? *His* mother?

"Through those genetic traits," Furness went on, noting MacCreedy's reaction, "came the strongest of both sides: the mental talents plus the ability to shift shape."

Max thought for a moment, then concluded, "So Nica and Tina can pass them on, but Oscar and I can't."

"That's right. The species has dwindled dangerously. I'm part of a preservation movement." He explained that through his work at St. Bart's, where Ancient children had been cared for along with humans, he'd established the means to observe those special offspring.

"For what?" Max demanded, suddenly suspicious.

"Abnormalities. Like Ben Spratt, where uncontrollable aggression takes over." The mild custodian had been exposed as a killer in the case Cee Cee had been working when she and Max first got together. "Or an equally dangerous psychosis. The fear of having these powerful, nearly unstoppable beings going unchecked divided us into two factions: one that seeks to destroy them before they endanger and expose us all, and one that wants to use them and develop their unique abilities."

"Like they did mine," Nica said softly. She'd silently come to stand behind MacCreedy's chair. She couldn't mistake the alarm in his gaze as it lifted to hers, as he saw what they'd all seen when looking at her. A freak.

"And which group do you belong to?" Max asked the priest.

"I don't take sides, Max. I want to protect our kind. My purpose is strictly to monitor, to record, not regulate. And to keep those who prove dangerous safe from themselves and others. I'd like your help."

Max recoiled. "As what? Lab animals?"

The priest chuckled. "No, of course not. I'd just like a genetic sample for our study. We use no names, just a coded entry. That will be cross-referenced with an equally anonymous code from whomever you procreate with, and so on with their offspring."

"I've heard of such studies," Nica drawled with contempt.

"These are in the name of science and preservation, not self-interest or greed," Furness promised.

"I have no great faith in your word, priest." She bristled, her attitude made pricklier by the way Silas still stared at her in mute distress.

"Why would we want to do this?" Max challenged. "Why should we care?"

"Because it involves all of you. Because Carmen Blutafino is part of a growing black market specializing in harvesting those with specific genetic markers."

"The women were chosen for a reason." Cee Cee mulled over her previous conversation threads, tying them together into a dreadful new pattern. "He's using

Shifters to pick up females identified as having those markers. Manny probably has no idea why they're so valuable. He's just filling an order and making a buck."

"So," Max summarized with a scowl, "it's more than just the Trackers from the North we have to worry about. There's a whole new underworld element targeting our kind."

"You can ignore the problem until it involves you or someone close," the priest concluded, "or you can get proactive now. Talk about it and let me know."

After he left, Max let his head drop back on the chair and groaned, "Like I need another problem." He scrubbed his hands over his face, then looked at Cee Cee. "Any comments, *sha*?"

Charlotte was deep in thought, her analytical cop brain clearly whirring. "How do they get the DNA samples? Clinics? They wouldn't have the manpower or the reason." Her gaze lifted to Max's. "It must be through the police lab."

That got MacCreedy's attention. "So who's getting the information? Who's giving Manny the list?"

"Shit. Shit, shit, shit. Someone on the inside."

Silas nodded grimly, afraid he already knew. A human cop with a reason to hate Shifters: Babineau. "Then we set a trap to flush him out. Dangle bait he can't resist."

Charlotte suggested, "I can have Dev put Chili Pepper's DNA sample in the system, substituting Nica's for mine. That should stir up some interest. We can watch to see who taps into the info and where it goes. My guess is, it'll lead back to Manny, and possibly to other black market links."

Maybe, maybe not, MacCreedy mused. If it was Babineau, he'd recognize the ploy for the trap it obviously was. But if it wasn't . . . "Babineau and I are ready on Manny's end. Nica can stay close to you."

Max smiled and took Cee Cee's hand. "The advantage of having a dead boyfriend is that no one expects him to show up."

Cee Cee grinned back. "I'll get Dovion to hold off on IDing the bodies in the morgue."

"And we'll set up a nice little surprise."

Cee Cee looked to the silent member of their group. "Nica? Are you in?"

She shrugged. "Sure. Why not?"

After Cee Cee and Max left, Nica assessed the situation critically. MacCreedy had changed the instant he learned she was an Ancient. He looked at her differently, as if the knowledge unsettled all he thought he knew.

"When did you find out?" he asked cautiously.

And suddenly she wanted him to know. To understand the things she'd shared with no other.

"I always knew. I wasn't like everyone else. When I stayed here Father Furness tried to convince me I could be, but that was a lie. I never heard a truth spoken until it came to me in a dream."

It had started as a teasing in her subconscious, she told him, like someone whispering in her ear, softly, seductively, things that made sense when nothing else seemed to.

Regarding the priest: *He's lying to you. He knows what you are. He's trying to keep you for his own purposes.*

Regarding her gifts: *You are more, Nica, more than this, more than them. They fear your strength. They won't let you discover your potential.*

About her future: *You could be the best. They would all look up to you. You could be free.*

That was the key word. She'd never known freedom. She'd never been in control of her situation, of her life, and at twelve she'd already seen how harsh the world could be when others made choices for her. She was young, angry, frustrated, and alone. All those things made her susceptible to believing the promise in those dreams. She could become powerful enough to direct her own fate.

"So I ran away from here, where I'd always been an outsider. There was a train ticket waiting for me."

"To take you where?" MacCreedy asked.

"North. To the camp where I'd learn how to make the most of all the things that made me different. Where I worked hard to become the best, to be recognized for my talents, to get to the place where I could demand they make good on their promises."

"And did they?" he asked quietly.

Nica glanced away. "Soon. They will soon."

MacCreedy leaned against one of the pews. Though obviously disturbed by what she'd told him, he reached out to hold her hand lightly as he asked, "So you went north to learn to kill your own kind?"

She pulled her hand away. "I have no *kind*. I have what I've always had: just me." That wasn't exactly true, but she couldn't divulge those truths, even to him. "I look out for myself because no one else wanted that job. And now I don't need anyone else. I do what I want, and don't look to anyone for approval or help."

"Does that make you free, or more of a prisoner?"

His question stunned her, then infuriated her because she didn't want to consider it. "Why do you care? It's not like we mean anything to each other."

He smiled faintly. "Now who's lying?"

"I don't need you, MacCreedy."

"Then why didn't you kill me in that alley last night?"

Nica stared up at him through eyes that glittered with desire and dread. "Don't question your good fortune." She turned and quickly escaped to avoid a truth she couldn't accept.

The importance of all he'd learned pounded in the back of Silas's head like a building low-pressure system. He went through the motions, linking up with Babineau to present a unified front when questions came flying. No, no news yet on Savoie, but no one had seen him since the accident. Detective Caissie was taking some personal time to explore her own leads. No, no reaction yet from the criminal community. They were all waiting for a confirmation on that body in that backseat.

Silas visited the lab under the pretext of following up on the Tides that Bind case. He chatted with the workers, who were quite forthcoming when he produced coffee and beignets. He learned about the chain of evidence, who handed what to whom, and, more important, who had access to their database regarding DNA. By late afternoon, his nerves were hip-hopping from all the caffeine and sugary carbs, and the mental pressure that had reached a throbbing Category Three.

He touched base again with Babineau, who he hoped against hope wouldn't get snared in the trap they were orchestrating; then he went home, desperately needing to unwind before his shift at the Sweat Shop.

There he found Brigit slumped on his sofa, her eyes swollen from fatigue and tears. He'd called her that morning to reassure her of his safety and to check on hers. She'd been listless then; now she was morose.

"Do you know yet if it's Daniel?" She sniffled as he settled beside her on the cushions.

"I've spoken to Savoie. The description he gave matched the one I got from you."

She made a mournful sound and turned away. Could she really have cared for the fool? Silas's irritable mood gave way to reluctant sympathy and he awkwardly patted her arm. "I'm sorry, Bree."

She shoved his hand away with a petulant cry of, "You are not. You're only sorry for the inconvenience it's caused you. If you'd taken care of things like you should have, instead of boning that nasty creature ... What will Kendra think when she hears of it?"

Silas gripped her shoulders, wrenching her around to face him. His expression was fierce, his tone cold. "And who's going to tell her? You? You would hurt her with things that don't concern her?"

"Don't concern her? You had an understanding ..."

"We had nothing, Bree. Nothing official, nothing even verbalized. I never led her to believe we'd have a future together, because I wasn't sure I could make it happen. You know that. Yet now I'm this horrible betrayer of promises never made? What was I supposed to do? Remain celibate all these years? Life isn't a fairy tale, Bree. It's not like *you've* stayed chaste in hopes of capturing that prince you used to go on about when we were kids."

"Of course not," she flung back at him. "Why are we even talking about this? Have you forgotten who loves and depends upon you? The longer you delay, the more dangerous our position becomes. You need to act quickly so we can get out of this place, so you can throw off whatever unhealthy hold it has on you. What would our parents say if they knew—"

He surged off the couch, all tension and fury. "They can't say anything about it because they're *dead*. I buried them, and I've been carrying the weight of their wishes ever since that day. I don't need you to add to it, Brigit."

He gestured angrily to the contents of her suitcase that were strewn across the floor and furniture. "Pick up that shit and put it in the bedroom. You'll be staying in there. I'm going to take a shower."

Silas stood under the cold spray, waiting for it to cool the heat of his temper and the guilt beneath it. She had no right to cheapen the depth of his feelings for Kendra. If he'd had his way, he would have mated with her years ago, and by now they would have had children and he'd have the warm comfort of family to come home to, instead of the cold emptiness of duty. He'd be living the joyous role of husband and father, devoting himself to whatever he could do to please those he loved, instead of struggling alone and satisfying no one, least of all himself.

Brigit was wrong to blame him for having failed to achieve his dreams. She knew doing so was beyond his control. As the son of a traitor, he wasn't a worthy match for Kendra. He held a name without honor, he was a male without status, his lineage had no value. He was nothing and would continue to be nothing, until he won back that respect through valor or blood.

He'd never made a declaration of love to Kendra. He'd never asked her to wait for him, though if what his sister said was true, she had. They'd only shared one kiss, of longing rather than passion. If she'd found another, he'd be hurt but he wouldn't blame her. Her happiness was more important to him than his own.

Silas cranked off the water with sudden clarity. He had to focus, and he couldn't when Nica had his thoughts and desires so fragmented. That had to stop.

When he emerged from the bathroom, he found

the mess gone from his living room and the door to his bedroom shut. With a sigh, he took out his phone. The sound of Nica's voice sent a shock of heat through him, like an electrical spark.

"Nica, can you meet me for dinner at La Bayou?"

"I have to eat."

He smiled faintly at her inescapable logic. "In an hour?"

"I'll see you there."

He tapped on the bedroom door. "Brigit, I need the clothes hanging on the closet door."

Silence, then the door cracked open just far enough for the hanger and his tux to come flying out.

"Thank you."

"Fuck you."

After he shaved and dressed, he paused at the bedroom door. "Bree, I have to go to work. If you need me, call me on my cell. Stay here and don't answer the door."

"Go to hell."

A fairly apt description of his destination.

Nica arrived at the restaurant early and got a table on the balcony overlooking Bourbon Street. To the left was the cleanly urban cityscape of the Central Business District; to the right was the historic Quarter, old, battered, and slightly seedy. Across the narrow street were clubs and shops selling any sin one could imagine, and in New Orleans one could imagine quite a lot.

In the doorway of one of Manny Blu's competitors

stood a buxom advertisement wearing a floor show costume, talking to a burly suit who was probably her manager. She called boldly to a young man passing by with his girlfriend, making his steps falter until the angry girl dragged him along after her. A family of four hurried by, directing their children's eyes toward the souvenir shops across the street. Nica smiled grimly. Everything was for sale: sex, honor, innocence, if the price was right.

Her senses tingled with awareness even before Silas came out on the balcony. Then her gaze traveled appreciatively over him. The polished tux accentuated his powerful masculinity. He slipped off his jacket to hang it on the back of his chair, then rolled up his shirtsleeves as he took a seat across from her.

"Have you ordered yet?"

"No. I've been waiting for you." *All my life.*

"I'm starving." His gaze buried in the menu.

"Me, too." She noticed how the late-day sunlight teased out red highlights in his close-cropped hair.

"What are you having?" he asked, glancing up.

She wanted to have him in the worst possible way.

"The chicken and andouille gumbo and crawfish étouffée. And a Sazerac." She needed the liquid courage.

MacCreedy handed their menus to the waiter, ordering for her and blackened redfish for himself. Then he leaned back to study the street.

Nica had thought of nothing but him all day. Of how he could alter the dangerous trajectory she was on, if she could just get the words out.

Her drink came and she took a quick gulp, letting the harsh liquid burn down her throat, sweet and bitter at the same time.

When their meal arrived to break the silence Mac-Creedy kept his attention on his plate, picking at his dinner while she devoured hers. He seemed remote, guarded, and ill at ease. Was he still bothered by what he'd learned that morning? Perhaps it was time to put his fears to rest.

"Busy day?"

"What?" His gaze flickered up, then quickly away. "Yes."

"Is your sister settling in?"

A wry smile. "Taking over like an invasive species."

"It's good of you to take her in."

He looked at her then, brows knit together. "Why do you say that?"

"She shows up, disrupts your life, invades your space. Most wouldn't be so obliging."

"She's my sister."

The simple answer said everything about him. He would always protect and support those he loved, regardless of circumstance. She found that remarkably sexy.

"Was the male who died her mate?"

"No, a lover. One in a long line."

"She seemed very distressed over the loss."

"She doesn't like to lose things until she's ready to get rid of them."

He was in a strange, unhappy mood. Still, she pressed on. "What are you going to do about the boy?"

His features grew more grim. "I'll finish what I started. That's what I do. I'm very reliable."

And very angry about something.

"Did you know Max and Lottie are a bound pair?"

He blinked at that, obviously surprised. "She's a human."

Nica leaned toward him to confide, "They can read each other's thoughts. It's because of the old blood."

"The blood you share."

"And you, as well."

He was silent, then asked, "You believe the priest?"

"I think what he said was the truth."

"That my mother was—"

"Like me? Perhaps. They say there are a few in every bloodline. She was a Guedry. An old and rich heritage."

"Why wouldn't she have told me?"

Nica's tone gentled. "Maybe she was waiting until you were old enough to understand it."

"She waited too long. And now it's too late." He looked away, his eyes blinking quickly. "I'm nothing like Savoie. I don't have any special talents, and neither does Brigit."

"I've heard that males have to be bonded before they reach their full potential."

He looked suspicious. "I've never heard that."

"We travel in very different circles. You also hadn't heard of those experiments the priest was describing. Record and protect, my ass."

That made him smile. "What else have you heard?"

Instead of answering, she asked, "Have you mated?"

He looked endearingly uncomfortable. She hadn't expected her fiery lover to be so conservative.

"When I was younger, when it was required, I was provided with a female. It was brief and unsettling."

"You didn't like it?" She leaned on her elbows, chin resting upon laced fingers, curious.

"She was a stranger, much older than me, and I was—"

"Scared?" she supplied.

He scowled at her. "Inexperienced. And you?"

She laughed. "I've never met a male I liked enough to let him go all fur and fangs over me." *Until now.* "I'm kind of a control freak."

He chuckled. "I've noticed."

She touched his hand, and his fingers spread so hers could lace between them.

He took a weary breath, the heaviness returning to his mood as he said, "Nica" softly.

Say it now. Just say it!

"Silas, what if you were to bond with me?"

His head reared back as if she'd slapped him. "What?"

She held his stare, laying out what she'd come up with in her desperation to keep him. "If you mate with me, if we're bonded, our abilities will be joined as well. I could share things with you that would make you as strong as Savoie, maybe stronger, since Lottie is a human. Think of it. You could have what you want. You could take what you deserve. I could help you."

"Why would you do that? Bonding is no casual thing. It's permanent. You can't try it on to see if you like it, then cast it aside."

"We like each other. We're sexually compatible. Most matches are made between strangers who don't have that luxury. We'd be starting off far better than most."

In his face, shock gave way to distress. Or was it distaste? Her heart began to race; panic squeezed about her chest.

"I want more, Nica."

It all clicked together in a devastating instant. His anxiousness, his somber mood.

He invited me here to give me the kiss-off.

And she was begging him for an eternity.

She laughed, a loud, rough sound. "I wasn't asking you to give me children. Forget I said anything. I'd forgotten that you were saving your precious seed to sow in your Terriot princess. I wouldn't expect you to scatter it about on fallow soil."

She tossed down the rest of her drink, blinking the moisture from her eyes. She wiped at them with a shaky hand, her laugh brittle. "I'm sorry I embarrassed you, MacCreedy. We'll pretend this never happened."

She rose from her chair but his hand circled her wrist.

"Nica, please."

If he said he was sorry, she'd lose it completely. Pity would destroy her.

Her eyes blazed as she snarled, "Touch me again and I *will* kill you."

She jerked away and disappeared, leaving him staring after her.

Silas closed his eyes and let out a harsh breath. His path was clear to duty and honor now, and the price was another burden on his soul. He could carry it, because he had to.

But that tragic look in her eyes, when she mistakenly assumed he didn't love her, might be the heaviest of them all.

Nineteen

Silas was off his game in more ways than one.

After he'd given away another huge pot in a long series of house losses, Manny came over, put a hand on his shoulder, and said softly, "Step out for a minute, Mac."

As he followed the hoodlum into his office, MacCreedy immediately apologized. "I'm sorry, Mr. Blutafino. My mind's not in the game tonight."

Manny pressed him down in one of the ugly chrome chairs and bent close to ask, "And what would get your mind right? A nine-millimeter to the frontal lobe?"

"I hope that won't be necessary," Silas was quick to murmur.

Manny laughed and eased his bulk into his throne-like seat. "What's going on with you? Something I can help you with? You've been a consistent moneymaker for me, Mac. I don't want to let you go."

As in .9mm to the brain. Yeah, he got that.

"I lost somebody close to me today. It shook me up more than I realized." How true that was.

"Do you want some time off?"

"No, sir. Thank you. I'm fine now. I'll get back to my table."

He just started to rise when the door opened and Francis Petitjohn entered. MacCreedy recognized him from studying his arrest jacket: Jimmy Legere's villainous cousin and Max's rival for Legere Enterprises International.

"Got a minute, Manny?"

"For you, Johnny? Anytime."

"I hope it's not too premature for a little toast to the former thorn in my ass that's now burning in hell." He glanced at Silas. "Fix us a couple of scotch rocks, kid."

"Yes, sir, Mr. Petitjohn."

T-John squinted at him. "Do I know you?"

"No, sir, but everyone knows you. Congratulations."

Preening at the compliment, he smiled. "On what?"

"Inheriting LEI. That's quite a coup."

Inheriting and *coup* didn't carry the same connotations, and T-John began to frown. Seeing his displeasure, Manny waved a hand. "Get the drinks, Mac, then get back to the game."

"Right away, Mr. Blutafino."

"Chatty bastard," T-John muttered as he sat down. Silas could feel his stare between his shoulder blades.

"So, Johnny, when can we get down to some serious business? I'm still a couple light on this latest shipment. When's the departure date? Do I have time to fill the load?"

"Everything's on hold for the next couple of days or so, until we get the official word. Then we can grease the right palms and be back to business as usual. The kind of business Jimmy was doing before Savoie let it all go to hell."

"I'm looking forward to working with you, Johnny."

MacCreedy placed their drinks on the desktop and nodded politely. "Good night, gentlemen."

As he resumed his seat at the blackjack table, he was relaxed and in control of his deck. He flipped the cards with crisp efficiency, noting, *Ace of hearts, eight of clubs, three of diamonds, queen of clubs,* as each settled facedown on the table.

He knew what the cards were. He'd always known. He figured some sort of fancy OCD imprinted the order in his subconscious as he shuffled. He'd always been good with numbers.

But no one was that good.

He studied the stacks before the players at his table. *Ace of hearts, eight of clubs, three of diamonds, queen of clubs.* Each card seemed to hold an energy from the last gaze that touched on it. He could *feel* it. He could *read* it as if the card had become transparent.

Because of the gift he'd inherited from his mother.

He spent the rest of the evening, into early morning, testing that theory. He never made a mistake—not once. By the time he rose up from the table to wish the players a good evening, he was able to look straight down through a deck of fifty-two and correctly identify each card in order.

A neat parlor trick that would keep a .9mm slug out of his gray matter.

What else could he do? he wondered, as he cashed in for the night.

The novelty wore off as he walked back to his apartment, the weight of Nica's humiliation dragging on him. She hadn't deserved to be treated that way. Especially not by him.

She'd taken him by surprise. Her suggestion had blanked his thoughts so completely, by the time he gathered them up again, his instincts had run away with him. *Bonded to Nica.* He'd blazed to life at the notion. The challenge of building a life with her, of having her beside him, at his back, in his bed. In one lightning strike, he'd seen the future he'd give anything to claim. And lost it just as quickly.

Just as well. His destiny was already in motion.

A destiny that met him at his door with a soft cry and silky arms about his neck.

"Oh, Silas. I've missed you so."

"Kendra?" he managed as he looked over her pale blonde curls to meet his sister's contented expression. *There,* it seemed to say. *Now all is as it should be, the three of us together.*

As much as he wanted to be angry with her for orchestrating this, a wave of tenderness swept over him for the little girl he'd loved, for the young woman he'd yearned for. He closed his eyes and breathed her in, resting his cheek on the crown of her head.

His sister sighed before saying, "Silas, Kendra needs to talk to you. I'll go in the other room so you can be alone."

Brigit's tone sounded serious, and Silas stepped back and tipped Kendra's lovely face up. He hadn't seen her for over five years, and her beauty still staggered him. Her dark, doe-like eyes were red from weeping. "Kenny, what's wrong?"

"Something awful," came her small voice, and instantly he got her over to the sofa and sat close beside her, her cold hands pressed between his.

"What's happened?"

She looked suddenly shy with him. "Bree said it was all right for me to come. She said I should ask for your help."

"Of course it's all right. I'll do anything I can for you. You know that." When she was silent for a moment too long, staring at the sight of their overlapping hands, he prompted quietly, "Why are you here, Kendra?"

"I'm one of the few eligible females of the Terriot line," she began softly, refusing to look up at him. "Because of that, I've gained favor in the House these last few years."

"Someone with your intelligence and beauty would be hard to ignore." It wasn't flattery, just fact.

Then her gaze lifted, and he could see the fear as she told him, "It would have been easier to be ignored."

"Has anyone harmed you, Kendra?" His voice was calm, but an eerie blue light flickered in his eyes.

She clutched at his hands. "No. I'm under Bram Terriot's protection. No one would dare. You saw to that for me."

He relaxed slightly. "So what are you afraid of?"

"Do you remember Bram's son Cale?"

Silas smiled fiercely. "Oh, yes, I remember him well. How's his eye?"

"I think his vanity pains him more than the injury. He's never gotten over how you shamed him."

"He's a brute and a bully, and he deserved to be taught a lesson." The repercussions had been well worth it.

"Apparently he'd like to teach you one, as well. When he learned you had a fondness for me, he asked his father's permission to take me for a mate."

Silas felt violent objection, protectiveness, and outrage. But not the possessive insult he'd expect.

Tears shimmered in her eyes. "I'm scared of him, Silas. He's little more than a beast, and I know he means to hurt me to get back at you. I'd rather die than live in misery bonded to him. You won't let that happen, will you? Please, promise you won't let him hurt me."

He quickly pulled her trembling figure close. "No, of course not," he murmured, his mind whirling frantically.

What was he supposed to do? Challenge the savage? Stroll into the Terriot stronghold and kill him? He would do those things if they would keep her safe, but they would only make him dead, leaving her at the vicious elder Terriot's mercy.

But Kendra's plan didn't involve fighting.

"Take me as *your* mate, Silas. He won't be able to have me if I belong to you."

He reacted with practical argument rather than delight. "Kenny, I have no standing in the Terriot court. Cale would just have me killed and take you anyway."

She looked up through those huge damp eyes. "Not if you bring them something they want, first."

And he felt Brigit's clever noose cinch tight about his neck.

She went on, "Bree told me about your plan to take that boy to them as an offering. She said they would deny you nothing. You could ask them for me." When he was silent, her confidence faltered. "She said you still cared for me. Was she mistaken?"

He stared into her eyes, looking for some hint of guile or cunning. But there was only the innocent plea of a frightened girl. He had no defense. "I have loved you my entire life, Kendra. And I will love you for the rest of it."

With a grateful cry, she collapsed against him. "I'll do everything I can to make you happy."

He was sure she'd try. She was pleasing, gentle, caring, and agreeable. Her mind was sharp and her tongue could be as well, when provoked. They'd been inseparable friends, sharing everything. It would be a good alliance and a satisfying relationship.

But she would never be Nica.

He patted her hair. "You need to get some sleep. You're safe here. I'll take care of everything."

She nodded, believing him totally. She relaxed against him, her body soft, her scent light and delicate. And as her eyes drifted shut from sheer exhaustion he simply held her, while inside, a terrible panic shook through him.

After her breaths had quieted, he carried her to the bedroom, where he was certain Brigit had been pressed against the door, listening. When he laid Kendra on the bed, his sister asked, "Should I leave?"

He glanced at her in surprise and said quickly, "No. I'll take the couch."

Brigit gave him a puzzled look but said nothing. She followed him out into the living room, trying to gauge his mood. "You're not going to strangle me, are you?"

"I should spank you the way I did when you were five," he said, resigned.

"I knew you wouldn't let her be taken against her will by that barbaric pig. You're doing the right thing, Silas. We can be together, a real family again. It's what our parents wanted for us."

Was it? Would his sweet, loving mother wish him to use her other child to further their success? Would his noble father want him to take the freedoms he'd given his life to protect, and give them away for a prison of security and comfort?

Would they want him to take the wrong woman to be his companion for life out of obligation, rather than desire?

When Brigit pushed into his side, his arm enfolded her without hesitation, but his quietness clearly bothered her.

"This *will* make you happy, won't it? It's what you've always wanted. We'll be safe, and I won't be such a burden to you."

"You're not a burden," he told her softly. "I love you, Bree."

"And you love Kendra."

"I do. I love you both."

The very same way. As sisters.

A cool, dry morning brought tourists and city dwellers by the score to indulge in café au lait and hot beignets under the awning at Café du Monde.

Nica slouched in her plastic chair, not hungry, pushing the plate of fried, confectioner's-sugar-coated dough toward Cee Cee.

At the moment, life in general sucked.

She'd met Cee Cee at the medical examiner's office to provide a mouth swab and blood draw. One of the few humans aware of Shifter existence, Devlin Dovion was fascinated by the detective's tale of genetic markers, and agreed to upload the substituted sample under the name Lenore "Chili Pepper" Charles into the DNA database. He also promised to keep tabs on who accessed the information, just as he'd agreed to delay ID of the mystery victim from the car fire. From there, they went to breakfast.

Charlotte had the glow of a woman who'd spent the night being thoroughly and exhaustively satisfied by the man she loved. And Nica resented the hell out of it. Her own evening had been spent slapping away the grabby hands of intoxicated customers, and lying on the floor of her condo, staring out through her skylight. She didn't dare sleep for fear of the dreams. Her system was shivering with tension, which meant things would happen soon. She always knew when it was coming, like a radar weather warning.

She didn't want to discover her reason for being in New Orleans, but she was restless and ready to move on. Anxious to complete her job, pack up, and disappear, quickly to be forgotten. Never to be missed.

"Thanks for saving us a seat."

Nica's gaze flew up as Alain Babineau and Silas joined them. Her glance met Silas's briefly before each of them looked away.

"Morning." Cee Cee used her foot to push out a chair for Babineau, then looked up at Silas. "Geez, Mac, you look like shit warmed over. Up all night?" Her eyes cut to Nica meaningfully.

"Tall man on a short couch. I've got guests."

Nica's attention sparked. Guests? Plural? She sipped her coffee, resolved to betray no interest.

"If it gets too bad, you can bunk over at my place," Babineau offered.

As Silas filled them in on his encounter with Francis Petitjohn, Nica glanced his way. He'd put on dark-lensed glasses and it made her uncomfortable, not being able to tell where he was looking. He wore a turquoise V-neck T-shirt that set off the tan acquired on his trip to the bayou and the powerful swell of his arms. His jeans were tight over muscular thighs and rolled into cuffs above white tennis shoes. He looked so damned hot, her eyeballs felt scorched.

Guests sharing his bed . . . she dragged her mind back to his words. His sister had just lost a lover, so it was probably another female. And she could think of only one he'd ever mentioned. Her coffee suddenly tasted like sludge.

"Lena Blutafino is stopping by the Towers for another visit," Cee Cee was saying, "and I think it's time for a little more girl talk. Nica, are you coming?"

"I can't. I've got an early shift. In fact, I don't think I'll be in New Orleans much longer. A job offer I've been waiting for should come any time now, so I don't want to make any plans. If you'll excuse me, I've got some errands to run."

She shoved back her chair, nearly knocking over a waitress with three trays stacked up her arm. Murmuring an apology, she waited for the way to clear, which gave Silas time to stand, as well.

She stared into the impenetrable blank of his aviator sunglasses, her expression stoic. *You had your shot, big guy. Don't you dare complicate things now.*

He simply stepped aside to offer her an exit, which she took gratefully, making very sure not to touch him in passing.

Cee Cee watched the interplay with interest. Mac-Creedy's gaze followed Nica's arrogant stride as she wound between the tables and dashed across Decatur. Placing the bottom of her foot on MacCreedy's very nice butt, Cee Cee gave him a push.

"You should probably go after her. She wants you to."

Silas hesitated, then said flatly, "No, I don't think so," in answer to one or both things. He resumed his seat and took off his sunglasses to rub his eyes.

If he'd looked like crap before, he now felt as if he'd been scraped off the bottom of someone's shoe. A size eight currently making quick time along the edge of the square.

"Oh, for fuck's sake," Cee Cee said into her coffee cup. "I'm surrounded by idiot men."

For the dozenth time since she'd begun her shift, Nica went all hot and cold and shivery. She had to stop and brace herself against the back of a chair until the swelling nausea went away.

"Hon, you look like you're about to toss your breakfast," Amber scolded, relieving her of her tray. "You need to go home. Jacques don't want you here when you're sick."

Nica wiped her brow with the rag from her back pocket. She was seeing double. "I'm not sick. I told you, it's a migraine. I get them sometimes."

"Is your migraine that six-three worth of hunky boyfriend over at the bar, pretending not to be staring at you?"

Nica turned to look but could only make out a turquoise blur. "Oh, hell. That's all I need."

"You want me to ask him to take you home with him?"

"No. He's got somebody else there with him now." Had that choky little whine come from her? Could she have sounded any more pathetic?

If it had been loaded, Amber's glare would have

knocked MacCreedy off his stool, and possibly through the wall. *"Bastard,"* she hissed. Her arm around Nica's waist, the buxom waitress steered her to the server's galley, where she plopped Nica on a stool and forced her head between her knees. "You want me to have Jacques and Philo knock the stupid outta him?"

"No. It's not his fault," she moaned.

"It's *always* their fault, hon. The boys'd be happy to do it for you. We take care of our own, sugar."

That protective sentiment spurred a flood of tears and embarrassment, until Nica was finally able to control her reeling emotions.

Amber blocked her from view of the bar like a mama lion. "I know he's a fine-looking piece, but there be plenty more out there that won't go breaking your heart. You don't need a man who makes you cry."

"I'm not crying over him," Nica sniffled, leaning into Amber's shoulder.

Patting her shaking body, Amber murmured, " 'Course not, hon. Cause he's not worth it."

Yes, he was. He was worth every tear, every cry that tore from her throat.

"I'm in love with him," she mourned wretchedly.

Amber did more patting, her voice soothing. "I know, sug. With any luck, he'll get hit by a streetcar over on St. Charles and have to drag his sexy, broken carcass into the gutter, where he'll rot and have his bones picked clean by vermin. Then we can ride by and spit on him. That'll make you feel better."

Nica had to laugh. She sat back and pushed the sweaty hair off her brow. "Maybe I'd better go home. I'm not doing anybody any good here."

"You want me to call you a cab, hon?"

"It's only a few blocks. I'll feel better when I get some air." She stood up, feeling shaky but less light-headed.

"Nica." Amber's tone was serious. "You should let him know that two more of my friends disappeared. I'm really worried about them. Janie Webb and Tandy Barrett. They're nice girls, not hookers. They wait tables at a club over in Algiers."

Nica agreed to tell him, then nodded toward to back of the club. "I'm going to go out through the alley."

"If he tries to follow you, I'll take out his kneecaps with that Louisville Slugger behind the bar."

Impulsively, Nica gave her a hug. "You've been a good friend to me, Amber. Thank you."

"You feel better now, hear."

The minute Nica stepped from the dim, air-conditioned bar into the steamy daylight glare of the alley, everything began to whirl in huge, sickening circles. She groped blindly for the door, reeling into a stack of liquor crates. She would have fallen with them if not for the sturdy support of an arm about her middle.

"I gotcha. It's all right."

It wasn't all right! Angrily, she attempted to pull free of MacCreedy's hold.

"Nica, stop. You're going to get hurt."

"Too late for that. Leave me alone. I don't need your

help. I don't need *you*." She jerked away, stumbled, and fell hard to her hands and knees, her head feeling like it was about to explode.

His hands were gentle on her arms. "Let me get you home," he coaxed. "You don't want to pass out in this alley."

The image of his bloated, maggot-ridden corpse in the gutter near the streetcar line made a semi-hysterical laugh come up, along with the beignets and coffee. Silas supported her until the spasms eased, then scooped her up in his arms. And that was the last thing she remembered.

Twenty

Nica slowly awoke cocooned in cool, dark comfort. She drifted in that gentle bliss for a while, unwilling to return to full awareness. Because then she'd have to reject the tender, healing stroke of MacCreedy's fingertips.

She finally opened her eyes and discovered she was lying on her couch with MacCreedy's thigh as a pillow.

His hand stilled. "Stay quiet," he said in a hushed voice.

Good advice. She closed her eyes and sighed as his light caress continued. "How did I get here?"

"I carried you."

"I don't want you to stay." But she was nudging into his touch, burrowing into the warmth of his palm.

"I don't care what you want."

"Obviously."

"I'm not going to argue with you." His thumb traced lightly over her lips.

"You'd lose."

"I think I might have a slight advantage at the moment."

She took another tack. "You didn't have to come in."

"Right. I could have left you hanging on the doorknob like a bag of dry cleaning."

"I'm fine now." She struggled to sit up and her head immediately began to throb. "See," she gritted out. "Fine. Go away."

"All I see is stubborn. And I'm staying until I'm sure you can take care of yourself." He got up and went into her kitchen, missing the spectacular scowl she sent him.

"I've been taking care of myself since I was seven. I don't need you here. I don't *want* you here."

Silence, then the sudden sound of shattering glass made her jump.

MacCreedy rounded out of the kitchen in a magnificent fury. His eyes glittered, quicksilver with flashes of blue fire. His voice rumbled like thunder. "Then by all freaking means continue. Take care of yourself. Rely on yourself. Live your own miserable life without ever giving a damn about anyone *but* yourself. You are the most—"

"I love you."

Her eyes were closed; she couldn't bear to look at him. She could feel his shock in the deafening silence. Finally, he stammered, "I—I broke one of your glasses," and returned to the kitchen. She could hear him pull the trash can out from under the sink, and the tinkle of glass as he tossed the shattered pieces into the pail. Like shards of her heart. Could she make a bigger fool of herself?

Nica got off the couch, wobbling. She took several cautious steps toward the hall, her focus on the bedroom door that she could close to escape this dreadful moment. The hallway tipped and warped wildly out of shape. A few more steps, then her legs gave out. Fueled by a humiliation that couldn't get worse, she crawled on hands and knees.

"Nica!"

She didn't stop. She couldn't. She couldn't see, couldn't breathe, couldn't struggle when he dropped down in front of her to gather her into his arms. Could do nothing but slump against him when he sat on the hall rug, back to the wall, cradling her to his chest and rocking her as he pressed rough kisses to her brow, her temple, her cheek. His breathing was as ragged as her emotions.

"Repeat that," he whispered.

"I love you, Si. But it doesn't change anything. Not who we are. Not what we have to do."

"Nica, I—"

She stopped his words with her palm. "No. I don't have the strength to hear it. Don't say anything. Please." Finally he nodded, lowering his head until his cheek rubbed against hers. She could feel the damp heat of tears. She didn't think she was crying; were they his?

After long minutes passed, Nica eased out of his embrace and settled beside him on the floor. They sat there, not looking at each other until she said, "I'm feeling better. I should probably just lie down for a while, then I'll be fine."

"Amber said you were sick. She told me you'd gone out the back, and that I should go after you to make sure you were all right."

So much for their man-hating sisterhood. "I'm not

sick," she told him testily. "I've never been sick a day in my life."

"Then what is it—" His voice broke, and his eyes became huge. He took a shaky breath, then ventured, "Nica, are you—"

"Pregnant?" She laughed. "Good God, no. I'm not *that* stupid."

"Oh." He turned away quickly, his jaw squaring as if she'd just offended the hell out of him.

Had he hoped—? No, of course not. Now she *was* being stupid. There had never been any question of forming lasting ties.

She puffed out a breath. "Thanks for bringing me here. If you could help me get to the bedroom, I'm going to nod off and you can go do whatever you need to do. If your hero instincts insist, you can call and check on me later, but I really think we should try to stay clear of each other from now on."

He just got to his feet and put down his hands to her. She placed hers in them without hesitation and allowed him to haul her up. When she swayed, his arm went about her waist.

"Lean on me, if your ego will permit it."

She did. She wouldn't have made it otherwise.

There were no windows in the room, just the illusion of it with draperies hanging down on either side of the wrought iron bed frame. When Silas reached for the light switch, she stayed his hand.

"No light. Just the fan."

He turned the rheostat down so just a faint glow warmed the room, and the ceiling fan stirred a pleasant breeze. With his arm still supporting her, he pulled back the covers, then eased her down onto the mattress.

"Let me get your shoes."

She started to protest but he was already untying and slipping off her athletic shoes, then her socks, his hands warm against her skin. She studied the top of his head, intrigued by the slight curl of his hair, by the dark fan of his lashes, the hard line of his shoulders, wanting to touch him so badly, her fingers knotted in the covers. *Not a good idea. Let him go. This can't end well.* Her bare toes rubbed over the top of his thighs.

"You never got to try out my bed," she said quietly. "It's much more comfortable than the floor." Her palm patted the space beside her. "Try it. Just for a second."

He eyed her warily, then sat on the edge of the bed. He looked at her in surprise. "What is this?"

"It's a feather pillow top."

He dropped back and sank into heavenly luxury. A heartfelt sigh issued from him as his eyes closed. "This is nothing like those hotel ironing boards I'm used to. I could hibernate in this for months. I'd never go to work again." He settled in, easing muscles that still protested the cramped night on the couch.

As his tension melted into the downy comfort, his thoughts drifted. It seemed the most natural thing in the world for Nica to lie down beside him, her head on his shoulder, her arm curled across his chest. He placed his hand over hers. And when he opened his eyes, it was four o'clock in the afternoon.

"Oh, shit!" MacCreedy turned his head to meet Nica's gaze. "Why didn't you wake me up?"

Her answer was simple. "You needed the sleep. I needed you."

Well . . . hell.

He should have jumped up and scrambled for the door. He should have done a lot of things. Anything other than lose himself in the vulnerability of that stare.

"This could be the last time we ever see each other," she said with a quiet calm. "I wanted to fill up on the sight."

The last time. Everything in him rebelled against that, but he didn't know what to say to her. He didn't know how to express the fullness in his heart, the anguish in his soul. Words couldn't explain.

I don't want to leave. I don't want to lose you. I can't bear to say good-bye. I don't have a choice. I have no control. There's nothing I can do. You're everything I need. All I've ever wanted. I can't let go. Don't let me go. Please, Nica.

He drew shuddering breath. "Nica."

"No apologies. No declarations. Just kiss me."

He touched her cheek, his hand unsteady. Her skin was so smooth. He combed his fingers back through her hair, a wild, dark tangle like the feelings raging inside him. Her eyes remained focused on his, so deep, so intense, endless heavens, bottomless seas.

She cupped the back of his head with her hand, and

he sought the soft part of her lips. Like the sinfully inviting mattress, he could sink into them and linger forever.
Her scent stirred all his senses. The taste of her intoxicated him: cool, inviting, silky yet complex, like the wine
they'd shared here. He drank deeply, desperately, until
she broke away, panting with a like urgency.

*Take her. Mate with her. Bond to her. Then no one can
ever take her from you.*

Her mouth slid along his jaw; her breath blew hot
against his ear until he was all gooseflesh and shaky. The
words she whispered inflamed him.

"I don't want you to leave. I don't want to lose you. I
can't bear to say good-bye. I don't have a choice. I have
no control. There's nothing I can do. You're everything I
need. All I've ever wanted. I can't let go."

Beautiful, passionate words.

The exact same words he'd been thinking.

His eyes sprang open and he looked into her soft,
dreamy gaze. *What the hell? Could she read his thoughts?*

"Don't let me go." Her voice was rough with emotion.
"Please, Silas."

He caught her wrists as he searched for answers in
her unguarded stare. Everything was laid bare for him;
the fragility of her love, the heat of her desire, the ache
of inevitability. And suddenly, starkly, an agonizing pain.

She cried out, her body stiffening, quaking. Then her
eyes rolled back and her breathing stopped.

"Nica!"

Was it some kind of seizure? He pressed his fingers

to her throat, where her pulse thundered. He patted her cheeks, lightly at first, then more sharply when she failed to respond.

Her eyes flashed open, filled with the cold, glassy fire he remembered from that night at Savoie's. With a snarl, she gripped him by the neck—damn, she was strong— and threw him across the room. As he got to his hands and knees she assumed a predatory posture on the bed, sinking low, muscles bunched, her teeth becoming fangs.

He was two heartbeats away from being dead.

"Nica, it's Silas," he said forcefully. "You won't like finding pieces of me all over your floor. It's *Silas*. You love me."

"Silas." His name rattled up from her chest and hissed between those lupine teeth. She shook her head, her long hair whipping like a dark mane. "Silas, don't let me hurt you. I don't want to hurt you."

He got to his feet and was moving toward her when she sprang. She hit like a wrecking ball, riding him to the floor. Her mouth was on his in a hard, ferocious kiss. Her teeth sliced his lips; her tongue lapped the blood away. "Love you," she growled.

And just as quickly, she was up and off him.

Cursing, he rolled to his feet and rushed after her into the living room, brought up short by the sight of her on her knees, smashing her head against the brick wall.

"Get out of my mind! Get out of my head!" she shrieked, making all the hairs stand on his arms and nape.

Seeing the blood streaming down her face broke his

trance. He grabbed her, throwing her onto her back so he could sit astride her, pinning her arms down with his knees. She spat and snarled and thrashed, it was all he could do to contain her. He gripped her contorted face in his hands, holding her head still.

"Nica, look at me. Nica!"

Her eyes swirled in raging aggression as she tried to bite him.

Now that he had her, what was he going to do with her?

His thoughts calmed, snagging on a memory from long ago, when he'd held a frantic, wailing child in his arms desperate to comfort her. Tina.

He took a deep, settling breath and let the ragged emotions leave him. He leaned closer, gazing deep into those fever-bright eyes, reaching beyond the madness to the anxious soul that had cried, "Love you."

His voice was low, a soothing cadence of persuasion. "Nica, look at me. Keep looking at me. Look into my eyes. Don't turn away. I want you to see me, just me. It's Silas. I'm here. I'll keep you safe. I promise. Just keep looking at me. Focus on me. It's all right, sweetheart. Nothing's going to take you away from me. You're safe. I won't let you go. Trust me, Nica. Trust me."

Her powerful, heaving struggles stopped. Her fierce panting breaths slowed and deepened. The dangerous shimmer in her eyes was softened by welling tears. And finally, she gave a raw swallow and whispered, "You should have run. Why did you stay?"

"I'm through running."

He rocked back on the balls of his feet to free her arms, which instantly hugged his neck. After holding her for a minute, MacCreedy carried her to the couch, settling her with a promise that he'd be right back. He returned with a wet cloth to gently clean her face and stanch the blood from the lacerations at her hairline. She sat quietly, somberly watching his expression. Her fingers touched his cut mouth.

"I'm sorry."

He lightly kissed and sucked at her fingertips, murmuring, "It's all right. Better now?"

"Yes."

"Okay, then. Here's where you tell me everything. *Everything*, Nica. Right now."

Her gaze shimmered anxiously. "You'll leave me."

"I won't."

A doubtful laugh. "You don't know what I'm going to say."

"It doesn't matter. It won't change anything. I need to know."

Her heart shuddered, and her courage faltered in the face of this monumental risk. "You'll hate me."

He shook his head. "I'm made of tougher stuff than that."

She saw the firmness of his jaw, the steady steeliness of his eyes. Maybe he was. She took a breath. "Could we have some wine?"

"If you need it."

A cynical smile. "I think *you're* going to need it, lover. Bring the bottle."

Nica had no memories of her family. She had no idea where she was born, where she lived, or what her parents looked like. When she tried to recall them, all she found were flashes of flames, pain, and fear.

"Did you lose them in a fire?" Silas asked after taking a big gulp of pinot gris. The thought of her as a child, alone, hurt, afraid, was unbearably painful.

"Maybe. I don't know. I've never been able to find out anything about them."

"Who raised you?"

Her smile curled. "Wolves. I grew up in a pack of Shifter children, some younger, most older than me. I was six or seven. We lived on the streets, surviving by whatever means necessary. They were the closest to family I ever had."

"Just children, alone? No adults?" He was horrified.

"We were resourceful. Sometimes we had to depend on adults to earn money or if one of us got in trouble. Those were lean, hard years, but the freedom was delicious. That's all I want to share with you about that." She gave him a belligerent look, daring him to push for more.

"Okay." For now. Children roaming the streets like savage animals. Someone had to know something. They had to come from somewhere. "Where was this? Do you remember?"

"In the North. I remember snow. Chicago, I think. It seemed familiar when I went there later."

Chicago, where the Chosen ruled. He kept his features impassive. "How did you end up at St. Bart's?"

"We traveled a lot, hopping trains. I'd go as a lookout for the older boys, because I seemed harmless and had more nerve than any of them."

His smile twitched at that. Silas could imagine her as a fierce, feral child and his sympathies clenched tight. But he couldn't let her see that; she'd hate it.

"We were brought down to New Orleans for a job. It was during Mardi Gras. I remember the parades and the easy pickings. And then everything went to hell." She sipped her wine, shadows darkening her gaze. "Something blew our deal and two of the boys died."

"Died? How?"

Nica shrugged. "They were shot. It happened sometimes." She continued as if the death of kids was an acceptable part of her early existence. "But they were the ones who had all our travel money. We had to scatter and fend for ourselves. That's when Tommy Caissie found me. He was a beat cop then. I was seven or eight and he dumped me at St. Bart's."

Thank God for Charlotte's father. For four years, she'd had a safe place to be a child.

But that wasn't how she'd seen it. It was a cage, to a predator used to freedom. She hated the rules, resisted authority, fought for everything she had, and sometimes for things she didn't need out of frustration and fear.

"I thought about escape every day. I wondered what happened to my friends, and hoped they'd come for me."

"But no one did."

She shook her head sadly. "I never spoke to any of them again. But I didn't stay at St. Bart's because they made me." She said it proudly, wanting him to know that it was her choice. "I wanted to learn. I didn't know how to read or do numbers. I wanted to know things, things that would keep me alive."

"Knowledge is power, my father always said."

Nica nodded. "Exactly. I spent all my time learning and staying strong. By the time I was twelve, I was doing the work of a senior in high school. Tommy Caissie let me come with them sometimes when he'd pick up Lottie. He taught us hand-to-hand and how to respect guns. He said I was a quick study."

Learning to be a quick and lethal assassin before the age of puberty—when other changes began to take hold.

"I started having dreams. I called them that because I didn't know what they were. Visions, maybe. Usually when I was asleep, sometimes when I was awake."

"Is that what happened today?"

A tight smile. "Wait for it, MacCreedy."

He finished his glass and poured more for both of them. "Describe these dreams."

Here's where he'd discover just how different she was.

"I'd be someplace else. I mean *really* someplace else. I could hear, feel, taste, smell everything around me, but the images were scrambled, wrong somehow. But they were real, Silas. I was really at these places."

"Okay," he responded, not rejecting what he was hearing. "Did you tell anyone about these dreams?"

"I told Mary Kate once. It scared her and she made me talk to Father Furness. I told him I made everything up. That's when he started watching me more carefully."

"What was it? Telepathy? Astral projection?" At her surprise, he shrugged. "I'd heard of these kinds of things before Father Furness enlightened us. I just never—"

"Believed in them. I didn't, either. Then one day I realized I could hear what some of my prison mates at St. Bart's were thinking, like I was right there in their heads. I could tune in the other Shifters without them knowing it."

"Can you read my mind?"

"Rarely. You're difficult unless your emotions are stirred up. Then I can catch glimpses. Not much."

Liar.

Nica could read that clearly enough.

"So what were these dreams about?"

She grew cautious. "They were warnings. About things that hadn't happened yet."

"You were seeing the future?"

"Things that *could* happen. Sometimes they were messages about things I was supposed to do. If I didn't do them, the messages would get stronger and stronger, more and more clear. And the headaches would start."

"Is that what happened in the alley that night? When

you dropped your knife? What were you supposed to do, Nica? What did you see?"

She looked him squarely in the eyes and told him. He never blinked. She didn't, however, tell him of the other vision—of the child he was carrying on his shoulders, a child she was now sure was theirs.

"Where do these dreams come from?" he demanded, more shaken now.

"Ahh, the big question. That's what I wanted to know. I wanted to know *everything*. I wanted to know why I was different, why Father Furness knew something about me but wouldn't tell me. He knew I was different. If he'd told me the truth—"

"You would have trusted him," Silas concluded.

And her life would have turned out completely different. Perhaps.

"I had to have the knowledge, MacCreedy. I had to know."

He nodded.

So she followed the dictates of her vision to Chicago. She was met at the train by a friendly couple who took her home, fed her, and bought her clothes. They talked to her about a community where she could belong and be cared for, where she could learn and excel beyond her wildest imaginings. Where she could hone her talents and never be afraid again. She could control her own destiny.

"They said all the right things. And I believed them."

"They lied to you."

A wry smile. "Not exactly. But they didn't tell me the

truth, either. That where I'd be going was like another prison, that I'd have to fight and earn every privilege, where freedom was the reward of the very, very few. So I fought and I learned and I was determined to be one of the very, very few.

"So here I am, MacCreedy, on the cusp of that freedom. And all I have to do to earn it, is kill someone I've grown to respect and care about."

Twenty-one

Over the course of the afternoon, into a second bottle of wine, Nica told him everything she knew, which altogether wasn't much.

She'd been an excellent student, one of the top five. She was a merciless combatant and a clever tactician, rising through the ranks to become the only female in her class, because she could do something none of the others could. She could change shape.

She was careful never to do it around any others. She'd only release enough of the beast to give her strength equal to that of the males. She thought she was smart enough to keep her talent hidden, but she hadn't known what the last step of her training involved.

They called it mental conditioning. Like the others, she thought it was some psychological mind game. She was seventeen, tough, lean, fierce, ready for anything that would allow her to gain the status required for independence.

"But it was really mind control," Nica told him grimly. "Instead of granting freedom, they took away all hope of it. They use the dreams to manipulate us. It starts with a subliminal message, repeated images that get stronger and more frequent until they're imprinted on the brain, until you can't separate your will from theirs."

"If you resist?"

"They hurt you."

"Could they kill you?"

"I've seen it happen. They're big on demonstrations. Watching someone's mind explode is a powerful motivator for compliance. If you do what you're told, the visions and the pain stop. If you don't, those increase until you die or they take you over."

A chill ran through MacCreedy. "What does that mean? What the hell did they do to you and the others?"

"Each of us was mentally linked to our own Controller. That Controller monitors our progress, relays information, directs our actions, and, if we're nonresponsive, doles out punishment until we obey or bend."

"Bend?"

"Let them assume control of our actions."

"Have you ever—?"

"No. I refuse to surrender what little free will I have. Once you do, it's easier for them to use you without your knowledge or consent, even though they're not officially allowed to. They're only supposed to guide you on specific missions and the rest of the time, stay out of your way."

The tightness in her expression clued him. "But yours didn't?"

"No. I was imprinted with a pissy little shit of a watchdog named Hawthorne. I've never seen him, but I can feel his dirty mind all over me. I imagine him whacking off in some dark room somewhere while he watches me undress. Our Controllers aren't supposed to spy on our private moments, but my shadow has become a bit of a stalker."

MacCreedy was very still, his eyes narrowed into dangerous slits. "If he's breaking the rules, isn't there someone you can go to?"

"Supposedly—if Hawthorne didn't have something to hold over my head to keep me in line."

"He knows you can shape-change."

"He does, but he's an opportunistic bastard and doesn't want to share that knowledge. He uses my skills to his advantage; my successes are his successes. That's not what he holds over me, though. He knows where my friends are, Si. He knows what happened to them after we split up all those years ago. And he'll harm them if I betray him." Her voice shook slightly.

"Do you know that for certain, or could it be an empty threat?"

"A few years ago, I was angry enough to call his bluff. He showed me a man being eviscerated in the basement of an office building. I found the building. The police had just gotten there. He was a security guard."

"How do you know—"

"He'd written a message to me in his own blood while he was dying. 'Kiki, don't trust the Shadows.' Henry was a year younger than me. He had a scar on his left shoulder that I gave him during a training exercise. He was like my brother." She turned away, struggling with her composure.

"This Hawthorne, can he hear us now?"

She shook her head. "I can block him most of the time, except when I sleep and—" She broke off.

"And?"

"He can't usually surprise me. I can feel him getting close, like he's breathing down my neck. I keep my guard up so he can't sneak in."

"Except?"

She met his intense stare. "A couple of times when I was with you."

Nothing changed in his expression. "At Savoie's and here, just a bit ago?"

"Yes."

He exploded up off the couch, a coil of deadly tension. "So we've been having threesomes that I didn't know about?"

She held his fierce glare without flinching. "Yes."

He whirled away and strode into the kitchen.

Silence. Total, terrifying silence. She could only imagine what was going through his mind. The disgust, the repulsion, the fury. Now he would leave, and she would never see him again. She wouldn't beg his forgiveness, how could she? She would have to let him go.

MacCreedy returned to the living room with a purposeful stride, his expression fierce, his eyes cool as glaciers. He crouched in front of her so their eyes were level as he said, slowly and with a deadly distinction, "I am going to find this man for you, and if he won't let you go, I'm going to kill him horribly while you watch. We're going to get you free of this mess."

He kissed her so deep and hard, she was sure he could taste her heart as it rose up into her throat. When he leaned back to wipe her tears off her cheeks, he told her steadily, "I promise you this, Nica."

"I want to have your children, MacCreedy," she said fervently.

He just smiled slightly and stroked his hands through her hair. "We have to be very careful. He's made a very big mistake in underestimating us. Nobody fucks with our families."

Nica's tremulous smile gained ferocity from his. For the first time in years she felt a sense of camaraderie, and with it came relief and a wonderful thrill of power. She let him enfold her to his chest, reveling in the courageous beat of his heart and the press of his lips atop her head.

"I've got to go. But I don't like leaving you here alone," he said.

She melted. "You could come back tonight. You're the only man I've ever wanted to wake up to."

A pause.

She'd forgotten. "Oh. You have guests." She pushed back from him. "Go."

"There are some things I have to resolve. I'll call you." He stood. "Lock up after me."

Her gaze followed him down the hall. As he opened the door, she called, "MacCreedy?"

He looked back.

"I meant that about having your children."

His grin flashed quick and wide. "I was hoping you did." Then the door closed quietly behind him.

Smiling, Nica started for the door to lock it, her thoughts tender and optimistic.

And no match for the sudden pain that dropped her to her knees, or the dream that sucked her under. A dream of blood and death.

Three hours later, MacCreedy ran out of reasons to stay away from his apartment.

He'd checked in with Babineau then Caissie, who reported that her new furnishings looked fantastic but her decorator was still close-lipped. Amber had given him two names at the bar: Janie Webb and Tandy Barrett. He called the names in to Dovion to see if they matched the DNA profile.

As he stood on the steps outside his building, Silas gave in and reached for his phone.

No answer. Right to voice mail.

Maybe he should go check...

Silas reined in the impulse and trudged up the stairs.

Brigit was pacing his living room. Her usually polished appearance was showing signs of wear. Her fiery hair was held back in a simple clip from a pinched, makeup-free face. It softened his mood toward her, until she spoke.

"It's about damned time. You could call, you know. Kendra just went out to pick up some food. We didn't know when you'd be—" She broke off, her eyes flaming bright as she inhaled. "You bastard! How could you do this to her?"

"Bree—"

"I will *not* let you break her heart, not after all she's been through. She can't know—"

"She *has* to know." He took her shoulders, squeezing to convince her of his sincerity. "Bree, I have to tell her."

His sister went very still, looking alarmed as she searched his features. "Tell her what? You've loved her since we were children. This is how things were meant to be."

"And I will always love her through the eyes of that child. Bree, I'm not fourteen anymore. Try to understand."

"What's to understand? You're not thinking with your brain or your heart. Don't throw everything away on a moment's lust."

"I want to spend the rest of my life with Nica, Bree."

Brigit looked over his shoulder, her eyes widening in dismay, and Silas turned to see Kendra in the doorway.

Hurt, shock, betrayal, and grief filled her huge, welling eyes as she stared at him. The grocery bags dropped from slack fingers. A choking sound escaped her, then she bolted for the bedroom.

Brigit glared damnation at him, shoving him out of the way to go after her friend. The slam of the door closed a chapter in his life that he could never reopen, one of youth and hope and innocence.

Silas went to wait on the couch, while the muffled sounds of weeping teethed on his conscience. He didn't look up when Brigit returned sometime later and sat on the arm of the couch next to him.

"I need to tell her how sorry I am," he said. He needed to find some way to relieve the crushing guilt that sat on his heart like a boulder.

"Believe me, she doesn't want to hear that right now. You can't make it disappear with a few regretful sentiments. What did you think would happen after you pulled her security out from under her?"

His head hung low, his sturdy frame slumped. "I never planned to hurt her," he said hoarsely. "I meant what I said last night. I wanted to make things work out. I tried to keep my promises, Bree. I really did."

The tremor that shook his strong shoulders shocked Brigit even more than his outrageous choice. She'd never seen anything come close to breaking him down. Not when they were children and he was their ever-indulgent guardian. Not when he'd come racing up the stairs that night, face blanched of color, to take the two of them in his arms saying, "Don't be afraid. I will never let anything harm you," in the low, fierce voice of the man he'd become at that moment. Not when he'd gone to his knees with a stoic determination before monsters, pledging loyalty in order to protect them. He'd bent, but never broken—which told her how horrendously he suffered now. Part of her coldly said, *Good*. But another would do anything to ease that pain.

She laid her cheek against his hair as her arms went around him, and she told him softly, "You're not the only eligible male in the world who'd make Kendra a good match." She kissed his brow. "She'll survive this. She'll find another champion."

He shook his head. "I tried to convince myself that it'd be enough. That I could take Kendra for my mate and live off the Terriots' charity. But how could I do that when I'd be everything this brand of shame on my wrist says I am? A dog, a slave, a coward—eating tamely from the hands of those who killed our mother and father right in front of me." His voice fractured. "Who made me fix the heads of our relatives on poles around their dinner table, so they could see through their dead eyes how far I'd fallen."

Brigit had never known that. Appalled, she hugged him hard, her tone protectively angry. "You're *none* of those things. If anything, they would have looked on you with pride. You refused to disavow our name and take that of Terriot, when it would have made things easier for you."

He was silent for a long while. Then he put his hands over hers to squeeze lightly.

"Tina Babineau and her son are our family, too, Bree. She's our sister—yet we were going to use her the same way the Terriots used our parents to try to get what they wanted. We should have welcomed them into our arms instead of selling them into slavery, just so we could have a greater taste of freedom. I don't want to live that lie anymore."

She swallowed down her fear. "What do you want?"

"I want what I've seen here—what I think Savoie is going to be able to do here in New Orleans. He has the kind of vision our father would have approved of. He's offered me opportunities I want to grab onto."

"Silas, he'll get you killed." Her voice trembled.

"I've been living on borrowed time for years, without really living. I've learned things in the last few days that have turned everything I believed upside down. I'm afraid I've trusted in the wrong things."

"And the right things are the son of our enemy and this girlfriend of yours?"

"Yes."

Brigit sat back, releasing him, fighting her panic. "So what happens to us, now that you have this new dream?"

He glanced up at her, his eyes so guileless and filled with hope that it wrung her heart. "You'll stay here with me."

Brigit gave his apartment a critical sweep. "Hmmmm, tempting, but not quite what I'm accustomed to. Here among the humans, with this lowly clan rabble to protect us? I think not."

A slight smile. "You're such a snob."

"Once one lowers their standards, there's no limit as to how far they can fall. And Uprights make me nervous." She straightened, concealing her fear behind arrogance, knowing she could sway him if he saw through it. Knowing he would make any sacrifice to take care of her.

So, she wouldn't let him see her distress. She owed him that, because she loved him.

She gave an indignant sniff. "Besides, I don't think Kendra and I would feel comfortable sharing these rooms with your future mate."

He suddenly frowned. There was something else troubling him. He asked, "Bree, do you have any talents that are . . . unique? Something you haven't told me about?"

"Other than the ability to attract the worst kind of male?"

"I'm serious."

She grew evasive. "A girl has to have her secrets."

"This is important, Brigit. Are there things you can do that others can't? Things beyond what normal Shifter females are capable of? Can you change shape?"

"What?" Her shock was genuine. "Of course not." Then she placed her palm to his cheek. "I'm painfully ordinary."

Silas knew she was lying to him. Irritation and concern made him want to both shake her and hold her close.

Then she asked, "Are you in love with that creature?"

"Yes."

"Are you sure it's not just a physical thing?"

He crooked a smile at her. "It's a soul thing. The kind you told me of when we were children. So you can say 'I told you so' now."

Brigit shook her head, clearly mystified. "I don't see

the attraction. You have Kendra, who adores you, is beautiful, kind, well-bred, and would never give a moment's grief. Yet you prefer that bold, rude, skinny bitch who thrives on making things unpleasant."

Silas smiled, tenderness in his eyes. "She makes me feel alive, Bree. Kendra's like a safe, peaceful place without distractions or complications where you can go to escape. It's nice for a while, but I'd get restless there." His eyes smoldered. "Nica is like a ride on a runaway train. Reckless, exciting, dangerous, and unexpectedly fun. Every second I'm with her makes my blood pound."

He looked up at Brigit earnestly, needing her to understand. "She gets me, Bree. She laughs at me and calls me 'Hero.' I don't have to be *more* than I am when I'm with her. What I am is enough. She makes me want to be selfish when we're together. Does that make any sense?"

She heaved a huge sigh. "She makes you happy. Damn. I guess I'm going to have to tolerate her."

"You can start by not calling her 'that creature' or 'that bitch.'"

Brigit wrinkled her nose. "Nica. An odd name. What did you say it was? Monica? I'll call her that. She won't like it."

"This means everything to me, Bree."

Brigit could see it did, so she surrendered. "She'd better appreciate you, or she'll have me to deal with."

"She'd be wise to worry." Then he looked at the closed

bedroom door. "What are the two of you going to do now?"

"We'll land on our feet. You're not the only clever one in the family."

His cell rang, and he answered, "This is Mac."

"How soon can you get over here?" Charlotte asked.

Twenty-two

She got here about an hour ago, beat to shit, with the little kid in tow."

MacCreedy peered into the bedroom. A battered Lena Blutafino was curled up in the huge bed with her arms about a small boy. Both were deep in exhausted sleep. He shut the door quietly and followed Cee Cee to the living room.

Things had changed since the last time he'd been in the apartment. It was an elegant work in progress with natural stone, deep, tranquil colors, and lush fabrics.

Cee Cee gestured to a pair of overstuffed sofas in dark teal. "Coffee?"

"Black, please." He settled into the comfortable cushions. "Why did you call me?"

"Max had to slip out quick. Alain picked him up. He's going to stay with him."

A wry smile. "That'll be pleasant for them."

Cee Cee appreciated his dark humor. "I couldn't reach Nica. I thought maybe she was with you."

"No."

She brought him a big mug filled with a brew so strong, the chicory scent alone was an adrenaline rush.

She noted his uneasy expression without comment. "You're a bright guy, already on the inside with Manny. Alain trusts you and I'm inclined to agree with his judgment."

"Thanks. What do you need?"

"Lena's scared, and she should be. She wants to get out of town and disappear in exchange for later testimony. She doesn't trust the system—especially the police."

"Smart girl," he muttered.

"She needs money."

"How much?"

"A lot. She can't touch her own accounts."

"We can't go through the department. Can Savoie give her cash?"

"Not from the grave."

"Ahh. I see the problem." He thought for a moment, then glanced up at her with a gleam in his eyes. "I have an idea. I need to discuss it with Max first."

Cee Cee smiled and nodded. "I like you, Mac. You're a good man to work with. I don't want that to change."

His features stilled. "Are we getting away from business?"

"Oh, it's business. Personal business. Max told me about Rollo, and how his greed ripped the figurative guts out of your family."

Not a muscle in his face moved.

"I'm glad the selfish bastard's dead," she continued, holding that fierce eye contact. "Max tells me the two of you are squared away. Is that how you see it, too?"

"Yes."

"You're Tina's half brother, Ozzy's uncle. That almost makes us related."

A twitch of a smile, but she could tell he was still wary.

"If you're like Max, there's nothing more important to you than family. Not your own personal agendas, not your own feelings."

"Where are you going with this, Charlotte?"

"Why did Nica come back to New Orleans, Mac?"

"She has a job here."

"Does that job involve killing Max?"

"I don't know. Really, I don't."

"If it does, could you stop her?"

"No."

"Would you try?"

"Are you asking me where I'd stand?"

"If a threat comes at Max I stand beside him, if not in front of him. I'm guessing that you feel the same about her."

His quiet growl threw the gloves off. "To my last heartbeat."

"If I have to go through you to stop her, I will."

"Understood."

Cee Cee leaned back on the adjacent couch with a sigh. "Well, this just sucks, doesn't it?"

"Yes, it does."

Cee Cee drew out her ankle piece, the one she kept loaded with silver. He didn't make a move as she placed it on the table between them.

"I don't want things to go down like this, Mac. I don't want anyone to get hurt."

He met her determined gaze. "I don't, either. I want to make a home here with Nica. She has no choice in the things she's doing."

"But you do, Mac."

"And I'd choose her every time. I want to work together to protect our family, Charlotte. She's in trouble. I'm trying to help her, but I can't do it alone."

"What do you need?" Right to the point.

His grateful smile flickered. "Time. Don't let Max force me to act in her defense, because I will."

"In return, I expect a warning if you can't keep things under control."

He considered that carefully, then nodded. "Fair enough."

MacCreedy stepped out of the rain into the quiet interior of St. Bart's. His footsteps echoed.

"Detective MacCreedy. I've been expecting you." The priest was sitting in the first pew.

Silas slid into the one behind him. "You said you knew my mother."

"She was a lovely woman who adored your father and her children. She was willing to make any sacrifices for them."

"Including giving one of them up to you?"

"Yes. It was an incredibly difficult decision for her to make, but with your father's support, she was able to."

"And it killed them."

"I regret that."

"Was saving Tina worth their deaths to you?"

Furness turned and placed a big hand on Silas's shoulder. "Is that the question you came here to ask?"

"If I protect the boy, it could cost me everything."

"Yes, it could. Is it that sacrifice that concerns you?"

"I've given over twenty years of my life to protect my family, and if I do this, it could be for nothing."

"Where's your faith?"

Silas laughed angrily. "My faith died with my parents."

"Did it? Or was that when it was born?"

"Don't play games with me, Father. I don't want to argue theology."

"Your father was a man of tremendous principles, as I believe you are. He saw things on a larger scale that made the more personal choices less difficult, but no less painful."

Silas took an anguished breath. "I will *not* let those I love suffer for some greater good. You know how I can save them. Tell me what I can do. Help me protect them."

That large hand pressed gently. "You have to let them go."

MacCreedy threw off his consoling grip. "No! I won't."

"You have a different path now—one they can't follow. Let them discover their own. Let them go. You can't deny your fate."

"Fuck fate. I don't believe in it any more than I believe in faith."

"Yes, you do." Furness smiled at him, not offended and not deterred. "It's brought you here, right where you need to be to do the things you must. You look like your father. He was a strong, decent man, determined to make the right choices. We had a similar discussion when he came to me with a broken heart because the child he thought was his had been fathered by another."

Struggling with fury and fear, Silas drew a calming breath. "What did you tell him?"

"I reminded him of Joseph and his decision."

"My half sister's conception was hardly immaculate. It was a rape of everything my mother believed in."

"I told him I had no answers for him. I told him they were already inside his soul."

With a curse, MacCreedy surged to his feet. "I've wasted my time here."

Furness caught his wrist, the one branded by the Terriots, and held tight. Unable to break free, MacCreedy glared down at the priest.

"He didn't need my answers," Furness told him firmly. "He already knew them. He came to me for permission to take the path he'd already chosen. Isn't that why you're here, Silas? You don't need my blessing any more than he did."

"But I love them."

"And the strength of that love will sustain them on their own journeys."

MacCreedy sank onto the padded seat, resting his forehead on the back of hands that clenched the pew back in front of him.

"There's a great darkness coming, Silas," the priest told him. "You have your mother's compassion, your father's wisdom, and your own courage of conviction. Max will need you if the community here is to survive. You will be his Michael—his sword of justice, his edge of reason."

"And Nica," he whispered roughly. "Am I supposed to let her go, too?"

Furness's hand clamped down on the back of his neck. Hard. "No. Her you keep close, as close as you can."

His gaze lifted, seeking answers.

"You need each other, Silas. Keep her with you."

"I don't know how to protect her."

"Yes, you do. Give her your strength. Earn her trust. I never could, and I've always regretted that. Don't let darkness control her."

"Do you know who they are? Do you know how I can get her free of them?" He gripped the priest's robes. "Do you know where I can find them?"

That rough hand gently covered MacCreedy's again. "Yes, and I will tell you. But first, you must save her from herself."

Nica paced the floor of her condo with restless energy, moving from room to room to keep the tension at bay.

Stop fighting.

She shook off the impatient voice echoing through her head. She wouldn't listen. She wouldn't give in.

Go ahead and call him. You know you want to. Invite him over. I don't mind.

"Three's a crowd, Hawthorne. Go get your kicks on the Internet."

The pain crested in a powerful wave, making her legs buckle. She stumbled but kept moving, staggering, leaning into the wall for balance. *Don't think of MacCreedy,* she told herself. *Don't think of how much you want him. How much you need him.*

Call him, Nica. We could arrange a delightful greeting for him. Couldn't we, darling?

Images flashed through her mind, gruesome, vicious visions of what Hawthorne wanted done. Horrible things of which she knew she was capable.

"Get out of my head, you bastard! I'm not calling him. I don't need anyone. Let's just keep it you and me, *darlin'.*" She smiled ferociously and swayed through the living room like a drunk. *Keep moving,* she reminded herself. *Out distance the pain. Walk it off. Move through it.*

Her cell was on the table. It held MacCreedy's messages. All she had to do was pick it up and she could hear his voice. A touch of one button would bring him to her side.

So that she could kill him.

Nica picked up her phone and flung it against the bricks, where it shattered into a satisfying number of pieces. Her wild, frantic laugh broke off at the sound of a knock at the door, and she froze.

Another knock, more insistent.

"Go away. Please," she whispered.

"Nica?"

"Nooooo. Silas, please just go."

"Nica!" Pounding now.

Had she remembered the dead bolt? The regular lock wouldn't keep him out. Nica started toward the door, reeling, running, reaching for the disengaged lock just as the door swung inward. She saw the tremendous relief in his eyes at the sight of her; then she was in his arms.

"Run," she panted against his neck. "Not safe here. Run, Silas, now."

She pushed him away, sending him back into the hall. Before she could close the door he had his shoulder against it, shoving his way in. When she strode away from him toward the living room, she heard him click the lock into place.

"What's going on?"

He was drenched from the downpour that beat against the skylight. His hair lay dark and sleek against his head. His shirt was plastered to the sculpted line of his body. He entered the living room and took in the phone debris, then he looked at her again, closely. Cautiously.

"I got tired of hearing it ring. I didn't want to talk to you. I don't want you here. I'm not good company, MacCreedy." She held his gaze, betraying nothing with her own.

"I was worried," he told her, coming nearer.

She put up staying hands, gesturing low for him to keep away, conveying what she couldn't in words. Because someone else was listening, watching through her eyes.

"I'm fine. I really need you to go, right *now*." *Run! Silas, run!*

His scent rolled over her, blending with those harsh pulses of pain, becoming one and the same, one constant demand. He was the cause of her misery. He was bringing the ceaseless agony that wracked her body, along with the conflicts torturing heart and mind. There was only one way to end it. Only one way to make it stop.

Nica turned away, pressing the heels of her hands against her temples, squeezing her eyes shut, but the message continued to stab through her head.

Kill him. Do it now. Quickly, then it will end. Now, Nica! Save yourself. Save them!

She whirled, tears on her cheeks, her nails lengthening into razor-sharp claws.

But he'd moved swiftly, sidestepping her attack. MacCreedy caught her wrist, twisting with surprising force. His other hand clamped tight about her neck, driving her down onto her back in a body slam that knocked the breath from her. But only for a moment. She was sobbing now. She'd wanted it to be a quick, clean kill, as merciful for them both as she could make it, and now it was going to get messy.

MacCreedy was astride her, pinning her arms and legs with the wrap of his own. His body mass doubled, the increased weight mashing her into the carpet, his expanding bulk ripping through the seams of his cotton T-shirt and jeans. The angles of his face altered, lengthening, stretching to accommodate the sharp teeth he bared. His eyes were on fire, bloodred and hot ice blue.

Here was the raw male power and strength she'd only guessed at. He was the most fearsomely arousing thing she'd ever seen, because he could have slain her in an instant, but refrained.

Something in the compelling brilliance of his gaze penetrated the fog of pain imprisoning her mind, scattering it like the blast of a gale-force wind. She gasped as he released one of her hands to clasp her jaw, stilling the thrash of her head with paralyzing pressure. His stare pierced hers like a surgical laser as he leaned closer to speak in a harsh, tearing snarl.

"Let her go, you son of a bitch. This is *my* female and you will *not* take her from me."

All the torturous pain and pressure disappeared in an instant, the sudden shock leaving Nica astonished.

My female.

She made a soft, wondering sound, then gripped the back of MacCreedy's neck for a savage kiss. Her claws ripped through what was left of his shirt as she rolled above him, never surrendering that fierce, biting, lapping kiss. He tore off her shirt, gripped the waistband of her jeans and rent them in half so he could possess her.

The feel of him pounding so close to the heat of her became an unbearable frustration. She yanked down his zipper and murmured an impressed epithet as they stripped off the remainder of their clothing. Then he sat up, his arms circling her in a possessive crush as he kissed her mouth, her throat, her breasts with hungry determination.

She gripped his wet hair, twining the new shaggy length of it in her fists, stilling him long enough to pant, "The bed?"

"Here," he growled. "I love this rug. I knew you were the only one for me from the first time you kissed me."

She leaned into his hard chest and even harder sex, rocking against him as her own physiology changed, becoming his equal.

His mouth was hot against her ear, her neck, her shoulder. Feeling her tense, he nuzzled her gently, whispering, "Are you ready for me?"

"Make me yours, MacCreedy."

With his touch, his kisses he lavished attention to her shoulders, along her spine, until any trace of apprehension heated into anticipation. When he lifted her hips, she was wet and eager to receive him. But even prepared, she hadn't expected the size of him, biting back a sharp cry as he breached her.

MacCreedy immediately stilled, panting with the effort. He couldn't bear to hurt her, yet he couldn't bear to let her go. Nica solved the problem by easing him in slowly, steadily. Her slender figure shook and quivered.

The feel of her around him was like nothing he'd ever experienced. Like he'd never known pleasure. His senses were so alive, they burned and tingled. Like the first time he saw her. The first time he recognized without comprehension that she was the one, the only one he would ever need to possess with this fierce, blinding urgency. To claim. To hold. Forever.

With a throaty rumble of satisfaction, Nica began to rise and fall in time with his increasingly ragged breaths.

Sensations, hot, primal, and glorious, swelled within her. Her eyes squeezed shut as a smile curved her parted lips because this was *her* man, *her* male, *her* mate taking this rough, wild ride with her.

Tension gathered into a tight, pounding beat. Instinctively, Nica rolled her head so her hair slid away, baring the curve of her neck and shoulder for the hot graze of MacCreedy's breath. Then his bite.

Piercing pain streaked to the heart of her. Nica tried to pull away but she was held tight, caught between the strength of his jaws and length of his sex. He bit down harder, drawing at the wound where he'd marked her, plunging into her, and suddenly her entire reality changed.

Nica's senses exploded outward, dazzling her with such splendor that she cried out, then again as a fierce orgasm shook her to the soul. The strong jolts of pleasure sent shock waves through the dreamscape surrounding her.

Unlike the nightmare Hawthorne sucked her into, this delighted her with strange flashes of light and snatches of sound as she spiraled through time and space and awareness. And Silas was with her, his scent stroking her like a caress, his panting breaths pulsing over her in a hot tide until the sudden force of his release sent her spinning on another giddy ride.

My God, it was wonderful!

All too soon, reality trickled back into her consciousness. She could feel the crushed nap of the carpet under her, the damp mat of MacCreedy's hair as his chest rose and fell. They were lying side by side, her head on his outflung arm. His heart pounded beneath her palm like thunder.

"Holy shit," she whispered as she began the incredible effort of opening her eyes.

"Holy shit," MacCreedy groaned beside her. His hand covered hers and they lay like that for several more minutes. He stirred at the sound of her husky chuckle, rolling onto his side, looking dazed and sweaty and gorgeous.

Hers.

That realization blossomed beautifully inside her.

"I am so glad you didn't let me kill you," she murmured with a lazy smile.

"I'm kinda happy about that myself." He leaned down to kiss her softly.

"I hope this experience was more pleasant than your first," Nica teased, sucking lightly at his lips.

"You inspired me to great heights of passion," he assured her, tongue flickering against hers until their kiss deepened.

Nica laughed again, her gaze lost in his. "You're *still* inspired, lover." Her admiring touch stroked over that apparent truth. "Should we take advantage of it?"

He kissed her tenderly before he whispered, "I'm thinking shower, bed, and lots more sex."

"My hero," she purred in surrender.

As thick, relaxing steam filled the bathroom, they washed each other behind the wall of glass. MacCreedy tended the already healing wounds in her shoulder, their significance filling him with a dizzying sense of possessiveness and devotion. He kissed her there, tenderly, then her mouth lavishly, until he'd backed her against one of the granite shower walls. Under the double rain forest shower heads, he drew her knee up over his hip so he could take her again more slowly.

And again as they were drying off. He cleared the edge of the sink with a sweep of his arm and set her there for another enthusiastic coupling, as hot and steamy as the room.

By the time they sank into the soft embrace of the bed, it was almost morning.

Silas cradled Nica in his arms, the feel of her so perfect and right he wasn't sure he could ever let her go. Her face was pressed into his shoulder, her body was trembling, and he felt the hot dampness of tears against his skin.

"You came," she whispered hoarsely.

He smiled into her fragrant hair. "Yes, I did. More than once. Thank you."

Her chest hitched almost painfully. "You picked the lock on my door."

"I'd have torn down the wall," he said huskily.

She fell silent, kneading the back of his neck and his upper arm with unspoken anxiousness. Finally she asked, "What happens now?"

Exhausted, yet so satisfied he couldn't stop touching her, he stroked the long velvety line of her back. "I'm moving in with you. I love this bed, that shower, the rug in the living room, and the company."

"What happens to us?" she asked after a pause.

Us. He rubbed his cheek against the top of her head, emotions swelling up so quick and full, it took him a moment to speak.

"I'm staying here in New Orleans. I have my job, and Savoie's proposed a couple of interesting ideas I'll want to discuss with you. You're not going to kill me or anyone else. You're retiring. Does that sound okay to you?"

"What about your family?"

He tipped her head back so she could see him. "You mean the rest of my family?"

Her eyes shimmered like precious stones.

"I want to get to know my sister and nephew. Brigit won't be staying. Things are too tame for her here."

"And Kendra?"

"She hasn't mentioned her plans to me." He stroked her cheek with his thumb. "And we're going to find *your* family and make sure they're safe."

Her expression stilled. "Don't make me promises, Silas."

"Why? Don't you trust me to keep them?"

"We wouldn't be here like this if I didn't." There was no doubt in her gaze. There was worry.

Twenty-three

Nica.

She stirred languidly beneath the covers as the low purr of MacCreedy's voice stroked through her. Delicious sensations of warmth shimmered just beneath the surface of consciousness, nudging away her dreams. Her hand reached across the sheet in search of him and her eyes opened. He wasn't in bed beside her. Nor was he in the room.

The television was on and she smelled good coffee.

Knotting the belt to her robe, she moved down the hallway and found her big, nearly naked lover at her table breakfasting on a fried egg on toast, yogurt, and half a grapefruit. He pointed at the TV screen with his spoon.

"They still assume it was Savoie in that car. I made coffee."

How annoying to have someone so wide awake and businesslike at six A.M., expecting conversation.

As she walked in front of the TV, his gaze lifted to linger on her. Now *that*, she liked. Hot coffee and a hotter stare.

Nica poured herself a cup, frowning slightly at the

clutter and juice stains on the countertop. He'd made himself at home very quickly. His attention was back on the television by the time she reentered the room and she paused.

How did this mated-couple thing work?

She wasn't a morning person. Was he expecting her to get all snuggly with him before she'd had coffee? She liked to begin her day in silence—not with network chatter and the pressures of civility.

MacCreedy toed out a chair for her while concentrating on his meal and the top-of-the-hour news. She took the seat with a scowl. Her shoulder ached, and she felt uncertain as to how their new relationship was going to mesh into her life. Tossing a man out the door after hot sex was a lot simpler than entertaining him in the morning.

What was she supposed to do? Should she have gotten up to feed him? Was she expected to pretend to enjoy the disruption of her routine? Did he expect cheerful conversation?

Apparently MacCreedy didn't expect anything. He finished his meal, carried his dishes to the kitchen, and did a quick, efficient cleanup before asking, "Can I get you something?"

"No thanks. Just coffee's fine."

As she was thinking things might be very fine indeed, he came up behind her and touched a light kiss to her nape.

"I hope the noise didn't wake you. I usually catch

the news with my morning coffee. I should have asked first."

"No, it's okay. It didn't wake me."

His big hands massaged her upper arms gently before he turned off the remote and went to settle on the love seat, leaning his head back and closing his eyes. Wearing just his undershorts, he was better than a jolt of caffeine. Her gaze drifted along his strong body in appreciation. *This* was something she could get used to every morning.

"Could I get you to do something for me?" he asked without opening his eyes.

The slight discomfort in his tone made her curious. She took her coffee and went to sit astride his lap, her arm going about his neck as she breathed softly into his ear. "What else would you like me to blow into?"

His eyes popped open and she had his complete attention. His blush charmed her. He wrapped his arms around her with a grin.

"That wasn't what I had in mind, but I like the way you think." He tucked her in beside him and kissed her brow. They were snuggling, and she was enjoying it. "I have no clothes."

"I like that about you. Can I keep you here as my sex toy?"

"Hmmm. I may have to rethink my request."

"Which is what?"

"Since what I wore last night is in shreds, I'm going to need some stuff from my apartment. And since I can't really go out like this . . ."

"You want me to go wrestle your belongings away from your sister and your fiancée?"

"Would you? I know it's a lot to ask." He frowned and looked even more uncomfortable. "I tried calling, but Brigit isn't picking up."

Nica kissed him soundly. "You're going to owe me for this, MacCreedy. I don't know much about relationships, but even I know this is above and beyond."

"Thank you, Nica."

"Talk is cheap, lover. You can thank me later."

Though she had MacCreedy's key, using it seemed too rude so she knocked.

The door was answered by a lovely little blonde with fatigue-smudged eyes.

"You must be Kendra. I'm Nica. MacCreedy asked me to stop by and pick up a couple of things for him."

The ex-fiancée stepped aside in a stupor of dismay to let her in. "Silas couldn't come for them himself?"

"He wasn't exactly in a position to." Nica cast a wary eye about the room. "Is Brigit here?"

"She had to run a few errands. She should be back soon. His things are back here," Kendra said in a fragile voice as she went down the hall.

In a surly humor, Nica followed. She wanted to fling harsh, defensively spiteful words at the girl. *I know where his things are. In fact, I know more about him than you ever will. I've already slept with him in his bed, and now he's in mine.*

Her jaw ached with the effort of silence as she sized up the tiny figure as weak and delicate, her manner as helplessly passive. Was that what drew MacCreedy, with his rescuing-hero complex? An aggressive jealousy shimmered through her, a feeling she had no experience with. Competition, she understood. Rivalry, she thrived upon. But how could she confront and overcome something as tenuous as emotional selfishness?

Instead of leaving Nica alone, Kendra sat on the bed and watched her like she was a thief intent on sneaking off with the family jewels.

Determined to ignore her, Nica went to the closet. When she pulled open the door, the essence of the man she loved flooded over her—his scent, the sight of his familiar clothing, the feel of his jacket. For a moment, she was lost to sensual pleasures.

Nica shook off the sentimentality. They were just clothes. She grabbed a couple of his suit coats and white shirts and tossed them onto the bed, then pulled a gym bag out of the closet. When she turned, she saw Kendra lift up one of the jackets, carrying it up to her cheek as dampness gathered on the fringe of her lashes. Nica froze, shocked, then rattled by the implied intimacy.

Why was she surprised? Nica chided herself fiercely. She knew they'd loved each other, that Silas had planned to take Kendra as his mate and share his future with her. And in truth, Nica probably knew only a smidgen of what Kendra did about the man she'd stolen away from her. Nica knew very little about him at all, especially why he'd leave a sweet child like Kendra in the lurch for a bad bet like herself. And that made her cross enough to want to rip the coat from the other's hands—or join her in tears.

Damn all men, anyway.

Nica stepped over the heaps of female paraphernalia that came with two houseguests. From his dresser she snatched out underwear, socks, and jeans, several T-shirts, and two ties.

"We grew up together," Kendra said quietly.

"Yes, I know." Her reply was sharper than she meant it to be.

"He was smart and kind and brave, my dearest friend."

"Was." Like he'd died or something.

"After my mother died when I was little, he was the only one who could comfort me. He'd sit with me until I'd fall back to sleep, sometimes for hours."

Nica didn't want to picture a young Silas rocking the little girl in his arms, charming her from her fears with his soothing voice. The same way he'd done with her. How could Kendra help but fall in love with him?

Another thought crept in unexpectedly. What a wonderful father he'd make.

"How did your mother die?" Nica asked stiffly.

"She—she was killed."

"I never knew my mother." The information was out before Nica could wonder why.

"I'm sorry."

Why should *she* be sorry? Nica whirled and stuffed

the clothing randomly into MacCreedy's bag, anxious to escape this uncomfortable discussion and those big, now curious, eyes. She hurried into the bathroom, finding his travel pouch under the sink and loading his toiletries into it, her insides shaking.

When Nica returned to the bedroom, she glanced from the now neatly arranged bag to Kendra's hands as she folded his charcoal gray suit coat, tucking it gently inside. Temper and panic quaking through her, Nica grabbed the bag, shoved in the travel kit, and jerked at the zipper.

"Don't forget this." Kendra took a denim jacket from the closet. "It's always been his favorite." She extended it, meeting Nica's stare fully for the first time. Then she said simply, "He must really love you."

Nica pushed the jacket back at Kendra. "I've got enough here. He can come back for that. I'm sure he'll want to spend some time with you and his sister before you leave."

Smiling bravely, Kendra clutched the coat.

Nica shouldered the bag, draped the freshly dry-cleaned tux over her arm, and grabbed his polished shoes off the floor. Then she rushed from the room, only to collide with Brigit at the door.

The redhead stoically took in the sight of her brother's exiting belongings. Then her gaze widened as Nica's T-shirt shifted from the bag's strap, revealing the marks on her shoulder. Marks of possession. Brigit made a stricken sound, then quickly moved forward. Her hands full, Nica readied for an attack.

Embracing her a little too tightly, Brigit surprised her by saying, "Please be good to him. He deserves to be happy." Then she rushed to the bedroom.

Nica stumbled down the stairs, struggling with an unknown upset. It was as if they were sending her off with his clothes to bury him. Was that how they saw her, as a fate worse than death? As if the evil stepsister had breached their fairy tale and stole the prince out from under them, toothbrush and all?

She rushed down the sidewalk, trying to outdistance her distress. By the time she collapsed into her elevator, she was a mess of raw emotions. She had to key the door three times for it to green-light. And after shooting the dead bolt on the outside world, the first thing she heard was the low rumble of his voice.

She followed the sound into the living room. He was on the phone, bending over the table to jot something down on the back of her phone book. The sight of him in his butt-hugging briefs gave her heart a quick kick start.

MacCreedy turned at the sound of his belongings being dumped on the floor and saw Nica disappearing down the hallway. Frowning slightly, he ended his call and pulled on jeans before going after her.

She was in the bathroom brushing her hair with swift, brutal motions until it snapped with electricity. As did her mood.

"Do you want me to camp out in the living room?"

The rhythm of her arm was interrupted briefly; then she continued the fierce strokes. "That would be foolish, since you didn't invite yourself to move in to sleep on the couch."

"Can I put my stuff away in your room?"

She glared at him, something dark and dangerous glittering in her eyes. "Where else would you put it?"

"From the mood you're in, I thought maybe you wanted it out on the curb."

"I wouldn't have dragged it all the way over here if that's where I wanted it."

"Just checking."

"And I'm not in a 'mood.'"

Oooookay. He'd grown up with two females. He knew when it was smart to back away without argument.

Silas retrieved his things. The bathroom door was closed as he passed by on the way to the bedroom. Her unexplained temper had him cautious, but the satisfaction of settling in with her soon overcame it.

She had surprisingly few possessions. He found an empty drawer in the dresser and plenty of available hangers in the closet.

As he was hanging up his jacket, Kendra's scent came tumbling out of the folds. The intensity made him think she'd held it close, not just touched it. That quickened his worry. It couldn't have been a pleasant meeting. Why hadn't he considered the feelings of these two females he loved more carefully?

There was no way to deal with Kendra's hurt and humiliation at the moment. But he did have a very prickly female right here who was undoubtedly rethinking their living arrangement. And regrets, he couldn't allow.

As he was shoving his empty bag into the back of the closet, it bumped into another piece of carry-on. Mac-Creedy drew out the battered backpack with its taunting lock, remembering the desperate gratitude in Nica's eyes when he'd returned it to her. He gave it a slight shake, hearing loose items rattle inside it.

"What are you doing?"

He turned toward the door with a guilty start. "I was just putting my things away."

Her glare filled with angry fire, Nica snatched the backpack from him. "This is mine. Keep your hands off it. If you think you can snoop around where you don't belong, you're mistaken. In fact, this whole idea was a mistake." Bag clutched to her chest, she whirled toward the door.

Nica, don't walk away. Trust me!

She stopped, her body tense and suddenly trembling. Slowly, she came about, her wary gaze lifting to his.

"I know this has been sudden," Silas began, his voice low and calming, as if he didn't realized he'd projected his thoughts. "I know you're upset and afraid and angry. I'm not trying to crowd you or control you, Nica. I don't want to change you. I'm not going to pry into your past or ask you to do anything you don't want to do. It's going to be you doing your thing and me doing my thing, until we can figure out how to make those things work together. I want us to *be* together. Fifty-fifty. Two halves, one whole. Is that what you want, too?"

A stiff nod.

"Good, because I'm in this for the long haul. I'm not going to leave you. I know it's awkward sharing space. For me, too." That was a lie. There was nothing Silas loved more than the sound of family chaos around him. He thrived on it. The surrounding sense of love fed his soul and he'd been starving for it. The loneliness was what tore him apart.

But that wasn't where Nica had come from, so he had to go slow and not frighten or overwhelm her. He could do that. He could do anything but let her go.

Slowly, he stretched out a hand to take one of the straps to her backpack. After a moment's hesitation, she released it and let him put it on the bed behind him.

"Trust me, Nica. Let me be part of your life. Let me protect you. Let me be strong for you. Let me be whatever you need, whenever you need it. All you have to do is ask."

Nica stood very still for a very long time, never looking away from the intensity of his stare. Finally, she said, "I need you, Silas. I don't want to do this alone anymore. I need you here with me."

He made a beckoning gesture with his fingers and she stepped into his arms. He simply held her until the tension finally left her shoulders.

"Silas?" she asked at last. "If we're two halves of one whole, what do you get out of it?"

He heard the wealth of her doubts and insecurities in that simple question, so he replied, "You. I love you. I love having sex with you. And I'm going to love coming home to you." He smiled, feeling her tremendous sigh as her cheek rubbed against his bare chest. A chest filled to bursting.

Then Nica pushed away and climbed onto the bed, pulling the backpack into the circle of her crossed legs. "In here is my whole life. My past. Everything that's ever meant something to me. I want to show you."

He sat on the edge of the bed while she worked the combination lock. When she upended the bag, he found himself looking at weapons and . . . junk. Broken bits and pieces, odds and ends of no value, except to her.

She handed him a chipped blue marble. "That's Henry. I won that from him. He boasted that no one could beat him. I did." She smiled softly as she took it back, rolling it in her palm before letting it drop. Then she picked up a yellowed ladies' dress glove and held it to her nose. He did the same when she passed it to him. A faint fragrance perfumed the fibers, like the one on Nica's skin.

"That's my mother. And this is my father." A valet parking stub from Michigan Avenue in Chicago.

Nica smiled as she showed a crumpled pack of cigarettes, saying, "Lottie," and then a tube of frosted beige lipstick: "Mary Kate." A plain gold cross with a broken chain. "Father Furness."

Silas picked up a token for the St. Charles streetcar. "Who's this?"

She smiled and took it back from him. "Amber." Pointing to a stained cocktail napkin, "Jacques."

As she identified the other trinkets that had belonged to her wild, young friends—a wad of gum rolled in its wrapper, a shoelace, a barrette, a pair of sunglasses with one lens missing, the tattered cover of a comic book—Silas saw them for what they were. Treasures.

He picked up an empty beer bottle, recognizing the brand. As he lifted a brow she reclaimed it, letting her tongue touch the rim. "So I could always taste you."

The bottle fell among the other precious memories as he caught Nica's face between his palms and pulled her into a deep kiss.

They used business as the means to explore the strange new link between them. Concentrating on an outside endeavor made it easier for Nica to allow MacCreedy's mind free access to her own.

At first she fought against the intrusion, scared of giving up even a tiny slice of control. But once MacCreedy turned it into a game and a challenge, she cautiously invited him in.

It began with the deck he'd picked up at a novelty store down the block. He'd focus on a card and she'd pick it from his thoughts. Sensing her reluctance, Silas let her come to him rather than pushing the information upon her.

Their first exchange was nearly his last; her initial attempt sent a blast of energy jolting through him like an electrocution. His system was still twitching with it when he explained how their new connection could be used.

"I had a plan for tonight but this is so much better. They'll never see it coming." He smiled slyly as he wiped his bloody nose.

"What's tonight?"

"A private poker game at Manny's. And an opportunity for you to wear that red dress again. If we're going to stay here in New Orleans, we have to clear out some of the obstacles in our way. We've got lots to do today, starting with a little surge protector control on your part."

They spent the afternoon working the cards. Silas had an obvious gift for them, a psychic talent for reading them, a physical talent for handling them with speed and grace. She liked that about his clever hands. Nica immersed herself in his game, serious and saying little. And with every hour they spent together, she learned more about him.

In some ways, she and Silas were just alike. Manipulators, schemers with smooth surfaces over deep, turbulent waters. They were ruthless predators who'd let nothing get in the way of their end results. Hers was freedom. His was his family's honor.

He'd managed to convince the Terriot clan that he was submissive, the NOPD that he was not only loyal but human, and the über-cautious Max Savoie that he was harmless. But as she watched him flip the cards, she could see exactly what Silas MacCreedy was: determined to win at any cost, but only to the limit of his convictions.

There was a big heart beneath all those glorious muscles. One that couldn't take advantage of a mother and child, one that couldn't cold-bloodedly murder despicable men, or blame a son for a father's misdeeds. Integrity held him back from taking that extra step that she'd been forced to. That step beyond conscience.

And that's what she loved about him.

Together, they gathered strength from each other. He was her steady moral compass. She was his heart to come home to.

And Nica began to believe there was nothing they couldn't do.

Manny Blutafino's invitation-only poker games, Nica learned, were the only time he invested his own funds at the table. The names of the players were kept secret, as was the location of the game until the last possible moment. Only two people were privy to the information in advance: Carmen's right hand, who made the reservations and arranged security, and Carmen's wife, who usually attended on his arm.

Babineau drove in silence to the parking garage of one of the pricey Central Business District hotels. Manny had sent him to pick his dealer up at seven. Silas purposefully hadn't involved Alain in his scheme, to avoid having to choose between cop work and clan business. Accountability was one reason. Unresolved trust issues were another. Mostly, was the fact that Alain was married to Silas's half sister and needed to come out alive.

Despite the danger involved Silas was relaxed and calm, but then, Nica knew he excelled under pressure. He'd kept himself and his family alive by balancing risks with a cool head and calculating reason, by knowing which alliances offered the greatest return. Now that scale had tipped away from the Terriots because of Savoie. And because of her.

She started when his hand settled lightly on her thigh, and her muscles bunched.

"Nervous?" he asked softly, looking straitlaced with his slicked hair and dark-rimmed glasses.

"Hardly. I'm a professional."

He chuckled at her stiff reply, his hand kneading gently. "And you're beautiful."

The compliment rattled her, making her heart flutter, though her answer was wry. "I try to fit the part I'm playing."

Since she wasn't beautiful, despite what MacCreedy thought, Nica had taken extra care to appear elegant. The red dress he so admired lent her a long, sleek silhouette atop the killer heels. To accentuate that she'd pulled her hair up off her neck, securing it in a coronet of small braids and loose curls he couldn't seem to keep his fingers out of. Imitation jewels sparkled at her ears and wrist, and a filmy scarf knotted at the side concealed the still visible scar of MacCreedy's mark.

She'd been bold with her cosmetics, drawing heavy

lines about her eyes and lips so they stood out in stark, dramatic relief. Even if she wasn't beautiful, she was striking, and just the seemingly harmless distraction the evening required.

And as they rode up in the elevator, his hand at her waist, his gaze lingering over her all possessive and pleased, Nica shivered with unfamiliar delight. Because in his eyes, she knew she *was* lovely.

The huge suite with its panoramic view of the city featured a stocked bar and a buffet, but the focus was the big round table in the center of the room. Babineau took them to the door, then turned them over to Todd, the bulky security man from the Sweat Shop. Todd returned Nica's smile, then pulled Silas to one side.

"Boss didn't say nothing about you bringing your lady."

MacCreedy leaned in to confide, "We had plans for tonight, and she's been giving me grief about never taking her anywhere. Give me a break, man. I just moved into her place, and I'd rather be sleeping in the bedroom than on the couch. Put her to work. Give her something to do. Just don't kick her out."

Todd gave Nica a lingering assessment. "Not much to her. A little skinny and a little too old for Manny's taste."

"She's done some waitressing. She can handle the drinks. C'mon, man."

"Something special, huh?"

"A real animal in bed," Silas confided with a wink.

Todd sighed. "Fine. Have her talk to Danny at the bar. Tell him I said it was okay."

"I won't forget this."

MacCreedy returned to Nica's side to whisper, "You're in."

With Nica chatting up the bartender, Silas sat down to get a feel for the table. He relaxed into it, letting distractions flow from his mind as the players arrived. Lena had filled them in on the guest list: Warren Brady, the police commissioner; Simon Cummings, developer and mayoral candidate; Francis Petitjohn, supposed heir to Legere Enterprises International; Virgil Johnson, sports promoter; and some pretty-boy actor whose name Silas had forgotten. Men with lots of money to burn and favors to offer.

Carmen Blutafino arrived with a bevy of spectacularly endowed working girls instead of his wife. He was all smiles as the gracious host.

MacCreedy glanced over and caught Nica's unguarded expression, and alarm spiked through him. He crossed over to her under the pretext of getting a bottled water. He could feel her tension as he placed a hand against her rigid spine.

"Nica, what is it? What's wrong?"

She turned away from the room, her body swaying into him. Her voice was low and shaken. "That man over there. I recognize him."

"Does he know you?" MacCreedy asked calmly.

"I doubt it. I was seven years old at the time. He's the one who brought us down to New Orleans, then betrayed us. The tall one with the dark hair."

Warren Brady. The police commissioner.

"You're sure?"

"Yes."

"Are you going to be able to do this, or should we stop now?"

Her posture straightened, then she gave him a narrow smile. "Game on."

MacCreedy nodded and returned to the table as the others took their places.

"Our dealer, Mac Creed," Manny said.

"Good evening, gentlemen. The game is five-card stud."

Twenty-four

Over the first four hours, luck fell evenly among the six players.

Manny was generous with the alcohol while touching little himself, and talk was as loose as the women who paired up with the men. After carelessly losing fifteen thousand dollars on a single hand, the actor, who seemed more interested in the endless flow of Dewar's and in getting a lap dance from his companion, excused himself to visit one of the bedrooms. MacCreedy wondered how much the fool would be willing to pay to make sure the secret filming Manny would have arranged for wouldn't go to the press or his high-profile wife.

Manny's orders were to let the cards fall where they might until the alcohol level was high and inhabitions low. Silas dealt by rote and covertly watched Nica.

Something was different since they'd gotten into the car at her apartment. She'd said little during the trip.

Nica?

Her gaze flickered toward him, her eyes overly bright. Her faint smile didn't quiet his concern, especially when she was quick to look away.

"I'd like to call for a short break," Silas announced as Cummings raked in a good-sized pot. "A fifteen-minute stretch."

Commissioner Brady and Johnson, the entertainment broker, took the opportunity to guide their lady friends into private corners while Cummings, Petitjohn, and Manny Blu went to select cigars. Silas caught Nica's elbow, steering her out onto the balcony and closed the slider behind them.

The night was cool, yet Nica's skin felt on fire.

Hawthorne was close.

"I'm fine," she protested as MacCreedy tried to put his arm around her. She pushed away, swaying slightly as she walked to the railing.

"You're not fine. If you're not going to be able to do this, I need to know now."

Her shoulders squared up. "I'm not going to fold on you, MacCreedy. Don't worry about me."

"I *am* worried." He stepped up close behind her, blocking her in with the brace of his arms as he gripped the rail on either side of her. He rubbed his cheek against her hair, then pressed his lips to her smooth throat. Her pulse was racing like a high-performance engine.

"I'll see the job through," was her curt response.

"I'm not worried about the job, Nica. I'm worried about you."

Her quick sidelong glance called him a liar. He couldn't continue with his plan without her and they both knew it.

Silas frowned and enfolded her in his arms. "If you want to go, we will. No questions asked. Okay?"

Slowly, her hands moved to cover his. She forced a smile. "I'll be fine. We may never get another chance like this. It's just a headache. I can deal with it."

He lifted one hand to his lips. "It's not about the job, Nica. It's about our future. We're doing this for us."

"Then we'd damn well better do it right." She straightened his bow tie, her fingertips stroking down the lapels of his tux jacket.

Silas leaned toward her, but she evaded his kiss to slip back inside, leaving him to frown after her.

The players drifted back to the table to continue the game. As T-John began to sit down, a hand stayed him. He glanced up and his face went pale.

"*Max.*"

"Francis, thank you for holding my chair for me, but I'll take over now on behalf of LEI."

Petitjohn hesitated, stiff with shock and fury as Savoie smiled at Blutafino.

"Unless, of course, Carmen has any objections."

Manny showed his teeth. "Welcome to the table, Max. You're looking well."

"As they say, the rumors of my death were greatly exaggerated." He took the seat and glanced up at T-John. "Good night, Francis. We'll talk tomorrow."

Petitjohn managed a quick nod. He cast a frantic look at Manny, who wouldn't meet his gaze. Finally, he turned and exited the suite. As the elevator doors closed he was on the phone making an angry call, most likely to cover his ass, which Max's return left hanging.

"I wasn't aware you were a gambler, Max," Blutafino said, nodding at Silas to begin the deal.

"I like a good game."

Manny introduced the way-too-drunk-to-see-straight actor and the sports entertainment mogul and was about to continue when Max drawled, "I already know Mr. Cummings and the commissioner. I look forward to taking your money this evening, gentlemen."

Savoie's presence definitely put an edge to the mood. He played a relaxed, rather conservative game while Cummings, Brady, and Blutafino grew more aggressively careless in their agitation. Soon the pot size was considerable and the actor withdrew, retreating back to the bedroom with two of the women. After watching close to eight grand from his pocket being scooped toward Cummings, Virgil Johnson also folded, thanking the other players for the education. That left a very tense trio and Max Savoie.

And MacCreedy was ready to get his game on.

Nica, are you ready?

Nothing.

He glanced up in search of her. She stood at the end of the bar, clinging to its edge, her face pale as ice and shiny with perspiration. Her eyes closed as she wobbled on her high heels. A shaky hand lifted to press to her temple.

Nica?

Her eyes opened, focusing, locking on his gaze. *Game on, hero.*

MacCreedy dealt the cards, never lifting his attention from the deck, his movements smooth and economical. As each one sailed across the table, he sent the image to Nica. *Jack of hearts, two of diamonds, seven of spades.* Just as quickly, Nica conveyed the information to Max through the minute hand signals Silas had taught her that afternoon. The original plan had Silas sending the signals, but using a third party lessened the danger of discovery. And Max went from being an adequate player to an unbeatable one.

With shrewd bets and folds, soon the table's wealth was split between him and Manny. Brady and Cummings dropped out to watch, like buzzards waiting for fresh carrion.

Max studied the cards he'd been given, his features betraying nothing. He pushed a stack of chips into the center of the table.

Manny took a long drink before seeing the bet and raising it. His available cash was dwindling, and Max was sitting on a mountain of it.

Very carefully, Silas selected the cards from the deck for each player. When he called them out telepathically to Nica he was met with a strange static, as if the station he was listening to had suddenly gone out of broadcast range.

Nica? Nica!

Silas . . . Si, stay with me.

Her voice was faint and distorted.

She was sitting on one of the couches, slumped forward as if she'd had too much to drink. Tendrils of her hair had come loose and trailed to the carpet.

Max assessed his hand, then matched the pot and raised, slowly and deliberately.

Nica!

She didn't move. MacCreedy couldn't reach her; it was as if she was moving farther and farther away. To pursue her in that unstable psychic plane would require all his concentration and drain his energy. He'd have nothing left. He'd have to break cover.

Nica, hold on. Just one more minute. Just one.

The two cards Manny called for landed in front of him. He picked them up, his pupils widening, then he added to the stack on the table.

Max hesitated.

Silently cursing, Silas pulled away from Nica and sent a single thought at Savoie.

Take him.

Max reached up to dab at a sudden trickle of blood that spilled over his lip. And he smiled at Carmen, pushing the remaining stack of his winnings forward. "Call."

Manny took a ragged breath. "Son of a bitch, that's over a quarter of a mil. I can't match that and you know it."

When Max reached for the pot, Manny stopped him with a frantic growl. "What do you want, Savoie?"

"I want our association ended. Our accounts are settled on the turn of these cards."

"Agreed."

Manny laid down his hand with a grin. A full house, queens on tens. Max placed his cards on the table one at a time, revealing a jack high straight flush.

Blutafino stared at the display, his face pale, then florid. Outrage shook through him, but he didn't dare act on it as Savoie picked up the attaché case he'd carried in with him and handed it to Todd, watching stoically as his winnings were stacked inside.

"Thank you for the game, gentlemen," he announced smoothly as the latches clicked shut. "Now if you'll excuse me, I need to place a call to have my men offload your cargo from my ship. Then I've promised Karen Crawford a brief interview concerning my return to the living. She's meeting me in the lobby. Good-bye, Carmen. I can't say it was a pleasure doing business with you."

As Max rose up from his seat, Nica also straightened and stood. Her features were composed, her eyes gleamed.

Nica!

She didn't glance MacCreedy's way, her gaze tracking Savoie.

Silas started out of his chair, but Manny pressed him firmly back into it as his guests hurried to slip out before the press swarmed the lobby.

"We need to have a talk, Creed. I think it's time to reevaluate your job performance." He hissed at Todd, "If he moves, kill him."

Helplessly, Silas watched Savoie leave the suite, crossing the hall to step into the elevator. Nica slipped in with him and her flat, emotionless gaze met Silas's just as the doors began to close.

Good-bye, MacCreedy.

Awareness came back in slow, sickening waves.

"It's all right. You'll be all right. Don't try to move."

Brigit?

Silas struggled to force his eyes open and his sister's features swam into focus. She was holding an ice-filled towel to his cheek and her eyes glittered with unshed tears. Two things became apparent. He was lying on the couch in his apartment, and he'd had the shit kicked out of him.

Carmen Blutafino packed one hell of a punch. His face ached in testament. Manny had delivered only a few blows himself. The rest of the beating was turned over to Todd, who didn't let friendship interfere with orders.

"How did I get here?" he managed to whisper without moving his probably fractured jaw.

"Your friend brought you, the pretty blond one."

Babineau? His senses began to sharpen into focus. "How long ago?"

"About an hour. He wanted to take you to the hospital but said you refused to go." She blinked several times. "Someone sure made a mess of you."

"Severance package," he muttered, closing his eyes to assess his situation. Cracked ribs, a smashed and gashed nose from where his prop glasses had been broken, multiple contusions, and a possible concussion. But no .9mm termination notice.

Agony shot through his hand as a cold pack was replaced. Every one of his fingers had been methodically broken. Kendra was kneeling beside the couch, gently tending to his grossly distorted digits, her cheeks wet with tears.

His feverish thoughts drifted back to another time when these two had put him back together after the Terriots' even less tender attentions. He'd heal from this, just as he had then. But time was a weighing factor and his energies were drained by the psychic exercise.

"Keep him still," Brigit said as she pushed her palm against his splintered side. He winced in pain, then a deep, soothing heat penetrated through his skin, muscle, and bones.

Then she took each of his fingers in turn, straightening them with a quick snap, mending them with that infusion of warmth . . . the same way she had repaired the damage done by the Terriots' brutal hands. He hadn't remembered that until now.

Silas opened his eyes as she laid her palms on his face, easing her fingertips over each bruise and cut. No special gifts? His sister hadn't exactly been honest with him.

Brigit smiled. "Better? Hurt anywhere else?"

He expanded his chest in a full breath, flexed his hands, then moved his jaw. "Maybe my pride. Why didn't you tell me, Bree?"

"I promised our mother I'd never speak of it. She didn't want me to be different, she said it was dangerous. But I couldn't sit by and watch you suffer. Not then, not now."

When her voice faltered, Silas sat up to embrace her, opening one arm to enfold Kendra as well. He kissed the tops of their heads. "The two of you mean more to me—" He broke off, and his gaze darted about the apartment.

"Where's Nica?"

"She wasn't with you." Brigit released him, keeping her arm around Kendra's shoulders.

Silas grabbed his ruined tux jacket off the coffee table, searching for his phone before remembering Nica had destroyed hers. Squeezing his eyes shut, he gulped down several panicked breaths before he could settle his heart and mind enough to reach out for her.

Nica, where are you?

A terrifying silence answered.

Nica, you don't have to do this. Please don't do this to us. Nica? I let you down. I'm sorry. Nica, please.

Savoie. He took another steadying breath and dialed. When his call was answered, relief shook through him. "Max, you rode down in the elevator with Nica. Is she still with you?"

"No. She took the money over to the Towers while I talked to the press. Why?"

"How long would it take you to pick me up at my apartment?"

"Five."

"Hurry."

He closed his phone and surged off the couch, stripping out of his bloodied clothes as he rushed into the bedroom to yank on jeans and a T-shirt. He sat on the edge of the bed to put on his shoes, but his hands were so shaky he couldn't tie them.

Then Kendra was there at his feet, brushing his fumbling hands aside to efficiently do up his laces. Regret and affection twisted through him as his hand stroked lightly over her hair.

"I'm sorry. I never meant to hurt you."

She straightened. No blame or ill will showed in her soft gaze. "We can't help who we love. You've been my dearest friend forever. How could I not be happy for you?"

Smile weak with gratitude, Silas leaned forward to kiss her cheek. At the last second, she turned slightly so that their lips met instead. Her hands clutched the sides of his face, prolonging the gesture far beyond what he'd intended. Finally she released him, rising up and turning away before he could see the tears he knew were on her face.

MacCreedy waited on the building's front steps for Savoie, finishing the raw burger his sister had given him along with a command to be careful. A motorcycle pulled up and Max tossed a helmet at him. Cinching it under his chin, he settled on the seat of the big BMW.

The instant he rested his hands at Savoie's waist the bike lunged away from the curb, rocketing toward the Towers with a roar.

In the rush, Silas had no chance to tell Max what he'd discovered.

Max wasn't Nica's target. Charlotte was.

Twenty-five

Lena Blutafino stared down into the suitcase of money, her mouth open.

"Where did you get this?"

Nica smiled thinly. "Some traveling money, compliments of your husband. Get dressed and get your things together. You've got a train to catch to Memphis, and from there, anywhere you want to go." She held herself stiffly as Lena's arms flew about her.

"How can I thank you?"

"No need."

"I'll come to Memphis with someone who'll take your statement," Cee Cee told Lena. "Then you'll come back to testify. That's the deal my friend in the NOPD got for you."

The bright blonde head nodded. With her hair down and no makeup on, wearing an oversize sleep shirt, Lena Blutafino looked like a twelve-year-old girl... with a huge chest.

Her eyes were shiny. "I can't believe we're going to be free." With a loud sniff, she hurried back to the bedroom to pack, and within ten minutes she was dressed in jeans and a blousy tunic. Her vibrant hair tucked under a ball cap, a single bag slung over her shoulder, she held the attaché case in one hand and her sleepy son in the other. Giles took them from her.

"Giles will drive you to Baton Rouge," Cee Cee continued. "Your train leaves in the morning. Wait there until I contact you. Don't call anyone; don't talk to anyone but me. Don't trust the cops—just me."

Lena embraced Cee Cee, then Nica again, before following Giles to the private elevator.

Cee Cee pulled off the red wig she was wearing and tossed it onto one of the end tables. "I hope that's the last time I have to put that thing on." She gave her scalp a vigorous scratch. "With Lena under wraps and those girls freed from the freighter, we should be able to put a tight noose around Blutafino's neck. We couldn't have done it without you, Nica. I'm so glad you'll be staying in New Orleans now. I haven't had a real friend here—" She faltered and took a breath. "Since Mary Kate."

"I'm not staying."

The bluntly spoken words came as a shock. "But I thought you and Mac—"

She shrugged. "No. It's all about the job. Anything else is just a distraction."

"That's not true."

Nica laughed, a harsh, cynical sound. "Of course it's true. It's the only truth I've ever believed. You can't trust anyone to put you ahead of their own interests. I know what I offer, and it's a onetime-only deal. I'm not into repeat performances.

"I should never have come back. There's nothing for me here. I'm the bad news people can't wait to see gone. That's just the way it is. I am what I am." There was no inflection in her voice, no emotion in her eyes.

Before Cee Cee could argue, Max's voice rang through her head.

She's been hired to kill you, sha. Run! I'm on my way.

Without hesitation, Cee Cee gripped a marble-based lamp and swung it with all her strength. It caught Nica in the temple, sending her crashing to the floor. Cee Cee raced out the door to dash for the stairs. When she pulled the fire door open, two things surprised her: three of Blutafino's thugs were trotting up the steps, and thick curls of smoke drifted through the stairwell below them.

"Ms. Pepper, Mr. Blutafino wants to see you. Something about a blood test."

"Tell him I gave at the office." She shoved against them, sending them stumbling over one another to the landing below while she jumped back, pulling the heavy door shut. She heard the ping of the elevator and sprinted for it.

Its door opened just as Nica reeled out of the apartment, and MacCreedy exited. He gripped Cee Cee's arm and shoved her inside where Max waited, then turned to intercept Nica's running charge.

She sprang, vaulting high to clamp his head between her knees, using a twist of momentum to throw him down onto his back. In an equally quick move he wrapped his legs about her shoulders, scissoring her to the carpet, where they both scrambled to their feet, panting warily.

"Nica?"

A slow, fierce smile. "Nobody here by that name, MacCreedy."

She feinted toward him. When he countered, she whirled and ran for the stairway, jerking open the door and plowing into the bruised henchmen. They didn't realize they had the wrong female until she literally punched holes through them with a stiletto-heeled shoe in each hand. When they fell back, clutching their puncture wounds, she leapt up onto the railing and slid in her stocking feet to the landing below. From there she headed down as fast as she could, hearing Silas pushing his way over the injured men to follow.

And then she saw the flames.

Tongues of fire shot up through the open stairwell, chased by thick curls of smoke. She flattened against the wall, too terrified to move. The surge of adreneline cleared the last of Hawthorne's influence from her mind, leaving her starkly aware of her position.

She couldn't remember much. The brutal, escalating pain in the hotel room. She'd tried to cling to her mental hold on Silas, but he'd pulled away, letting her fall into the seething dreams. Horrible visions. Horrendous truths telling of death and misery. Of Silas weeping inconsolably over the mutilated bodies of his sister and best friend.

It can only end badly, Nica. Hawthorne's insidious

whisper was a serpent's hiss in her ear. *When they're dead, who will he blame? Let go. If you care for him, let him go with them. You have work here. Just this last job before you see your friends again. Or do their lives mean so little to you? Is this what you want for them, Nica?*

Images burned into her mind, flashing like the flip of MacCreedy's cards. Henry disemboweled in that cold basement. James beheaded, outlined in separate parts by police tape. Colin run through as he stepped from a limo. Jilly garroted from behind. Silas with their beautiful child on his shoulders, both cut down in a hail of bullets. It was too much, too awful. Her doing. Her fault.

Everything lost.

Her spirit broken, her will folded like that house of cards. And for the first time, because she couldn't obey, she bent under the crushing emotional pressure, letting her Controller take her over. Letting him use her as others always had.

After that, all was a blur until the fire slapped her awake.

She heard MacCreedy rounding the landing above her, but he stopped when he saw her situation.

"Nica, come up here to me. Don't run. You won't make it. All of the seventh floor is burning. Don't be afraid. Trust me. Come up or I'll come down to you."

Afraid? Such a weak word to describe the horror clawing through the haze of her memories—a horror locked away just out of reach, but so very, very real. Panting, beginning to cough, she forced her paralyzed limbs into action, going up the stairs to where MacCreedy was waiting to slip his arm around her and hurry her back up to eleven, avoiding the thugs on twelve.

Once the fire door to the stairwell shut behind them, sealing out the heat and smell, Nica struggled to escape him, toppling them both to the floor. Silas simply held on to her, letting her kick and slap and scratch.

"Let me go, MacCreedy!" Her voice was raw from smoke and emotion.

"Walk out with me. I'll keep you safe. I'll protect you."

"Savoie's here to kill me, and he'll go through you if he has to."

"Then he'll have to. Nica, stop fighting me, dammit! Let me help you."

She went still, gasping and trembling. "You can't, Silas. You can't protect me. Either let me go or let them kill me. Those are your only choices. I won't destroy you."

"I don't accept those choices."

"I can't stay with you. You have to let me go or you'll die. They'll *all* die. Take Kendra and your sister to Nevada. Be safe and live long—or stay here and die soon."

"I'm not letting you go." He hauled her up into his arms and she sagged against him, sobbing miserably.

"You have to. You're not strong enough to fight them, and I can't bear to let them kill you. Please, Si. Just let me go."

"Together, we're strong enough." He buried his face in her hair. "Don't give up, Nica. I'm so sorry I let you down at the hotel. It's my fault that bastard got a hold of you again. I thought I could do both things and I was wrong.

"There's just you now; nothing else matters to me. I'll find a way, Nica—just stay with me. I love you. You're my heart, my life. I can't lose you. I won't let you go."

She was quiet for a long time. Then she whispered, "I don't want to go."

He pressed a kiss to her temple. "Let's get out of here."

As they got to their feet, Nica looked about, puzzled. "Why aren't there any alarms? Why isn't the sprinkler system working?"

"I don't know."

Concern sharpened her tone. "Silas, there are families living on this floor. Jacques has a room here. We have to warn them." She gripped his hand and started pulling him.

Halfway down the hall, the lights went out. A haze began to thicken in the air. Nica started running, her fingers flying over the room numbers until she cried, "Here it is!" and started banging.

LaRoche answered the door in a pair of gym shorts, holding a powerful flashlight. "What the hell's going on?"

"There's a fire on seven. We have to get everyone out," Nica told him.

"There's a flight of stairs to the right and straight back. Only two through four and ten and eleven are occupied," LaRoche told them.

Silas volunteered to help Jacques on the floor below, where the danger was closer and the need greater. Nica hugged him, struggling with her terror of the flames and her reluctance to part from him as she said, "The only good hero is a live hero. Don't you dare let anything happen to you. I want your promise, MacCreedy."

"I promise."

His kiss sucked the remaining oxygen from her lungs and left her reeling. Then she turned to face her fears.

Max and Cee Cee stood with a member of the fire department, checking every person who left the building against the occupancy chart. The blaze was nearly under control but the damage was horrendous—a crushing setback to all Max's plans. His mood was raw, his temper short. So it wasn't the best time for one of Blutafino's men to approach him with a message: nobody fucks with Manny Blu.

Max's fingers were around the man's throat instantly. "You tell Carmen that the only game I play better than cards is life-and-death. Ask him if he can afford to lose *that* one."

As Max shoved the gasping man away, his furious gaze caught on the sight of soot-smudged Nica Fraser, picking her way over the snaking fire hoses in the parking lot, carrying a child and a plastic hamster cage. She was kneeling down, comforting the little girl, so she didn't notice his approach. But suddenly MacCreedy was in his path, presenting an immobile obstacle.

"Back off, Savoie. She just helped save half your tenants."

"And I'll be sure to thank her after I break her neck."

The palms braced against his chest sprouted claws, and Silas's snarl displayed impressive fangs. "I'm not going to let that happen."

Max gripped his shoulders to fling him out of the way, but MacCreedy pushed back with a startling amount of power, his arm hooking about Savoie's neck, taking him down to one knee and holding him there.

No one was more surprised than Silas at the strength surging from a source he didn't recognize. Then he felt Nica's hands on his shoulders, and he knew: from her. From his bond with her.

"Silas, don't," she cried softly. "Let him up."

The instant MacCreedy's grip lessened, Max shook him off and was on his feet, braced and ready.

Cee Cee stepped between them. "Both of you, stop."

Silas gave her a regretful glance, keeping Nica shielded behind him. "This is that time we were talking about. I can't let him harm her."

Cee Cee looked to Max to petition quietly, "Max, they're mated. They're a bound pair. He's not going to back down, and I don't want you to kill him."

"Well, hell, I don't want to kill him either, but she's out of control. She's dangerous and I can't risk her attacking you. Give me an option. I'll listen."

"Help me," MacCreedy said. "Help me free her, and I'll accept your offer. I'll work for you and your clan. I'll stand with you against any odds."

Max was silent for a moment, weighing MacCreedy's value against Nica's threat. But it was the expressive plea

in his own mate's eyes, as she stood with her hand resting upon MacCreedy's shoulder, that decided it. "Work
with me," he amended, then sighed. "Bring her out to the
house."

Silas nodded. "We have to make a couple of quick
stops first." Then he added, "Thank you."

Nica followed MacCreedy up the stairs to his apartment. He was worried about his family after his falling-
out with Blutafino, and his first instinct was to gather
them close.

He stood in the center of the empty apartment, too
dismayed to react.

They were gone. All their clothes, their belongings,
everything, without a note, without a word.

The touch of Nica's hand at the small of his back woke
him from his stupor. He snatched out his phone, walking into the bedroom as he punched in the numbers. His
voice was rough and shaky as he demanded, "Bree, where
are you? Are you all right? The airport? No. No, Bree,
don't do that. Wait for me. Bree—

"Kendra, what's going on?" He started to pace, the
movements quick with agitation. "Don't. You don't have
to do that. Let me—Kenny, please, don't do this. Just
wait for me. I don't want you to do this. Please. Not for
me. Don't—"

He came to a stop, breathing hard, struggling for
words. Nica had never felt so helpless, so excluded, when
he whispered hoarsely, "I always will. You know that."

His eyes squeezed shut and then he continued more gruffly, "This is insanity, Brigit. What are you thinking? Stay here. I can—" He swallowed hard. "I love you, too. If you need me for anything, call me and I'll be there. I don't care about that. Yes. Yes, she's here." A ragged laugh. "I know. I will. You be careful. Don't do anything—" Another laugh and a twitch of a smile. "Any more than usual. Call me. I'll answer."

He stood for a moment, put the silent phone back in his pocket, then shoved open the window and stepped out onto the balcony.

It was very dark, not yet three in the morning. Nica could only see him in shadow where he sat on the steps, elbows on knees, head in his hands. The snag of his breathing was breaking her heart.

"Where are they going?"

"Reno."

Back to the Terriots.

"There's still time. You can still go with them." Her tone was level, but her insides trembled as she waited for his reply.

He looked over his shoulder to where she sat on the the windowsill, his eyes glittered in the darkness. "My life is here. With you. I have to let them go." He turned to stare out over the lights of the Quarter.

Relief caused the firm set of her features to collapse. "Isn't it dangerous for them to return to the Terriots? Should we stop them, Silas?"

"We? You want to bring them back?"

"They're family. We can protect them—"

He reached up for her, drawing her down beside him. Her arms banded about his middle as he held her head to his shoulder. "They're safer where they're going. She's going to accept an offer from the Terriot heir. The mating will give her security and power, if nothing else."

"Brigit?"

"No. Kendra. She's going to bargain for Brigit's protection from the Guedrys and for my freedom from their service."

Nica blinked in surprise and admiration. The kitten was a lioness after all.

"Will they keep their promises?"

MacCreedy shrugged. "Depends on how much Cale Terriot wants her. My guess is he'll give her anything she asks for."

And they'd be out of reach of Hawthorne's retribution.

"They'll be fine, Silas."

"I know." He drew a heavy breath and let it out in a shaky gust. "I just wanted to see them before they left. I never seem to get the chance to say good-bye."

Before going to Max's they returned to her apartment and showered together out of necessity, so weary they had to cling to each other for balance. MacCreedy cast a wistful look at the pillow-top bed as they dressed, longing to sink into it with his mate beside him. *Soon*, he told himself. Soon they could start the kind of life together that he'd only dared dream of. He sat on the edge of the mattress and tried to calm his thoughts by watching her.

Nica was quiet as she braided her damp, heavy hair. She'd dressed simply in the skinny black jeans and white ribbed tank top. But instead of seeing a sleek, strong warrior readying for battle, he noted the slight tremble of her fingers and the unsteady shallowness of her respiration. She'd made herself vulnerable because of him—because she loved and trusted him. To be worthy of the faith she'd placed in him, he had to keep his word to free her. A shadow of anxiety gnawed at his determination. If he failed . . .

Nica caught his intense study, then stepped between his knees to cradle his face in her palms.

"It doesn't matter what happens," she softly told him. "I never expected to have anything like this, ever. It's scary and amazing and wonderful. If this is all we have, just this moment, I have no regrets. I want you to know that."

She bent to touch her lips to his.

MacCreedy gripped her wrists, his eyes glacial gray, fierce, and full of cold fire. "Well, it's not enough for me. I want every minute of the rest of our lives to be together. I'm going to have sex with you every night on this bed until we're too exhausted to move, and wake up beside you the next morning. I'm going to drink your lousy coffee out there at that table while I watch the news before I go to work. I'm going to fill you with my children, and we're going to get old together watching them grow up happy and free. I'll be damned if I let anyone take a single second of that from us. I won't let you down, Nica."

Nica's eyes darkened with belief and desire. "I love you, Silas. Give me those things."

It was midmorning by the time Silas drove through the gates on River Road. The mood was grim and tense between them when they climbed up onto the porch, Nica's hand clasped firmly in his.

Oscar fell eagerly in step with his uncle, filling them in on all the news of the fire. Arson was suspected, but miraculously there'd been no loss of life. Fire investigators were on the scene picking through the rubble. Max and Charlotte had gotten home only a few hours ago, detained by endless questioning.

When the boy ran ahead to announce their arrival, Tina approached with a nervous smile. "I've given a lot of thought to what we talked about," she told Silas. "New Orleans is Ozzy's home. I spent my entire life on the move from one place to the next and I don't want that for him. I want him to grow up with family around him, with a sense of permanence, if not the most ideal security. I hope you can understand that."

Silas put an arm about her shoulders and lightly kissed her brow. "I do. And I think it's the right choice, if not the safest one. Nica and I are staying, too, so you can count on us for anything you need. I take family seriously."

She sighed in relief, leaning into him. "Thank you."

"And I still have hopes that your fool of a husband will grow a pair *and* a brain and take care of you the way he should."

Tina stepped back, her smile rueful. "We'll see."

With Oscar leading the way, Max and Cee Cee came out to join their guests in the foyer. MacCreedy's hand tightened about Nica's as Max regarded her unwelcomingly.

"Abuse my hospitality, assassin, and I'll be taking you and MacCreedy on our next boat ride out into the bayou."

She showed her teeth. "I'll be on my best behavior." But her posturing faltered when Charlotte strode up to pull her into a fearless embrace.

"Don't worry about him, Nica. He has no social graces."

"Lottie," she whispered, "it wasn't personal."

"I know," Cee Cee said as she stepped back. "If I thought it was, I'd be piloting that boat." She grinned up at the glowering MacCreedy. "Let's get to work. We've got to do some creative report writing to make sure all the necessary asses are covered." She glanced back at Max. "Especially those I'm particularly fond of."

Max chuckled. "I always knew you were after me for my assets."

They set up shop in Jimmy Legere's old office. Nica sat outside on the porch, where Silas could keep a watchful eye on her as she dozed in the sun.

Seeing his attentive look, Cee Cee gave him a nudge. "Things okay between the two of you?"

He smiled grimly. "I've promised her it will be."

"I'm familiar with those kinds of promises. The huge, grand gestures we make to those we love, without the slightest clue how to keep them."

"I have to keep this one."

"You two have good, powerful friends here, Mac. We'll take care of you."

He stared at her as if confused by the offer, then his shoulders relaxed. "Okay. Good to know."

"It's going to be a reciprocal arrangement, so don't thank me yet. Wait until you hear about the mess you're stepping into when you come on board with Max. He trusts you, and he doesn't trust easily. Don't fuck him over."

"I won't." A small, genuine smile. "So, what are we dealing with?"

She laughed. "I don't know where to start." She smiled at him, thankful for his presence because it gave her an unbiased opening into Max's business, where she'd formerly had only cursory access. MacCreedy's involvement would bridge both worlds: hers of law enforcement and Max's with the clans. He'd be the solid, dependable voice Max could rely on with knowledge and experience in both places. "I'm glad you're here. I'm going to enjoy working with you."

MacCreedy's grin was wry. "Just don't try working me, Charlotte. I don't like being fucked over, either."

She grinned. "We're going to get along fine, smart guy."

Over chicory coffee and tasty crab salad sandwiches, they talked police and clan business. Silas brought Cee Cee up to speed on his dealings with Max, with how he'd met Nica, on Brigit's ill-fated affair with Daniel Guedry, and then laid out what he'd learned working undercover with Manny Blu.

She was stunned to hear of the commissioner's involvement both currently and in the past, but she wasn't surprised that Cummings wasn't snow white.

She filled him in on the bad blood between the mayoral hopeful and Max, and Max's claim that Cummings had had dealings with Jimmy and his own father. She suspected that there was more Max wasn't saying and seemed so unsettled by that, Silas decided to say nothing about Cummings's questionable dealings with Babineau. He wanted to talk to Max and to Alain himself, verifying what the evidence was telling him, before going there with her.

Regarding Carmen Blutafino, Max had taken the drugged Shifter females off his vessel so he'd have no ties to human trafficking. Giles had returned early that morning after putting Lena and her son safely on a train for Memphis, where she'd go into hiding.

The fire was another matter. Arson was a given, but the potentially deadly code violations that had been exposed were quite another. Max, his attorney, and the site engineers would be pouring over the blueprints at his office in the City in an effort to escape hefty fines and even possible criminal charges. Cummings displayed horror and outrage at the news, carefully removing himself from any backlash.

And then there was the matter of who had hired Nica to kill Cee Cee, and why. Those answers, MacCreedy hoped to have that evening.

When Cee Cee received a call from Devlin Dovion Silas went outside to check on Nica, whom he found sleeping, her lunch untouched. He walked down the long porch, to check in with the lab about who had access to the DNA samples of Charlotte, Nica, and the kidnapped girls. And what he learned rocked him.

Only two people had pulled the information on all the names given. Commissioner Warren Brady. And Detective Alain Babineau.

Twenty-six

Nica opened her eyes to see MacCreedy sitting on the foot of her chaise longue. He was looking out over the lawn, his expression pensive and faraway, probably in Reno by now. She watched him, her emotions thickening like a simmering roux.

He'd stayed with her and was going to remain with her. And while that was the most beautiful, romantic thing she could imagine, it was also the most foolhardy. Chances were good that he was going to die tonight in a futile effort to save her, and there was nothing she could do to stop him. Chances were also good that she'd be the instrument of his death. She couldn't stop that, either.

There was nothing to do but trust him and whatever he was planning, but the uncertainty had her sick with dread. He'd told her nothing, afraid the information would leak to Hawthorne and give him warning. MacCreedy was a smart man. She'd placed her trust wisely.

She rubbed her toe along his thigh so he'd turn and look at her. She loved his face, the strength in it, the way a smile curved the edges of his lips, the heat that thawed his steely gaze to a warm pewter. And his voice, that deep rumble that made her quiver in response.

His hand settled on her leg, squeezing gently. "Hi. How are you feeling?"

Everything about him was calm and confident. She wanted to fling herself into his arms and lose herself there forever. *I'm feeling scared*, she wanted to whimper so he would comfort her. *I want you desperately*, she wanted to growl so he'd take her upstairs and screw her blind. *I want you to run while you can, to get on that plane to Reno*, she wanted to wail, knowing he wouldn't go.

So she smiled at him and lied. "Fine."

She could see he didn't believe her. He pointed to the plate of sandwiches. "You didn't eat anything. You need to keep up your strength."

"You're my strength. Besides, I didn't think I'd be able to keep anything down."

He gestured with the curl of his fingers. "C'mere."

She scooted down to straddle his lap, clutching him tight with her knees and the fierce circle of her arms, her head tucking under his chin.

"Don't be afraid. I won't let anything harm you."

Didn't he realize she wasn't going to be the one who was harmed?

"I'm not afraid," she told him. "I'm terrified beyond the capacity for rational thought."

She felt his breath stir her hair as he whispered, "Me, too." And her heart spasmed with her love of him, for his bravery, his sense of sacrifice and honor, his drive to protect her.

She pushed back so she could openly adore him as she said, "What do you mean I make lousy coffee?"

He blinked, then his grin broke wide. "It's really awful, but if you make it, I'll drink it."

Her eyes brimmed to overflowing. "My hero."

They shared an awkward meal in the dining room. Nica's head pounded so furiously, just the idea of food had her nauseous. She sipped her water and held Silas's hand tightly while Oscar cajoled him into telling stories about himself when he was his nephew's age. They were adventurous, amusing tales, filled with the love of family and especially the adulation of a boy for his father. Tina dabbed discreetly at her eyes, while Cee Cee stoically studied her nearly untouched plate.

And Nica smiled, imagining again the beautiful blond-haired child riding on Silas's shoulders. Their son. Their future. The vision was shattered by a sudden stab of pain that made her knock her glass over, sending water and ice across the table.

When she jumped to her feet, nearly blinded by the hammering behind her eyes, Silas pulled her down to his lap, holding her close as he continued his story as if nothing was wrong. He stroked her hair and rubbed her shoulders as her hands knotted in his T-shirt, twisting, then tearing.

Tina started to get up. "I'm going to take Oscar upstairs."

"No," MacCreedy interrupted. "Please let him stay. I

need him to stay. Father Furness will be here in a minute."

"What's he coming here for?" The harsh question came from Cee Cee.

"Because I asked him. Because I need his help. I need all of your help."

Max nodded, understanding. "He needs our energy. Bring her into the study."

As they moved out into the hall, Giles approached, looking haggard and distressed. He said something to Max, then went to answer the door, admitting the priest.

"You told me I could free her," Silas called to Furness. "Make good on your word, Father. Help me do it now."

By the time he laid her on the leather couch in Jimmy's office Nica was thrashing, drenched in a sweat of pain. Silas knelt beside her so she could focus on his face and his voice.

"Shhh, Nica, I'm right here. Look at me, keep looking at me. Just listen to my voice and don't be afraid. We're going to do this together. I need you to trust me. Is he here?"

"No, not yet," she panted. "I'm trying to keep him out, but it's so hard."

He smoothed his palm over her damp brow. "Don't fight him. Let him in."

"What?" Panic crackled in her voice. "Don't let me go, Silas. Stay with me!"

"I'll be right here. I won't be far. I need you to relax

and let him take over. Don't fight, Nica." He kissed her and whispered, "You won't be alone. I promise."

Her breathing slowed and the tension eased from her muscles. He brushed his hand over her eyes to shut them, whispering in her ear, "I love you, Nica. Let go."

When he straightened from her limp form, he looked at Max. "I need to follow her. I need to know where she's going. What do I do?"

Max squatted down next to him, putting one hand on Nica's shoulder and the other on MacCreedy's. "Close your eyes. Relax. Big breath. Another. Big breath. Relax your shoulders, your arms. Slow your heartbeats. Breathe. Let ... time ... stop."

Dizzy from the hyperventilation, feeling weightless and disconnected from everything, Silas heard Max say, "Open your eyes." When he did he sucked in a startled breath, because he wasn't in the study anymore. He was ... someplace else.

"Take a second to get used to it. There are no boundaries here. Think your destination and your consciousness will follow. Do you understand?"

"Yes."

"Look for her, Silas. You're connected. Feel her."

Nica?

There were cold, strange flashes of light without color. When Silas glanced down, he saw himself bent over Nica and he faltered.

"Don't look back. You have to let go. Reach for where you want to be."

He reached out his hands, his fingers stretching, losing shape and solidity, becoming pure light, sheer energy. Then there was a tremendous rush of movement, like the plunge from the highest roller-coaster peak.

Nica, help me find you.

Silas?

She was suddenly everywhere, her scent flooding into his pores, her breath filling his lungs, the whirl of her thoughts tangling with his in an instant of exhilarating chaos. He pulled back, easing away from her strong, vibrant signature. He could see her, transparent and slightly distorted against a field of explosive color. She was in a room, a sterile, clinical-looking place. Her mouth moved, speaking his name without sound as her hand stretched out to pass right through him with a blast of cauterizing cold.

He gasped and withdrew, pulling back through the walls of the room, down corridors, through the shaft of an elevator, out through walls of steel and brick into space.

Slow! Slow. Where is this place? Where am I?

A city. He could see the skyline, the distinctive spires of Chicago.

Signs. Look for signs.

Streets. The building, glittering against the evening sky. Hard to see past the lights, so bright. Then a name.

Silas, don't leave me!

MacCreedy opened his eyes. He was on his back, his heart was racing. A cold, cramping sensation twisted through him, bringing his dinner up in a rush into the waste basket Cee Cee held. Weak and shaky, he tried to sit up but he had no control over his muscles.

"Give it a minute. It's rough on you the first few times," Max said.

"Deveraux Clinic." Was that his voice, so thin and strained? "Waverly and Plymouth. Chicago." He was finally able to move his hands and dragged himself up to his knees. "It's a medical facility of some kind. I have to go back."

"Not a good idea," Max warned.

"I have to go back to help!"

Father Furness crouched down by the sofa. "You'll need someone to channel the energy for you or it will scramble you like an egg."

"Can you do that?"

"It's been a long time, but I should be able to filter it. You'll have to tell me if it gets to be too much. Believe me, you'll know when it's time to pull back."

"Fine. I will." Anything to get him back there before Nica thought she'd been abandoned. He took her limp hands in his and closed his eyes.

Nica, don't be afraid.

And he was instantly there, the transition so abrupt, he had mental whiplash. He was back in that searingly white room where Nica huddled in its center as a hallucinogenic collage flashed across the walls. Brainwashing? Was she even now being fed images that would direct her actions against her will?

He went to kneel beside her, unable to touch her as her vacant stare fixed upon the poisonous pictures. Of Nica calling his name, him turning toward her, her slashing his throat, over and over in a brutal loop. Of Charlotte spinning, her weapon drawn, firing with cold accuracy, the bullets tearing through him and the blond-haired boy on his shoulders. Their child? *Oh, Nica, he's so beautiful!*

And then that voice, soft and sinister. "She's going to kill them, Nica. They're going to die unless you get to her first. She's going to murder them right in front of you. If you don't act now, you won't be able to save them. Their blood will be on your hands. She's going to steal your future from you unless you stop her. Do it now, Nica. Do it *now*."

"Wake her up when I tell you," Silas called to Furness, "and keep her from Charlotte. Give me that boost *now*."

He felt energy snap and sizzle through him like a jolt from jumper cables. He waited until the voice began again, latching onto that wave of psychic power, then cried, "Get her out of here!" as he rode that whip of energy back to its source. To a trendy apartment filled with art and music, to a neatly dressed middle-aged man with thinning hair, a pencil mustache, and a soft midsection, seated at his dining room table twirling spaghetti on his fork, who stared, jaw dropping, eyes bulging.

"Are you Hawthorne? My name's MacCreedy. Don't say I didn't warn you."

Silas let the image he projected shift, becoming huge,

with intimidating muscles and fur and fangs. His claws sank into the tabletop, ripping through the cherrywood inlay.

Hawthorne shrieked like a little girl as a gigantic paw snatched him from his chair, shaking him as the monstrous face loomed, drooling strings of saliva onto his petrified features.

"Who hired you to kill Charlotte Caissie? Tell me!"

Hawthorne continued to scream and struggle against a demon his mind told him wasn't there, even as razor-sharp claws shredded his designer shirt and skin.

The effort of holding the illusion built pressure inside Silas's head as inside an egg boiling in the microwave. He pulled more strength through Furness's conduit, drawing from Max and Tina and Oscar, ignoring the pain and scalding heat surging through him. He stared down into the frightened eyes, looking through those huge pupils, tearing through the splinters of memory, digging determinedly even as his absent body began to seize and shudder.

"Silas, come back now!"

He fought against the summons, his eyes rolling back, blood streaking like tears from their corners, streaming from his nose and ears as he burrowed into Hawthorne's brain, powered by the unstoppable energy that was ripping him apart. Searching as Hawthorne tried to elude him, tried to hide that truth as his system sizzled and scorched. Because he couldn't stop until his promise was met. Even if it killed him.

———

Nica's eyes snapped open, wild and glazed with fury. They fixed on Cee Cee like a missile and with a snarl, she lunged. Max's elbow caught her in the forehead, dropping her onto the couch cushions with stunning efficiency. His hand went around her throat, pressing her down as her eyes blinked and cleared. She immediately began to thrash and fight him, but in her weakened state she was no match for him. Until he understood the reason for her frenzy.

"Silas!"

Released, she scrambled to the other end of the couch where MacCreedy sat on the floor, his head lolling against the seat cushion as Furness shook him. His eyes were open, pupils blown, swimming in blood.

"I can't bring him back!" the priest said. Nica shoved him aside to take the colorless face between her hands. She calmed the terror banging in her chest to speak to him softly, firmly.

"MacCreedy, I don't want a dead hero. I need you to keep your promise. I need you to stay with me. *Stay* with me."

He took a sharp breath, blinking several times until his eyes were once again clear. "I'm right here," he told her, voice hoarse. When he spoke, smoke wisped from between his lips. Then he looked at Max and Cee Cee, and said, "Petitjohn."

Francis Petitjohn sat at the desk in his small office at Legere Enterprises International, scanning the early

edition as was his daily habit. His lips curled in a contemptuous smirk as he read about the fire at the Trinity
Towers. Arson. *No shit.* No casualties. *Too bad.* Possible
criminal negligence for cutting building costs in viola-
tion of code. *Try talking your way out of that one, you son
of a bitch.*

There was a tap at his door, and it opened to that huge
dumb stump of a bodyguard who followed Max around.

"Morning, Mr. Petitjohn."

"What do you want, Giles?" He stabbed a finger at
the article he'd been reading. "Looks like I've got a lot of
damage control to get to, so make it quick."

"You sure do, so let's get right to it."

T-John scowled as the big thug set several sheets of
paper in front of him. "What's this?"

"Something the boss man wants you to sign. I'm to
make sure you do before we go."

"Go?" He glanced at the top sheet and went very still.

*I, Francis Petitjohn, being of sound mind and free of any
coercion, do hereby confess . . .*

"What the hell is this?"

"Just a little something Max put together to explain
why you all of a sudden up and disappeared. I'd read
through it if I were you."

Nervously, Petitjohn moved his gaze from the casually lounging muscleman to the damning list. Pocketing
kickbacks after changing spec codes Max had agreed on
for the Towers, changes that resulted in extensive damage due to substandard materials, faulty sprinklers, and

a failed alarm system. Conspiring in human trafficking with Carmen Blutafino. Hiring an assassin who died in an abortive attempt on Max's life.

"These are lies."

"Maybe in actual fact, but not in the spirit of things."

"I didn't keep two sets of books on the Towers," he argued. "Max signed those invoices."

Giles shrugged. "Let's see what turns up."

"I didn't hire anyone to kill Max," he sputtered furiously.

"Maybe you should have. He'd have been a lot more forgiving if you'd gone after him instead of Charlotte. They'll find your wire transfers leading to that crispy fella in the morgue."

When Petitjohn said nothing, Giles continued, "Why go after Charlotte? I put a lot of thought into that when I was driving back from Baton Rouge yesterday morning, after dropping off a real nice lady and her little boy. It's a shame there was a fire in her hotel room in Memphis. Kinda like the one at the Towers, except this time there were casualties. Nice place. The receptionist made the reservations at Charlotte's request. She told me you were asking about the arrangements. I bet Mr. Blutafino was right grateful for that information."

Petitjohn stopped reading, his face very pale.

"Anyways, I figured if you went for Max, everyone would know it was you and that it was business. But if Charlotte's killed it would point to Manny because of her undercover work, and Manny'd have no choice 'cept to take out Max to save his own skin. Leaving you free and clear."

Petitjohn remained silent.

"But you know how I knew it was you? Because being the sneaky, vicious little spider you are, you'd want Max to suffer as much as possible before stealing LEI from him. And that's what would do it."

Francis sneered. "I'll be damned. You've got a brain along with that brawn, after all."

"Yeah, I do. Sign that paper so we can be on our way."

"To where?" He was starting to sweat.

"If I was still working for Mr. Legere and he told me to pick someone up, I'd know exactly what he meant. One-way trip, no return. But this being Max, he's gonna give you a chance to run. I figure you've skimmed enough from LEI to live real comfortable in some nonextradition country. Signing those papers will make Max a lot more charitable about it."

Petitjohn picked up his pen. "No one will believe it."

"That letter was composed on your laptop and printed up on that printer right over there. And you'll be gone. What's not to believe?" Giles checked his watch. "Let's get a move on. I've got things to do."

After a little frantic thought, Francis figured, why not? He did have plenty of cash, and things were getting dicey with Manny now that Max had shut down his transportation avenues. Better to run while the getting was good. That was a mistake Jimmy never would have made. He never let his enemies escape him. But then Max Savoie was no Jimmy Legere.

He signed. Why not? He'd had a good run. He'd be sipping champagne in South America by dinnertime on LEI's dime. He'd just bide his time until someone else did him the favor of taking his nemesis out.

"Let's go out the back way," Giles suggested. "No need for anyone to see us."

Thinking about the calls he'd have to make to get a fake passport and a new ID, T-John rode down in the service elevator and followed Giles to the big town car with tinted windows. Giles opened the rear door for him, waiting for him to slide into the dark interior before getting behind the wheel.

As the car pulled out of the dim parking garage Petit-john saw that he wasn't alone, and he gasped.

"Hello, Francis," Max drawled from where he sat at the other end of the seat. His eyes flickered eerily. "We're going to play a game. You're going to run, and I'm going to chase you. I'll even give you a head start."

And he smiled, his manner and attitude very Jimmy Legere—except for the very sharp teeth.

Charlotte Caissie sat in a pew at St. Bart's, hoping to find some comfort. But Mary Kate wasn't here. The ever-present smells of candle wax and polish didn't evoke her spiritual presence any longer, they only brought sorrow. With so much weighing on her heart, Cee Cee was desperate for counsel. Max had gone before she woke or she would have turned to him, something she'd been doing more and more often. And Nica had left to take Mac-Creedy home after dropping an unsettling bomb.

"You asked me about Mary Kate," Nica had whispered to her. "I think I know someone who can help you."

But just because she *could* do something didn't always mean she should. Cee Cee's desire to bring her friend back from the coma where she hovered crossed all sorts of moral lines Mary Kate might not appreciate. But if there was even the slightest chance to bring her back, why was she hesitating?

Then there was the other news she received in her phone call with Dev Dovion.

"Lottie, this is a nice surprise," Father Furness said.

She looked up, her expression guarded. "I've had all the surprises I can handle, Father. Thank you again for your help."

"Why do I get the feeling you're not here to thank me?"

Cee Cee struggled to keep her voice level. "You were always like a saint to me, Father. My rescuer, my friend. I couldn't believe the things Nica was saying about you, that you were a manipulator, a liar, a deceiver. But now I'm beginning to think she's right."

She closed her eyes to shut out the look of dismay on the priest's face. Or was it guilt she wondered, as Dovion's conversation came back to her. Two things had been discovered from the blood sample she'd given the lab.

She was pregnant.

And the Ancient gene present in Nica's blood was also in hers.

Charlotte opened her eyes and looked at the priest who had guided and possibly misdirected her entire life. "Why didn't you tell me about my mother?"

Twenty-seven

He was either dead or dreaming. MacCreedy couldn't decide which.

Then the warm figure pressed against him in their cozy feather-filled nest moved, stirring up proof that one part of him was very much alive.

A light touch stroked his unshaven cheek. "Are you awake?"

He turned his head to take in the most beautiful sight imaginable. "I hope so."

Nica smiled, her eyes softening to a deep, just-before-sunrise blue. "Feeling better?"

"Than what?" He'd experienced a world of pain he never wished to revisit, as if he'd been lying at the bottom of a vat and enthusiastic vintners were stomping away, trying to mash his blood and bones into wine. He had no idea how she'd managed to get him home.

Home. Where this delightful bed and this delicious woman resided.

"Did I hear the phone earlier?" He looked at the clock. Nine A.M.

"Your partner called. He wanted to remind you of some meeting this afternoon. I told him if he showed up at our door I would vivisect him on the spot. You think that was a little over the top?"

"I think I love you."

He closed his eyes. Alain Babineau: his sister's husband, his friend, the human who had his back on the streets. A problem he wished he didn't have to deal with. A bad cop? Instinct said no, despite the damning evidence.

"And your sister called."

"Tina?"

"The wicked sister."

Brigit. "Is everything okay?"

"She said she'd call you with details tonight and that you weren't to worry."

Which meant there was something to worry about. *Hell.*

"Silas?"

The fragile note in Nica's voice brought his eyes open. Hers were shiny.

"No more hero stuff for a while. I don't think my heart can take it."

"Okay."

"You came back for me. Thank you." A soft kiss. "But you almost died. What good would freedom do me without *you* here to do me?"

He grinned. "I'm gonna need a rain check on that, at least until after breakfast."

She was still chewing on something. Finally, she looked him in the eye and asked, "Are you happy?"

"What?"

"Brigit said—"

MacCreedy finished that sentence with a kiss, pouring all his passion and joy and gratitude into her until she purred like a sleek, pampered cat. When he pulled away, she was smiling contentedly.

"You have an amazing way with words, MacCreedy."

"Only one thing could make me happier."

"What's that?"

"You making coffee while I catch another ten minutes of sleep."

"Done."

Nica slipped out of bed and MacCreedy's gaze followed her as she crossed the room to shrug on his white shirt. Lust and love filled his chest with rib-cracking intensity.

Happy? There wasn't a word big enough for what he felt for her. Which was why he'd risk anything to fulfill his promise.

Silas closed his eyes on a deep breath. Time to settle things.

That slimeball Hawthorne was pouring a cup of very nice smelling coffee. When he turned, the cup fell to the floor as he lunged back against the counter, eyes wide.

"We didn't get to finish our talk last night," MacCreedy said with a threatening smile. "I know where you live. I know where you work, and I know how to get into your head. Unless you want me to show up here in person to do all the things you threatened to do to my mate and my family, you're going to do as I say."

"Anything you want!"

"You're going to report that Monica Fraser was killed in New Orleans and that the man who contracted her job is also dead, so there's no need to complete her assignment and no refunds are necessary. You can keep your percentage and your miserable life—*if* you leave us alone. Agreed?"

When Hawthorne hesitated MacCreedy's energy force hit him, driving the breath from him with the sensation of crushing cold. Like death.

"All right!" he screamed. "I'll do it."

"Have the names and addresses of all Nica's friends ready when I come to see you again."

"But I can't— All right. All right!"

"Don't fuck with me."

Pain scissored across Hawthorne's face, and blood welled up from the slashes scored from ear to chin. MacCreedy had made actual contact with him! Impossible!

The scent of hazelnut coffee was replaced by a more pungent smell as Hawthorne wet himself.

"Here's your coffee."

Silas opened his eyes and smiled despite the acrid aroma, sliding his hand down the curve of her hip.

Noting the tenting action under the sheet, Nica said, "I see you've changed the menu. And I have a very strong appetite. Is that blood under your nails?"

Silas glanced down. "Must be from last night." He distracted her from any other questions by slipping his hands under her shirt and up her smooth skin.

As she sank into his kiss, her hands showing him what she was hungry for, Silas reveled in his good fortune.

Tonight he'd fill the coffeemaker himself and set the timer.

Nothing about his future was going to be bitter.

Turn the page
for an exciting sneak peek
of the next irresistible novel
in the Shadows series
by Nancy Gideon

Coming soon from Pocket Books

The club's interior was pitch-black and quiet as Susanna hurried down the hall toward the open office door. A faint light glowed within from the fixtures she'd left on low. It was 5:00 A.M. She had only a few hours and was anxious to boot up and resume her research. As she crossed to the big desk, the overhead fluorescents flashed on, blinding her like a lightning strike as a thunderous voice boomed behind her.

"Where the hell have you been?"

The sight of Jacques LaRoche blown up into a thunderhead of temper rooted Susanna to the spot.

He was magnificent in his fury, brows lowered storm clouds over those blue eyes, nostrils flaring like something wild and dangerous scenting a fight . . . or a female. His posture was all-aggressive male, leaning in to intimidate and squared up to accentuate his impressive dimensions. In a moment, he'd be beating his chest and letting out a conquering roar.

And Susanna had had enough.

She'd been bullied and threatened and submissive for the last time. Fists on her hips, she drew herself up, placing her at eye level with his sternum.

"Who do you think you are, taking that tone with me?" she snapped with the fierceness of a terrier attacking a rottweiler.

Her retaliation only fueled his anger. "I'll take any tone I please. This is *my* place and you are a reluctantly invited guest here. Where have you been?"

It registered in the back of her mind that he'd been worried, but she couldn't get past the arrogance of his snarling masculine entitlement.

"I don't have to check my schedule with you," she countered. "I'm only using your computer. That doesn't make you my babysitter or master."

"When you're supposed to be here and you decide to be elsewhere, you *will* check with me," he growled. "You're my responsibility, whether I want it or not."

And he didn't want it—or her. Her pride rallied against that hurtful jab. "You don't owe me anything. I don't want your sense of obligation hanging on me like chains. I've had all of that I can tolerate. Now let me do the work I came here to do." Frustrated, she put her hands flat on his chest and shoved. Set like a mountain, he didn't budge.

His huge hands curled about her wrists, making her pulse jump. Suddenly, his hot gaze dropped, sweeping her from head to toe, taking in her new haircut and clothes. His deep voice became a gruff rumble. "What have you done to yourself?"

Uncertain if his tone implied approval or disgust, Susanna rebelled against it. "Nothing for the likes of you."

He flushed with angry insult and something else that she both feared and hoped was desire. The sudden darkening of his eyes warned he'd been pushed beyond his limit, and he yanked her up against the unyielding wall of his body.

The contact shocked them both. With their panting, their gazes held in helpless attraction and dismay. Then Jacques bent down to her, slowly enough that she could avoid it if she chose to.

She didn't choose to. *Oh, yes. At last.*

His kiss was pure heaven, forceful at first because she'd stirred his passions into a frenzy, then quickly softening to a yearning so sweet, she ached to her soul. The familiar cushion of his full lips, intensified by the prickly outline of facial stubble, had her lost in a delirious haze. Nothing had ever felt so strong, so right, as the emotions crowding up inside her.

Before she could respond to the hunger surging through her, Jacques abruptly jumped back to regard her through wide, stricken eyes.

Unable to catch her breath, Susanna lifted a shaking hand to her mouth to marvel at the delicious bruising of her lips. How had she existed for so long without this crazy zing of feelings, her skin tingling, her blood hot and heavy, need pooling damply at the apex of her thighs? Her body cried out for more—but one look at his frozen features told her that wasn't going to happen.

"I'm sorry," he whispered in horror as she stared blankly up at him, trembling in what he probably assumed was shock. "I never . . . I would never . . . I don't know what happened."

And Susanna realized then that she couldn't allow them to fall into such a dangerous relationship. It wasn't fair to either of them. She deliberately made her words cold and concise.

"You overstepped yourself, Mr. LaRoche, and it *will* not happen again." Her conscience writhed as she watched him assemble his scattered thoughts behind a self-preserving wall.

"Don't worry, Dr. Duchamps. I'm not the kind of guy who has to force himself on females."

"I'm sure you're not. You have them trailing behind you throwing beer and gumbo in your path. But I am not one of those females. I have a mate and a child back home in Chicago. I have no interest in the kind of dalliance you might offer."

He told her with a prideful stiffening, "You have no idea what I might have to offer, and I'm not about to enlighten you." Then he surprised her with a gruff admission. "I would never do anything to disrespect you or your family. Again, I apologize."

Susanna's resolve and tone thawed, despite her intention to keep him at arm's length. "Accepted. I'm here to work and I appreciate the offer of your facilities. In return, I'll do you the courtesy of letting you know when I'll be here and when I won't, so you won't feel obligated to worry."

He didn't deny that he had been. He gave a brief nod

and turned to escape his office, shutting the door behind him.

Susanna sagged into the desk chair, her knees unable to support her any longer. This couldn't happen again. She couldn't hurt him like that, taking advantage of the instinctual pull between them that went cross-grained of his conscience.

The decision she'd made seven years ago must stand firm. She had let him go then, and she had to stay away now. She couldn't interfere in the life he'd made for himself—the life that didn't include her. She couldn't destroy him with the knowledge that had her heart breaking.

Damien Frost wasn't her bonded mate. Jacques was.

Jacques threw open the hinged pass-through at the end of the bar, gratified by the loud *bang* as it hit the counter.

What the hell is wrong with me?

He stopped at the small bar sink and twisted the cold tap, filling unsteady hands and splashing his face with the bracing chill. But it failed to cool his overheated body or his wildly inappropriate thoughts.

He refused to glance back up at his office window, where she was probably shivering in dread and disgust. Because he was exactly what she feared.

A rude brute. An unmannered beast. An untamed animal. Growling and grabbing at what wasn't his to take or desire. A primitive, inferior species unable to control his carnal needs.

He stared at his face in the mirror. Seven years ago,

he'd had no idea who those features belonged to. He could have been anything, anyone.

What he did know was that he'd belonged to *them*: those pitiless users in the North who'd obviously trained him and directed him to serve their capricious whims. The scar between his shoulder blades told him that. Had he pleasured their females? Had he hunted and killed his own kind? Had he been a mindless drone who went about his business with blind obedience? Was he so conditioned to their commands that he had no self-control, even now?

Maybe the riotous emotions spiraling through him had been programmed there, to protect their kind from his natural impulses.

Resentment simmered as he paced.

Why can't I get a grip? This isn't what I've made of myself. Why am I letting her get to me? She's one of theirs—not one of mine. She belongs to one of them, not to me. Not to me.

So why did every pulse of his blood deny that fact?

There was no explanation for the way his heart had stumbled when he'd looked into his office and discovered her gone. His mind had instantly blanked with alarm, thinking some harm had come to her. The crippling fear had almost taken him to his knees. The response came from no place he recognized, but he'd been there before. When he'd seen that Tracker place a gun to her head.

He would never stand for injury to come to any female, to anyone weaker or defenseless. Not in his place, not at his bar, not in his presence. He just wouldn't tolerate it. But his instincts were so fiercely overprotective where Susanna Duchamps was concerned, they defied logic or understanding.

Adrenaline still had him shaking inside and he stalked behind the bar, circling from one end to the other like a wild thing in a cage, trying to settle his churning emotions. The need for violent action burned in him, because sex was out of the question.

Sex was what he wanted. Sex with that maddeningly irresistible female in his office. The taste of her burned through his blood like grain alcohol, frying his thought process, enflaming his lust. He'd felt her heartbeat leap beneath his fingertips, and for a moment had believed it was due to passion.

He would have taken her right there on the floor with the slightest encouragement, without a thought to who she was, what she was, or who she belonged to, so lost in mating madness that nothing mattered but finding a way inside her as fast as possible.

You'd think he was a rutting youth sniffing out his first female.

You'd think he'd discovered his one and only all over again.

But the fragile Chosen doctor was not his chosen mate, despite what his pounding desires told him. He'd lost that treasured female when his memories were torn from him, her fate unknown to him. He'd failed her, and he couldn't go forward, because there was no going back to right whatever terrible mistake he'd made that had erased her from his future. There was only here and now. And at the moment, he couldn't bear the bleakness of that knowledge.

Jacques lifted a bottle of liquor and carried it to a table. The first long swallow was as harsh as his mood, burning his throat, wetting his eyes. After that, it lost the power to hurt him.

Susanna gave up trying to work. Her thoughts were fragmented, her emotions were in a knot. Fatigue and sorrow twisted with the sense of blame that refused to leave her alone.

Seven years ago, she'd done the only thing she could to save them all. There'd been no other choice, no options. If she hadn't let him go, he'd be dead.

But knowing that didn't lessen her pain.

Tears burned in her eyes as she watched his restless pacing, knowing he struggled against feelings he couldn't understand. His desire for her wasn't natural, not like the earthy affection he had for his female staff. Yet it couldn't be broken by distance or anger or the drink he finally reached for. Its power couldn't be explained or denied. She knew—she felt it, too.

She could still taste him, feel him, smell him. Desire growled through her like a hungry beast, terrifying in its strength, devastating in its potential.

She had family; he had a life here. There was no hope for a future now, any more than there had been seven years ago. She'd thought there was, once, but she'd been young and giddy with passion. Now, she had no excuse. Only relentless guilt as she watched him find solace in alcohol.

She shut down the computer, unable to endure another minute of the self-destructive torture. On a cocktail napkin she neatly printed, "Have gone home. S."

The dawn air felt good against her skin as she walked the quiet streets, and the exercise eased the tension twining through her. She couldn't ever go back there. She'd ask Nica to find her another place to work, one without the danger and distraction of Jacques LaRoche. She couldn't afford to be near him again, lest both their wills give way.

She hadn't come to New Orleans to relive her illfated past. She'd come to guarantee a future for the child she loved more than herself.

As she walked along the uneven sidewalks, Susanna's focus returned with a renewed purpose. As she climbed the stairs to her borrowed apartment, she formulated the direction of her next research study. After she slept, she'd be ready to attack her work with new vigor.

She unlocked the door and stepped into the dark living area. Dim light filtered in from the large windows on both ends of the narrow apartment, and she made her way to the small table to place her satchel there. Then she gave a slow stretch to release the tension in her shoulders . . . and caught the glitter of broken glass on the floor beneath the windowsill.

Something moved behind her, a shift of shadows without sound.

Before Susanna could turn, a rough hand clamped over her mouth, stifling her scream.

Susanna sat on the couch, her slight figure in shadows. Her head lifted when she heard Jacques come in, giving him a brief glimpse of her pale features before it lowered again, masking her face behind the curtain of her mussed hair.

"I should have listened to you." Her words were quiet and inflectionless. "I didn't and I'm sorry."

She was sorry? She thought *she* was to blame?

When Jacques was able to speak, his voice growled like thunder. "Get your things. You're coming home with me."

No argument. No hesitation. That in itself alarmed him as she shouldered her bulky purse. She wouldn't meet his gaze as she approached in silence, adding weight to his guilt.

She stopped when his hand touched her shoulder. "Do you trust me, Susanna?"

She glanced up then. "Not at first, but I do now."

Her admission wedged up in his throat, forcing him to clear it. "Do you need to get anything from the apartment?"

Her shudder was slight but unmistakable. "No. I don't want to go back there."

If she'd been his, he would have snatched her up close and held her. But she wasn't.

He stepped back, letting her precede him to the car parked in the rear alley.

———

Susanna sat still and silent while Jacques drove. Her only sign of agitation was in her quick, shaky breaths.

He frowned at the sight of blood on one of her hands. "Are you hurt?"

She blinked up at him in confusion.

"Did they hurt you?"

She shook her head, then followed his nod to her fingertips. "I scratched one of them on the neck."

"Did you see their faces?" He was careful to keep his tone level as fury began to boil up inside him.

"No, it was dark and they surprised me. I'm afraid I'm not a very good witness."

His jaw clenched tight as he kept his eyes on the road. "I'm sorry," he said.

She looked startled. "About what? None of this was your fault. I was careless. You have every right to be angry."

She was taking the blame for his own mistakes. She'd been sitting there expecting him to chew her out, while he was close to drowning in shame.

"I'm not angry with you." He drew in a savage breath. "I didn't answer your call."

Again, the guileless blink of her eyes. "There was nothing you could have done even if you had." After that cool logic, she turned away to stare out the side window, dismissing any further apology or explanation.

When Jacques brought the Caddy to a stop outside his construction trailer, his humiliation twisted into a tight knot.

What was he thinking, bringing her here?

Susanna was obviously from wealth and privilege. He imagined her horror at being cloistered in his dingy bachelor accommodations, and almost put the car into reverse. But where would he take her?

Well, she was his responsibility. She would just have to make do.

"Welcome to my humble abode," he drawled ruefully. "Emphasis on *humble*."

Inside, she paused in the center of the main room to look around. There was no sign of disgust on her dainty features, just curiosity.

"You work here, too?" she asked, touching the stack of invoices he'd left on the stained formica-topped table.

"Yeah, it's convenient. I like to be on-site so I can keep an eye on things."

Susanna picked up and examined the magazines scattered across his couch: *Entrepreneur, Time, Bloomberg Businessweek*. Thankfully, Philo had five-fingered his latest "pictorial" magazine to admire the tri-fold air brushing.

"You have interesting taste," she commented.

"My *Metropolitan Home* and *Food and Wine* come next week."

She smiled, and glanced at the books he'd stacked on the floor. "When do you find time to read, working two demanding jobs?"

"While I'm not sleeping. The bathroom and bedroom are down there."

He rummaged through the tiny linen closet for clean towels as she went down the hall, looking ready to drop from fatigue.

After he set the towels out, he found Susanna seated on the edge of his bed. She looked up through eyes swimming with distress.

He dropped down onto one knee so they were eye-to-eye and made his tone low and soothing. "It's going to be all right."

Tears finally streamed down her cheeks. "I hate being afraid all the time. I feel so safe when I'm with you."

She leaned forward, her arms going about his waist, her head nestling beneath his chin as if his chest made the perfect pillow. Jacques brushed his lips across her hair, then rested his cheek there with an odd feeling of familiarity. What in hell had he gotten himself into?